WANDERLOST

BEN OLSON

Illustrated by Zach Hagadone

ALPHAR PUBLISHING

Copyright © Ben Olson, 2006

Wanderlost was originally published as a series of four articles in the
Sandpoint Reader titled "Notes From the Rails," and also contains por-
tions from "American Standard" in *The Ides* literary journal—both written by Ben Olson under the influence of hubris and Wild Turkey. This
paperback edition contains significant changes and revisions from the
first edition (i.e. all the dumb mistakes were fixed and illustrations added). All copyrights for pieces printed at the end of the book are owned by
the writers listed; Erin Brannigan, Adriane Albertowicz, Jenna Bowers,
Jenn Witte and Josh Hedlund. Some pieces were previously published
in *The Ides* literary journal.

LIBRARY OF CONGRESS CATALOGING IN PUBLICATION DATA
Olson, Ben
WANDERLOST
1 Title
ISBN 0-9786024-1-3
ISBN 978-0-9786024-1-3 (13-digit)
2nd Printing (paperback)

Cover illustrated by Zach Hagadone and designed by Ben Olson
All photographs by Ben Olson

What readers are saying about Wanderlost:

••

"Reading your novel is not in the cards for me I'm afraid."
  -Tom Robbins

"The journey takes the reader not just through evocative descriptions of the changing landscape, but through the highly charged and personal musings of a young writer as he grapples with which direction he wants to go. Gritty and at times graphically intense, it is also a witty, insightful and humorous exploration of how to balance freedom with obligation and what it means to be a young American in the 21st century."
  -*The Sandpoint Reader*

"Here is a writer howling at the American landscape and destined to become an American writer of significance. The torch has been passed..."
  -Nathan Jordon - Jack Kerouac School of Disembodied Poets

"Ben Olson... has seen and done more in his 25 years than most of us will ever do."
  -*North Idaho Lifestyles Magazine*

"PLEASE buy this book... get this fucking guy off my couch!"
  -Marisa Fenarjian - Allows Olson to Sleep on Her Couch

"This man will not live to see 30... It's a new movement, a movement like I've never seen before... Art for bums... Ignore his hard drinking, his distorted politics and his hair-brained theories, his utter grimness, his cathartic experiences, his constant cycling between satori and ennui and go straight to the humanness of his work, wherein Max, this uncommon common man, makes common mistakes in a messy world."
  -Erin Brannigan - Former Professional Racquetball
      Player, Art Thief, Master of Bullshit,
      An Ordinary Man Himself

"Never heard of it."
  -Chevron Station Attendant - San Francisco, CA

To the Others... and Z

ILLUSTATOR'S FOREWORD

When Ben Olson sat down to write this book he was somewhat shocked, as were his close friends. Not because we thought he couldn't get it published, or that it was a bad idea, but because he'd tried and failed to finish about four other books within the same year – one of which was already called "Wanderlost" (or "Wanderlust" until he found, to his horror, that Danielle Steele had already used it).

As I write this, the "Illustrator's Foreword," I'm sitting on the Blue Line Trolley bound for downtown San Diego, wondering how I got into this. When we arrive, Ben and I will hop into his battered truck and head north to Los Angeles where "final edits" will be applied to this paperback edition of "Wanderlost."

We completed the work during a grueling three-day stint at El Portal De Rosarito – a clean but cheap place on the busted main street of Rosarito, Mexico.

It was there, also, that I produced about 20 of the illustrations contained herein. That's a lot of work; especially when spicy Mexican food is introduced to my lily Gringo innards and doused with innumerable bottles of Dos Equis beer (not to mention the terrible Mexican cigarettes).

It was accomplished because Ben is a cruel task master. And his Spanish is infinitely better than mine. He had the power to withhold food and drink; failing that, he could leave me in that dusty burg of sirens and car alarms. I was at his mercy, and that's why we went there in the first place.

That and to escape his bitch-mistress Los Angeles. He was mired in work problems - the first and primary problem being that he *had* to work - and couch surfing, as is his habit. These stresses, compounded with the stress of trying to revise "Wanderlost," led him to heavy drinking. Even by his standards. It was when he dipped into the Absinthe that we both knew L.A. was not where "Wanderlost" should be re-mastered; so we did what we do best and got the Hell out of Dodge.

It worked, and in so doing, proved a few things about this book - mainly, and I think this is the moral but Ben would slap me for saying as much, that just because you're going in the opposite direction of your problems doesn't mean you're running from them. The tonic of freedom, ultimately, is perspective-enhancing and can help jar a person out of their insane ruts. I say "insane" thinking of the old adage: "Insanity is defined by continually pursuing a solution you know doesn't work," or something like that.

That's certainly something Ben knows and something this book exemplifies. But he's no saint, and neither am I. We're poor, desperate and cheap at heart. He still can't pay his bills, and mine are sitting on a table, also unpaid and late, somewhere in Portland. I hope this book helps remedy this situation, which means, put in a less mercenary way, that I hope the reader finds these illustrations enjoyable, or entertaining or, dare I say, enlightening. Most of all, though, I content myself with these illustrations being merely illustrative.

I'm not an "artist" by trade, just a fellow traveler who happens to know a little about how to wield a pen. Plus, there was only room for one writer on the Amtrak lines that winter; I'm glad it was Ben instead of me.

Zach Hagadone
2.7.07 - San Diego, CA

AUTHOR'S NOTE

(OK, here's the deal: "Wanderlost" was supposed to look like this for the first edition. But things happened fast (as they usually do) and I was forced to write the damn thing in 37 days, drunk on whiskey and stir-crazy as a shithouse rat. Zach was going to edit it and draw these illustrations and it was going to be our grand Opus to finger at the world. Then we'd sit back and drink expensive champagne, hire some midgets to type our manuscripts and waste away until death escorted us to immortality. It was going to be a good life. But, since we're both degenerate, broke assholes, he failed to edit the book at all (except for one day of drunken attempts at the bar) and didn't draw anything but cover art. I couldn't pay him anything to do it. He'd been hired to edit a magazine and needed the money for rent. As a result, character names were flip-flopped, misspellings occurred, and nonsense passages that would've normally been cut were included.

Essentially, I published my first draft.

Apologies to all of you who bought it (probably less than 150 people, you poor supportive fools). To the rest of you, disregard these first three paragraphs. You're seeing this book as it was intended. Now buy more copies, you cheap sonsabitches.)

This book evolved from years of struggle. Years of gut-wrenching poverty. Years of butting my head against the walls of mediocre art. For too long I've seen my society, the "greatest society," deflating and dumbing down the masses to fools. I wondered if it was still possible to write a great novel.

And if so, was there anyone left to read it?

This is not a great novel. It will never be on any best-seller lists. Oprah won't select it for her book club. I don't want her to. I didn't write this for Them. I wrote this for the Others of the world – those who don't fit into the American version of what's "good" (i.e. what sells – who cares what it really says, right?). Right. Elitist? Sure.

This is a truthful account of a common man's life in a dirty, shitty, exploding, apathetic world, and that is why it has merit. I believe in something that will never die – the notion that you can still live free in America, and do whatever the fuck you want between the poles. Write obscene words, drink whiskey, sleep with loose women, drive fast on the wrong side of the road, stay up til dawn doing hard drugs, piss on streetcorners, throw rocks through real estate windows, fall in love with ghosts... I live how I want to live. I capture the moments I want to capture, and I know it is Art. I know it is Truth. I am just like you, and I'm so confused. I was born in the wrong era. I should be a pirate or a rum-runner or a goddamn Roman gladiator. Instead I'm just a dipshit among dipshits. A bum inside the gates. I'm just a poor bastard who has read too many great novels and copied too many great styles. I've rejected the American Dream... it means nothing to me now. Who the hell wants to raise a family and get a real job and punch a clock 50 weeks a year? Not me. It's just futile effort and early death.

I know I'm full of shit. I know I have my head up my ass, and I know you do too. So be it. There's a literary renaissance occurring now – people are tired of reading and watching and listening to empty confection. This is my attempt at something real. I didn't write it to make money or become famous... I wrote it because I had to. I wrote it for you.

Enjoy it.

I'll be dead soon.

Ben Olson
3.12.07 – Sandpoint, ID

WANDERLOST

Ben Olson

Illustrated by Zach Hagadone

ALPHAR PUBLISHING

poop

PROLOGUE

IT WAS WINTER AND I WAS SLIDING down, down into the decline of my middle twenties—lost in an endless cycle of high and wild nights, jaded dreams, and terrible booze shits between.

The nights filled with faux hipsters screaming poetry in piano bars, jocks, thugs, and meatheads on the prowl for cheap sex in pool rooms reeking of stale cigarettes and stale life, ditzy girls in jeans sipping mixed vodka drinks, bullshit barroom philosophy in corner booths, and late-night prophets in scarves sitting cross-legged on the carpets of after-hours pads smoking joints as the sun pierces through the cast-iron dawn, discussing politics, books, culture, Our Generation, and how we're all doomed to burn out in a flaming echo.

Unwilling cogs in the vast machine, we chased the end of the night like we chased immortality—satisfied by neither, forever seeking the justification for all.

Rambling up and down rainy 1st Avenue streets in groups of talking and arm pulling from one bar to the next—Northsaint, Idaho; the small mountain town you've never heard of where this story begins… it could be anywhere, though. We breathe the same air.

ONE

THE 419, ACCORDING TO MY FRIEND FLANNIGAN, is like "an opium den with cowboys instead of Chinamen." It's a dingy redbrick bar wedged between real estate offices in downtown Northsaint. There's a bar like it in any small town across the West. A dented metal door underneath a neon martini glass brought you inside, where natural light never shined and the handful of songs playing on the jukebox kept time frozen and hazy.

Decades-old Christmas lights hung from dusty wagon wheels, tables with cattle brands burned under yellowed laminate, and thousands of burn stains from neglected butts fallen from ashtrays. Leather high-back chairs surrounded a worn bar, leading to the "Smut Corner" by the front door; where sat a shrine to old patrons in various poses of drunkenness, all of them clutching either a cigarette, a beer mug, or both. Most were missing teeth and all the men wore grimy caps. The air always smelled foul with cigarette smoke, mixed with dried whiskey on leather jackets; a stale, musty smell that lingered in your hair, clung to your clothes, and served as a morning reminder to where you'd been the night before.

North Idaho characters lined the bar; aging 30's white trash women with lips pinched around Misty 120's, cackling next to bearded loggers in greasy jeans drinking Budweiser from the bottle; young college kids back on winter break pounding mugs of PBR and high-fiving each other constantly; booths full of middle-twenties locals; ski bums, construction workers, small business owners. And the Corner Booth—a giant circular nerve center of cracked leather seats that stretched from one corner of the rectangular room to the other, always filled with ten, fifteen, sometimes twenty shouting figures piled on top of one another, grouped around in chairs, guys with their arms around two blond girls, empties littering the tables, dirty ashtrays overflowing despite the hustling cocktail waitress' best efforts to change them, notebooks and cocktail napkins out on the table with all different handwriting, the common tablets that get passed from one hand to the next without any word of instruction or explanation—the unsaid rule was to read the last line and go from there—but it didn't matter, just write whatever you wanted and pass it on. Flannigan kept all these notebooks in great stacks under his bed, and I had no idea if anyone ever read them once they ended up there.

The Corner Booth, where grand adventures were hatched and quickly forgotten, where road trips were planned, gossip was spread, and stories were told over the crashing din of the night. It was an altar of sorts, to pound out our righteousness with faltering fists. It was our place to be young and stupid and full of piss. It was a meeting ground for the agitated youth fed up with the mediocre world that raised them.

We were a Non-Generation, caught in the amber of the curious transformation from post-college to adulthood, raised in a soulless era of crass pop culture exploding like a shit mist over everything, brought up in a world of spin and catch phrases, morally bankrupt politicians waging pointless wars, and restlessness for something real, something more, something pure.

We were the Others; the writers and musicians and

painters and poets. The dope fiends. The shabby dressers. The ones who didn't fit into the order of society and success, American style. We'd all graduated from high school and went off to out-of-state colleges to seek institutional wisdom, then gradually trickled back into Northsaint to take jobs serving booze and staying up all night; riding old beach cruisers around town with backpacks, sitting around big bonfires on the beach with guitars and bottle rockets.

But Northsaint wasn't the same town we'd left those many years ago. Once a small community of loggers and hillbillies and hippies escaped from suburban sprawl, now just another "destination resort" like Aspen or Vail, Durango, Lake Tahoe, Jackson Hole. Doesn't matter anymore, each town is exactly the same as the last. Hollow. Cookie cutter. Empty.

Land developers "discovered" Northsaint and bought up all the lakefront real estate. These dirt pimps, land rapers, and small town Napoleons gobbled up the land like Monopoly deeds and set about planning for the "future." They built giant, soulless housing complexes on sacred Native American land and the population boomed. Everyone wanted in. Soon the box stores moved in, picking up the scent of Progress like sharks on a blood trail, and the local markets slowly folded up their window shutters. The tiny airport expanded to accommodate direct flights from larger cities around the West. Old pickup trucks with dogs in the beds gave way to shiny black Hummers clogging the downtown streets. And that is how you build a resort town in the West.

The virus of Progress hit Northsaint like a shit-bomb, and the only jobs left to those not willing to sell out for the dollar in real estate were in the service industry—slanging booze at the many downtown bars, operating chairlifts at the local ski resort, waiting tables, and selling wine to foo-foo tourists and amenity migrants. We were catering to the very people who ruined our town and scrapping over the tips and crumbs they left behind.

We were defined merely by what we *weren't*, what we *didn't* believe in. We yearned for a voice… a way to sound off against what was happening to our community, to our world. We read poetry at open mic nights, wrote long rambling articles in the independent newspaper, attended underground warehouse parties with drugs and deejays and house dogs sniffing for scraps of leftover food. We argued about small town politics at coffee houses, read old Beat novels on grassy lawns with Bob Dylan in our ears, organized art showings, and listened to young local musicians at hippie bars until closing time.

People came and went, like I did, in search of adventures away from the shroud of acceptance that existed in Northsaint. But they always drifted back. There was, and still is, something about the town that got into your blood, a magnetic mystery, for too much exposure sent you flying away, and too little dragged you back.

I'd first come home after a three year stint working in the film business in Los Angeles. After dropping out of college my sophomore year, I moved to Hollywood to become "rich and famous" like all the rest, but ended up working in television commercials. I finally had to flee when I felt myself turning into a cow-eyed lemming; chasing after a soap opera version of success that would only come at too great a cost.

I rented a small cabin across the lake from town and began a strange lifestyle of bohemian bliss that lasted several months at a time before I had to drift back to Los Angeles for quick bursts of cash to pay the rent. I got used to this lifestyle, always in constant flux, rambling back and forth from Idaho to California, escaping one extreme for the other, always running from something. I never saved any money and I never lasted long in either place—I was addicted to the space between; the Open Road, the motion, where I was neither here nor there—always seeking something I could not define, but knew was out there somewhere.

The Life PT. 2

- PSUEDO-RELATIONSHIPS WITH DENNISON'S
    OF SMALL TOWN WOE

I'll have a distinctional relationship
please.... i mean a famism.

but let this as small town brings us together
        please let this small town
        tear us apart?

I DON'T HAVE ANY ONE - LOVERS RIGHT NOW.
    DIARRHEA of THE MIND.

↑ SPECIAL GUEST APPEARANCE BY DON NICKLES.

AND THAT'S ALL SHE WROTE.

DMS

THE LIFE
        (ON A NAPKIN)

BIG SIP, LITTLE TOWN

My life's a reband

I try and I try

THIS DRINK IS WARM. — I'M COLD.
like the street, like the night,
This blood is just waiting to feel thin again
IT'S NOT BLOOD, IT'S SOUP!
Its true
    I'm twisted in you
        you make me feel blue.
    is the soup that i believe in

It was Wednesday at the 419, and I had just returned from another two months in L.A., working on television commercials for Lexus, Jack in the Box, and Tampax. The latter was especially demeaning.

We were all crowded in the Corner Booth, hyped up after Open Mic Night across the street and tossing back our drinks with brio.

Jack Oglethorpe was there, the great mind of Northsaint, his tall, bony frame hunched over a mug of PBR like an old vulture. As always, Jack wore his black wool cap and tightly-knotted black scarf tucked into a West German field jacket. His knees poked out of shabby khaki trousers he'd worn since high school. Everything hung from his thin frame like sad sacraments of poor-man pride. He was a newspaperman.

"*Stupid* people talk about other people," I heard him lecturing some drunk woman, his long finger waving in her face, "Average people talk about things... *brilliant* people talk about *ideas!*"

Jack moved back to Northsaint with his fiancé Guinevere after college to start a weekly newspaper called the *Northsaint Reader*. They argued about politics and history and literature—topics they both shared equally frightful master of—and fixed great big pots of pasta in the middle of the night to feed the blathering "illiterate" that lounged on their thrift store furniture after the bars closed, listening to old jazz records or watching atomic bomb explosions on the black and white television that sat on a milk crate in the corner.

At one point, while he and Guinnie were in college, they broke up because of a disagreement over Leninist Bolshevism versus Goldmanite Anarchism.

"It was late at night and I was clutching a plastic bottle of Smirnoff vodka or some shit," Jack said in his deep, monotone voice, lowering his chin and peering over his spectacles.

"I got shit-can drunk and stormed over to her dorm room to listen to Russian folk music, but we started arguing about politics. She started quoting Goldman and I got really pissed off, because anarchism is such *bullshit!* Have some fucking knowledge of the system before you try to overthrow it, you jackasses! So I finally stood up and yelled, 'I can't *be* with someone who *thinks* this way! This naiveté is out of *control!*' and stormed out of there."

"We broke up for a whole year because of that," he continued, laughing at the absurdity. "It stood in for a lot of other things, I guess—we were both really hung up on our own egos," he turned to me, "You probably know something about that, eh?"

Good ol' Jack, who burns eyeballs at you behind square spectacles and grits his teeth. Who never likes anyone unless they earn his respect. Who gives intelligent, no-bullshit responses peppered with classic historical rhetoric, quoting Nietzsche, idolizing Lenin, drawing cartoons of Nazis and doom… he's like your favorite cranky old grandpa transplanted into the body of a 25-year-old that wore the same pair of clothes every day. It was Jack who convinced me to finally move out of Los Angeles and write for his newspaper. He said he'd pay ten cents a word to write, which he never did, of course, because the paper always made just enough money to publish the next issue. But I still came.

"Then, a whole year later," he went on. "I went to Ireland just to see her and we got back together… and now we're getting fucking *married*."

They were intellectuals caught in the day-to-day struggle to pay rent and keep the newspaper afloat, while still having a little leftover for some drinks at the bar.

"What are you gonna do with *The Reader* after you guys get married?" I asked.

"Bah, fuck the newspaper," he snorted. "I'm so sick of that goddamn thing. Every week I have to deal with the same old boring hack articles… I'll probably just sell it off or something."

"What?" I slammed my mug on the table, "You bastard! You can't just *abandon* it! What about all the work we've put into it? What about all these people that *depend* on it every week?"

"Ah hell, Max, nobody'll give a shit… these people are all just a bunch of blathering booze-shitters anyway." He cocked an eyebrow at me, "And what do *you* care anyway? You haven't written anything for me in *months*."

"Well shit man, I've been in L.A. this whole time," I said defensively, "I can't get anything done while I'm down in that cesspool, you know that."

"Nyeh."

Little brown-haired Wrenn slid into the booth next to me and put her arm around my shoulders. Her cheeks were red and eyes watering from walking in the cold.

"You're back," she said, squeezing a lime in her drink. "How was the drive up?"

"Oh, pretty uneventful," I sighed, patting her on the leg. "My tire flew off in Portland though."

"Flew off?"

"Yeah, I forgot to tighten the damn lug nuts after changing my brake pads, so the fucker just came right off when I was going about 80 miles an hour… went right into a ravine. Other than *that*, it was pretty uneventful."

She shook her head and giggled quietly. Wrenn designed tee-shirts and wore plaid, hand-me-down skirts with ballerina shoes. She sat erect in her seat with neck stiff and drink straw in hand and waved her arms eloquently when making points, hiccupped all the time, and sighed into the ears of boys she liked but never had the courage to act on.

"Well," she said, "You have a pretty loose definition of 'uneventful.' How long are you staying in town this time?"

"Until my money runs out, like usual," I sighed.

She reached up and scratched at my beard, "This is getting pretty thick."

"Jesus, she's right," Jack nodded. "You look like some hack American version of Che Guevara."

"*Viva la revolución!*" I yelled and we all drank.

"Yess!" I heard Flannigan, the wide-eyed, thick-sideburned Irish poet, yell from the other end of the booth. He bent over the composition notebook open on the table and scribbled a few words, then threw it over to a group of huddled hipsters talking in the corner: "*Write* something!"

Flannigan had a three-day beard growing underneath those sideburns and specks of foam in the corners of his mouth from long-winded conversations without pause or cause. He was always running from one group of people to the next, darting his head back and forth and honking like a goose while people spoke and laughed and cursed, capturing it all down in the little notebook for some purpose yet to be determined.

"Jesus, Max," he rubbed his forehead, "I wasn't even gonna drink tonight until you ordered all those shots of Wild Turkey at Open Mic and got me all excited about this idealistic lifestyle we all live," and so on, the way that Flannigan talked. He seized onto concepts and ideas, mostly intangibles, and devoured them, threw them into the air, knocked them around, examined their innards, picked apart their meanings… not to resolve them, but to hear them spoken, hear them said, to give them life.

"Christ, that reminds me, we need s'more shots!" I yelled and sprang up to the bar, where JUDE!, the bartender was standing with bitch-beater tucked into jeans and muscular arms clenched like Wolverine from X-Men. He was a spoken word poet who insisted on writing his name in all caps and an exclamation point. I asked him why one day and he replied, "Dude, if a man wants to eat horse, let him eat horse." He recited raunchy diatribes at Open Mic and made low-budget soft-core porno movies at the seedy motel he owned outside of town. In fact, he always smelled strongly of sex.

"We need some Turkey over here, JUDE!" I banged on the bar.

"Course you do," he shouted back, lining up the shot glasses with that all-knowing smile of a bartender. "Dude, I got this new idea for my next film… it's a drinking and dating reality show where we follow people home on one-night-stands and film them havin' sex. Whaddya think?"

"You wanna do that in *this* town?"

"Yeah, why not?" he shrugged.

"Well, I'll be damned if I'm gonna take some chippee home and bend her over one night only to see you lurking around outside my window with a camera."

"It's the wave of the future, brother," he handed me the shots and jogged to the other end of the bar, picking up empties along the way and blowing smooches at his girlfriend Gyna, who used to date Flannigan, who is now dating one of the guitar-playing Darling twins.

Essentially, everyone has slept with everyone in North-saint, if not directly, then within one or two degrees of separation.

I meandered back through the crash and roar to the Corner Booth, where Flannigan was yelling at two punk-rocker kids wearing spiked bracelets and chains.

"But *see*, all you're doing is conforming outside of conformity, y'know?" he said. "You wear your chains an' paint your fingernails black an' wear NOFX tee-shirts an' sneer an' all that shit, but *look*, you all look *alike*."

The punk-rockers stared at each other dumbly while Flannigan continued.

"If you *really* want to be non-conformists, you'd just be naked, or maybe wearing a shroud of hemp or some shit—all you're doing now is telling everyone 'lookit me, lookit me…

lookit how *different* I am.'"

One of the punkers tried to interject, but Flannigan just ignored him and waved an arm out, spilling one of their beers all over the floor, "Shit man, they prolly printed up, like, ten *thousand* of those shirts, just like that and sold 'em at concerts or whatever, so there're like ten *thousand* other kids just like you guys wearing that same fucking shirt who think they're all being 'modern retro punk' by wearing a mid-nineties NOFX shirt. You guys should just listen to some indie folk and chill the fuck out."

Before the punkers could reply, Flannigan was scooping a shot glass out of my hand and running back over to the Corner Booth after stumbling into two fat women mauling a hillbilly in a John Deere hat, "Hoo! Wake up you bastards, Max just brought us some more shots!"

On and on the night moved, the clock ticking closer to closing time and the conversation losing coherence. Red-haired Arianna ducked her petite body into the booth and grabbed my arm while telling me about a poem she'd written for next week's Open Mic, cooing in my ear and asking what she should order for a drink.

She sat in the wings, smiling at everyone beneath her puffy vest and flowery dress, wearing a wool beanie she used to cut the winter chill while walking down the streets with stacks of medical books under her arms.

"I just dissected a *pig* heart today," she sing-songed to me, wrinkling her cute little forehead, a comic look of despair in her eyes. When she talked, she caressed my forearm with little delicate fingers.

"What for, your anatomy class?"

"Yeah," she moaned. "It felt so weird just hacking into something's *heart!*"

"Well, you wanna be a doctor, you gotta hack into body parts," I said. "Just wait 'til you get some old homeless cadaver and have to chop *him* all up."

She giggled and scrunched her freckled face.

Gyna came over, skirts flying, hair hanging loose, looking like a painting come to life, a painting of a Woman; the curves, the femininity, the eyes. She set her Bushmills down and slid in, resting her head on my shoulder for a moment before joining the conversation.

"Word," she said into my ear.

Before long, the whole table was involved in an earnest discussion of the last time we'd all pissed our pants—I had no idea who brought it up or why. Flannigan recorded everything in his notebook.

When it came to my turn, I said, "Welll, I actually have *two* stories about pissing my pants."

"The very *last* time I peed my pants was across the street, at A.J.'s," I said. "I was shit-faced and this 60 year-old woman was hitting on me all night. She even stuck her *tongue* in my mouth!"

Everyone groaned and grimaced but I waved them down and continued.

"It's *true!* Anyways, after that happened, I ran to the bathroom to escape and stood there at the urinal, but I forgot to unzip my damn *pants*, so it all just dribbled down both legs. I had to walk through the whole bar again with piss all over myself, and the old battle-axe *still* tried to hit on me, piss stains and all."

"I *remember* that night!" Flannigan broke in, "You were all fucked up on mushrooms, right?"

"I dunno, *maybe*," I shrugged.

"What was the other time?" Wrenn leaned in with an eager smile.

"Ahh, the *other* time was in L.A. last year, when I was working on some bullshit Hormel Chili commercial. I brought a pack of Depends to my friend's 30th birthday party, and there were all these big-wig Hollywood producer types and hanger-on'ers at the party getting wasted and name dropping, an' all that, and one of them wondered if Depends really worked an' I said, '*Course* they work,' and the guy sez, 'Prove it!' so I just stripped off my clothes right there and put on the diaper, pissed like a sumbitch right in front of everyone, and by god, they *did* work! Those people had no idea *what* the hell to think!"

"Oh my god!" Gyna doubled up, tears in her eyes, "I think I just peed a little right *now!*"

Shawny and Liam appeared from their piano bar across the street, where we read poetry. They moved over from Boston a year before and bought the place so Liam could play music. Northsaint accepted them like natives.

"Closed down early, eh?" I said to Shawny.

"Yeesh! Finally, all those artsy-fartsy fuckers are outta my bar! C'mon, we're playing darts—me and Liam against you and Jack," Shawny demanded. She ordered Liam, her quiet, bespectacled husband to the bar for drinks.

We went to the back room where a few sullen drunks played pool and said things like, "Wail, caught me a nice cutthroat out past the Monarchs last week with Dale," and slobbered over mugs of cheap beer between shots.

"Oh Shawny, our Philistine booze slanger," I said as she chalked our names next to the dart board. She was short, dark and stubborn, with her hair tight in a ponytail for convenience.

"I'm not a Philistine!" she protested. "I just think all those artsy-fartsy fuckers are a bunch of whiners."

"Well, there's your problem," Jack grinned, hand on hip. "You *married* an artsty-fartsy fucker."

She regarded Liam at the bar, paying for the drinks, nodding his thanks to JUDE! "Yeah, but he's not like all these little punks—they all whine about, 'oh, my vagina,' or 'oh, Bush sucks,' and all that shit, but they never really *do* anything except get drunk and make asses of themselves. They're just privileged little punks." She struck a match, lit the tip of her cigarette and waved it out.

"So what makes me any different from the 'privileged little punks'?" I asked. "I get up there and read stuff too, sometimes."

"Well, I *like* you, but shit man, you're still an artsy-fartsy fucker," she grinned and yanked the darts out of the board aggressively.

Shawny throws darts like she's sticking daggers into the hearts of heathens. They fly through the air with no arc—just line drives—and bury deep into the corkboard with a heavy *thwack*.

"Where would we be without art, eh?" I waved my arms in the air, spilling beer on the floor. "We wouldn't have any music, any paintings or good books… it'd be a sterile world."

She lunged three more darts in the board, arm reaching back for maximum velocity—*thwack thwack thwack*—and yanked them out irritably, "Yeah, but if you could just see all this from behind the bar where I stand all night—every night—serving everyone their drinks and listening to the bullshit conversations, you'd realize that you all look ridiculous."

"Shawny's just angry because she doesn't have a *thing*," Liam said with a quiet grin.

"*You're* just angry cuz I beat you at *darts* all the time," she shot back. "The only way you can win is if we're on the same team."

"What do you mean *thing?*" I asked.

Liam started to answer, but Shawny cut him off.

"*Look* at you guys," she said, *thwack thwack thwack*, "Flannigan has his quiet, beat poetry *thing*, Gyna has her feminine vagina poetry *thing*, Jay has his indie folk singer *thing*, you have your anti-everything *thing*…"

"I'm not anti-everything," I frowned.

"You all have your thing and you do it over and over again, every Wednesday night," she continued. "And I have to stand there and listen to it."

"Ah, you just don't have the balls to get up there and do your own thing," I said snidely.

"Fuck *you*," she shook her head, "I'm just sick of everyone jerking each other off, thinking they're all great or something. And I'm sick of people referring to me as 'Liam's wife' or as 'the bartender.' I have a fucking Master's in anthropology! Everyone thinks I'm some kind of idiot because I own a bar and serve booze... because I don't get up in front of everyone and show off. I have to pay *bills!* I have to keep this bar afloat! I don't have time to sit around all night writing *sonnets* about my fucking *vagina*."

"Ho ho!" Jack hooted, "I bet that would be something."

"I just think you guys all live in this little dream world," she continued, *thwack thwack thwack*. "You have to realize the real world doesn't give a shit about you or your poetry or your music. Sooner or later, you're going to have to get a real job and pay the bills, cuz nobody makes any money being a mediocre poet."

"So don't *be* a mediocre poet!" I yelled. "Be a *good* poet. It's still possible to earn money doing something you love—not everyone has to work jobs they hate just to survive. You ever hear of Sisyphus?"

She shrugged and nodded.

"He was that dude who was banished to roll a huge rock up a hill for eternity, but every time he rolled it to the top, it would fall back down and he'd have to start all over."

"That's a *simple* version of the Myth of Sisyphus," Jack snorted, forefinger upturned.

"Ah, go fuck yourself," I barked at him. "Anyways, that was his penance for sinning or whatever... rolling this rock up a hill for eternity. But we're all doing the same fucking things every *day*, punching a clock, pushing a rock, working shitty jobs we hate just to make money, and we're all doing this not because we sinned, but merely because we exist."

"So what are you trying to say?" Shawny asked, *thwack thwack thwack*.

"What I'm *saying* is, why don't we just let the fucking rock *go* and climb up the hill alone, despite everyone telling us we can't? Why don't we just try to find a way to make a living doing something we love? It's absurd, this rock."

"Yeah, but how many people actually accomplish that?" Shawny asked. "How many people are actually doing what they love and getting paid well for it?"

"Hardly any," I nodded. "But that doesn't mean it's *impossible*. Why push this rock? Why?"

"Well, I'll tell you one thing," Jack pointed to the dart board, "You're never gonna make a living playing darts, you ass-hat… they just *beat* us."

"Ha!" Shawny high-fived Liam and then she stuck a finger in my chest, "Write a poem about *that!*"

Into the bathroom; smells of urine and stale cigarette smoke, mixed with decades of dried vomit in the grouting of the tiles. The wooden stalls were covered with unintelligent bathroom graffiti, like "Quit looking here, the joke's in your hand," or some guy who wrote his name, and another in different pen wrote "Sucks!" underneath it. I heard snorting from the single stall, and then Bama, the bleary-eyed southern trust-fund drug fiend stumbled out and ran into me while I unzipped.

"Ooop, hey dare Max, y'all want summa dis?" he drawled, waving a bag of coke in my face.

Bama's existence was small and hazy—a terminal coma of Xanax bars, coke and whiskey. He told long, uninteresting stories about times he got drunk and hurt himself, fish he'd caught, women he'd dated years ago. There was an underlying stupidity in him, one that guaranteed that whatever idiot thing he got into, Mom and Dad would bail him out with their money. But he wasn't completely unintelligent. He started a publishing house in Colorado a few years back, but moved to Northsaint for a rehab program that involved teaching kids how to build barns. We'd had a falling out some time ago, and I rarely talked to him.

"Nah."

He cleared his nose and stood there weaving while I finished pissing, then cleared his throat, "Y'all think we can be friends ag'in?"

"No," I flushed the toilet, "I don't."

A flash of clarity broke through his glazed eyes, just for a moment, then faded away. I pushed past him out the door.

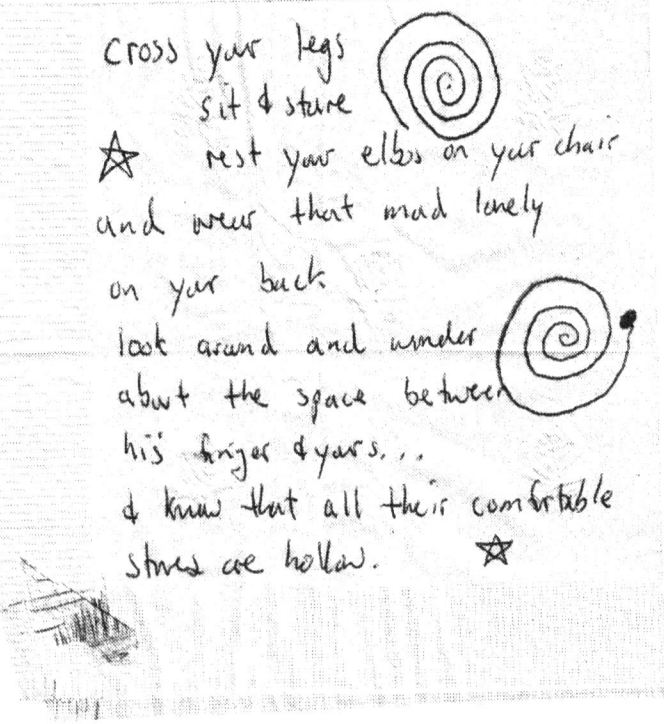

A funny thing happens at the 419 around closing time. Stumbling, drooling cowboys saunter closer to the unclaimed harridans swaying in the "Smut Corner," hoping to take one of them home for a night of cheap, abbreviated sex in some backwoods trailer or cat piss apartment in the low-rent section of town. Heavily intoxicated college girls tug at each other's sleeves and argue about whether or not one should go home with the goateed restaurant worker waiting awkwardly at the bar, watching both of them with tapping foot. Ubiquitous drunks vomit in the bathrooms and get dragged out by Tony, the 300-pound bouncer who writes dirty limericks and reads Bukowski while working the door.

"Hey Tony, what you got for me tonight?" I called to him from the Corner Booth.

He waddled over with smug smile; a slow, mannish strut he used to wag his dick in everyone's face. Up close, he's as big as an ox, head as big as a prize steer.

"I got one for ya," he said and cocked his head to the side with thumb on chin:

> *There are many a sexual diversion*
> *And as many an unnatural excursion*
> *But of all the proclivities*
> *And related activities*
> *Abstinence is the strangest of perversions."*

"Nice nice," I clapped.

"Thanks, now get your feet off the fucking table," he then shuffled back to the door to flare his nostrils at the booze-shitters lining the bar.

Most of our friends had cleared out. Only Jack, Flannigan and myself were still in the Corner Booth, slumped over our mugs and crushing butts into the ashtray.

"God, *look* at this fucking place," I scowled. "These

people… I've only been back a few days and already I'm disgusted again."

"Shit, at least you got to get *out* for a while," Jack grumbled. "I haven't taken a trip since we went to the Testicle Festival last fall."

"You know something I thought of while we were playing darts?" I said. "Do you realize that we're *both* living our dreams right now?"

Jack frowned, "What do you mean?" Flannigan scribbled away into his notebook, listening to the conversation, half-detached, also scanning the bar for drunk women he could take home.

"I mean, you own your own newspaper, you live in your own place with Guinevere and you guys are getting married in a few months. I live in my little cabin in the woods and write all day, eat burritos for breakfast, travel around wherever I want as long as I got enough money. You and I are both living our *dreams* right now and we're just as broke and miserable and lost as all the rest of these fools."

"You're damn right we're miserable," Jack pounded his fist on the table and leaned forward, "That's the way it *is*, man… all you fucking post-modern fools thinking the world owes you something… at least you still *have* a dream. Think of all those idiots out there who've just given up."

"Yeah, but I feel like I've outlived it," I said. "I mean *shit*, I work on fucking *television* commercials, man… that's how I make my living. I always thought it would be so glamorous in Hollywood, but it's just as depraved as everywhere else. I don't even *watch* T.V.! I'm a goddamn hypocrite."

"Well, you recognize it," he grumbled. "Most people deny it."

"I dunno," I sighed and finished off the last of the warm beer in the mug. "I don't think I can keep going back and forth from L.A. to here like I have been… every time it gets worse and worse. I just need to take off, y'know?"

"You got some money, right?" Flannigan said, "Why don't you just take a road trip or something? Hell, I'll go with you."

I stared at the big screen T.V. across the bar for a moment, struck by the vision of the open highway; silent, passing, sweet grains of asphalt, lonely winds in the desert, strangers eating in diners, truckers passing on freeways at night, sunrises over rolling wheat fields, yellow and white lines cutting beneath my fenders, power lines rising and falling out the side window.

Oh, there is nothing more beautiful and pure and perfect than the warm wind coming in through the open window as I burn down the road somewhere far away, with grasshopper wings clapping, where nothing can catch up to me and nothing can hold me back.

On the T.V., an old Danny DeVito movie played on mute. He was sitting on a train, staring out the window at the rolling scenery. It was that moment that this whole thing began, which is ironic, because it stemmed from watching T.V.

"That's it!" I yelled. "I'll get a train pass! I mean, I'll just hop on that fucker and GO, doesn't matter where! Why didn't I think of that before? I'll just spend a whole month on the rails."

"That's probably expensive," Jack turned his mug in a puddle of condensation.

"Fuck, I don't care how much it is," I huffed, feeling alive again just from the thought of it, electricity in my bones. "Whaddya think, Flannigan? Let's do it."

"Ahh, I dunno, man," he licked his cracked lips. "I don't think I can get more than a week off work."

"Fuck work!" I yelled. "What do you care about that stupid job anyway? All you do is sit in the bathroom and write text messages with your cock in your hand."

"Yeah, but ever since I stopped slangin' dope, I gotta rely on that paycheck, man," he said, hesitated, then wrote a line in his notebook.

I looked over at Jack eagerly, but he waved his hands in front of him, like he was swatting away a pesky bee, "Oh no, don't even ask me; you know I'd love to go, but who the hell's gonna run the paper? Plus I only have twenty-seven dollars in my bank account and that has to last me another week."

"Well, fuck it then, I'll go alone," I nodded. "I'll leave tomorrow night—I need to get out and see something *real* again."

The overhead lights blinked on suddenly and everyone shrieked—the horror!—there is nothing more horrid than a brightly lit bar at closing time.

"Awright, finish your drinks, clear your tabs!" Tony yelled, pushing people out of chairs and swinging his dick in everyone's face, "Bar's closed! Get the fuck out!"

"Let's get the fuck outta here," Flannigan snapped the notebook closed and shoved it in the back of his pants. "The homies are all at the Green House right now, let's cruise over and smoke some herb and listen to Jay play some music and stay up all night talking about trivial bullshit, as if it even matters in the first place."

On the way out, Jack murmured like Bogart and shoved his hands in his pockets, "Nyeh, I gotta go edit the rest of the paper... you guys gonna stay up for a while?"

"Course, man," Flannigan said. "Least 'til sunrise, you know us."

"Right, I'll come by when I'm finished," he said and shambled down the sidewalk to his office, hands deep in pockets, looking like a bony tramp searching for a hot bowl of truth.

Flannigan and I beat the other way down the frigid sidewalk with the rest of the rabble that collects like flotsam outside of bars at closing time. Girls detached themselves from unsuccessful attempts at their nether regions and two meth-heads brawled a half-block up, with hipsters stepping over them nonchalantly, cell phones attached to their ears trying to find the coke connection for the night.

"Hel-*lo* Maxy boy," came a boozy, oily female voice behind me. It was Jesse, a fuck buddy of mine, and she was swerving back and forth on the street corner. "What are you up to tonight?" she asked with cocked eyebrow.

Flannigan turned away, visibly annoyed.

Her red hair was frazzled and hung in front of her freckled face, and there was a beer stain on her low-cut blouse showing everything but nipples. She sauntered over and rested her hand on my hip, giving me the horny eye.

"I *really* wanna fuck you tonight," she breathed in my ear, smelling of gin, swaying her hips back and forth, rubbing up against me.

A police car suddenly appeared with lights flashing. Two stocky cops ran over to break up the meth-head fight.

"Fuckin' tree-huggin' *hippie!*" one of the meth-heads yelled. "I *saw* you! I saw you beatin' on *women!* Goddammit, lemme out'ta these cuffs, you pigs! Fuckin' *hippies!*"

Jesse poked me in the stomach and whispered again, "So...whaddya think? Take me home and fuck my brains out."

"Ehgh," I sighed. "We can't do this anymore... your boyfriend."

"*Fuck* my boyfriend," she scowled.

"Well, that's what you *should* be doing," I nodded. "I don't wanna get mixed up with this anymore, okay?"

"But I *need* it!" she pleaded.

I've lost my taste for this cheap love... these 2 a.m. hook-ups... everything half-felt and dirty. I shook myself away from her sad, lost glance and trotted to catch up with Flannigan.

"Surprised you didn't go off with her," he grumbled.

"Well, I didn't need it that bad."

We reached the Green House and saw Bama passed out, face-first, on the front porch—a broken beer bottle in his hand.

"Jesus, man," Flannigan shook his head. "Lookit this asshole. BAMA! Get up!"

He kicked him a few times in the stomach, but Bama didn't stir.

"Ah screw it, man, I've seen him like this before, just leave him," I said, pushing my way in the door.

The night flew on as so many had before; sitting cross-legged on the living room floor passing around bowls and talking into the morning. Jay wandered into the room, looking like a small child lost in a department store, quietly lugging his guitar. "I want to play a few of my new songs for you guys," he said softly, and sat carefully on the mantle to play for us with his feet turned inward and insecure, a voice so soft and yearning, ready to dismantle at any moment, ready to burst while soothing all your jagged edges, searching for the answer we're all looking for, and you can see him get misty when he sings about the girl he once loved or a time he lost; songs we wish we could capture and play in our headphones on lonely nights in the rain. Songs that speak about Our Generation, about our mundane existences... songs about letting your hair grow long, about the death of our small town, about the great American Knot bunching around our necks, getting tighter every day.

Someday Jay will be playing out there in front of millions. By all rights, he should be. But instead he works every day at a music store and goes home to take his vitamins and write another song—one of hundreds of originals—and plays for free at Open Mic Night while the girls sit at his feet, their doe eyes blinking up at him releasing his art, his pathos, and they sigh when he finishes a song and sometimes even shed little tears. He plays for the joy of playing, he plays for the need to play, he plays for Us. He is a musician. He is an Other.

Jay understood what it meant to be an Other, just like Flannigan and Jack. It meant you dedicated your whole being—every breath—to your art. It meant a half-hour discussion when someone asks a nonsense question like, "What do you do for a living?" It meant the sacrifice, the hunger, the sadistic fever… cuz we're never gonna get there, but that doesn't stop us from trying, from dying, from explaining, from observing.

After he'd played a few songs, Jay got up and said, "Well, I have to go take my vitamins," and walked to his room in the back of the house. We put Bob Dylan on the hi-fi and resumed our chatter—Jay coming back to brood in the corner with a full beer.

Jack stumbled in and poked his head through the door around four a.m.

"You guys know Bama's out here with a big piss stain on his pants?" he scowled, leaning through the door.

"Ha!" Flannigan honked and beat the arm of the couch. "I guess we know the last time *he* pissed his pants!"

Jack grabbed a beer out of the fridge and sat down on an old leather chair in the corner with audible relief. The chair was one of those that looked old and uncomfortable, and was, in fact… a chair for looking at, not for sitting. Nobody knew where it came from.

"I think it's hilarious that only my dad and Jack sit in that chair when they come over here," Flannigan said, curled on the couch in a blanket, knees in his hands.

"That's cuz they're both old men," I chuckled.

"I'm *not* an old man, dammit!" Jack sat forward. "Why does everyone have this fascination with calling me an old man? Because I know history? I'm 25 years *old*, man!"

I left as grey light came in through the window curtains, walked back downtown to my car, the wonderful feeling of wandering down the middle of the street at dawn with winter birds chirping their morning wake-up and a car whizzing down a side-street, everything looking new and misty, and I drove home with a pink sun coming up over the mountains to the east, a fresh powdered sprinkle of snow at the tops. Oh, how many times have I driven this bridge across the lake as the sun came up, silent and new? How many times have I stumbled into my little cabin with bugs smashed all over the windows and desk cluttered two years thick with all manner of manuscript papers, dirty dishes, cocktail napkins filled with ballpoint gibberish, spare change and cigarette ashes, and collapsed into bed as daylight broke and the Normals went to work?

I was getting lost in this cycle… this *scene*.

I lost the ability to have normal mornings. I spent every night chasing after something I knew would never come, then I'd sleep 'til the afternoon, just in time to watch the daylight fade in these short, dark, Orwellian days of winter.

My writing was slipping. I was lost inside my own voice, no longer observing things purely, but attaching my own filter of bullshit onto them.

Everything just fell apart. All I could do anymore was hide in my cabin for three, four days at a time, writing insane, rambling gibberish in fits and spells. Hundreds of rejection letters from publishers and magazines and literary agents littered the desk and floor of my workspace. I wrote back to magazines that had rejected my work in obscene, brutally angry tones, denouncing them and their whole staff, wishing they'd all get herpes and die of scurvy.

I just wanted to disappear and watch things happen again—not as an actor, but an *observer*. Some call it a quarter-life crisis, some just think it's the natural progression into looming adulthood. I thought it was the point in a person's life when they realize that to succeed in life, they needed to join the Machine, or die from malnutrition away from it. This train trip was the loophole—a back door perhaps, where I could just sit and watch, make my own assumptions, gather my own wisdom, and see what everyone else in the world was doing.

I'd had enough of this self-serving orgy of acceptance from my artsy friends. Maybe Shawny was right; maybe we *were* all just sycophants and morons. I was tired of my parents' constant questions about exactly how I made a living writing mock articles about Killer Bee attacks and getting wasted at the bar. I was sick of running into my high school friends' moms at grocery stores and having to explain "what I've been up to all these years."

I wanted to find the Soul again. The substance. I'd always believed inherently in the beauty of human nature, but everywhere I looked I saw evil. I saw lethargy. I saw passionate indifference. I saw these greedy, smarmy, apathetic sheep moving through life with self-snapped chains around their feet, afraid to stand out, too proud to fit in, masking their darkness with the wheels, the wheels, the wheels spinning mad, turning us round, all directions, right back to where *they* began... never escaping the cycle. Is this all we are, America?

The morality is gone, and so is the fun. Now we've entered the mediocre, the trite, like bland fast food that tastes the same in Kansas as it does in New York. All we want is the illusion of sustenance, to be entertained, to be showered with attention and then left alone.

Enough!

I packed four changes of clothes, one leather notebook, several pens, a dozen books and a computer, a camera and travel tripod, my sleeping bag, a ratty Mexican blanket and toothbrush, a portable camp stove, one aluminum pan, several packets of ramen noodles, cans of soup and beans, a rain poncho, and two pouches of rolling tobacco; everything I'd need on the road and nothing I didn't.

I called Jack and asked him for a ride to the train station the next evening, then walked up the hill to my landlord's place to drop off my rent check (three days late, of course) and admired his view of the lake. My cabin only looked out on trees and the abrupt incline of the hillside.

"You're *leaving* again?" he asked. "You just got back, didn't you?"

Thirty days to see my country again—four corners bending onward. Spine heights of the Oregon coast to terrible brown California valleys stinking of rotten vegetables and rotten history, leading up into the Sierras into mile-high continental divide unfurling all the way down through dreary plains of Nebraska, Iowa where the corn grows high and the farmers sigh, Illinois, jumping Chi-town, sullen Philly, Boston, New England shining in the mist and on down the eastern seaboard to Florida wetlands, where land turns into emerald sea.

I needed a serious cleansing from this toxic lifestyle. For too long I was chasing after a dream that was never going to come. For too long I was sitting idly by, writing thousands of words into my computer late at night and hoping against hope that maybe someday I could escape this Machine and actually succeed and do it *my way*, instead of quitting the simple way of life and getting a real job. Punching a clock and pushing a rock.

I just wanted to remove myself from everything—to watch life speed by without me in it. To *observe* again. Maybe I was just escaping the fangs of reality. Maybe I was just bored. I don't know. It didn't matter… it was something that had to be done…

Here we go…

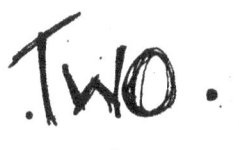

Two.

Rainy dusk when we left—me in the passenger seat watching the darkness roll, tapping my feet, clearing my throat, tugging at my beard—Jack hunched over the steering wheel and squinting through the windshield, "Goddamn these wipers! Can't see a thing!"

He thrust a gloved hand outside and wiped the windshield clear of ice, blurring it even more in the process. We used Guinevere's car, as his had been parked in the same spot outside of their small house for the past two years.

Jack is nervous behind the wheel, which is why he usually leaves the driving up to me during our many road trips. But this time he was at the helm; his black leather gloves wringing the wheel, West German field jacket buttoned neatly over a knotted scarf—standard winter uniform.

I tapped my hands on the dash with the feverish urge I always get right before a big journey.

"Hooo-ah, can't wait to get on that ol' train!" I yelled.

"When's the last time you went back east?"

"God, I dunno… I guess it was when I was a kid, with my dad," I smiled as the memory came back. "He used to drag us along on these epic trips around the country every summer, the only real purpose was to watch baseball games at parks that were being torn down. He wanted me to be able to say I visited every state in the country, and I *have* except for damn Hawaii… can't drive there."

"How's he doin' anyway?"

"My dad?   He's hangin' in there," I stared up at the moon, following along behind the pine trees, sticking to our motion—that big blue moon over us all. "He's getting real thin and frail, especially this last year. It's only a matter of time, y'know?"

"I bet he liked the idea of you going on this trip, huh?"

"Well, I dunno… I don't really talk to him that much anymore."

"Did you even *tell* anyone you're leaving?" he asked.

"You and Flannigan are the only ones who know," I smiled. "I kinda like it that way."

Ray Charles sang and banged on his piano inside our speakers while we discussed the brutish facts of our little world; whether we wanted to write for a new magazine in town that may be funded by a real estate company; drawing in more tourists and smarmy second-home-owner yuppies ("What the hell would I want with *that* magazine?" I ask, and Jack says, "Well, they're paying ten cents a word, man," and I bounce my head and say, "Okay, I'll think about it.") We covered the gamut—drinking too much, staying up too late, ideas for the next article in the *Reader*, plans for a graphic novel that I would write and he illustrate—one of our many projects discussed in length but never completed—whether we were ever going to pull out of this rut and create something great like we always planned.

The Amtrak station was quiet at midnight—lonely and desolate, with a few bare streetlamps burning hard shadows across the parking lot. Lazy snow blew in and night sounds moved across town. A handful of sullen passengers sat waiting with bags between their legs. This; the lull and still-life of travel.

It was quiet with echoes, as all train stations are late at night. The dim-witted Amtrak attendant behind the counter looked bored and inexperienced.

He sold me the 30-day rail pass with some difficulty, having to run into the back room to scratch his bald head and speak with a supervisor several times by the end of the transaction.

"Where do you wanna go first?" he asked finally, hands poised on the keyboard.

"Oh, I'm not even sure," I scratched my beard. "How 'bout I start in Denver? I got friends in Denver."

He clacked away, humming to himself, then stopped and clicked his teeth.

"Oop, looks like the train coming in from Montana just had an engine go down. Looks like you'll have to take a bus to Portland, then the Coast Starlight will get you to Sacramento, then the Zephyr takes to east to Denver."

"A bus?" I scowled. "Oh well—bus, train, cabbage truck—it don't matter, s'long as I can go... anywhere but here."

"All right then," he pushed the tickets over to me. "Have a good trip."

We walked outside into the cold just as two buses pulled up and hit the airbrakes with squeals and honks, piercing the night with that lonely sound, that forgotten sound of motion on the way.

"Which one do I take to Portland?" I asked the chubby baggage attendant.

"Either one," he grumbled, loading suitcases with head down. "This one here is a charter bus with a Christian fellowship on board—it's only half full, and t'other is the regular Greyhound line with only a coupla seats left. You'd prolly be more comfortable on the Christian bus—more room to stretch out, y'know? Either one is fine."

"I'll take the full one." He nodded and threw my giant

rucksack underneath with the rest of the bags, grunting and reaching for the next person in line.

"Well, I guess this is it," I offered my hand to Jack.

"Yes sir."

"Take care of the booze-shitters while I'm gone."

"Right," he nodded and gave me one last look—a look that stays with me. I think of it often, Jack's looks when I depart and enter the big blue world, and he stands right on the cusp of familiarity with feet planted, and firmly shoves me off. Like so many moments before and so many yet to come, I stood there at that edge, that razor's edge of familiar and unknown, separated only by the conscious decision to leave one in search of another. I turned and left him standing on the asphalt.

"Careful out there," he glowered. "See you in a month."

Fifty pairs of eyes watched me for split-second judgment when I boarded, then looked away lethargically. The only open seat was in the very back, next to a bathroom and an old woman I thought was dead until she suddenly broke into a coughing fit and wetted my cheek with her spittle. I sighed happily and watched Jack walk erectly to his car, look up at the bus one last time, then pull out of the parking lot with tailpipe smoking, cigarette glowing, back to his sleeping fiancé, back to Northsaint, back to our little Shire.

It was 1 a.m. when the overhead lights dimmed and the bus pulled out, grumbling and cussing through the quiet downtown streets of Spokane, onto the freeway, climbing up the hill south of town, entering the darkness out there, in the great beyond... hot damn, on my way.

The worst place to sit on a bus is right next to the bathroom. I was not only nudged awake by every sweating goon stumbling back to deposit their McDonald's goo in the miniature toilet, but also by a sick woman who ran back to violently vomit every 10 or 15 minutes. For six hours.

"I'm sorry," she said every time after exiting the bathroom, wiping chunks from her chin. "I have the flu, I think." The passengers still awake gave her acidic smiles, all wanting to bash her in the face, no doubt.

So, lulled by the sounds of disruptive bowels and car sickness, the bus sped blue through the moonlit night, cutting south into Tri-Cities in eastern Washington amongst those endless expanses of farmland—girded by lines of power poles like stitches across the tundra.

Finally, we broke into Oregon and headed west along the gusty Columbia River Gorge, stopping briefly in The Dalles for fuel around 4 a.m. I hopped out into the frigid air and smoked a cigarette with two or three grubby travelers.

"Hey man, can I give you a dollar for one of them cigarettes?" asked a toothless man, holding out a crumpled, soiled bill.

"How 'bout I just give you one for free?" I handed him one and lit it.

"Awright, lessgo!" yelled the driver, and we were off again, before the man could even take two puffs off of his cigarette.

The vibrations of a bus leave something to be desired. The trip is filled with the whiny drone of that big mother diesel engine, rising and falling at the whim of the driver's steady toe. Every imperfection on the highway rattles your spine, jabs your hips, rocks your stomach like a paint mixer. Passengers snore on top of one another in that half-asleep, half-awake, half-miserable, half-beautiful traveling state of consciousness. It feels more like you're in the crew bunk of a submarine than in a charter bus.

But a train—riding a train is like riding on white noise, a swooping serenade of background motion that soothes your soul and opens you eyes, letting it all come a-rushin' in. The engine a half-mile ahead, barely heard back in the coach cars... sometimes you hear the whistle far off, from a dream. Buckles in the track and clackety-clack, we're on our way Jack.

We reached Portland at dawn—the city of stone bridges and smoking chimneys. Gulls picked at the roofs of small tin shacks by the rail yard while bleary-eyed drunks roused to greet the steely grey of a new day.

A city is never more itself than in the Great Hour of Waking.

I had five hours to kill before the Coast Starlight line cut through, so I checked my bags at the baggage counter for $2 and took a great hobo nap at Union Station.

All urban train stations are the same, no matter where you go in the country. The echoes of hushed voices in high-ceiling buildings built in another time, in another era, varnished curved wooden bunches polished by the asses of so

many Traveling Sams, etched with their lonely initials and dirty limericks—always a sickly yellow-colored wood that reminds you of vomit and old times. So much woe, so much optimism, so much ennui has rested a bony haunch on those pillars—incredible to think.

I shook awake after a bit and took a stroll outside, through Chinatown with all the beat characters of the early morning emerging like worms after a heavy rain.

Bums in rags squeezing quarters off the sharply dressed businessmen rapping their expensive pace en route to chic office buildings. Ancient Chinese merchants sweeping their front steps in dirty aprons, nodding hello as I moped by with great fried smells wafting out from the back. Crazy morning joggers in headbands and iPods, insulating themselves from the world with music. Hungover Portland hipsters in Saturday night clothes, walking home from all-night parties to make pancakes and read the funnies with pounding temples—the Curse of the Non-Generation.

All these characters of American Life—each one slipping past, occupying a moment in my life, showing me their fantastic anonymous faces and walks and bench-sitting postures. They show me so much.

But the thing about watching people is, you lose track of time. Rush back to the station, smoke a quick butt along the way and leap on the train just in the nick of time (how come they don't yell "All Aboard" anymore?). Stow the bags, settle into the seat, kick open a nice thick book and watch it all go burning by—a fantastic rolling slideshow outside my window, just for me.

We wound through central and southern Oregon all covered with snow—stopping in Salem, Albany and Eugene, then Chemult. Me staring the whole time out the window at everything and trying to write it down as fast as possible without thinking—not even looking at what I was typing.

Telephone poles crooked in an ochre sky, men in black woolen caps and brown jackets, climbing into GMC pickups and trundling away from industrial slag yards festooned with decaying farm machinery and old washing machines.

Midget horse ranches, droopy old hound dogs chained to the grills of snowmobiles, moldy stacks of hay hidden underneath ancient blue tarps. Billboards stuck like neon daggers beside the road; advertising used car dealerships, A.M. radio stations and housing developments moving into the area. Barbed wire fences with scrap wood posts stretching along the tracks for dozens of miles before suddenly cutting north and disappearing far across the horizon. A golf course in fabulous shades of Oregon green all glinting with golden sidelight from a late afternoon sun slowly drifting toward the big blue Pacific, looming somewhere out there, due west.

The Oregon Trail commemorated with three huge, covered wagon statues the size of buildings, blue garbage cans placed at the curb for the, yes, there it is now, the garbage truck; manned by two men in grubby overalls, one driving, the other hanging off the back. They scoop up the muck we give them week by week, and I could almost swear one of them had a smile on his face.

Little brown-haired kid waving at me as we parallel the highway, except I don't wave back. I just stare at him with my gloomy face and watch him drift away in the passenger seat of his father's construction truck, piled with ladders and power tools and flapping tarpaulins.

And there you are sun—thought you'd given up for the day behind those Bob Ross clouds trying to shade us all from the light. Canby, Oregon now, still moving steady and sure like a winter chill off the back of a high and mighty mountain, picking up kinetic energy to expend just as soon as I think of what to expend it on, see? Yass, I'm sure you see, but do *I* see? Where *is* the sea? Can't see it from here… must be too far inland. River's flooding though—trees growing out of the turbulent water.

Ah me, all this shit to see and I can't keep up—I can *never* keep up. Too slow, too fast, wrong direction—ack ack, it's never enough, it's too much… one day. *Some* day.

I took a short nap and woke up quick as the train slowed into a nondescript station—Zang!—I put on my shoes, scarf, hat, jacket, and went galumphing up a few cars to see if I could sneak out and smoke off one of these joints I smuggled in the bottom of a pouch of Drum rolling tobacco, but no, the conductor stopped me and said, "Ho there buddy, this ain't no smoke stop—you're gonna have to wait 'til Klamath Falls." So I beat back down the aisle past the bored passengers reading books and eating pre-packaged meals from the deli or just staring out the window blankly.

Through the night into Dunsmuir, California after traversing the pristine Siskiyou Mountains. Full moon the only source of light outside my window pane, but all I see is the dark, lonely reflection of this train car, my lost face staring back with eyebrows pulled back. There's a movie playing in the lounge car, but I don't wanna see it—I'd rather stare at my stupid face and the black night—every once in a while passing a night watchman's shack with solitary lamp post, the poor bastard seen blowing into his hands and watching a tiny television set through the small window covered in ice and snow. Even out here in the boonies they crave the neon connection.

The two people in front of me yakking on and on—the guy talking about how much he pays for his cell phone bill, how much his breakfast cost, how much the price of gas has risen, how much, how much. Oh, poor man—forever stuck valuring everything based on how much money it costs to obtain. One of those "how much" guys who can't think in terms of anything else, and can't think of anything else to talk about, so they set their blinders and go full speed back-wards, complaining about it all.

The weird part is, the lady he talks to actually seems *interested* in what he says. She's probably lonely too—when people don't hear their own voices for a while, they get a little batty and desperate. They put up with just about anything so that they can add their insignificant little input to the world.

"*Six dollars* for two eggs, coffee and juice!" he bellowed. "I could go to Denny's and get three *times* that amount of food for the same price."

"Yeah, I know," the woman replied. "It's terrible!"

Redding, Weed, Chico, and finally Sacramento at dawn. I hadn't uttered a single word to one person the whole time except for that guy who bummed a cigarette on the bus. I wasn't ready to talk yet—just observe.

The light grew to the east as we slowed into Sac-town. A boy of about 8 or 9 years walking by the tracks lifted his hand as if to wave at us, but dropped it suddenly and bent his little head down to watch his foot falls. Must've thought better of it at the last second. Wonder what strange deeds his heart is up to at 7 o'clock on a Monday morning.

Sacramento. I got off the train listening to the "How Much" guy still blathering, now about how much his car in-surance costs. "I can't *believe* it, they just *raised* it $100 this year because of a speeding ticket I got a few months ago, I *tell* ya, it's getting to be too much for anyone to handle anymore. How we s'pose to *live?*"

I stowed my bags at the counter and ambled around downtown to stretch my legs. Just like the previous day in Portland, the great brown, smelly city of Sacramento was rousing itself awake, like a whore the morning after a hard night of fucking.

Fat, sloppy government workers waddled down the sidewalks with swinging plastic ID badges around their chubby necks, eating Filet-O-Fish sandwiches from McDonald's, tartar sauce oozing onto their fat fingers. This is who mans the halls of government? Phooey.

Later, while sitting on the courthouse steps, writing down my thoughts next to a fountain, I was mistaken for a homeless man and shooed away—like you'd shoo a dog who just pissed the rug.

"You can't sit here," the government man sneered. He wore a cut-rate suit jacket with ID badge clipped self-importantly to his lapel.

"What do you mean?" I looked around. "Why is this huge *bench* here if people can't sit on it?"

"This is government property," he sneered again. "Move along please, or I'll be forced to call the police."

Instead of arguing, I just smiled to myself and walked away, thinking that I probably made more money than he did last year, then feeling ashamed for thinking that.

It was like that all over downtown—bums lining the streets hitting people up for quarters and the Suits walking by without taking notice.

"Hey man, you spare some change for a vet?" they'd say. "I fought fer yer freedom! Now gimmie a damn quarter! How 'bout a smoke?"

But the Suits marched on, blathering on cell phones and punching important details in their PDA's, stepping over the legs of sleeping vagrants lying in their own piss. And when I met eyes with these bastions of success and American Worth, they looked at me not like one of them as I had been accustomed to, but like I was just another worthless bum littering their city streets. I was an outsider—another freeloader scamming the system. Just more hair clogging the bottom of the drain.

Maybe it was my hat that caused people to scowl. I stole it from a paint store in Fresno some years ago on my way up to Yosemite. I remember seeing it there on the shelf, a light khaki pork-pie hat with short brim, and thought it was the ugliest hat I'd ever laid eyes on. I put it on my head and walked out the door with it, tag hanging down and everything. I don't know why—I don't usually steal things except for food and drugs on occasion.

Now, several years later, it had acquired a brown rim of sweat stain around the brim, grease from changing tires on freeways, tears and burn holes from campfires, and the bill just hung down flaccid, having lost its ability to stand up anymore. It was full of bad Karma and I took it with me everywhere. If I was a hat, I'd look like this one.

Feeling sad and ponderous after all the homeless people, I moped back to the station, stopping briefly to read the headlines from the Sacramento Bee:

"MAJORITY SUPPORTS IMPEACHING BUSH FOR WIRETAPPING."

"FORMER VP GORE DELIVERS REMARKS ON 'DANGEROUS' CONSTITUTIONAL ISSUES."

"US MILITARY DEATHS TOP 2,000 IN IRAQ."

"37 SLAIN IN SHIITE MOSQUE CAR BOMBING."

"BRANGELINA TO HAVE BABY!"

"MAJORITY OF AMERICANS THINK MOST OF CONGRESS IS CORRUPT."

"BUSH'S APPROVAL RATING DROPS TO LOWEST POINT OF PRESIDENCY."

I shook my head and looked around at the faces coming and going, the cars honking at FedEx drivers with flashing hazard lights, the ratty bums with ratty dogs on makeshift leashes, the musicians with guitars strapped on backs… we all read the same headlines of disaster and nonsense and it just drifts past our desensitized eyes, more fodder for the apocalypse.

The black locker attendant back at the station lugged my heavy rucksack up to the counter and panted, "Lawd me, you in the Army or somethin'?"

"Nah, I'm a writer," I smiled.

"Oh."

Outside the people lined up by the train and passengers finished quick butts on the platform. I stepped aboard the California Zephyr heading east and sunk back into another seat with my nose on the window pane, ready to watch.

Goddamn, there's a huge tent city of hobos there in a brown gully by the tracks… the things you don't see from the highway, or anywhere else for that matter—all manner of bums and homeless living like animals next to the muddy overflow of the Sacramento River. These inland no-man's-land California swamps in the throes of winter, scenes of green and brown whipping by—a dog walking party there—an old woman on a bike with hoody sweatshirt grey and black, a scowl on her face in split second snapshot. Wal-Mart, Costco, Radisson Hotels—back to civilization again. The strip mall paradise of the American West. One big homogenous happy family. Our American cookie cutter architecture—everything the same, always the same.

Cars streaming underneath our train bridges, big orange box trucks trundling their loads on the road running parallel to the tracks—it's a yellow and orange world today… stopping briefly by the off-ramp leading onto some unnamed highway system cutting across the outskirts of dingy old smelly old Sacramento.

There's a decrepit, burned-out lawn chair—green, like the one I used to have but caught on fire trying to dry it over a midnight bonfire at the lake—but this one's sitting here in a gully ditch beside the road by a construction mess, set up on its collapsible legs pointing right at me, as if there's some phantom sittin' there pondering up at me like I am at him. Pondering at an empty chair, what the hell am I doing?

The ebb and flow of traffic. The ebb and flow of life—just a barren world waiting for a seed of something fantastic to bloom and blossom to take away this monotony, this emptiness, this dull state of affairs, this ennui of the human spirit we all seem to be suffering. How can I find this stopped scene—while a Burlington Northern passes us on the other track—so fascinating? Because I have nowhere else to look? What if I were three cars up, looking at that strip mall those poor bastards in the sleeping cars are seeing?

Agh, my knee hurts… been hurting for days. This travel is no good for a bum knee. And a bum knee is no good for a bum me… and that's what I'm trying to do, I suppose; try to look like a bum with all my high-tech gadgetry and such—what a fool I am.

Ah me, moving now—saw a purple glove perched high in a barren tree. Yes, now more scenery; white half-moon shaped buildings containing something to be kept dry—lumber perhaps. Big silver culverts waiting to be installed somewhere they don't have any business being, field of orange tractors lined up, soap on the windshields, it's a farm sale, derelict stacks of railroad ties, blue garbage dumpsters, trailer parks in the distance, oh here we all go…

Gradually making our way east, high up into the Sierra Nevadas all crisp and white with untouched happiness. Up and over Donner Pass with a shudder. Old mining towns zip by, now ghosts and tourist attractions—brown highway signs point the way. Mini-vans stopped on the side of the road there, swarms of jacketed tourists snapping pictures with slim digital cameras—their breath smoking.

Well, hidely hee, here we be, rollin' on into Truckee, white-washed with every chimney a-smokin' and all the wrapped and bundled people warm and smiling beneath their layers. Red-cheeked and warm-hearted, it seems.

Now following the old Truckee River on down past Lake Tahoe to the south, winding down the mountain 'til we arrive in Reno so I can step off this mother and smoke another holy Drum stick. Animal tracks in craters of the Truckee moon.

There *is* something odd about the way people stare at a passing train—almost like they're staring at the past, or at a myth suddenly brought to life.

There's one now; an old grampa with a little terdy grandkid in his arms, the gramma waiting demurely off to the side as they both go a-watchin' the train whiz by. Yeah, there sure is something magical about a train. Can't quite put my finger on it—it's like they represent movement in the old sense, before everything became so hung-up on instantaneous results. I've felt it since I was a kid. I used to ask my dad to take me to the train station just so I could watch the people coming and going, here and there. It was almost as if their act of movement was contagious, and I could catch it as some sort of strange side effect and be off on my own wayward journey. I always wanted to go somewhere. Cuz I can't stand the stationary—like sharks that suffocate when not moving through the water.

These small western towns boomed because the railroad came steaming through bringing more people, more money, more idealists and capitalists and entrepreneurs—this east-west route across the country taken both ways for hundreds of years, by those seeking something great to find or those escaping something that has found them. By those looking for another chance, a last chance. By those born into this world with an idea of something better. And these trains still rumble along, like the last brown buffalo loping around the hills, waiting for their ultimate demise. One last archaic piece of history amidst an era of sweet, hollow confection.

Secret furtive glances at my fellow passengers, always on the lookout for cute girls to talk to. No luck this trip—mostly old people clearing their sinuses and a few true characters that would take *pages* to describe. No suits here. No bankers or lawyers. No bleached-teeth doctors or spastic Hollywood actors. Just real people. Some overweight, some wearing rags, some starving, some in wheelchairs, some mysterious, some predictable, some lonely, some chatty, some wealthy, some poor—all different, all the same.

People that travel by train seem to have one major thing in common; they are people who enjoy time to watch, to think... time just to *be*. Seems that it gets more and more difficult to obtain that time anymore when we're too busy trying to save it.

Oh well—rolling beside Highway 6 now—which begins in Bishop, California and ends some 3,200 miles later at the very tip of Cape Cod, Massachusetts. Kerouac's "holy red line" across America—passing cars now and then, their curious faces peering over at me sitting here writing about them.

Down, down the pass, still heading toward Reno all twinkling with neon dreams—but not so fast! About 20 miles outside of town, the train stops and sits idle. According to the conductor, we almost collided with a speeding freight train heading the other direction.

"Nothing to worry about folks," he said with kid gloves to the train car. "We had a close call with a westbound freight, so we'll have to wait here for a little while until the congestion clears up."

"How long is it gonna take?" a kid in Cincinatti Reds cap asked.

"We don't know yet," the conductor answered. "Could be an hour, could be longer."

We ended up burning four hours stopped beside I-80, waiting for some switchman or conductor to get the signals right. Bellyaching from the passengers about this and that while I sat silently observing them like a lonely botanist stuck watching humans instead of trees.

"They can't just keep us cooped up in here," a housewife complained. "I knew I should've flown."

A strange yoga girl began hanging upside-down by her knees from the overhead compartment shelf beside me, attracting strange glances from other passengers. She then climbed around on all the seatbacks up and down the train car, saying, "Gotta do something to break the monotony," and all other manner of bullshit. I listened to her talking for hours before and grew annoyed with her: "I don't eat meat, or *any* animal products, actually. I don't even use *soap*. I just like to live natural and not put any toxins in my body," and so on… I just sat there pouring Wild Turkey from a bottle I found in my rucksack, smelling my own body odor and wondering how bad *she* smelled if she never used soap. I wondered if her aura was purple.

An old hoary man sitting behind me started spitting and swearing about the conductors not letting him out to smoke.

"This is kidnapping!" he screamed to nobody in particular. "I ought'a write a letter!"

No one listened to his complaints, though he didn't seem to care one way or another—just passing the time by bitching. A Midwestern soccer mom sat knitting lethargically and eating dried apricots. A baby cried somewhere in the back of the car. Two Chinese women sat opposite my seat, the closest holding a cross medallion. She hadn't stopped fidgeting with it the whole journey—a spiritual woman.

But that's the price you pay for all this… this… this what exactly? The train is never on time. It doesn't go half the places you want to go. The attendants are surly. The dining car food is bland and expensive. All in all, it's an archaic way to travel, second only to the Greyhound Bus… but still, once you get on board, none of that matters.

No one seems to travel by train anymore. Why would they when it's so quick and easy to take an airplane? So economical? Why spend three days on a train when you can cross the country in a matter of hours by air?

In the pressurized tube of a jetliner 30,000 feet in the sapphire sky, the human stain upon the earth appears infinitesimal—like insects. Especially while moving at such an incredible velocity.

All the grit is lost beneath the ever-fleeting space between. All reality slapped by the hushed airless void, isolated, blind, shooting through the stratosphere—21st century explorers with no more frontiers.

But traveling by train is like traveling inside a black and white photograph. There is so… much… time… time that you may have thought impossible to obtain. When else will you have 30 straight days just to read books, look at people and ponder out the window at the whole hep world whizzing by? An orange and blue dream.

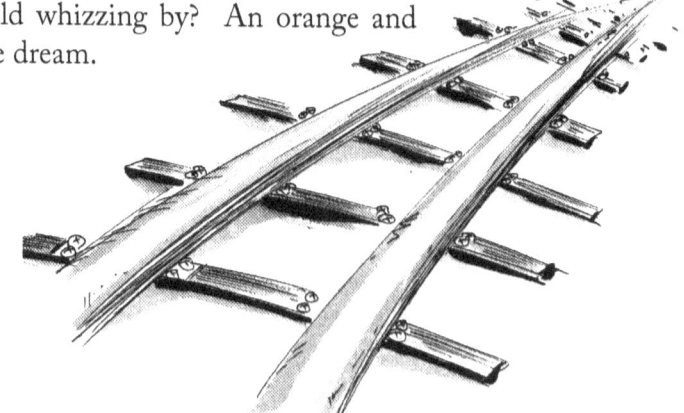

THREE

I slept through the post-apocalyptic decay of northern Nevada and woke at the border town of Wendover. I had a flat here once, about ten miles east of town. The auto repair shop that towed me in and changed my flat for $200 whizzed by. Old memories from the loony past.

And here we go again—11 a.m. in the Wasatch Range, Utah—everything covered in white-filled beauty. Little green trees poking out clean, winter haze creeping low around the hilltops, Provo up ahead—on our way to Grand Junction, five hours behind schedule.

Shanty little towns in nowhere Utah; piles of broken-down junkyard cars in front yards, a faded yellow bus frame listing to port side—neat little cottages with wrapped chimneys and rabbit ear antennae sticking out of the roofs—the closer to the rails, the beater they are. Water towers with small town names painted in large letters, floodlights poking over some boxcars from a nearby baseball diamond—stopped in… hell, I have no idea where we are right now. Some podunk Utah town where they won't let us out to smoke cuz they want to make up the time we lost in Reno. Fuckers.

I can see the heat rising out of the vents on the ol' Union

Pacific engine parked on the tracks next to us, shimmering and radiating the mountains beyond—thick, tall sandstone bluffs that look as if they'd all come tumbling down if you pulled one rock from the base—dotted with tumbleweeds of sage, blackbrush, pinyon, sprinkled with powdered sugar snow here and there. Wile E. Coyote spires.

Ho ho, an entire field of port-a-pottis... hundreds of 'em, pink, blue, yellow, orange, green—every color under the Mormon sun. Off in the distance the line of houses crawl up the mountain like a growth of algae. Like a line of viral mutants. Like a rising tide that never recedes. Cranes perched silently in the grey sky, looming over skeletal births of giant buildings, freeways taking shape, paths moved, rivers diverted, the asphalt covered with orange cones and plywood barriers, caution tape and surveyors. In America, we've entered the age of constant construction. Can't build it fast enough.

Ah, moving on down the line—three hours to go until we get to Grand Junction where they let us out to smoke— Helper, Utah—that's the name of this town. Strange name.

Closed-down gas stations, nondescript redbrick buildings built a hundred years ago, every window boarded up or shielded with rusty bars. All of them shrouded with delicious momentary mystery. It's a sleepy town where maybe someone is sitting in a closed room, pondering about all this road going and all this life moving. Find your way.

There's a couple of old ghost boxcars—Golden West Pacific—one red, one blue—sitting in decay next to the outskirts of this little burg, camo-painted Chevy Blazers for hunting, junk junk junk junk everywhere, feed houses in every back yard... god, all this junk. Why do we keep it? Is it the measure of our worth?

Ah, but what the hell... listening to Bob Dylan as this train makes its way further and further east, going nowhere, going everywhere, staring my sad green eyes out at this world I've only begun to see.

In the sightseeing car with my feet up, watching the high desert of Utah slowly turn into the Rocky Mountains of Colorado. Climbing this plateau, bending onward toward the Continental Divide, tip of the world down here, for water's sake, and down into Denver—holy Denver—where I planned to hop off and spend a few days bumming around my old college haunts.

At times like these, it doesn't matter that we're five hours behind schedule. It doesn't matter that I haven't showered in three days. It doesn't matter that I'm hungry, that my bum knee hurts, that I'm tired of sleeping in a train seat while the fat man ahead of me talks on and on to some poor old Japanese woman next to him ("An' so my *third* wife divorced me last year and now I'm tryin' to get custody of the kids cuz she's datin' a *crack* addict…").

None of these trivial things matter because I'm not traveling to *get* anywhere. I'm just going to *go*.

Dogs laying in the bright winter sun, lapping their little doggie tongues happily, little trailer houses on blocks just feet away from the tracks—the poor families who have gotten used to the rumbling of this steel ghost and the piercing cry of her whistle. Bronze statue in a park; an old man holding a little boy's hand—wonder if it's Catholic?—ho ho.

And look there, a little stream with a kid's jump that he built for his bike… following along with old Highway 6 again, moving at a good speed. The wide, brown valley extends for miles, hemmed in by great heights yet to come.

Houses up there on the bluff overlooking the whole valley—maybe the rich'uns? Distant church steeples—the whip that keeps Utah in line.

I'm consumed by this strange conversation occurring at the other end of the sightseer car. Same fat John Candy type guy who kept hounding the Japanese woman, hopping from one end of the train to the other, seeking out people to talk to and almost acting like some sort of queer saint, making people feel as if they have something amazing to say to his gol-LEEE way of speaking. I don't know exactly what's wrong with him, but I can tell exactly what his deal is... he finds a new person or couple or whatever, talks with them for a little while after offering his pudgy hand, lays down all of his problems, all of his fears, all of his worries, and listens while they unload all of their psychobabble canned wisdom... Train Therapy. He knows he'll never see them again. He purposely tells them everything and maybe even lies a little to spice it up. Mostly talking about his ex-wife and his soon-to-be ex-kids, his money woes, his being fired from a job, and his reason for this train trip, which was either to get a new job or to kill his entire family.

The John Candy guy now talking to a couple from Texas who lived in third-hand slogans: "Just do it," "Live for the moment," "Take days one at a time." His dumb wife or girl-friend backed the Texan up with her equally stupid wisdom: "We all have our crosses to bear," and, "Don't dwell on the past so much," blah blah blah. Two blowhards who think they know the way of the world, just because they read a few self-help books. SELF-HELP BOOKS ARE FOR LAZY PEOPLE. They think they have it all figured out... it's easy to regurgi-tate a bunch of nonsense and wrap it up in a perfumed rag, but a turd is a turd, as my father always said.

I'm amazed at the level of talking going on—and I'm also saddened that I feel like I can see through this fat guy's game while these dupes keep talking and talking. Before the Texas couple, it was a brown-haired lady with an ugly mole on her cheek. Before her it was my smelly yoga friend that sits one seat behind me. He just hops from one group to the next, telling the same self-deprecating tales and expecting them all to suddenly cry out and hug him, shower him with attention and guidance.

Here's what they're saying to the Fat Man, so you un-derstand what I mean: "If you were flying an airplane and you got off the controls, odds are you're gonna die. If you stayed at the controls, odds are you're gonna land it. You gotta stay awake, stay alert, realize that you are your own best friend, don't fall asleep at the wheel," and so on. "You have goodness in you, you have personal issues from when you were younger, it's up to you now. It's time. It's your job now.

"Yeah, but," he interjects, his knees shaking up and down. "How can I convince my wife that this guy she's dating is no good?"

"Thought you said she was your *ex*-wife?"

"Well, yeah, that's what I *meant*," he grins sheepishly.

I guess we all take the train for different reasons. For some it's the saving of money. Others it's the sights, or maybe they're afraid of flying, or don't like the confinement of an airplane, or want to hide from the Man—no, the Fat Man just happens to be taking the train because he needs some sort of psychiatric help—therapy—someone to tell him their colloquial bullshit so he can get away with talking about himself. Because that's all he really wants to do anyway—talk about himself. It's the character we think we know best. Every time somebody strays from his problems, he quickly interrupts with an anecdote or story or reiteration of a previous point already smashed to death. Just like we all do in America —me! That's what this is all about: ME!

Riding right alongside I-70 now… south a ways, over the expanse of brown and yellow desert, lies Arches National Park, Moab, Canyonlands and the Colorado River. I used to backpack around here every spring, in the carefree days, whizzing along Highway 191 with some beef jerky, talking into my tape recorder, pondering into the sun and deciding where I was going to go, what I was going to do, and who I was going to see—standard decisions of the nomad life.

Three days on this train and I still haven't really talked with anyone yet—the last train trek I took from Raton, New Mexico to Los Angeles was filled with talking. I sat next to a couple of old grandmothers who smoked their way from Florida to the Pacific—this before they got rid of the smoking cars. Then there was that Kiwi snowboarder girl I shared a J with in Albuquerque and told my life story and heard hers in return that night and sleepy morning. I asked her what she did for a living and she just said, "I'm a traveler." I liked hearing that.

I was returning to L.A. after taking a strange trip that began with my radiator exploding in a column of white smoke right on I-10 in rush hour. Somehow I managed to get it to Palm Springs and ditched it at my friend Moe's house, where we continued on in his Subaru to go hiking in Canyonlands for a week. The only way I had to make it back was by airplane or train, and flying is so boring and stupid and easy that I refuse to do it unless I have to.

But now, I don't really feel like talking with *anyone*. I just want to sit here and watch everything. I hate that I see through people so easily—like I'm not even giving them a chance. I just don't want to waste a few hours hearing someone talk about how they did this or that or whatever—it's like trying to have a conversation with Bama—you say one thing and they interrupt and say, "Oh yeah, I remember this one time I used to…" blah blah blah. Always searching for some little gem of the conversation that they can blow and polish and jam up someone else's ass whether they really want to hear it or not. We no longer possess the skill of pure listening—just waiting for the hesitations in conversation so we can jump in and steer the direction back to ourselves. Always trying to fill the silence. I'm sick of talking about my stupid life—trying to explain to people, "What I do for a living." To hell with them and their Dr. Phil bullshit.

Christ, there go the Texans again, spilling their gibberish to the Fat Man over and over again, who keeps the conversation going long after it died. "Follow your heart." "Just because you don't know the solution doesn't mean there isn't one." "Come from integrity everyday." "These are our challenges, you're never going to stop having them."

If I had to hear this bullshit, both coming from Fat Man and from his savior Texan therapists, and actually *respond* to it, instead of just sitting here eavesdropping on them while my computer charges up from the only outlet on the train, I think I'd probably smother myself with this tiny little pillow the conductor gives you at night.

These little slogans are so obvious, so cliché. Anyone with half a brain knows these things, yet those who dispense such knowledge do so as if they're leaking out confidential life information. Really, they just saw it on Oprah or read it in *Conversations with God*.

"You act like you're the shit, people think you're shit."

"You got one foot in the past and t'other in the future, it means you're pissing on the present. Yuk yuk yuk."

"Accentuate the positive, eliminate the negative. That's from the 'Jungle Book'."

"What would you do if you had four years to live, four days, four minutes, four *seconds*… that's your life calling."

Back in my seat finally, away from psychobabble land, just sighing and staring out the window again, and ahh, much better… solitude. Golf course in northern Utah, the grass dead and bent over brown with winter's stain—a curvy playground slide out in the middle of nowhere, strange place for a park. Dilapidated old wooden shacks leaning in the hard sun—radio towers gleaming with little lights blinking on top—hard gritty desert sand with rattlesnakes, lizards, scorpions; varmints of every kind.

I know this terrain well—I feel it in my bones. These long flat valleys between the sandstone bluffs, the random desert cows hobbling around in the tundra looking for something to eat, the endless span of power lines stretching from here all the way around the goddamn country. The *silence* of the desert.

Guy just passed by with one of those "mid-life crisis" ponytails and said, "Whatchoo writin' there? Lonely Highway?" laugh chortle laugh. Hyaw hyaw hyaw. I didn't get it.

"Yeah, something like that," I said.

He then walked away, but hesitated and came back, "You put the railroad tracks in there and you can have a (something I didn't understand)" laugh chortle laugh, hyaw hyaw hyaw.

"Yeah," I mumbled and bent my head back to writing.

Goddamn people—I love them as long as they don't talk to me, as long as they don't show their soft underbelly weaknesses. As long as they don't show their dark side, their weak side, their bullshit side... goddamn, now I'm hungry. I won't eat this train food—no sir—but I *will* pop open a can of beanie weenies and eat the fuckers cold. Why not?

Yeah, so there—I just did. Ate the fuckers cold and they tasted just fine. Now I'm gonna take a whore's bath in the teeny tiny toilet and maybe change clothes—these old rags are stinking terribly. I've been wallowing in them for days now—ever since, well, shit, ever since Friday morning when I put them on. Now here it is Tuesday, four days later, four days of sitting, traveling, smoking and just living hard, getting my stink on them. How does that girl smell so good that just whisked by on the way down to the dining car? She must've just gotten on. Or maybe she's sitting atop a perfume bottle. My my she has a wonderful ass. Mmmm. I wonder if women realize how many times men are watching their asses when they walk by.

"Hey, lookit that!" the man sitting ahead of me said. He had sandy blond hair and a wily mustache, wore simple tweed clothes in earthen tones. We hadn't spoken a word to each other, but I noticed his habits. A crossword puzzle sat on the tray table, half-completed, right next to a bone-handled knife he used to slice up bits of apple and feed them under that mustache. Edward Abbey novel spine-up on the seat next to him and a green army tin kept filled with coffee from a rusty thermos.

I took him for an old farm hand, or a fly-fisherman, or maybe an eccentric high school economics teacher.

"Lookit those elk out there!" he motioned with his knife, standing up in the seat ahead of me and nodding out the window.

The herd was enormous—probably around 500 head, some big bulls with impressive racks. They were all bent over a quiet section of tundra, feeding on scrubs of wintertime.

"Aren't they magnificent creatures?" he shook his head slowly and then clicked his teeth.

"Y'know, when I was living up near Estes Park in Colorada, we used to see herds three, four times as big as this, right on our front lawn that sloped up and away from the house," he said. "Sometimes my wife would leave apples in patterns so they'd stand in certain poses, then she'd take their pictures like this—spelling out words, making happy faces. It was marvelous when it worked."

"That's great," I smiled, imagining what dirty words I could spell out in the fields with elk bodies. "Estes Park is beautiful."

"Oh yeah? You from 'round there?" he asked, settling the conversational elbow on the back of his chair.

"Well, no, I'm from north Idaho," I replied. "But I went

to school in Fort Collins. We used to head up to Estes all the time to go hiking and camping, y'know."

"Hell yeah, shore a pretty place," he clicked teeth again. "That where you're heading now?"

"Nah, I'm a-goin' to Chicago," he said simply, then sunk back in his seat.

I sat in silence for a moment and almost began writing again in my journal when he reappeared and stuck his hand into my face.

"I'm Frank, by the way," he said. "Where *you* headed?"

"Ohh, I dunno... I'm gonna stop in Denver for a few days and then move on east. I'm spending a month on the train, going around the country."

"Oh? What for?" he raised his eyebrows.

"I don't know really. I just wanted to go, y'know?"

"What do you think you'll find out here?"

"I dunno... maybe nothing," I shrugged. "Who says I'm even looking for something in the first place?"

Frank let a wizened old chuckle slip from underneath the big mustache and grinned, or rather, the mustache *stretched*.

"Oh, everybody's a-lookin' for something," he raised his eyebrows and sat back down in his seat once again.

The snow-crusted tips of Moab bluffs now running past the window—the same ones I've stared at many times in the past. From Canyonlands parking lot, from the top of the Maze Overlook heading down-canyon into the wash 1,000 feet below, from my car as I drove away from Utah and back into Colorado... these same mountains that run through my mind in the urban life, the city days.

Oh, and we pull into the growing sprawl of Grand Junction and all I see are boxes—stores that look like boxes, tractor trailers towing boxes, boxy restaurants, boxy streets, different colored boxes, long boxes, wide boxes, littered boxes by the track—a city of boxes—a world of boxes—a nation in a box—for we are slowly becoming just like all the others—or rather *they* are all becoming just like *us*—a lady standing outside her boxy car hitting the car alarm box a few times to make sure it arms before trundling into the box store to purchase boxes and boxes of whatever the fuck she came to buy so she can take it home to her boxy pre-fab home and open up the box and throw it into another box, which is then scooped up and hauled away in another box—we live inside a box. And it seems to be shrinking.

Farm equipment in multicolor ambiguity across a field of asphalt, "Soap n' Suds Laundro-mat," broken-down Conoco station left to rot, power lines, power lines, we're all bound by these power lines—the crackling undercurrent we don't even notice anymore it seems. Just gimmie my power, my T.V., my toaster, my Internet, my cell phone charger. Tin men stretching across the horizon—bound by the electric chain.

Damn, the light is nice right now—everything has that sunset look to it—"magic hour" they called it in the film business, the only term I remember that instantly fills me with such dread, for in magic hour, if you miss the shot you're *fucked*, can't duplicate the lighting—so everyone's on edge and tryin' their damndest not to screw up and it's a tense monkey-fuck most of the time. Such a stupid way to classify a sunset. But, it's an industry overrun with stupidity.

"Oh shit, oh shee-it!" came the laughter of a black man a few seats back. "He heh heh, awright, awright, an' you remember that parrot he had? You 'member that parrot? Talked all dirty an' shit."

"Shee-it!" said his friend.

They were rocking back and forth in their seats, laughing and slapping the seat backs ahead of them. "Taught that mo'fucker to say 'shee-it' he did, shee-it!"

"Sheeee-it!" the other said.

Ooop, just stopped the train—freight congestion again—parked next to a power pole of all poley things. Let's describe it and everything beyond it: Tapered cracked deep brown pole 'bout oh, maybe thirty feet tall, black transformer box with chipped paint cracking off perched on the right side with a coupla little brass space-rod gizmo things and a wire coming out the top and a white buffer thing leading up to the main wire—and, to boot, a wee little sparrow perched right on the tip top of this pole, cocking his head over at me with a little "Waassss goin' on?" expression, "Whassis *train* doin' stopped here?" Oh and there I am staring out at him like a mad heretic, listening to his thoughts, trying to silence my own… the curious sparrow perched above this slag yard, an off-white wood house all dilapidated and sagging with age and sorrow, yellowish water stains on the siding, surrounded by dead aspen trees and a field bejeweled with scrap metal, old trucks, car parts, railroad ties, washing machines, farm equipment, gutted boxcars, and there he is, the junkyard man himself—exactly like I would picture a guy living in a plot of land like this—big sloppy belly covered in a grimy green sweatshirt, thick Jeremiah Johnson beard and Davy Jones wool cap—walking around his junk heap with a small cigar in his fat jowls, piling junk in certain stacks— there's an order to it! All this time I thought these junkyard hounds just threw shit in piles and let them rot, but now it seems that junkyard man, Jeremiah Junkyard they call him, has a *method*… oh, to know this method, to hear his thoughts beside Interstate 70 and the cross-country railroad tracks, wedged between the two arteries of long-haulers and living in a world his own—a man living out on the edge of it all, off the grid, smoking a Backwoods cigar and pondering at a small camp trailer he's been looking at the past few minutes, spits onto the ground, stamps his feet, wearing old work boots, and hitches up his pants with a Civil War-esque light grey stripe running up the vertical side of the leg—pacing up and down the trailer, checking out the front, the ball hitch, kicking the tires, a yapping dog at his heels, stamps his feet again and kicks at the old scraggy mutt as the conductor puts us into GO and Jeremiah Junkyard, my junkyard prophet, my dirt farmer of the sun, I'll see you again perhaps—Lord of the Junkyard—and now he's gone... just a snapshot. *My* snapshot.

FOUR

THE SUN DIED AND DARKNESS REIGNED. Back in the sightseer car again with headphones plugged into computer, computer plugged into wall socket, wall socket plugged into train and train plugged into these rails leading us all wherever we go—east, west, north, south—it don't matter, just s'long as it ain't here, now, where I'm standing, sitting, lying, moaning, sighing, rubbing my hands together and feeling my beard for about the five-hundredth time today… just keep me moving, keep me free.

And hot damn I'm starting to get the Denver excitement again—I should'a been there about two hours ago if trains ran on time, but instead I'm not even to Granby yet. I'll roll into the Denver station at midnight and my old college roommate Liz will be waiting there in her Subaru Outback, probably wearing a scarf and an expensive black leather jacket, make-up, hair thrown back expertly casual, and then topping it all off with some god-awful ugly pair of workout pants—a weird dresser that Liz, like she just pulls garments out of the dresser at random. Then we'll zoom off to her place, maybe the same one as last time I visited (last year? Two years ago? Christ, it's been awhile) and drink beers into the night—her going to sleep to wake up for work in the morning, me probably just staying up cuz my sleep routines are shot thanks to this damn train, this beautiful train, this holy train where I sleep only when my mind shuts down and these fingers stay silent.

I drug my cell phone out of the depths of the rucksack and called Liz to tell her when I'd be in. She was angry with me for not giving her more notice, but said she'd be there to give me a ride from the station.

There are others from my old college days still bumming around Colorado. Ani still lives in Boulder. Ani with her Cheshire grin and olive skin, Ani who I fell in love with during a sailing trip to the British Virgin Islands some time ago, Ani who is also the younger sister of Mitch, my other roommate from college, who lives in Ohio and who I will meet up with sometime next week. And Regan lives in Winter Park. Regan my friend from high school days of drinking in the woods on weekends and camping next to bonfires as the sun went down, Regan who enlisted in Americorps and was just kicked out because she dated one of her crew members. They actually sent her home from rebuilding homes in New Orleans because she held the boy's hand and went to a movie with him.

All these wonderful sensations of crazy wild nomad wanderlust with a friend at every twinkling city along the way to share a beer, share a story, share a memory of the last time I came barreling through on some other loony mission of the past. All these friends of mine that I can't wait to see again—Liz in Denver; Regan in Winter Park; Ani in Boulder; Mitch in Ohio, with his soon-to-be wife Joanna; Seda in New Jersey washing linens and preparing for my arrival next week, I hope, cuz I'm gonna make her sweat and scream for days; wise old Ed in Florida; Nathan in Houston devouring his books and writing his manifestos; Chuck in Los Angeles barbequing burgers—goddamn it's a free-for-all, I tell ya…

I'm just gonna keep going and I'm not gonna stop 'til my pass runs out, then I'll just turn around and go somewhere else. What the hell else is there to do?

Such a long, impractical journey—I could've made it in 17 hours by car, but instead it took me three days by train— but hell, if I were driving I'd probably be upside-down in a ditch by now cuz my tires, they be bald, my oil hasn't been changed in 13,000 miles, my mind hasn't been right ever since I started smoking this schwag green weed that I bought in a huge quantity from Rick in L.A.—me zipping up to see him the day before taking off from L.A. back to Northsaint and him handing me this big turd of a bag full of shake and charging me $250 for an ounce—not a bad price, but I saw why so cheap when I smoked the shit—barely makes me high—I could smoke two of them damn joints in a row and just barely feel something tickling the back of my brain.

Ho ho, what's this—a hot springs—it's been pitch black out here in this damn beautiful part of Colorado for hours and now we just passed by an enormous lit-up resort with steam hanging in the air, naked women prolly frolicking around in the hot water drinking canned beer and flicking each other's nipples, dumb thick men sitting at the edges of the pools watching with wide-eyed wonderment, not making a peep so as not to disturb the lovely scene—then, just as quickly as it cometh, it vanishes into the night—just a split-second revelry—momentary distraction of the mind and back to the rumbling void. Sometimes I don't even know if we're moving forwards of backwards—not many lights out there to guide the way. And cars? Cars aren't moving down this highway, cuz we ain't *on* any highway now, see, we're off in the snowfields on a bumpy section of track prolly laid down in the mid-1800's in that great swooping push for Union Pacific to meet up with Burlington Northern to drive that golden spike where the two met at Promontory Point, Utah and open up the land once and for all—Manifest Destiny—an' I been there, with my dad, back in the days when I was just a staring little boy trying to gather everything into my silly little head as quickly as I could. I remember it now in sepia tones—we slept in the car outside of Dinosaur National Monument the night before cuz I remember waking up in the frigid Utah air startled to see a goddamn T-Rex looming over the car with jowls wide open, as if he meant to eat us whole—this before Jurassic Park when kids were forced to think of such scenes out of pure imagination— nevermore—but it was just metal and we both lurched over to the ditch and took steaming pisses at T-Rex's feet—two puddles of piss at a dinosaur's feet, one large and man-like, the other small and childlike. Then drove down further into Utah and reached the Golden Spike Museum at lunchtime—wandered around the area for a few hours and snapped some pictures and read some plaques and watched a historical re-enactment of some silly railroad tycoon man driving the final spike, the magical golden spike that sealed the fate of the east and west, one golden spike into the railroad tie with a prop sledge hammer as sullen crowds of tourists stood idly by, clapping politely. Turns out later the real spike was stolen by some bandits, so they replaced it with a normal one and put a *fake* real one on display in the museum for snot-nosed kids to sniffle over and parents to point at with babies in their arms carrying loads of poo in their bucket asses. Oh how I love history… memories… tawdry hours in the night when there's no one around except me and my words, my music, my thoughts—my excitement for a wild night in Denver, my anxiety at seeing Ani again and trying not to fall foot into mouth in love with her again, and happiness at the thought of a few days off the train and into the arms of my friends that are so good and so pure it makes me feel as if I'm taking advantage of them if they hadn't offered everything in the first place… I don't know what I ever did to deserve them—maybe the fact that I recognize that they are wonderful and holy and true and just exactly the type of people that I want to waste my time with is enough, because I can't help it, when I find someone that I consider a "kindred spirit" like Flannigan or Jack or whoever else—someone I consider to be a cut above the rest because of their sheer ability to make me shut up sometimes and think a bit instead of holding court with imbeciles that don't have any fucking idea what I'm saying in the first place (and neither do I, for that matter). It's friends like these that make enemies impossible, I say. And in just a few short hours it's on—It's on, it's on—one more memory to throw onto the stack, one more experience to think about the next time I come shambling back into Denver (or *anywhere* for that matter) and it's snowing—just saw it in the lampposts by that chainsaw shop all lit up next to a café called the "Wagoneer" or some god-awful thing like that—people still cashing in on the pioneers. When will they learn? Ace Hardware, Pearl Chinese food sign yellow and red, the standard combination of colors psychologically proven to make folks hungry, but not me, I say, I just had a Cup o' Noodles from the snack car and a big old smelly moist bagel that almost made me yak—no hunger here, thanks. OK, we're stopping now—time to rush outside to smoke off a Drum stick followed by a cigarette so I can make it these last hundred miles or so into Denver, these last joyful, soulful pure miles of snow-covered space and time... hooah.

Ah hell... false alarm... smoke stop is thirty minutes down the line at Winter Park... this is Granby. Hell. Guess I'll jess have to keep on gesticulating my fingers as an extension of my tired mind, the fellaheen prophet with nothing to add to this woeful world 'cept my silly words and this horrible case of gas that keeps slipping out—sorry fellow trainsters, next time I'll try to be more coy with my bodily functions, next time I won't eat Beanie-Weenies on the train.

Shore wish I could spend some time in Chi-town—the city of my father's youth—where he cut school and work on the farm to speed off to Wrigley Field in an old '32 Ford with a coupla buddies and a bottle in his breast pocket—watching the Cubs lose (yes, lose, for they have *always* lost, which is why I love them from the depths of my heart). Where the great Chicago gangsters immortalized walls with their Tommy guns. Where the great bop musicians 60 years ago in the heyday of jazz blew their horns and poured their sweat to the beat night as characters like Kerouac, Cassady, Ginsberg, Burroughs and all the rest jumped and swayed and danced in the crowd with the whole country's soul ripped open wide before them and the raw unfolded vagina of their discontent seething, and the whole crazy world of potential over their heads, for they all came out all right if you ask me; Kerouac dead with his insides exploded from living too much life, Cassady's heart giving out from exposure on the railroad tracks in Mexico, Burroughs finally succumbing to death after living 70 years too long and Ginsberg bowing to a failed liver. That's why I sometimes wonder if all of this is worth it—maybe I don't want to live fast, get STD's and die young. All for the glory that I know is out there, but if I didn't try to capture it, I'd be a faker. *And* a failure. This is my true soul, my purpose, my duty—to write, to observe, to capture what I can and put it down onto the page in such a way that stays true to the way I saw it as well as the way that those choose to read it—destiny and fate and all that other happy horseshit—I can go on about it all night and all the way across this swollen continent, but the facts remain the facts: I can't do anything except *live* and then write about it—it's my only talent, my only true ability—I'm no good at anything else… not working as a film producer, not a golf pro, not a busboy, not a bartender, not a driving range attendant… all these have been *jobs*, *gigs*, ways to make *money* and move the fuck on. Writing is the Way. It is the Light. It is Jesus Christ, God, the Easter Bunny, and Wilt Chamberlain all rolled up into one soulful burrito and ingested in a fit of starvation then vomited back up onto the page in letters and words and paragraphs and sacred god damn pieces of work that try to capture this moment for others to lose themselves in years from now—maybe centuries—maybe when the Bomb drops and we've all turned to mutants, these words that humans wrote will remain. It is my method, just like Jeremiah Junkyard had his back there in the Grand Junction junk heap—he piles his junk over there in that manner, I pile my junk over here in this manner... we're all running parallel lines that intersect, though you may have read that can't happen, but it's all hooey—who the hell cares what mathematicians and biologists and all those square fools have to say about the world—this train ride may be happening because of math—the weight ratio to the pressure exerted, the horsepower, the thrust, blah blah, yak yaaaak, but it runs on something greater than numbers and their products—it runs because of the need for people to *go*. To *move*. To cross the country, to cross the state, to go from Denver to Chicago, from New York to Florida, from here to there, it don't matter—this train runs because people are seeking the Word in a place not their own, they choose to drift and run and this old faithful train comes and scoops them up every day—check your timetable, it'll appear in a town near you, perhaps perhaps, ahem... I mean *hell*, the conductors still wear those square hats too... if everything were left in the hands of the capitalists, they'd be wearing storm trooper helmets, frisking us at the doors, and finger-fucking the weak in their seats, for I admit, I'd be guilty—I'm a drug smuggler, running schwag joints in through the bottom of my pouch of Drum rolling tobacco—I don't mean anyone harm by it, I just want to smoke them. I just want to live how I want to live without feeling like a criminal. There's about ten of the buggers hidden there inside the tobacco, one of them burning an absolute hole in my pocket right now as that Winter

Park stop looms closer and closer ahead, oh my, how I love everything… these fingers o' mine are cramping up and I don't care—if they can't keep up I'll just lop the fuckers off and start jabbing at the keys with bloody stumps—gotta get this message out—gotta keep this thing flowing.

I suppose I'll hit a wall sometime in this long and dangerous narrative without any structure or scope—but I don't give a fuck really—that shit's all up ahead and all I gotta worry 'bout now is the present, according to those Dr. Phil rip-off Texans earlier—telling the Fat Man how to live his life (the Fat Man, incidentally, is named Don. I know this cuz when I was wobbling through the aisles back to my seat—always weaving and stuttering like a drunk at the curves in the track—he was talking to some *other* idiots, prolly about the same damn problems, and he said, "And this guy's pretty quiet, I see him writin' all the time in that little book. I never even met him yet," meaning me, of course, and I just rose my eyebrows mysteriously to let him wonder a bit more and kept on walking—he caught me on the way back to my seat, though, when he stuck his fat paw in the air and said, "I'm Don." "Max," I said. "What? Alex?" "No, *Max*." "Ah, pleased to meet you Max, Where're you—" and then I just walked off—not even giving the portly bastard a second to spew his train-wisdom-seeker game on me—hell with that and hell with him—aw, but I get down on Fat Man, er, *Don*, too much because I don't like the way he does things—but that's *him* and that's his trip—oop, train's stopping, it's on…).

Aaaaaaaaaah, hot damn hooooo-ey! Praise God for Victory! Now down to nine of those wonderful little schwag Drum sticks. Winter Park snowy and cold and dark and pulsating with that excitement, that adrenalin you always feel in the pit of your stomach when entering a ski town—always aware that somewhere, not far from these gentle hamlet lights twinkling at the street corners and gas stations is a giant damn mountain that Man has cleared and attempted to Master. I see the snow cats now—little ant lights like stars on the distant slope grooming nature's payload for the weekend warriors, the amateur athletes and the snow bums humping this windfall for bread and kicks.

Ani called just as the train came to a halt—I threw a scarf around my neck, rushed through the train and downstairs, out into the falling snow, talking loudly with her and listening for that laugh, her wonderful laugh and her "aaup," and her "naaah," and her thousand other little words and noises and sounds that make Ani one of the most desirable, most amazing little chicks I've known—I'm really so hopelessly in love with her, but it was always doomed from the beginning… since when do cliché shipboard crushes ever work out?

"Well, what in the hell are you up to now, you old crazy bastard? A train trip, eh? Aaup," she said.

Oh, Ani… she travels around the world every summer with a backpack just to see what there is to see, she once wrote down all the German pronunciations of animal sounds for me so I could talk to the toddler of a German couple we met while in the islands. She still dreamed and still dedicated herself to giving beauty to others. The mere sound of her voice threw me right back into the trance, my fantasy about a girl who exists only in the suspended state I left her during those two weeks at sea.

We agreed to have a drink before I left Denver. Ah, Ani… we're a lot alike, see—turned on by the same zest for life that we both discovered in each other while sailing—me at the helm swinging the wheel around like an old salty sea captain with an English L&M pinched in my lips and a strong glass of Mount Gay rum and ice in my hand. Her lying under the boom in a dark brown bikini, olive skin that glistened in the sun, lying on her stomach with head of sandy brown hair on one arm resting on a small journal—the pen perched delicately in her fine mangrove fingers—oh how I long for that moment again—there are not many regrets that I carry around in this old battered suitcase of my soul, but one will always be not grabbing her like Dick Tracy and kissing her with all my grit and everything I got—it doesn't matter if Mitch, my best friend, is her big brother. It doesn't matter that Mitch is a very *protective* older brother. It doesn't even matter that he's seen me dog a few girls in my day (oh, and I just recalled that time in the dorms when I snuck a girl in and fucked her in my bed as he snored not five feet away), though I'm pretty sure he thinks I'm a good guy at heart (the fool!). Things like that shouldn't matter—if I met her under different circumstances, or if she wasn't Mitch's sister, of if if if, aaah whatever—maybe that's the attraction behind it—I always want what I can't have. I always want the horizon, the next dawn, the view from the next peak—I always want to punch the sun. Girls like Ani don't fall for guys like me, because they are too smart. They realize that I'll spend my life forever pining after something I'll never have and will never appreciate what I do.

The last time I saw her, she invited me to crash at her place in Boulder, a sweet little cottage with a hot fireplace and a couple of cool roommates and a stone back porch where we sat and smoked cigarettes and talked about our schemes, our dreams, our ideas and inner passions—me talking about traveling into Asia, sailing through the Caribbean again, writing books someday, and never giving up the nomad life—her talking about living in Mexico with the Navajo tribe that summer, her best friend that was in a coma from a car accident, her lethargic life in Boulder, how she wants to leave sometimes and never come back.

Goddamn, I can't get all hung up on this shit again—once again I'm obsessed with one of the few things I can't accomplish in this world—and I say that with no sarcasm... I truly believe and *know* in fact that if I really want something to happen, chances are, it will happen—I saw this with the golf course job I had back in Northsaint, I saw this later after I moved down to Pebble Beach and got hired right away— even after they laid off ten percent of their work force after September 11. I saw it later when I got hooked up in the film business and met all those exciting people that were always working and always needed a hand on various film shoots, it happened yet again when Mick asked me to produce his $1 million photography book. I was never trained to do anything. Everything I've ever done was something I'd just stumbled into—I would just wedge my toes in the door and wriggle myself in, conning everyone I could into thinking that I really knew what I was doing when, really, I didn't have a clue... I can usually make my way in such a *different* manner than the rest and still manage to make money at it. I haven't really had a normal job, unless you count working as a busboy in high school, or maybe those couple months working at Foley's Department Store in college, wearing a suit and tie every day and folding fucking clothes that people mussed up and selling blenders and microwaveable bacon cookers to Okie grandpas—I guess those were "normal" jobs, but they were only temporary. I always saw the end of them in sight. Then I set out for L.A., bound for greatness or failure—tired of living a life I knew was sub-par—tired of wanting—tired of reading about people doing and not doing anything on my own. I guess that worked too.

I can still return and work down there any time I want... in fact, if I could take it, I could probably be pulling in a hundred grand a year and driving a BMW like all the other morons... I could've been comfortable down there. I could be paying my bills every month, buying the new cell phone everyone's excited about, hanging expensive pieces of art above televisions and never looking at them again. I chose to give these comforts up and live bohemian in Northsaint, only returning to work the occasional commercial when the money ran out. It always ran out. It always got hard. And I never missed the comfort. Surrounded by all those bastions of American success in Los Angeles, they naturally thought I was one of them, but I wasn't. I'm not. I'm just hanging on for dear life, jabbing this mother bitch in the eye and seeing which direction she slaps me—sipping that expensive Jameson-on-the-rocks (classic hipster drink) at the Standard lounge where the materialistic whores scan the crowd for fat wallets, thick nostrils and mediocre conversation. Anything to fuck them up. Anything to get them high. I'd stand there and scowl at them all. Then I'd drive drunk all the way across town to the ocean and sleep in the front seat of my car because I couldn't find the key to my friend's house in Venice where I crash on the couch from time to time—some big shot I was.

But still, I was once exactly like them—a "yes man" in the purest sense—not thinking about what the "yes" really *meant*, just agreeing to it on terms of pure desperation and excitement and wonderment at the methods of man. I wanted IN and I got it, by god. Money, drugs, fast nights, and confused morns. Hipsters on Hollywood Boulevard, indie rockers in Los Feliz lighting cigarettes and whooping after a show, the hoochi-mama's on Sunset wearing tight skirts and carrying rainbows of rubbers, the jocks in Lakers' jerseys, the sad artists kicking cans on the streets of Santa Monica, the street performers in Venice, the surfers of Huntington, the businessmen in expensive suits strolling all over Century City, the foo-foo celebrities in the Hollywood Hills and the hanger-on'ers all over the stinking valley from Thousand Oaks to Reseda all the way over to Agoura Hills that catch fire just about every two, three years, the Malibu beach community Fascist and racist and bigoted, but "oh, it's so beautiful," and the long PCH drumming up the west coast of California, of America, of the whole Western World, leading on up and out of L.A. to greater points beyond the horizon…

Yeah, I came down to that whole stinking mess and bitch-slapped it right in its warty, pimply, piss-eyed face.

Los Angeles is my bitch—I didn't become famous, I didn't make a lot of money, I didn't write anything spectacular or take any poetic photographs or invent a hit reality show… I didn't really do *anything* notable. But I lived through it. I sunk so far down into the pit of the true degradation of that city—the rotten filthy corrupted entertainment industry—made my money, saw how it all worked, observed the other side and got the fuck out before it caught me broadside.

Oh—God—yesss—the lights of Denver spread out like an electric pinpoint carpet below. We're really far up, aren't we? Can't see a damn thing outside except that expanse of twinkling suburban lights—must be Fort Collins, Boulder, Longmont, and early Denver I'm seeing. I'm riding those mountains that I used to stare up at when sad and lonely in college, perched above the Horsetooth Reservoir and writing into my first journal. I remember that night I was sitting there writing in the dark and the cops came pulling up outta nowhere and I got all nervous and jumped out of the car and they drew their guns and ordered me to put my hands above my head, then they found a *keg* of all things in the backseat—an empty beer keg I had forgotten to take back to my friend who bought it for another raging party where everyone vomited and the women walked home bowlegged, wondering if they'd just contracted an STD—and they asked me what I was doing up there and I told them I had just broken up with my girlfriend and was trying to sort some things out—this they understood tenderly and let me go with a warning—always wondered why I said that, instead of saying that I was just sad and lonely and wanted to look up at the stars with tears in my eyes while I wrote words I couldn't see, hoping they'd be good, but reading them later, realizing they were not only illegible, but lacking in creativity and emotion—words—fuck 'em—waaall, no, don't get all huffy there speed king, words are your only tools.

five

We pulled into the station somewhere around midnight. A few bums moped around the rail yard, bent to the wind, moving onto wherever they would sleep that night. The neon sign for a brewery shone across the street appealingly, several people smoking cigarettes in parkas outside the front door. Large buildings twinkled in the distance.

"Good luck on the rest of your trip," I said to Frank, the mustache man.

"Hey, you too man," he looked up from his novel. "I hope you find what it is you're looking for."

"We'll see."

The stars were diamonds in the moonless sky. Liz wasn't there to pick me up, so I sat on the bench outside the station and peered inside the windows. Passengers waited in line to catch the train I'd just disembarked from, each face sadder than the last—midnight boarders going east, propelled by the events of their varied lives. A young jail kid biting the end of his experimental mustache, a college girl bobbing her head under earphones, a fat old woman with a sneer on her face, two little black girls fighting over a bag of Doritos, a Suit pressing important words into his Palm Pilot.

Where do these people go at midnight in Denver? Are families at the end of the line? Jobs? Adventure? Are they just passing through? Will they ever return?

A black man came out the front door and pulled the collar up on his jacket. He wore work pants and boots, and carried a small duffel bag over one shoulder. Deep creases in his face and a hangdog way of standing told of long days of hard work in his past. He stood there; stamping his feet against the cold, blowing into his gloveless hands, looking at the buildings downtown across the freeway, finally fixing his gaze on me. I didn't look away.

"Got another one a those?" he pointed to my cigarette.

"Uh, yeah, they're roll-your-own's, though," I offered him the pack of Drums. Then I remembered I had a bunch of joints packed in there. "Actually, you can have this one, I'll roll another for myself."

I gave him the smoke I'd just lit and he nodded thanks.

"You comin' or goin'?" he asked.

"Just got here. Waiting for a friend."

"Long trip?"

"Ah, well, yeah kinda," I said. I licked the gum on the paper and rolled the cigarette closed and stuck it in my mouth. "Started in Spokane a few days ago and I'm just stopping here for a few days."

"Oh yeah? I just came up from Grand Junction. You been to Denver b'fore?"

"I went to school in Fort Collins."

"Ahh, Colorado State," he smiled. "*Fine* lookin' women up there."

"You bet."

"*Mountain* women… *healthy* women," his eyes shined.

"Mm hmm."

"Where you headin' after this?"

"Well, I dunno… wherever I want, really," I said. He wrinkled his forehead. "I got a 30-day pass and I'm just traveling around the country. I think I'll head to Chicago next, then New York."

"No shit!" he said, a new twinkle in his eyes. "Tha's a *great* thing to be doin' for a guy your age. I bet you havin' the time of your life, eh?"

"It's been interesting."

I looked at the gap between his teeth and his smile and realized it was genuine; a genuine smile from a real person. Seems like such a long time since I'd seen a smile like that.

"Damn, I tell you what, I'd rather be out there doin' what you're doin' than what I'm doin', shee-it," he sighed, his smile turning into a grimace. "Got me a wife lives here in Denver, wants a divorce an' I finally agreed to it. So now here I am, got off work for a day just to meet with her an' sign those papers an' say hello to my little baby girl."

"Really? Sorry to hear that."

"Ahh, she's a bitch anyways," he spat. "Never was happy with her. Don't know why I even married her, y'know?"

He searched into my eyes as if I *did* in fact *know*. I could only shrug.

"Well, just let that be a lesson to you, kid," he said. "Don't ever get married."

I laughed with him and offered my hand.

"I'm Max."

"Max, pleasure to meet you brother, I'm Hank," he said. He sat his hands on hips and sighed into the air, his breath forming silver crystals hanging over our heads from the flood lights of the station.

I wondered what I looked like to this man in Denver that I just met and will never see again—what characteristics he'd remember me for. My ugly sweat-stained hat? This heavy green rucksack sitting beside me on the bench? The Drum cigarette I gave him? How would he describe me to his friends if he had to?

Hank with his upturned collar; a meager shield to the winds of misfortune, but it's all he has. Divorcing his wife, returning to Grand Junction to do whatever he does there. Life in motion that I see for only a split second, and vice versa. But sometimes the snapshot is what captures the moment best, when words and thoughts and emotions fall short and lose meaning. Sometimes you learn more meeting a stranger for two minutes than knowing a close friend for twenty years.

"Well, I 'spect I better get on," he said finally, breaking the silence. "Gotta walk a few blocks down an' catch the bus over to my cousin Rickey's place."

"All right Hank, well, good luck signing those papers."

"Oh yeah," he smiled. "Signin' them papers. Just remember what I tol' you 'bout marriage, now, y'hear? You too young to be getting' tied down by no girl just yet. You got things to do, I can tell."

"I hear ya."

"Good luck on the rest of your journey now, a'ight?"

"You too." He turned and walked away. I watched him hesitate at the brewery, then head down a dark street, disappearing behind a building. He never looked back.

Liz arrived some time later in a new Subaru Outback. She honked frantically at me, sitting with my head bent over my journal.

"I *thought* that was you!" she yelled, her black hair pulled back in a bun. "I knew it was either you or a homeless guy!"

"A *homeless* guy?" I yelled back.

She ran over and met me halfway. We hugged and kissed each other on the cheek.

"You look like *shit* man, lookit that *beard!*" she squealed.

Liz wore a heavy University of Colorado sweatshirt and blue pajama pants with dragons going up either leg—the same pants she wore every night when we lived together in college that I teased her for endlessly. She's built like a slim barrel, with thick, heavy upper-body muscles from years of swim meets, beady eyes, jaws clenching aggressively, always waiting to inject her opinion in every conversation. Liz exudes an air of brute authority with everything, but acts like a goofball most of the time to cover it up.

She athletically hefted my leather day pack and computer case off my shoulders and carried them over to the trunk. After tossing them in, she struggled with my 50-pound rucksack.

"Oof, what the hell's in here?" she grunted. "You really need all this shit?"

"You never know," I shrugged.

We shoved it in the trunk and shut the door, then hugged again.

"Ooooh, I can't believe you're here! It's so good to see you! How long are you staying?"

"Oh, I'll probably stay a couple days if that's cool."

"Of *course* it's cool, stay as long as you want… I just got a new place with a big comfy couch and everything, cable, hot showers, big balcony to smoke cigarettes and watch my fat neighbors having sex, it's great… c'mon, let's go, I'm freezing my nipples off out here."

We made our way down Colfax, through my old sleepy downtown Denver with cold brick buildings and tailpipes smoking in waiting cabs, late night walkers going somewhere, anywhere, ah it was so good to be mile-high again.

"So why the hell are you taking this trip?" she asked irritably. "Are you doing it for that photographer guy's book?"

"No, I'm not working with him right now. I just got restless and had to go, y'know?"

"Hmph. Must be nice to just take off for a month and

cruise around America," she accelerated away from the light, jamming the shifter in gear. "*Some* of us have *real* jobs, y'know, we can't *all* live like rock stars."

"*Rock stars?*" I cried. "You think I live like a *rock star?* I just got done sleeping on a train for five days without showering, how's that like a rock star? You should smell my balls!"

"Eyuuk, gross. I don't wanna hear that," she swatted me. "How are you paying for this trip anyways?"

"I still had a little left over from my last trip to L.A. I spent two of the shittiest months of my life down there working like a dog."

We stopped at a red light. Two bar-hoppers strutted across Colfax arm-in-arm, drunken smiles and blank eyes. The man reached down and squeezed the woman's ass.

"Yeah, well at least you're not sitting behind some stupid desk all the time, like I am," she said.

"How's that going anyway?" I asked, suddenly forgetting exactly what Liz's job was. Something to do with nursing, or hospitals, or mortgage loans… shit. Something like that.

"It's all right, I guess. They're opening another office in Westminster and putting me in charge of it next month, so I'll get a pretty nice promotion."

"Good for you."

"I just don't know what the hell I'm doing, though," she sighed. "I just sit behind a desk and deal with stupid shit all day, nine to five, and attend morning meetings and write memos and Excel sheets and price breakdowns an' all that… I couldn't care less about any of it."

"Whatever happened to that idea of yours to open a thrift store coffee shop? I thought you were getting the loans and everything."

She squinted her eyes and smirked, pleased that I remembered, or pleased at an old idea she'd forgotten about.

"God, I haven't thought about that in *years!*" she exclaimed. "I had all the paperwork and everything, we were gonna open it in Boulder, but my friend Kelly, who was the other partner, backed out at the last minute. I didn't have enough cash to do it myself, so it kind of just went away."

"That's too bad," I shook my head. "I thought it was a good idea."

"We had such a perfect location too," she slapped me on the knee. She was always swatting people to make her point. "Right in the middle of campus, on the hill by all the bars. My dad was going to donate all the old books in his library, and we were gonna have this big literary section. You'd have loved it…"

We rode in silence for a moment.

"It's not too late, y'know," I said.

Liz mused over this for a second, her brown nose and goofy smile, freckles and pencil in her bun. My old college roommate. The girl who used to wake me up deliberately in the dorms every morning on her way to swimming practice at 5 a.m., banging on the door. The girl who introduced me to all of her hot swimmer friends (a few I'd slept with, before realizing that swimmers never shaved their legs until a competition, so they get hairy and prickly in places where you don't want to feel hair and prickles). The girl who used expressions like "What the H?" and giggled foolishly when being goaded, who would take all the dishes I'd failed to wash and pile them in front of my bedroom door as a not-so-subtle hint to keep up on my housework.

The girl I knew from college now this woman who wears pant suits and answers phones all day and makes important decisions concerning either nurses, hospitals, or mortgage loans. Awkwardly living an adult life like a robin learning to fly in winter.

"I know," she said at last.

We pulled up to her building on 14th and Fillmore, a sturdy brick tenement with squat elm trees curling branches around the first three floors. Covered in snow and darkness, it looked like something out of Kafka's night dreams.

"Here we are," she waved her arm up at the foreboding building. Wind whistled through the alcove of the back door, dark under a burned-out bulb.

"Nice place," I said uselessly. I never know what to say sometimes.

"No it's not," she slammed the key in the knob and wrenched the metal door open with a horrifying shriek. "It's dark and scary and I love it. It costs a fortune, too. C'mon, I got some beer in the fridge, let's go."

And we galumphed down the hallway, me carrying just my leather pack and leaving the rest in the trunk. Up the stairs smelling of old people, down another hallway. White walls with drab grey carpet—the same carpet they had at my elementary school. The same carpet you see in urban libraries, living rooms of old folks homes, mid-level managers' offices, mental institution waiting rooms and old Denver apartment buildings. Stains of life.

"I live by myself now, so you don't have to deal with my crazy roommate this time," she said, opening the door to 5B.

The room was spacious, with a neat kitchen and sitting bar on the left, large living room and overstuffed couches next to sliding glass doors of a balcony. A modest library of books neatly stacked in an Ikea shelf, right next to a big screen T.V. and a pile of celebrity magazines. She had obviously picked things up a bit for my arrival. I remember her living habits from college. Or had she changed?

"This is great, Liz," I stood in the middle of the room, gazing at everything warmly. It had been a long trip already and I was happy to be in a comfortable room with someone I knew—an old friend.

"It's not bad," she harrumphed. "*Speaking* of my ex-roommate…"

"Yeah?" I hesitated. I knew what was coming.

She popped the top off a Red Stripe beer and handed it to me. I nodded my approval at the brand.

I remembered the ordeal with her ex-roommate. Vividly. I was scouting for the photography book I'd been hired to produce, and was in Denver for a few days. Liz had just gotten a job at the Gap, so she wasn't around much. Her roommate Katie had just gotten fired from Starbucks for stealing money out of the till, so she spent most days lounging around on the couch watching Court T.V. and thumbing listlessly through the classifieds. She was remarkably attractive.

Katie and I invariably spent several hours a day talking with each other, mostly about how she was tired of working dead-end jobs and getting fired because she was a klepto.

It all collapsed one night when Liz told me she was staying with her boyfriend and wouldn't be home until the morning, my last day in town.

Katie and I drank beer and smoked cigarettes all night on the back porch, tip-toeing around the fact that we were both drunk and horny and had the whole apartment to ourselves. When it came time to go to bed, she simply took my hand and led me into her room. We tore each other's clothes off and fucked a half dozen times until dawn. She was a screamer—one of those women who yell and moan at the top of her lungs when you really give it to her. Loudest fuck I ever had. I'm sure the *neighbors* had to smoke when we were finished.

Right before we met with Liz for breakfast the next morning, Katie pleaded with me to take her with me on the road. She thought she was in love with me until I finally convinced her that we were just two cauldrons of hormones that spilled over one night and nothing more.

"But how can you make love to me if you don't *love* me?" she asked.

"Katie, I *didn't* make love to you, we just *fucked*," I said.

"I don't even *know* you. How can you say you *love* me?"

My visit ended with an awkward breakfast at some foo-foo organic café; Liz and her boyfriend Saul sitting across from Katie and me, talking amiably. Before I got in my car to drive away at top speed, Katie stole my old tattered copy of *On the Road*—a treasured possession—and told me to go to hell.

"You're such a *slut*, I *swear!*" Liz shook her head.

"Oh, you're just jealous," I said with male smugness. "I see through you… you always introduce me to your hot friends and then I have sex with them and you act like you're all offended and shocked, but *secretly*, you do it because you've always wanted to have me yourself."

She choked on some beer and spat it into the sink, staggering back to the counter dramatically.

"Sorry to disappoint, but that's all you little fantasy, I'm afraid. I *have* a man and he treats me *good*… better than *you* ever could."

I started to object, then thought better of it.

"Who's this boyfriend anyway?" Is he worth anything? Not like that *last* one, I hope."

"Who, Saul? Ha!" she hooted. "Yeah, he turned out to be a total prick. He cheated on me with his ex-girlfriend—I caught them in *my* bed."

"Jesus, what a bastard."

"Yeah, fuck him… Mark's a good guy, you'll meet him on Thursday. Oh, by the way, I got tickets to the Nuggets game tomorrow night if you wanna go," she ushered me out onto the balcony. "C'mon, let's share a stog."

"Do you remember that stupid bench you hauled all the way down to our house sophomore year?" she said on the porch, shivering. "Do you still have that?"

"It wasn't *stupid*," I snatched back the cigarette. "That was my senior bench from high school, *course* I still have it—it's under a tarp waiting to go on the back deck of my house someday."

"Yeah right, you'll never settle down enough to have a house," she waved her arms at me. "You're gonna be some 45-year-old bum sleeping in his car and chasing things around the country just like you are now. Some things don't change."

"Yeah, well some things do."

"Speaking of, you know Mitch and Joanna are getting married, right?"

"Yeah, isn't that *crazy?*" I said.

"Everyone's marrying off," she shook her head. We shared the house our sophomore year with Mitch, who I'd spent freshman year with in the dorms. Just recently he'd moved back to Ohio to take a marketing job for his father's company and prepare for marriage and domestic life.

We went inside and Liz lit up a bowl and we talked for another two hours about everything, about nothing.

"Dude, you remember last time you were in town, you got *arrested?* When we had that party at Kenny's house?" she bundled on the other couch with a blanket wrapped around her neck. "You'd better behave yourself this time."

"Ah, whatever, it wasn't that big of a deal," I wagged my head smirking.

"They took you away in *handcuffs,* right when we got there. I remember Mitch looked over at me and said, 'Well, I guess Max hasn't changed much,' or some shit like that. What the hell did they *stop* you for? You weren't even *driving* anywhere, were you?"

"No! I was just walking out to the car to get a six-pack of beer. The cops drove up and shone a flashlight in my face and got out all of a sudden, asked for my ID and said I matched the description of a fucking *prowler*."

"Ha haa! That's right, they thought you were a burglar!" she swatted the arm of the couch.

"An' I told him, 'So, how is looking at my ID gonna

prove I'm a prowler, officer?' and he just sneered at me and said, 'Just quiet down while we run your name.' I was so pissed off. Then he turned to me after listening to the radio in his ear and smiled, 'Welll, looks like you have a warrant out for your arrest, Mr. Manchester,' and put me in fucking handcuffs. He wouldn't even tell me what I was being arrested for, just that I had a warrant out. It wasn't until I got to the station, after being hauled away in front of everyone at the party, that they told me it was for not paying that damn noise ticket we got for that Halloween party right before I dropped out of college."

"They almost held you all weekend, the guy told me. Said you were being all uncooperative and everything."

"I just didn't want them to take my fingerprints. Once you get printed, you're in the System, and I didn't want any of that shit. Now I'm in there, in a big file with all the rest."

She grabbed another couple of beers out of the fridge, hesitated in thought over one, then handed it to me.

"You ever regret dropping out when you did?" she said.

"I never regret anything."

"No really," she rolled her eyes. "Do you ever think things would've been different if you'd have stayed and finished school?"

"Well, of course it would've been different," I leaned back in my seat. "But does that mean it would've been *better*? I just hit a point when I didn't need any more institutional knowledge. I wanted to experience things for myself. I wanted to do, not just read about doing like all those other assholes. I dropped out and moved to L.A. to tempt chance, to become rich and famous, to do something worthwhile. Now I'm here; poor and unknown, but at least I made the decision for myself. *I'm* responsible, no one else."

"Yeah, but don't you feel like you're gonna need a degree if writing doesn't work out?" she pulled the blanket around her neck again and huddled on the couch.

"A degree in *what?*" I threw my arms in the air, suddenly defensive. "How is a piece of paper and a huge student loan debt gonna make me any better of a person? What the hell am I gonna do in my life that requires a degree? I don't need one to produce T.V. commercials. I don't need one to write for the newspaper. I'm never gonna be a doctor or a lawyer or anything like that. It's of no use to me. It only shows that someone has successfully done exactly what is asked of them by the powers that be. That they can be maleable."

"I just think you should have some kind of a back-up plan, y'know?" she said meekly. "What if you never make it as a writer? What are you gonna do then?"

"I guess I'm going to die broke and unhappy," I sniffed. "Because I'd rather chase this dream all the way 'til I die a stone broke failure than give up and plague my soul with earning money by selling out to the Machine."

She thought about this for a second, swishing the beer around in the bottle.

"Do you think *I've* sold out?" she asked pointedly.

"We *all* sell out, Liz," I said. "Some more than others, but we all sell out to the Machine, one way or another. I make television commercials. I help big corporations get bigger. I help fool the masses. Even though I don't even watch T.V., I'm partly responsible for how it affects our society. It makes me sick."

"But you're saying that I've sold out too, right?" she squinted her eyes. "That I have this corporate job and shit, and drive a nice car and have a comfortable apartment... that's because I've sold out, huh?"

"I'm not just talking about *you*, Liz," I tried to explain. "I'm saying that we've *all* sold out. It's our *nature*. It's what we *do*."

"What do you mean, 'the Machine'?" she asked.

I sighed and took a long swig from the bottle.

"I dunno... it's like the mechanism in place that gathers up all creative thought and channels it straight out the sewer pipe. It's the American Dream. It's the reason people make money and buy houses and get married—not because we *want* to, but because it's been ingrained in us since the beginning. We're all supposed to *succeed!* If you're working, you're doing well. You're making it. Doesn't matter what you're doing, just that you're punching a clock. But success is just another stupid label we all throw around, just another catch phrase. You're a Republican, I'm a liberal, he's a progressive, she's an anarchist, they're rich, they're poor—we don't all necessarily disagree on everything, but society has labeled us and categorized us into neat little groups of Us and Them. Just like our child president; that 'if you're not with me, you're against me,' mentality. Anyone who asks questions against our government or rebels from this system or status quo is labeled 'anti-American.' Anyone who defies the norm and does things their own way is labeled 'eccentric.' Anyone who actually participates in their democracy is a threat. Anyone who just wants to live simply and travel around the world and write silly words in his notebook and pop in on friends whenever he wants to have a good time is unacceptable... doesn't fit into any pattern. It's just useless to anyone who matters. Anyone but me, that is. My lifestyle is obsolete and impractical, but it's *true* and that's why it's beautiful. The Machine wants us to abandon Truth and accept the root ugliness of a useless, wasted existence."

"Yeah, but how is going to college and getting a job selling out to the Machine?" she asked. "Isn't it just survival? We all need to *eat*, we all need a place to *sleep*, right?"

"Sure," I nodded. "But do we need to eat hamburgers from McDonald's just because everyone else does? Do we need to sleep in fancy apartments with $500 bedspreads because that means we've succeeded? We don't need a college degree to survive."

"Oh please!" she shook her head. "What are we supposed to *do?* Just live in the woods like animals and not be part of society? That's a pretty simple answer."

"I don't *know* what we're supposed to do! If I *did*, I wouldn't be taking this trip around America right now. I'd be sitting in the sun on some Caribbean island undoing the strap of some floozy girl's bikini and drinking mojitos. I'm not saying that I'm *above* the Machine, or *beyond* it in any way… I'm stuck *inside* like everyone else. But I'm trying to find a *loophole*… to *sidestep* all this bullshit. There's got to be a better way. I'll probably never find it, but what the hell else am I gonna do? Just bend over and take it up the ass? Just give up? Just accept it and die with a smile on my face? I want to enjoy my suffering before my society hollows it out."

"It just seems like you're making things harder than they need to be."

"You bet I am," I pounded my fist on the coffee table. "And why not? Maybe I *want* things to be difficult. Maybe I *want* a wall to bang my head against. Maybe I'm *tired* of being a privileged white male in America. Maybe I *like* the struggle. If being 'successful' means giving up on my dreams and falling in line with the rest of the fucking lemmings, you can *have* success… I'll take failure."

Around 3 a.m. Liz suddenly threw the blanket off with kicking feet and gasped in frustration.

"Rrrgh, I have to go to sleep Max… you make me constipated," she stumbled over the coffee table. "I have to work in six hours. The Machine is calling me."

"Look, I'm not saying this stuff to piss you off or anything," I said. "I just wonder sometimes why we do the things we do, y'know? Why we have to work jobs we hate to survive… why we have to subscribe to so much bullshit just to be productive and useful in society… why we have to sacrifice happiness to seek happiness."

She rubbed her eyes and yawned noisily.

"My brain's full, Maxy. You and your damn ideas."

"Awright. Thanks for picking me up and letting me crash here and everything."

"Yeah yeah… I'll leave the keys to my car on the table if you wanna use it tomorrow… I'm getting a ride to work with my friend Tawny."

"Yeah, that'd be great Liz."

"Don't wreck it or roll it or catch it on fire or anything," she glared back at me. "I'm going to bed, 'night 'night."

Silence and ticking of the heater. A lonely car *whisssh-ing* by on 14th Avenue. I got up and looked out the sliding glass doors at Denver below, shrouded in darkness, the holy mile-high city where the innocence of youth gave way to the corruption of adulthood. All those soldiers of Sisyphus sleeping in their Egyptian cotton sheets and goose-down bedspreads all across the city, the country, the whole brown world; resting in order to wake up and push their rocks again in the morning. Will we ever reach the top? Are we all doomed to repeat ourselves until we die neat deaths and fade away, leaving bank accounts and mortgages and unpaid parking tickets in our wakes? Isn't there a better way? Am I chasing after a ghost?

I sunk into her beautiful couch and the silence swept me away. I dreamt I was six years old, running through fields of snow.

Liz tried not to wake me when she left around eight, but I heard her scraping toast angrily and then drop the car keys on the counter. The door clicked shut and I drifted back to sleep for another few hours, stretched out like a cat.

Suddenly, around 11, I sprang up as if by a surge of electric current in the cushions, ran around the room for a second to get my bearings and puffed a cigarette out on the balcony. It was bright and clear outside—another beautiful Colorado day.

I walked around the corner and spat off the edge. An angry woman was throwing clothes out onto the lawn, where there were coffee tables, recliners, T.V. sets, dresser drawers and cardboard boxes piled at the curb. A man chased after her, picking up the clothes and yelling, "C'mon, stop throwin' my stuff around in the snow, dammit, c'mon honey, just let me *be*, dammit, let me *be*," and her answering, "I don't *care* about yer fucking clothes, you son of a bitch, I just want your shit *out* of here, get it *out!* Go stay with your *whore!*"

Another domestic dispute. Another broken home. Another failed marriage. More gloom. But hell, it couldn't penetrate my sunshine. I dashed the cigarette out and ran back giggling, rubbing my hands together. I was in Denver and had a car and a whole beautiful day at my disposal. What to do? Where to go? Ahh.

I stripped naked, turned Liz's bathroom radio up loud and hopped into a steamy shower, moaning along with the words to some Steely Dan song I didn't know. Amazing the power of a good hot shower—I emerged like a Roman gladiator and danced around the living room naked, rummaging through the pack for clean clothes, brushing my teeth, deodorant under the arms, then out the door and down the drab grey halls, outside the alcove and into the day; scarf wrapped tight around my neck and pack aback, ready to go, always ready to go.

Up Colfax toward the big buildings downtown, the sewer grates in the road venting steam into the air and cars running over the plumes, leaving a fractured wake—my eternal vision of downtown Denver—and hell, I didn't really know what to do, where to go or why, so I just kept driving, kept whistling, kept going. I-25 north out of the city, past Boulder, Longmont, Loveland, and eventually all the way to Fort Collins, my old college town.

Rolling through the old points of familiarity, looking at them all blankly… the gas station where I was pulled over that time freshman year and almost got a DUI. The "25-cent Adult Arcade" across from campus where Mitch and I used to joke about getting a job. The plasma donation center where I went three times a week for $27 to pay for beer and cigarettes. My dorm building, Corbett Hall, where Mitch and I lived freshman year and spied on the girls playing tennis across the street and snuck beer up in backpacks and played Mario Kart and cooked Pizza Rolls and ate Flavor-Ice and smoked pot and blew the smoke through toilet paper tubes stuffed with dryer sheets to mask the smell, the towel placed under the crack of the door, of course.

I drove by it all, staring out the window at everything and feeling enormously sad and old, pathetic, like an old man revisiting scenes of his jumping youth. All the kids strolling across the student grounds with notebooks and backpacks over their shoulders looked so young and naïve. Did I look that stupid when I was them?

And I see where they tore out the old drive-in theatre and put up a Wal-Mart, and I feel angry, because I always liked cruising by the drive-in and remembering the date when I watched the "Blair Witch Project" with that girl, Jody, my freshman year. Progress marches on. Now people can buy shotguns and toilet paper and bean bag chairs and canta-loupes and laundry detergent at low, low prices. Always.

I stopped at a bagel shop I used to frequent near campus and got in line behind a giggling group of girls that I felt crim-inal for looking at. I looked like some sort of child molester in my stupid hat, surrounded by healthy, bright young wom-en with perky breasts and low-cut pants riding low on their thin hips, smelling of sex and chapstick and J-Lo perfume.

"Brittney said that Donna said that the Sigma Chi's were gonna have a *massive* party Friday, but I think the *Kap*-pas are gonna be there," one of them blathered.

"Ugh!" another one added with theatrically rolled eyes. "The *Kappas?* God, they're so *mean*. What's that *one* bitch's name? Mellanina? Melanoma? What?"

The whole flock giggled and the line lurched forward.

I ordered my usual: turkey and cheese on a parmesan bagel with a Nantucket Lemonade, then sat down to eat in the middle of students talking about exams and chemistry quizzes and blowjobs and the like. They were chattering on cell phones, thumbing through the campus newspaper, writing into notebooks, telling loud stories about who got drunk at that one party and laughing—all safe in their institutional bubble still.

I chewed my food sadly, listening to conversations, watching cars driving by outside, glancing at notices posted on the walls. This used to be my home. Now it's just a cobweb… just an echo.

All of these people at Colorado State—some 25,000 students perhaps—and all the others going to school at CU in Boulder, DU in Denver, CSU at Colorado Springs, and then all the people going to college all over the country, eating bagels and talking about assignments and tests in coffee shops, getting drunk and having sex with each other, stumbling to class tired and bowlegged, barbequing with friends in the quad, bending their heads over thick books at the libraries, playing frisbee golf, taking bong hits in basement rooms… all embraced by the institutional hand, getting the knowledge it takes to *succeed*. To get a *good job*. To *make money* and *be something* when you're older.

None of them had a fucking clue, really.

That wide hand slapping us all in the face, one by one by one. Learn this, get a degree in that. Hang a diploma on your wall and make something of yourself. Succeed.

My phone rang.

"Max! It's Regan, what the fuck is *up*?"

"Regan! What're you doing? Are you drunk?"

"*No!*" she giggled. "It's eleven o'clock!"

Regan and I went to high school together and met up from time to time on our crazy loops around the country. She's just as restless as I am. She was a wanderer too. After quitting college, she'd spent a couple years fighting fires in Montana and then building houses with Americorps in the south, then volunteering in New Orleans after Katrina hit. She wore jeans and thrift store tee-shirts faded with the sun. She drank and spat and played a mean guitar with her brown hair pulled back and tied out of her face and twinkling blue eyes shining with a sense of adventure. She left sing-song messages on her friends' voicemails. She sent old Yeats poems on the back of postcards from her travles. We used to march through the woods back home with backpacks full of clinking beer bottles to catch sunsets and listen to the Grateful Dead.

Her latest stopping point, after being kicked out of Americorps, was Winter Park where she worked as a lifty.

I told her I was in town and had tickets to the Nuggets game with Liz's yuppie friends if she wanted to come down.

"Drive up to Winter Park and get me, I don't have a car," she said. "Fuck it, I can handle the yuppies. I'll pick up some beer for the drive down, okay?"

"Okay, I'll be there soon."

"Better hurry, there's supposed to be a butt-load of snow tonight," she warned in sing-song tone.

Just like that, plans for the night altered and I accepted them as they came—just as Regan my kindred spirit didn't think twice and accepted her new assignment for the night.

The bagel shop was making me feel old and a little criminal. I tossed the rest of my food into the trash and loped out of there, energized now by a plan of some kind, a mission.

The sky showed no signs of the big storm Regan said was coming, but I knew she was probably right. I've seen the snow in June and I've walked around in tee-shirts on January mornings—never know what to expect in ol' Colorady.

I drove the pleasant hour back into Denver listening to Nick Drake's soft voice of pain and eventual suicide and then caught the 70 going west toward the mountains and Winter Park. The snow started falling once I entered the mountains, but Liz's Subaru handled sharp and clean the whole time—not one skid or moment of anxiety.

Regan was waiting for me outside a small liquor store in Fraser, a sleepy Colorado mountain town with a handful of stores and houses at the foot of giant mountains that seemed to rise into the heavens. She wore a hoody sweatshirt and a big flowery skirt and had a woven bag full of water bottles and chapsticks and spare pairs of panties and bottles of booze—Regan was always a walking junk drawer.

We drank beer and smoked a J down the mountain, laughing and yelling of old times.

"I'll never be able to look you in the eye again after that time you jumped off Ally's back deck topless on New Year's Eve," I said.

"Oh my *god*, you even *filmed* it, didn't you?" she squealed.

"You bet I filmed it—I think it's on YouTube now."

"Well, they're great tits, what can I say?" she waggled her breasts in her hands.

Old memories—the ties that bind. Was it Emerson that wrote: "It is one of the blessings of old friends that you can afford to be stupid with them"? Wise man.

"Oh, I almost forget—I got you a present," she said when we were almost in the city.

She stuck her little rump in the air and rummaged in the back for a minute. I swerved all over the place deliberately to upset her balance.

"Stop it!" she screamed, giggling.

Then she pulled a damn Viking helmet out of her bag, with horns and everything.

"I got this is Vegas last time I was there—I figure you're the only one crazy enough to wear it."

"Holy shit! Gimmie!" I put it on my head and snarled into the rear view. Oh it was *on* now.

"Who are these people anyways?" she asked. We were pulling off the freeway and entering the surface streets. "Are they like us?"

"Ho ho, I doubt it," I laughed and threw another empty bottle in the backseat. "We'll have to stick together. Don't let 'em smell fear."

By the time we finally met up with Liz and her friends at the bar next to the Pepsi Center—Brooklyn's I think it was called—we were both shit-faced… me cocky and waving my arms at everything, storming around in my Viking helmet and yelling at passersby, and Regan a swerving, stuttering, giggling mess.

We barged into the bar and scanned the tables for Liz's crew, the milling crowds of people halting their conversations mid-sentence, glancing over at me with strange looks. I saw Liz surrounded by a group of clean-looking people with shirts tucked in and shiny shoes, and she waved us over—a mortified look on her face.

"What the hell are you *wearing?*" she yelled, ushering us over to the table, where she introduced me to all of her friends. Regan accidentally hugged one of Liz's blond friends I didn't know and howled, "Heeey Liz, so nice to finally meeeet you!" "No, *I'm* Liz." The women were all mid-twenties professionals and the men wore standard-issue striped shirts with open collars and gel in their faux-hawks, shiny flat-bottom shoes that they must issue everyone under thirty who makes over $40k a year. They all looked like a bunch of assholes. Everyone was somewhat taken aback to be shaking hands with a bearded drunk Viking and Regan, whose eyeballs were each pointing a different direction.

"Um, this is my friend Max," Liz told them meekly.

One of the Gel-Hair Pricks tilted his head and upturned his smarmy nose at me: "What are *you* supposed to be?"

"Drunk," I barked, then turned back to Liz. "You think we have time to order some chicken wings? We'd really love some chicken wings. We're *starving*."

I rubbed my belly. Her friends all gave each other knowing looks.

"Maybe if you were here like a half-*hour* ago when the *game* started," the Gel-Hair Prick muttered.

"Hey, American Idol, am I talking to you?" I shot at him. He cowered back.

Liz just stood clenching her jaw.

"Uh, well, the game *did* start a half-hour ago, so we should probably get going, huh?" she said, but Regan was already stumbling up to the bar to make the order. She pushed aside two businessmen with surprising force and waved her arms at the bartender, hooting and yelling, "Halloooo! Yoo hoo! Chicken wings!" to get his attention.

"Why don't you guys just go without us and we'll meet you there in a bit?" I said.

They left for the game in a huff—Regan and I finished the wings and a couple of beers before catching up with them in the upper deck. It was the Nuggets vs. the Cavs, but I didn't really give a hoot in hell who won, lost, tied, or whatever—sports are lost to me. I kept shouting "Go Vikings!" and spilling beer all over everyone, and even made it on the Jumbo-Tron at one point.

"Ha! Lookit yooo!" Regan elbowed me and pointed at the massive screen where 20,000 people watched me make a fool of myself.

"Yaaaargh!" I bellowed. I heard a wave of laughter go through the crowd.

"Hey, 'member that time Shea was on the Jumbo-Tron in Fresno? When you stacked all that shit on her head?" Regan said.

"Oh shit! That's right—what a helluva night *that* was," I elbowed one of Liz's smarmy friends and told him the story, even though he tried not to listen.

"Our friend Shea got all wasted on vodka one night when we were passing through Fresno—drank the whole fuckin' bottle—and we decided to go see a hockey game, so she ends up passing out in her seat and I started stacking shit on her head—y'know, nacho containers, beer bottles, my *shoe*—the stack was like three feet high and it was perfectly balanced, and all these people started noticing and laughing, pointing over at us and shit, and then the Jumbo-Tron shows her picture up there and the whole damn crowd cracks up and gives her a standing ovation. She woke up and it all toppled over and this cop tried to arrest us, I think. He thought we drugged her or some shit!"

"Hmm, that's *great*," the faux-hawk prick huffed, turning back to the game.

Liz's friends all hated me, naturally, and kept sighing and groaning every time I shoved my way down the row of seats to empty my bladder.

At one point, while getting more beer at the concession stand, I passed a throng of CU sorority girls wearing sailor caps and little grey tee-shirts with "Delta Gamma" printed on the front over those perky mounds—those firm asses in low-rise pants, belly buttons, and sexy stomachs showing as they wriggle and shake their little hips about the place. I couldn't resist running up to them and shouting, "Yaaaargh!" scaring the hell out of all of them.

"Ohmygod, ri-ght!" one of them giggled as they ran, screaming, away.

The game was down to the wire with only a few minutes left, but Regan and I decided to cut out early to go to

Sancho's, a Grateful Dead bar on Colfax not far from where Liz lived.

"You're *leaving?*" Liz yelled. "We're down by two and there's only a couple minutes to go!"

"Ah, fuck this game!" I stood up and shouted to the crowd: "You're all lemmings! All of you! Ah ha haaa!"

"Sit down!" a guy behind us shouted. He was wearing a Nuggets Jersey and acted as if his whole life depended on the outcome of this game.

"Heeeey man, how come you're sitting up *here?*" I shouted back to him. "Get *down* there, man, they *need* you! C'mon, you *got* the jersey! Two points down!"

He started to get up but Regan ushered me out of there quickly. We ran down the escalator out to the parking lot hooting and screaming at people.

I tore across town sideways, running red lights and swerving all over the place—turned the wrong direction down a one way street and pulled the e-brake to power slide into a parking spot, which I did with expert efficiency some-how—hoping to hell there wasn't a cop about.

"Holy shit!" Regan stumbled out of the car. "You fucker, we almost crashed!"

And then she slipped on a patch of ice and landed flat on her butt. I tried to help her up, but we were both laughing too hard and I slipped too, the two of us now sprawled in the middle of the street laughing like maniacs, cars honking at us impatiently.

We got a couple of Good Times burgers, took them into Sancho's and ate the shit out of them on their fine old beat couches with Yonder Mountain String Band playing loud over the house speakers and Colorado hippie girls getting out of their seats to dance and shake their hips with arms in the air and hairy pits beneath—the Colorado bluegrass way—ah, how I love this state. Sitting there in Sancho's with the posters of the Grateful Dead all around; beanies, ponytails, and barefooted dreadlock dudes with dogs tied to the pole outside and longboards leaning against the walls, women walking around with marijuana chocolates for sale, five bucks apiece.

"Give me the cheapest, most rot-gut whiskey you got!" I yelled to the bartendress, who just smiled and grabbed a well-worn bottle with a few inches left—oh those brief moments between bartender and drunk we all love. By this point I'd lost one of the Viking horns and must've looked ridiculous—like some kind of unicorn Viking—but she served me just the same.

Regan's friend called around closing time and said he could give her a ride back to Winter Park if she wanted—he was in Denver after dropping his sister off at the airport.

"Come with me if you want," she said when he showed up. "I have a hot Romanian friend who would *love* you."

"Nah, I can't get mixed up with some Romanian chick!" I pushed both arms at her. "I went on this trip to get away from all that, dammit, and here I am drunk again. What the hell's wrong with me? Whaa? Who? Hmm."

"Well, we can drop you off at Liz's place," she said slowly. "You prolly shouldn't drive anymore."

"Okay, let's go quick, 'fore I change my mind."

Out to her friend's car, me not even shaking his hand or paying attention to him at all, just hopping in his front seat and ordering him where to turn. I've been told by some that I "cast a large shadow" when I'm drunk and I'm sure it's true—I was being a complete asshole all night. But is it my fault that I am high on the night? He had to pull over once for Regan to stick her head out the window and vomit, right on Colfax Street.

"Ah, same ol' Regan," I shook my head and lit up a cigarette. "Just like high school."

"Uh, would you mind not smoking in here?" the friend asked. "This isn't really my car, and the girl who I borrowed it from is allergic to—"

"Yass yass, it's just up here a bit, two more blocks," I exhaled out the window.

They dropped me at Liz's building without fanfare and sped off for the hour-long trip back up the mountain. Liz was already asleep when I crashed through the door and collapsed on the couch, high on weed, booze, the night, and life—all come to a fine sloppy head at the top of the world. One mile high.

All this space to cover and never enough time to see it all—never enough. So many days, so many nights... so many miles to cover until I can't go anymore.

I awoke still wearing the Viking helmet, now missing both horns. Luckily, before passing out, I ate six Aspirin and drank about a gallon of water, so the hangover wasn't too bad. But I remember a horrid dream—I tossed and turned and squirmed all night on the couch because of it. I dreamt about these little crawly things like scorpions, but they were flat and microscopic, little crab lice or something, that fastened onto our water glasses and entered our stomachs, then grew large and somehow escaped our bodies, growing at an incredible rate, until they got so big they started running people down and killing them with huge claws or pincers—and the end of the dream was me running running running for all I had and watching one of those damn evil monsters grow to the size of an alligator and overtake me finally. It was like watching a cheetah run down a gazelle on one of those nature documentaries. I awoke at the moment its pincers started to close on me, drenched with sweat and a scream squelched in my throat.

But, lo and behold, when I shuffled outside to smoke my morning butt, I saw it had snowed about a foot with more coming down fast—what the fuck?—it was so *clear* yesterday... so sunny... and now this. "Only in Colorado," I heard myself saying, wishing I hadn't, for that is so cliché. That's the type of thing old feed store cashiers tell farmers on their way out the door—but I said it and luckily no one heard me.

Into the shower and out again, remembering that Liz's car was parked somewhere near Sancho's on Colfax. I dressed quickly and bundled up, then walked out into falling snow—down 14th, down Fillmore, down Colfax for blocks and blocks—little white mustache on the brim of my hat piled up quickly and efficiently. I finally reached the Subaru after digging the snowed-in Denver streets—the white-knuckle drivers splashing through the muck, the homeless prophets stamping their feet under the awnings of furniture stores. I thought there was going to be trouble—maybe the car got towed (I really don't even remember pulling it into a *space* last night, just hopped out when it stopped sliding), or maybe I got a ticket, or or or, hung up on these old tricks again, cuz when I got there everything was fine and dandy just like it always is—just a shapeless lump sitting serene and silent on a Denver side street covered in a foot of snow. I wiped the windshield clear with my gloves and hopped in, drove back to Liz's with a dumb smile on my face that only I saw in my reflection.

"Well, what do you do today?" I said to the rear view.

Back at Liz's place, I opened my laptop, pirated a WiFi signal, wrote an email to Jack telling him about my trip so far, then read a book on the couch for the rest of the day— the only day since the beginning where I didn't do anything; didn't go anywhere, didn't do anything—just vegged out on the couch. And it was glorious.

I picked Liz up from work around six o'clock. She motioned for me to get out of the driver's seat with a boxer's glare, and acted very cold on the drive back. We didn't talk for several moments.

"Look," I broke the awkward silence. "I'm sorry I got so wasted last night and pissed off your friends. I didn't really mean anything by it."

"You *never* really mean anything by it," she blurted. "You just storm into town and insult all my friends and think it's *funny* or something."

"Oh c'mon," I moaned. "Those people are *really* your friends? They're a bunch of douche-bags."

"Yes, they *are* my friends, and you made me feel like a total idiot in front of them."

"Geez, Liz, we used to make *fun* of people like that in college—"

"Well, we're not *in* college anymore!" she glared. "Things *change*, Max. Some of us have to grow up and get real jobs and sell out to your fucking *Machine*. We can't all just ramble around the country and leave when things get too real. Who are *you* to pass judgment on them? What makes *you* any better? You run away from everything. You're an escapist."

"I *said* I was sorry, Liz, what else do you want me to say?" I felt like such a lecher sitting there as she sped through traffic pounding the steering wheel. She was right, of course. Everything was falling apart again. God dammit.

"Max, I love you and everything, but you really embarrassed me last night," she said with an even tone. "And on top of that, I was late to work this morning because you had my *car* all night. I don't even want to know if you were driving drunk."

I looked out the window and sighed, "I'm sorry, I didn't think you needed it this morning."

"No," she shouted. "Of *course* you didn't think I needed it, because you never think of anyone else. You only think about *yourself*. You just take and take. I let you stay at my apartment, borrow my car, buy you and your friend tickets to the game and you never even *thanked* me, then you act like a total asshole in front of my friends and just take off. How am I *supposed* to feel?"

"Okay, just let me out here," I demanded suddenly, fed up with being harangued. "I'll walk the rest of the way back."

"Don't be ridiculous, it's freezing outside."

She glanced over at me with sad eyes; the eyes a mother gives a wayward child. I pursed my lips: "Let me out."

"Fine, suit yourself, run away," she pulled over. "I'll be at my apartment when you stop acting like a child."

I jumped out of the car, slammed the door and watched her skid into traffic. I had no idea where I was... somewhere downtown. The snow drifted down sideways across the red-brick as the sky grew dark. Streetlamps flickered and caught finally. This day was winding down.

Huddled beneath a store awning, I pulled out my cell phone and dialed Ani's number with nervous fingers.

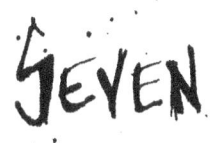

SEVEN

WE ALL HAVE AN ANI INSIDE OF US… a fictitious person that existed once, in reality, in a certain place and time. It might be a man you met in an elevator on Park Avenue, or a girl you spent a weekend with in Singapore during the 60's. Mine was a beautiful little brunette I spent time with on a sailboat in the Caribbean Sea.

Put them into reality and it never works, because these are the attractions that will never be cultivated into anything more than a figment of your imagination—they exist only in the mind, where you're always back on that sailboat with the Cheshire grin by your side. You never want it to be real because it served a better purpose as a fantasy.

And I suppose that's why I felt the way I did—because I knew it wasn't real. I knew it was impermanent. I knew it was pure fiction. It was safe for me to feel this way because I'd never have to face the reality of the situation.

"Ani? It's Max," I said into the phone.

It was cold, I was nervous and she sounded distant. There was an unspoken thing hanging in the air over our heads, but I couldn't put my finger on it. I asked if she wanted to meet up for a drink.

"Oh, *tonight?* Shit, I *can't* tonight, my uh, my boyfriend's *parents* are in town and I promised I'd go to dinner with them… are you gonna be here tomorrow?"

Boyfriend? I frowned.

"Aah, no… actually I'm taking off tonight around eight or nine."

Boyfriend?

"Man," she groaned. "That *sucks*, I wanted to *see* you."

"That's okay Ani, I didn't give you much notice."

"Well… when are you gonna be back through?"

"I dunno… sometime I guess."

She apologized again and hung up, leaving me standing there in the cold, dark night.

"God *dammit!*" I threw the phone down the street into a snow bank. A moment later, I ran after it quickly and fished it out, then dried it off on my jeans feeling foolish.

I'd spent the past five days daydreaming about what I'd say to Ani when I saw her again—wondering if she ever sat up in her room daydreaming about me… and it finally dawned on me, out there on the anonymous cold street corner, that she didn't love me, she never did… she didn't think of me, she didn't lie awake at night wondering what I was doing, what I was thinking about, who I was with. I was nothing more than an old friend who'd come into town at a bad time for her. Reality caught up to the fantasy and clubbed it over the head.

There was an old beat coffee house up ahead with a couple of yawning patrons dreaming out the windows, watching the snow fall and me mope by underneath the flakes all forlorn and haggard. They didn't care about me either… no one cared. And why should they?

These are the consequences of living too deep in the

fantasy. Oh, why do I always fall in love with people I can't be with? Doesn't she know that we're perfect together?

Why did I get out of the car? I don't even know where I am. Wonder how far of a walk it is to Liz's house… and why did I have to get so drunk and make a fool of myself last night? Why do I have to drink to feel confident, to feel like I belong, to *feel?*

No answers came. Just the bitter wind and *clomp clomp* of my shoes on the freshly fallen snow. I made it back to Liz's around 8 p.m., already late for the train. It was probably late though. The train never runs on time.

She opened the door slowly and shook her head at me, sopping wet and standing there hangdog in the hallway.

"I'm…" I stuttered. "I'm late for the train, Liz. Do you think… you could give me a ride to the station?"

She just sighed and put on her coat, grabbed her keys and pushed past me, slamming the door behind her without saying a word.

At the station the passengers were rushing in through the front door clutching duffel bags and carry-on suitcases, laptop cases, purses, messenger bags, cardboard boxes, and bottles of Pepsi.

"Thank you for the ride," I fidgeted with the strap on my pack. "And for letting me stay and everything else… I'm… I don't know what to say."

"Just say you'll be better behaved next time you come into town," she gripped the steering wheel methodically.

"I promise I'll try," I said with relief, grateful that she let me off the hook, and hopped out into the falling snow. I was halfway to the front door with my pack when I heard her shout behind me.

"Wait!" she called out and ran after me. "Max, call me when you get where you're going, all right? I worry about you, y'know?"

I nodded and we hugged for a long moment. No *pat–pat*

on the back with this hug. This was a *real* one.

She skidded away from the station with me standing in the doorway staring after her—back to her life, to the pantsuits and ringing phones, back to the fake smarmy friends and looming adulthood carrying us all away from the past, into the void. Onward. What is it in those last moments of watching someone go when you understand so much and still haven't a clue about anything? It's like you have the answer there at your fingertips, but only for a moment's time. Before you realize what it was, it's gone.

So that's Denver—I reached one more finger out into the abyss. Never regret a good time and never discount a disaster… sometimes they're all we have left.

Turned out the train was delayed four hours because of the snowstorm, so I just sat in the station next to my ugly pack and studied a cute girl sitting across the bench from me, reading a Hunter S. Thompson book and tapping her foot impatiently on the tiled floor. She didn't belong in this era either. She wore little black reading glasses that matched her black, curly hair, and had the dopest little body when she got up to fill her water bottle in the fountain by the bathroom. I hoped that we'd get stuck sitting together on the train. She seemed to be the type of girl who had theories about things.

I plugged in my laptop at an outlet across the large room and sat back down. Before long, a security guard ambled over to it, kicked the black, bulletproof, waterproof case with his toe and looked around suddenly with alarm. I got up and loped over there.

"That's mine," I said. "It's just my computer charging."

"Hmph," he grumbled, feeling a little foolish. "Just what I love to see, a mysterious black box plugged into the wall."

I guess he thought it was a bomb or something—but

then again, why the hell does anybody do anything?

Before long I was back on the rails, settled into my seat and closing my eyes as we sped east out of Denver, the mile-high edge of the phosphorescent west, the continental divide, where the water chooses to flow east along the rusty plains, through the cornrows and scablands into the muddy Mississippi backwater, through the humid tire-swing nights of the east, beyond the fireflies, beyond the factories, beyond the swirling madness of our first coast where this whole thing began, into the junkyard sea of Gulf storms and Atlantic fury where marlins crest in the fall of dusk… or West, the way of the wanderer, the way of our pioneers, Manifest Destiny, down the rocky foothills and waterfalls and green forest valleys, the snow-crusted mountain tops, the deserts and salt flats shining in pale daybreak, past the old frontier towns and mining camps, past the logging trails and fire lookouts, the river trout leaping at flies, the VW vans parked at trailheads, the apple orchards and artichoke fields, the bent migrant workers sweating, the dappled California valleys, the crusty oceanic rocks with hermit crabs and sand fleas, the dunes, out to the old blue Pacific shining like an answer just waiting for the right question to unleash it. Here was the great continental crossroads. Here I stood and looked in both directions until the sky met the unattainable dawn. Here I saw both seas in one wide, sweeping glace. Here the land opened up and spread her virgin petals to my stamping feet. Here is where I learned the way I am, and the way I always should be; mile-high. Here. *Here* I was king.

Eight.

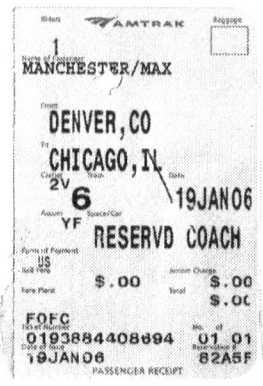

I WALKED UP AND DOWN the train car as we pulled out of the Denver station and frowned—every row was occupied by sleeping passengers sprawled across both seats. The conductor told me that I'd just have to wake one of them up if I wanted to sit down, so I picked one that looked harmless and shook him awake.

"Oh mannn," he groaned, smelling of whiskey and body odor. "Why don't you sit somewhere else? How am I supposed to *sleep?*"

"I'm sorry, there's no other open seats," I told him. Even strangers hated me.

"Ahg," he grumbled, clearing off the aisle seat theatrically, like a snot-nose kid stamping up the stairs to his room and rolling over on his side away from me. All I could do was sit in silence and try not to move a muscle—my penance for all the evil tricks I'd pulled in Denver and elsewhere in life. It was two in the morning and there was nothing but darkness outside the windows, punctuated every so often by a front range street lamp throwing wide arcs of blue light onto the snowy fields of the Colorado plains. We left the mountains behind and I drifted away. I closed my eyes to the sadness, hoping it would be gone in the morning.

Hooooo! Rose from a rolling dream as we slowed into Lincoln at daybreak—Off the train and smoked one of the coldest cigarettes of my life. Bitter wind blew in from deep in the prairie. Hot damn, dash that fucker out and run back upstairs. Lincoln, Nebraska! Middle America!

Everything is grey and exciting this morning... no more of the Denver sadness—the flat expanse of this sleepy Nebraska city spreading out over the earth, tilting at the edges of the horizon, rust-colored train station roof, dirt rail yard and brick buildings red like the earth with old dates stamped in their façades.

A wiry old nomad got off at Lincoln and left an open seat, so I ran up there and stretched out wide—happy to have my own row finally. I watched him walk from the station toting an old Salvation Army pack and several carefully wrapped packages, rolling a rusty ten-speed bike with him from the platform—his long, thin beard whipping in the amber waves of dawn.

I suddenly noticed I was sitting on something and fished out a bar of soap he left behind. It filled me with sadness to think of that old road man roaming around the world without his bar of soap. But I just shoved it in my pack and sighed as we began moving once again.

Everything was so new, so flat, so rural... this is Middle America, with her small roadside diners filled with beat farm pickups in the parking lot and warmth inside through the windows, red-roofed and twinkling, "Arby's now hiring" it says in the window next door—"Traveler's Café Bottomless cup o' coffee." Her windmills turning listlessly in the distance and heaps of junk and gutted cars and washing machines filled out the foreground—why so many gutted washing machines out here in America?

Now outside of town, pushing along like a strong plains wind with just about everything on my mind... planning to close my eyes again and sleep more than the three hours I got the night before. It was bleeding into afternoon.

Some hours later, I put on my scarf and hopped off for a cigarette in some no-name Iowa town. The conductor stood at the platform checking his gold pocket watch, his big white mustache twitching back and forth comically, like a squirrel tail. I walked down to the end of the train into the sunshine and stumbled upon a man taking a hit from a glass pipe.

"Ooop, hey... how's it goin' man?" he said. The sweet-smelling smoke slipped out of his mouth. "You want some?"

"Sure."

He offered it to me and I lit it up.

"I been dyin' for this all day," he scratched his stubbly, angular face. "They should have smoking cars like they used to back in the old days."

He looked like any other road wanderer we all pass by in our lives never really taking the time to notice them with our hurried eyes. A face that blended into the backdrop, with no features that stood out. Young, late twenties, black wool cap, jean jacket with paint stains on the sleeves, hard, cracked hands with dirty brown calluses on the tips, blackened fingernails from hammer smacks, soiled tee-shirt tucked into brown workpants and nondescript boots that carried him from one point to another with sad footfalls—boots that have clomped in construction yards and unemployment lines, boots that live in pool halls and on dirty sidewalks, bustling diners at dawn, rail yard garbage can fires. Boots that feel the weight upon them and groan silently with every fall.

"Yeah, last time I rode the train they still had the smoking cars," I handed him the pipe. "I remember spending most of my time in there, chatting with everyone. I haven't talked to hardly anyone today."

"Boy, ain't that the truth," he nodded. After whipping his head around to make sure the coast was clear, he bent back down and took another hit. "You the first person I talked to all day. I'm Kenny, by the way, Kenny Deemer from Kentucky."

He offered his cracked hand and I shook it.

"Max," I answered. "Good to meet you."

"Where you from?"

"Oh, a little town in north Idaho. Before that I was living in L.A. How 'bout you?"

Kenny's dark, grubby face grimaced quickly. It was as if I'd just told him his mother had herpes.

"God *damn* that L.A.!" he flared. "Ever' time I go there I get my ass in trouble, boy!"

"It's a rotten place," I agreed, watching him curiously. "I used to work in the film business, you know? I made television commercials. Buncha assholes."

"Board!" yelled the conductor. The milling smokers clogging the doorways all inhaled deeply and pitched their butts underneath the grumbling locomotive. Like cattle, they slowly climbed aboard. Kenny gazed at me with his head nodding—like he was sizing me up.

"Hmph… well, sounds *inneresting*," he spat, then clomped away on those old boots of life's decay. I lingered in the sunshine for a moment longer, feeling the burning rays red through my closed eyes, the red turning to purple finally when I turned back into the shade and watched Kenny hitch up his jeans and step aboard. I thought maybe I found the only person in the world who hated L.A. more than I did.

Once we left Denver and started rolling across the plains, time seemed to have stopped and lost meaning. I slept through the bottom nub of Nebraska and through half of Iowa as well, waking up a few times here and there and noticed the names of towns I'd passed through years before at different stages of my life—Creston, Osceola, Ottumwa.

I found a 110-year-old woman living in Ottumwa last year for the photography book. The whole idea of the book was to put together fine art portraits of the oldest people in the world—pictures of their faces real close up so you could see all their wrinkles and liver spots and aging scars. My job was to bum around America scouting for them, book the shoot and travel with Mick while he photographed them.

We took portraits of eighty people in the year I worked on the book—all of them over 100 years old and a third that were over 110. From the reservations of Arizona to old folks homes in Minnesota. From tenement buildings on Hollywood and Vine to old sharecropper farms of Mississippi—I sought them all out, one by one.

Those were some of the best times of my life out there on the lonesome highway—bumming around from one rural town to the next, checking out nursing homes and newspaper articles for puff pieces about old people turning 100, camping by the side of the road next to some river and eating beans by a crackling fire. Spending whole entire days sitting at a roadside picnic table, reading books and sighing. But, as with everything else, it ended too soon and I was left right back where I started—working for commercials again in Los Angeles, the city of the migratory soul. I hadn't saved any money—hadn't thought about what would happen after the job ended. I never do. I never book round trip tickets, save money in banks or think things all the way through. Nothing's permanent in this world, except for death, and all those old people we photographed are dead now... just faces in a book and memories in my head.

Darkness again outside these rain-streaked windows—indigo darkness broken only by the occasional street lamp and rising din of this little town of Princeton, Illinois, population: who cares? I can see the mighty billboards on the highway across town—the strange corporate glow rising and falling into our consciousness, dreary motel courts with a couple of sagging old Buicks and pickups with rust peeking through to dirty undercarriages caked in hard crust of life's heavily trod path—a momentary lull and lapse in time here in Princeton, no one getting on, no one getting off—on our way again, leaving it all behind and breaking through the plateau of darkness on the plains ahead, winding our way up this bread desert all the way up to shining Chicago by the lake; windy, homely, run-down Chicago smack dab between the east and west—great hub for the long-haulers heading one way or the other, a collection point where we gain our escape velocity and blast off in our different directions. Such is life on the long-haul trail—this train originating in the foggy outcroppings of a Frisco night and ending its run on the Loop, with the Midwest woe piercing softly from all around and saxophones blowing somewhere in the night.

Wonder what all my friends are up to now? In Northsaint, L.A., Ohio, Denver, Boulder, Reno, Las Vegas, San Diego, Frisco, Portland, Seattle, Thailand, New Zealand, all over the land and all across the sea—my web of comfort, my myth of validation…

They're all out there, just a phone call away, just an email, just a postcard, just a letter—just a shout from a closed room—they're all out there living in their own fashion, making their mistakes, waking with hangovers, pissing on the toilet seat, dropping the fork down the garbage disposal and wincing at the *clattery-clank-scREEEEK* sound that comes pouring out. They're hunched low over their checkbooks, they're staring blank into a computer with tired eyes, they're bursting in through the front door of some familiar bar, they're writing poems and reading want ads—and here we all go, living our sad, pathetic comedies out for the world to see, but the world doesn't care.

Fucking hell! Already five hours late and now we're stopped again, so close to Chicago, caught in this eternal "freight congestion."

"Sorry folks, we've got to wait for three trains to pass through, so we'll be stopped for at least forty-five minutes," Mr. Mustache conductor said. Everyone groaned.

So far, on every leg of my journey, the train has lost many hours due to this mysterious "freight congestion." The double-edged sword of prosperity. Here we are in America, the "greatest nation in the world," and we can't even figure out how to make our trains run on time. In Russia the trains run to the minute, in Germany, in France, in every developed nation of the world. But here in our land of sour milk and cream, the trains are bogged down and pressing against the walls. They are running out of room. All this commerce riding from east to west, north to south, shore to shore—all these goods shipped to consume, all this motion… no way to make it work for passengers to ride along too… *they should be taking airplanes!*

At some point in the small hours of the morning, as we sped blind through the tundra, I stumbled up to the sightseer car, passing bodies sprawled about the seats in every imaginable form.

I put on my headphones and listened to sad music for a while until someone tapped my shoulder.

"Hey man, you got a lighter" a kid asked.

"A *lighter?*" I asked. "For *what?* You smoking down there?"

"Yeah, there's a hatch that we can pry open."

I gave him a green lighter out of my pocket.

"C'mon down if you want," he said, wagging the lighter in my face. He was a stocky kid in his mid-twenties, just like me, wearing a Nike shirt and jeans, close-shaven head.

I followed him down to the snack bar, which was closed at this time of the morning. He introduced himself as Tom.

There were two people sitting in a booth drinking beers next to the window. They both turned their heads toward us—one with a bald head and thick goatee, the other a petite Mexican girl with long brown hair and thin, sexy lips.

"You get it?" the bald guy asked.

"Yep," Tom showed them the lighter.

"C'mon, let's spark it up, quick," the girl urged.

The bald guy opened a square hatch. The cool, subterranean night whooshed by. He pulled a joint from his jeans pocket and used my Bic to light it, then handed it to me.

I took a long drag and blew out. It tasted leafy, schwaggy, dirty… but it clicked that corner of the brain and got me high. Tom, who was standing in the stairwell on guard for conductors, waved his hands suddenly.

"Put it out, put it out!" he hissed. I crushed the cherry, slammed the window shut and slipped the roach in my pocket. We all rushed around in a quick circle and assumed casual poses.

Mr. Mustache conductor appeared in the stairwell and searched our eyes for a moment, like a disappointed school principal. His conductor's cap was tilted low over his searching eyes.

"What's going on down here?" he asked us. *Twitch twitch* went the mustache. "You kids haven't been smoking *cigarettes* in here, have you?"

"No sir," the bald kid said. The rest of us shook our

heads—who, *us? Smoking? Never!*

"All right then," Mr. Mustache said at last, breaking the awkward silence. After another moment he turned his heels and walked sadly up the stairs.

"Whew!" Tom wiped his forehead. "That was close." He then turned to me.

"You didn't throw that out, did you?"

"Nah, it's right here."

"Good," he nodded. "Hold onto it for a second. This is Luigi and Emily by the way. This is Max, you guys."

I nodded to both of them.

"Where you headed?" Emily asked.

"I was supposed to go to Cleveland, but I think I'm gonna miss my connection."

"Yeah, fuckin' freight congestions, eh?" she grinned.

"We're both going to Cleveland too," Luigi said. "I hear they might put us up in a hotel in Chicago if we miss it."

"Really?" I said, then turned to Emily. "What about you? Where you going?"

"I'm going to Milwaukee, but I think I'm gonna miss mine too," she said. "Looks like we might all be stuck in Chicago tonight."

We sat and told our stories—Tom and Luigi were friends from San Francisco traveling to Cleveland to see Tom's family and Emily was heading from Fresno to Milwaukee to see hers. They asked what my deal was, to which I said I was trying to make it to Columbus for Mitch's surprise birthday party.

I pulled out my bottle of Wild Turkey to break the ice and pretty soon we were all high and happy—whooping and banging our fists on the tables with whiskey on our breath and joy in our hearts. Chi-town loomed up ahead big and beautiful, the crossroads of America, where east meets west. The Mississippi River of cities.

"Last time I took the train this chick got booted off because she was smoking crack in the bathroom," Tom shouted with the whiskey bottle in hand. "They actually stopped the train and kicked her out, right in the middle of nowhere!"

"No way!" Emily shouted. "They can't do that, can they? What if someone gets stranded?"

"Well, they did," Tom assured her. "And this other time they caught these two dudes having sex in the bathroom—big, huge, fat dudes too… I have no idea how they both fit in there in the first place."

"Gross!" Luigi yelled. He propped his feet up on the table, wearing fuzzy wool slippers.

"It's funny, you meet the weirdest people on the train," Emily said. "You don't seem to meet anyone interesting on an airplane."

"Yeah, and if you do, they're all too afraid to talk to you, or they're so fucking boring they won't stop," I said.

"Right, like how we're all afraid to look at each other when we pass on the sidewalks," she said. "I'm glad I met you guys, though. I'm having fun."

"Yeah, this is great!" Luigi smiled, then turned to me and explained, "We all got on in Sacramento the other day."

"And you don't know each other?" I pointed from him to Emily.

"Well, Tom and I are old friends from high school. He asked me to come down from Alaska to go to Cleveland with him. We just met Emily down here yesterday, when she caught us trying to smoke a spliff."

"Kinda like how *you* met us," she smiled.

"What do you do in Alaska?" I asked Luigi.

"I'm a commercial fisherman," he said. "I operate out of Seward and Homer mostly, crabbing and salmon sometimes, depending on the season. I'm glad to be traveling again though. It was a tough season."

A few hours later, after the conductor had confirmed we would all miss our connections, I walked up to Tom and Luigi's seat in another car.

"Looks like you were right, they're gonna put us up in a hotel," I told them.

"Hell yeah," Tom put down his Maxim. "They're even gonna give us some money for cab fare and dinner. I think we're gonna go out and have some drinks with Emily—you wanna come?"

"Definitely! We should go to some old run-down blues club or something."

"Are you gonna catch the train to Cleveland tomorrow night?" Luigi asked.

"No, I think I'm gonna try to take a Greyhound or maybe rent a car," I told him. "If I take that train I'll get in at like three in the morning, and that's too late—I gotta try to make my friend's surprise party."

"Dude, what do you think about sharing a rental car and dropping us off in Cleveland?" Tom asked. "We can split the cost and everything."

"Yeah!" Luigi yelled. "That's a great idea! Probably won't cost more'n thirty or forty bucks apiece. Let's do it!"

"Why not?" I shrugged.

We pulled into Union Station in Chicago and were quickly ushered into a waiting room with the rest of the sour-faced passengers who'd missed connections. There, the Amtrak attendants gave out hotel vouchers for the Best Western on the Miracle Mile and $50 spending money apiece. We all shared a cab over to the hotel and planned to spend the rest of the money on booze.

As the rest of the passengers checked in at the hotel counter with sullen grumblings, we met in Tom's room to smoke before hitting the town.

"I can't believe I'm sitting here in a hotel room with three strangers I met on the train," Emily said. I lit up a cigarette and stared out the window. A great blizzard had blown in with sideways snow pounding on the backs of huddled Friday night crowds hopping over curbs to waiting cabs, winshield wipers pumping, all life moving. Chicago!

"Well, we're hardly strangers now," Tom said. "We hung out on that damn train for like three days straight, y'know."

"But you don't know *everything*," she grinned secretly.

"Oh?" Tom scrunched his forehead. "Like what?"

"You guys wanna know why I'm *really* going to Milwaukee?" she asked, eyebrow cocked. We all nodded.

"I'm a drug trafficker. I'm running weed up from Mexico to Milwaukee—I have two bundles in my baggage now that weigh 22 pounds each."

"Jesus, I *thought* something was up," Tom wagged his finger at her. "You seemed like you wanted to tell us."

"Well, not on the *train*."

We talked briefly about the in's and out's of her operation, the risks, the payoffs—it was fascinating. I'd had relations with runners in the past, and never had they been so candid about the business angles as she had been. I wondered why she was telling us all this, why she was breaking the secrecy that runners abide by.

"Well, I'm a gigolo," Tom blurted.

"What!?" we all cried at once.

"It's true!" Luigi pointed suddenly. He sat up on the bed and leaned forward. "He just slept with some 55-year-old woman for $100 right before we got on the train."

"We're not just going to Cleveland to visit family either," Tom said, the rush of Truth coming out like a dam bursting. "My brother's all hooked on heroin and my parents asked me to come home to help him kick it. I asked Luigi to come too. That's why we're here."

"Why not?" Luigi shrugged. "We didn't have anything else to do? We just got wasted one night and booked a train ticket, because it was like $40 cheaper than a plane."

"What about you?" I nodded to Luigi. He was finishing off the last of the J.

"What do you mean?" he coughed.

"Are you like some kind of Russian spy or something? What's your story?"

"Heh, no, I'm just a fisherman like I said on the train."

When they asked me what *my* real deal was, I just said that I was traveling around the country for a month, writing about what I see.

"So you're a writer, eh?" Emily asked, suddenly interested. "You gonna write about us?"

"I dunno, we'll see how tonight goes."

There we were: a writer, a fisherman, a drug-runner, and a gigolo. Four strangers running wild in the mad streets of Chicago on Amtrak's dollar—all of our strange separate journeys converging into one. Banded together. For just a moment. The *satori* of aimless lonely restless travelers and seekers in this New America, same as the old one.

We caught a taxi outside the hotel lobby and told the cabbie—a sweet old Nigerian man—to take us to a dueling piano bar called "Howl at the Moon" the hotel clerk recommended. I wanted to see live music—after all, we *were* in the Mecca of alley blues and street chords. It was out there somewhere, blowing in the night.

I asked the Nigerian if he'd been to the place before. He shook his head dully.

"Well, where's a good place to go see some music?" I asked.

"You gotta go to da 'Bodyguard'," he said, concentrating on the stormy traffic.

"What's that?"

"Blues club."

We pulled up in front of "Howl at the Moon" and frowned at a bunch of foo-foo people stamping their feet in line outside. They all looked like weekend-drunk bankers and lawyers and tourists. A surly bouncer stood at the door and determined who was hip enough to enter.

"I don't wanna wait in some goddamn line!" I yelled to the Nigerian. "Take us to a *real* place! You guys wanna go to that 'Bodyguard' place?"

They all seemed a bit nervous for some reason, but nevertheless let me direct the show, so we slid off in the helter-skelter snowstorm traffic, cabs and buses sliding all over the road just barely missing each other. We couldn't see any-thing—just a white torrent flustering across the buildings.

"Bodyguard" looked beat and fantastic—nondescript exterior with a blue neon sign that read "Live Music" with the first "I" flickering and burning out. We threw money at the Nigerian and piled out of the cab.

The man at the door asked for ID's and tickets. He was an enormous black man the size of a Clydesdale.

"Tickets?" I screamed. "The hell we need *tickets* for?"

"Buddy Guy," he said. "$25, standing room only."

Tom reached back for his wallet immediately, "Damn, I'll pay twenty-five bucks to see Buddy Guy!"

We rushed in the door, ordered shots of Wild Turkey at the bar with beer backs, and flowed into the crowd. There he was, Buddy Guy, the unsung blues legend himself. He played on a small beat stage wearing old blue overalls and a red pinstripe shirt, screaming into the microphone, jumping up on the balls of his feet, cocking his head.

"I can't believe we just walked into a Buddy Guy show!" I yelled to them.

Rumor had it that he began his set in the men's bath-room at the end of a long guitar cord and made his way through the crowd to the stage, playing the whole time.

There were a couple hundred people crammed in the small club, watching this man, his bald head pouring sweat and straining under the soul-drenched blues of the Chicago streets, originating in the bayou clubs of Louisiana. He bent the strings of that old black and white polka dot guitar, tak-ing his hands off and clutching them in the air to sing the high notes, playing behind his head, with his teeth, with his feet, throwing it into the air and catching it without miss-ing a note. He's a performer by nature. The be-hatted bass player thumbed the strings with a frown, the drummer beat tubs with anger and force, but a dedicated force unleased in small, rhythmic doses. The back up guitarist bobbed his head and tried to keep up with the 70-year-old cavorting all over center stage. It was loud and hot and wonderful.

He *owned* the crowd. They jumped and waved their arms in the air, sweat splashing all around and drinks shattering across the floor. Women danced like rag dolls, men lit cigarettes and sang along while he crashed through one song after another in his flamboyant style—the same that influenced the greats like Jimi Hendrix, the Stones, Clapton. I clinked glasses with my new buddies and we yelled to each other and slapped backs over the raw sound radiating out from the small man with that big grin. It was a mad night.

Then he stepped right off the stage, and ambled through the crowd, two bodyguards with him shining flashlights on his head. One cleared a path and the other held a microphone to Buddy's mouth. He kept jamming away at that old guitar; wandering through the crowd playing for squealing, clapping, gyrating older women; and eventually right out the front door. The music still played and his voice still carried through the speakers, but there was no sign of him. People looked around with mouths agape.

"Where the hell did he *go?*" Tom yelled with comic expression. Shit, I didn't know, I shrugged and ran over to a side door looking out on the street and saw one of the most thrilling sights of my life. Never saw anything like it before.

There he was, standing out on the sidewalk of Chicago singing into that microphone in the middle of a blizzard, spotlighted by a single flourescent streetlamp—cabs splashing by and passersby stopping and staring with confused looks and golly smiles. I watched him through the door and clutched my face in awe, dripping in sweat, caught between the blizzard and the glass. This is what the night is all about, this is what I'm seeking. He even reached into his pocket and dropped a handful of change into a bum's tin mug. Hoo!

Buddy finished jamming on the sidewalk and the body-guards cleared a path back into the club right through that side door. When he passed me, he stopped for a second, played a riff and looked me right in the eye and brought the chorus back together, and crooned, "Heeeyaaaoooo! Riiiiide Sall-lly Ride!" with the crowd shrieking along the words and the back-up band coming together in a crescendo of melody and I almost burst. All I could do was jump up and down and clap my hands—he was the greatest.

He made his way through the crowd to a bar along the back wall and ordered a drink, downed it quickly, and threw a handful of money at the bartender—all without missing a note on his guitar.

How could such a man go unrecognized for the majority of his life? He'd inspired the greats, but Buddy Guy didn't enjoy the fame and fortune the others did. He lived most of his life outside the limelight while those who had stolen licks from him and mimicked his stage antics went on to make millions. Like so many visionaries and pathfinders, Guy was overlooked, while his followers received all the recognition.

And when he got back on stage and waited for the applause to die down, he just grinned into the sharp glow of a spotlight with smoke thick in the air and cocked his head into the microphone and said, with angelic breath, "If you don't think you have the blues, jes' keep livin'," and the house erupted again.

He finished his set to a thunderous ovation and simply walked off the stage, retiring to a section of seats cordoned off to sign autographs and sip his drink quietly, accepting handshakes and praise with a humble, sweet bow of his head. The house lights came on and we all looked around at each other's sweaty faces.

"C'mon, let's go get some more drinks!" I shouted.

We filed out into the storm, stopping briefly to shake hands with the Man. I bowed my head to him on my turn.

He nodded his head and smiled that big modest grin.

Outside, the snow was wet and beautiful and just perfect for packing—so I threw a snowball at Tom and ran ahead shrieking, high on some drug called the Night. They all yelled and returned fire, hitting me several times, once right in the back of the head. I turned around and stuttered a bit ("The great Stutter Step!" Tom yelled later) and deliberately fell ass-down in a big puddle of snow and water—I didn't care about anything at that point.

I ran all over the street, chasing after cabs and hooting into the alleyways. Luigi hopped over puddles, wearing the sopping-wet wool slippers he'd worn on the train because their baggage was held in Chicago. He didn't have any other shoes. I saw a cab plodding across the street and threw a snowball at it, yelling for him to stop, which he did. We piled in and told him to take us to a bar—any bar.

"What's yer name?" I yelled to the cabbie.

"Muhammad Ali," he replied, to which I said, "Oh *man*, you've always been one of my heroes," or something stupid like that.

He smiled and dropped us off at a place called "Hugo's Frog Bar" and it turned out to be a quiet place with a few people sitting around drinking martinis and gin and eating late-night fish dinners—mostly well-dressed blacks and middle-aged banker-types. We just yelled and screamed to each other and spilled our water glasses and ordered cheeseburgers and I ordered two rum and cokes at once.

"You guys know what? We're 'that table' right now," I said, and they all got my meaning. The whole restaurant was aware of us. We couldn't get over what a fantastic night it had turned into—how random and serendipitous it all was. In fact, I was thinking that very exact thought when I walked back to the bathroom and heard the 10,000 Maniacs song called "Hey Jack Kerouac," and smiled while I peed all over the urinal cake. I knew that everything was going to be all right, as it always had been and always will be. I knew that I felt that mystical sensation of being out in the world, unafraid.

"You guys got an early start tonight," our waitress observed with a grin. She carried our cheeseburgers on a platter in her hands.

"Hooey, not near early *enough!*" I yelled. "Why don't you clock out and join us, huh?"

She blushed and rested her hand on my shoulder.

"Oh, I can't... I, I have a boyfriend," she said, but hell, I could tell she wanted to come along. Emily watched me with her brown, beautiful eyes while nibbling into her cheeseburger.

We finished our drinks and burgers and cabbed back to the hotel just before closing time, tipped the guy five bucks even though we only went a couple blocks, and scrambled back up to Tom and Luigi's room to smoke another J.

Tom laid on the bed and read an article I wrote a few months ago that blasted our stupid, apathetic generation. It was called "Curse of the Non-Generation." I'd brought along a handful of clips from my past articles in the *Reader*, back when I wrote regularly.

He read slowly and stumbled over words, put the wrong emphasis in all the wrong places, but I was too righteously high to correct him except when he blatantly fucked up. They all listened eagerly and nodded their heads at good lines.

"So, you're really a writer, huh?" Tom said, looking up at me with a newfound respect.

"Well, I guess," I shrugged. "I've never been published anywhere except that newspaper, but I've been rejected by the best publications around."

"Are you really gonna write about us?" Emily asked.

"Of course," I said. "I write about everything."

Somewhere around four a.m., I was standing in the middle of the room telling them about a time I ran into a swarm of killer bees in Arizona. It was a ridiculous story.

"And I was just driving along on the interstate with the window rolled down, thinking, 'god, what a nice day,' when this huge black cloud of insects suddenly appeared and I smashed into them going about eighty."

"No *way*," Emily exclaimed.

"*Yes* way!" I screamed. "There were thousands of 'em, all smashed and caked on the windshield! I couldn't see shit, they were so thick. I just kept plowing into them."

"Did any of 'em fly inside your window?" Tom asked.

"I'm getting there," I waved my arms around and emphasized every point, J in mouth. "So I pulled over to catch my breath after I passed through the swarm and sure enough, there was one of the little bastards, climbing up my seat and getting ready to sting me right in the back of the head! Jesus Christ, I grabbed everything I could and smashed the hell outta that sumbitch—I *hate* bees! I got stung like sixty times when I was a little kid, throwing rocks at a beehive."

"Well, serves you right," Emily flirted with her eyes. "They were probably ancestors, coming back to settle the score."

"So what happened next?" Tom beat the bedcovers.

"Well, after I'd killed that fucker, I remembered that I saw this ad on a billboard a few miles back... place called 'I'll Kill It Pest Control' or some shit, so I found the number and called it and tried to convince this dipshit that a swarm was heading for Phoenix. An' he was all, 'Wail shee-it, whattaya expect *me* to do about it?' and I was all, 'Fuck man, *you're* the expert!' He just hung up on me, so I sat in the rest area and wrote up this mock news alert for my newspaper back home, warning of a killer bee attack that's gonna spread through Phoenix, Las Vegas, and eventually to north Idaho. And the best part was, my friend—the publisher—was so damn desperate for something to fill the paper that week that he actually *ran* it. It was fuckin' hilarious!"

"Do you have a copy of it we can read?" Tom asked.

"Funny you should ask," I smiled, pulling the folded article out of my back pocket. I was just beginning to read the first paragraph when we heard a knock on the door.

I froze, turned about ten directions all at once, jumped in the air and darted my eyes about the room for a place to hide the joint burning in my hand. I ended up crushing the roach in an ashtray and putting it in the top drawer of the nightstand on the Bible. Right.

It was the night manager of the hotel, telling us to quiet down.

"We've had several noise complaints," she told us.

"OK, no problem," Tom slammed the door in her face.

He then turned and smiled at me.

"What the hell was that triple take all about, Max? A little paranoid?" he laughed. I took the ashtray out of the drawer and sparked up the J again. I read my article and they all laughed and cheered. We kept shushing each other like kids at camp, but it was no use. Soon we were yelling and banging around the room with empty beer bottles clanking on the floor and the manager appeared a second time.

"If I have to come back up here again, you're all out," she warned us sternly.

"Okay okay, sorry," Tom slammed the door.

"I guess it's getting pretty late, huh?" Emily said. She gave me a strange look.

"We're definitely renting this car tomorrow, right?" Tom asked me.

"Yeah—I think we should try to get an early start, too."

"What time?"

"Oh, I think we should try to leave by eight," I said,

looking at my wrist with no watch, "Which is in… oh, 'bout three hours."

"I'm horrible at waking up," Luigi yawned.

"Don't worry dude, I'll call the room and wake you fuckers up… I won't sleep in. We got a long haul tomorrow."

"Ohhh, I wish I was going with you guys," Emily cooed. "This has been one of the best nights I've had in a long, long time."

We all agreed and dispersed to sleep—not on a smelly, stuffy old train car, but in our own free, king-size beds in an expensive hotel in downtown Chicago.

I was just about to drift off when there came a soft knock on the door.

It was Emily. We looked at each other for a moment, her in the hallway and me in my boxers. I opened wider and she slipped inside.

"This is our little secret," she whispered in my ear.

"No one here but us," I whispered back.

I woke up to a ringing phone at 8:30. It was Tom.

"Mornin' Max," he said sleepily. "Thought you never slept in."

"Ooog," I sat up in bed, noticing Emily was gone. "I just decided our new departure time is 9:30."

We met in the lobby awhile later and cabbed back over to Union Station. Emily passed me a little note and smiled, then we all hugged goodbye and watched her board the Greyhound to Milwaukee with her 44 pounds of weed.

On the way to the rental cars, I pulled out the note.

It had a phone number next to the words, in childish scrawl: *If you're ever in Milwaukee again.*

"What's that?" Tom leaned over.

"Nothing," I smiled, tucking it back in my pocket with

hazy memories of her beautiful brown body in my arms.

We stormed up to the counter and I yelled to the clerk, "Gimmie your fastest car with the loudest radio."

He ended up getting us a sputtering Ford Taurus with a non-working radio.

ART ISNT ART WHEN you use it to get laid. it's just another tool on the path of mediocrity. Do i really want to have sex with her again? i've already conquered that... why do i keep going back to tread over the same ground? when will i be free of this desire? this never-ending need to live the life they think i should lead? when will i stop being a pawn to my own desires?

TEN

THE SUN WAS SHINING and the snow that fell just hours before had all but melted on the busy downtown streets of Chicago. I blasted the rental through the red lights and wound my way to Interstate-90, which would take us all the way to Cleveland.

"This fucking radio doesn't work!" Luigi yelled, banging it with his fist until something snapped inside the dashboard. "Goddammit, we gotta go all this way with no radio? Hell! You know where you're going?"

"*Course!*" I said. I didn't have a fucking clue, "My dad grew up here."

"Just watch our for killer *bees!*" Tom yelled from the back seat.

I took several wrong turns, ran a red light and cut someone off before finding the on-ramp to the freeway. Tom and Luigi grabbed the "oh shit" handles and held on tight.

The roads were clear all the way out of the industry-laden outskirts of Chicago into Indiana. We stuck to the interstate, stopping at the toll booths and passing weird service stations that were totally self-contained, like rest areas with fuel, fast food restaurants, and car repair places. It felt good to have a steering wheel in my hands again—to be in control of my own velocity and direction. To be in a part of the country I hadn't been in years.

"What should we call this hunk of shit car?" Tom asked, darting his head around to examine the interior. I was digging into my pouch of Drums for a J and swerving all over the road.

"Hmm, I dunno," I said. "This is a Taurus, right? How 'bout… Ferdinand?"

"Yes!" Luigi yelled. "Ferdinand the Taurus! *Vamanos!*"

We passed around the J and the sky turned a deeper shade of blue. Alongside the highway, vast expanses of farmland and cattle ranches drifted by, small rural houses with barns and baseball-cap-wearing farmers driving tractors that left small dust trails in the air. The Red States in winter. The middle of the country, where those who pushed west for glorious opportunities gave up, settled in, raised pigs and corn, and fly flags on their front porches.

We told stories the whole way; drunken tales and escapades of years passed. Most of the talk was about the previous night, though. We laughed at funny moments over and over again, passing around the J until it was gone and lighting up another.

"I don't think I'll ever forget that stutter step when we hit you with the snowball," Tom howled. "God, you were *soaked!*" He pantomimed me getting whacked with a snowball and falling into the puddle.

"Yeah, well, so were Luigi's feet from wearing those damn *slippers* all night, you fool!"

"That Emily was a little hottie, eh?" Luigi rubbed his belly. "Sure wish I could'a been stuck in *her* room last night."

"Yeah," I smiled to myself.

I figured out the time it would take to reach Columbus and realized I would be arriving too late for the beginning of Mitch's surprise party, but I'd show up later when the novelty had worn off and zang him again—two surprises in one night. He had no idea I was anywhere near Ohio.

"Hup, looks like you need to fill up, eh?" Luigi said, leaning over to look at my gas gauge, which was well below a quarter tank.

"Bah, we still got fifty miles left on that tank," I threw my head back. "I should tell you guys, though, I have a tendency to run out of gas. One time, while I was towing a sailboat from San Diego to Idaho, I ran out three times... in one trip. One time was in the middle of Nevada and I had to hitchhike 40 miles to a gas station and back."

"Jesus, man! *Three* times?" Tom laughed. "What the hell for?"

"Well, I dunno—I always want to see how far I can go on one tank. And I figure, if you fill up less, you spend less money on gas."

Luigi looked confused, "But you still spend the same amount, man. You go the same distance."

"I know, but if you stretch an extra, say, thirty miles out of each tank, by the time you die, you'll have saved like ten tanks of gas... it makes sense, trust me."

They just sat there blinking at me for a moment, and Luigi said finally, "I get the feeling you're not the safest person to travel with."

"I should tell you about my invention," I went on. "'Gas In a Pouch' I call it. It's this Capri-Sun looking pouch that holds a gallon of gas, and it's got rubber an' metal an' shit to give it strength, and it fits somewhere in the spare tire compartment, see, so any time you run out of gas, you always have an emergency little bit to get to the next station."

"Well, why wouldn't you just carry gas cans instead?" Tom asked.

"Fuck man, do *you* want to carry around cans of stinky fucking gas in your car? Hell no, nobody wants them all rolling around and spilling and shit. This would be a special attachment to every spare tire, and whenever you needed to use it, you'd just pull out a little valve and squeeze the gas in the tank. It's genius! I'd market it to the car manufacturers and they'd make them standard in every new car. And if you use one, you can buy another at Schuck's or Checker or wherever."

"You've spent a lot of time thinking about this," Luigi blinked.

"Well shit man, why not?" I shrugged.

I passed the next three stations, just to give them something to worry about, before finally stopping after the gas light started blinking. We were about a half-hour west of Cleveland.

Tom and Luigi ran inside to buy beef jerky and cigarettes and I sat on the hood smoking to the horizon, enjoying the moment.

It was a good trip. Once we hit the open road, I felt everything melt away and entered the state of motion that defines my life. Tom and Luigi turned out to be exactly the same. We were all nomads, really—our whole generation, or at least the Others of the Non-Generation. Seekers in mid-twenties stages of life, always picking up and moving down the road to find one thing and escape another—finding our own answers instead of just accepting them from the denizens of the mainstream.

"I don't know if I'll ever find a place to settle down," Luigi said, now in the backseat. "I been crashing around the country for so long, I don't know anything else. This job in Alaska is pretty good—I work three months and leave with a big fat paycheck—but I know I'll get sick of it soon and have to move on."

"Yeah, but don't you *see?*" I banged the steering wheel. "That's the best way to *be*. Do you really want to buy a house and raise an ugly family, change poopy diapers, drive to soccer practice, watch the evening news every night with disgust and eventual apathy, and sleep with your fat wife and hear her fart and moan in bed? Christ, who the hell wants *that?*"

"Well, I wouldn't mind getting married soon," Tom said. "In just a few years, I'll be 30, then I'll be 40, then I'll be eating Jell-O through a rubber spoon and shittin' my pants on purpose, just so a little blond nurse can wipe it up."

"Why don't you just marry one of your old women?" I cracked. "I don't see anything wrong with havin' a sugar momma—especially if they're old and ready to die soon."

"You'll think differently when you see 'em naked," he shuddered.

We bypassed Cleveland on I-80 and headed south on back roads towards Tom's house in Akron. It was a modest home in a housing development where each place looked exactly the same except for the color of the siding. Tom pointed to a pastel yellow one and told me to pull in there. I helped unload their shit out of the trunk and we stopped suddenly, realizing the end was upon us.

"Well boys, it's been an interesting trip," I offered my hand to them.

"Thanks for driving the whole way, man," Tom said.

"Hell, I don't mind driving at all. Keep slayin' those fish Luigi, and Tom, well… you keep slayin' those old women. Maybe one'll keel over soon and leave you the farm."

"And *you*," Tom wagged his finger at me. "You, you crazy bastard, you keep doing whatever the hell you're doing… seems to be working just fine."

They still owed me $60 for their share of the rental car, but I didn't ask for it. I didn't really care about $60—the trip was worth it.

We exchanged phone numbers and email addresses for the future, in case we should ever meet again, and I tooted

the horn at them while pulling out into the confusing housing complex cul de sacs. They faded in the rear view as I sped
away, pointing Ferdinand south by southwest on Highway 71
all the way into Columbus with the Ohio sun setting behind
stoic clouds lined with salmon, ochre, pink, and heaven.

Eleven

It was dark when I reached Columbus. Mitch's surprise party was happening at a place called the City Club, which was described to me as "a cabin by the lake with a really freaky-looking driveway that looks like it's out of 'Children of the Corn' or something," by Joanna, Mitch's fiancé.

We'd been communicating secretly over the past few days to touch base on when I'd be in town. Sure enough, I found the driveway and heard the tires munching gravel as it wound downhill toward a lake somewhere out in the night.

The City Club turned out to be a small wooden cabin that wealthy people rented out for special occasions. It had total privacy and was shaded by tall trees in all directions but one, which bordered the small lake—a perfect place for a party. It was built very well. I walked up to the crowd of well-dressed people and saw Mitch throwing horseshoes down by the bonfire—he was wearing his old beanie and a sweatshirt, yelling at someone.

I found Joanna and she rallied Mitch's parents so that we could surprise him, then we all walked down to the fire like an intervention group. I walked right up to him with a big goofy smile on my face. He scrunched his forehead and cocked his head forward, trying to recognize me… realized it was me and popped his eyes out, dropped his jaw and yelled, "What the fuck are *you* doing here? Holy shit!" and we hugged and laughed and slapped hands and everyone got a tingle of magic and snapped pictures—the shrouded traveler arrives. Everyone grouped around and wondered who I was, where I came from, and why I looked so scroungy.

His hair was cut short and it looked strange—Mitch always had long, straight hair that he tucked behind his ears with index finger and thumb. When he laughed, his whole body laughed—arms flailing everywhere, legs kicking, head wagging, and it was a laugh that infected those who heard it. When Mitch drank, his big lips constantly formed comic expressions under rosy cheeks and his voice boomed. His eyes saw the joy we're all trying to get out of life.

Franklin was also there—Mitch's cousin (a fledgling actor now living in New York) who was on the sailing trip to the BVI's also. Although he was only 26, his hair had almost completely fallen out except for a thin wisp on top. He wore a clean pink polo shirt and jeans, looking fit and tidy.

"I see you still have some hair left, Frank," I rubbed his bald head.

He punched me in the shoulder, "Yeah, there's a few of 'em still up there, how are you man? Long time."

"I can't believe you're *here*, man," Mitch said drunkenly, leading me around with his arm around my neck, introducing me to friends I'd never remember the next day. "I can always count on you for turning up in strange places."

"Well, that's what I do," I beamed.

We spent the rest of the night drinking Mount Gay rum and beer around the bonfire—throwing frisbees around in the grass, playing horseshoes, strumming on guitars and grazing on the snacks laid out inside the cabin.

Mitch's parents tottered around refilling drinks and asking how relatives were, how school was going, how work was… they were wonderful parents who cared about their kids and the friends that surrounded them. I always wanted a family like that.

Tall, blond Joanna with her muscular legs from running marathons and hiking up mountains, threw her arms around me and thanked me for surprising Mitch. "We pulled it off, Max!"

They met in college some years ago, right around the time I dropped out.

"Hey! Get yer hands off'a my woman!" Mitch yelled over the fire, then lumbered over and threw his arms around both of us, swerving and all of us tumbling over in a laughing heap—the big goofy bastard.

"Did you pass through Denver on the way here?" he asked later.

"Yeah, I stayed with Liz for a few days," I said, throwing another piece of wood on the fire. "I think I pissed her off, though."

"Well, that's not hard to do," he chugged his drink and threw out the ice. "What'd you do? Sleep with her room-mate again? Fuck man… F-Faaaack!"

"Nah, I got all wasted and made fun of her stupid yuppie friends at the Nuggets game."

"That sounds about right," he smiled, then waved his arms to the rest of the party, "You can make fun of my yuppie friends if you like, they don't give a shit."

The hour grew late. People began to leave. We decided to head over to Mitch and Joanna's house they just purchased in Columbus for late-night beer and hot tub revelry.

Right before we all rallied to go, Mitch lurched over to his bright red jacked-up Jeep covered in silly string and started driving around in circles—laughing and waving his arms in the air, hanging his tongue out the window and spitting gravel everywhere. It was his birthday, his night to be stupid. Everyone stood around in a smiling circle, pointing at him and shaking their heads with hands over their eyes. Franklin chased after him and finally wrestled him out of the driver's seat.

"You bastard," he panted, bent over with hands on knees. "I don't care if it's your birthday or not, I'll beat you silly, fucker!"

Franklin climbed in the driver's seat and I followed them into Columbus in my rental, drunk myself.

Halfway back, Franklin pulled off the road in a residential neighborhood and put on his hazard lights. I pulled up next to him and rolled down my passenger-side window.

"What's up?" I yelled. I heard sounds of puking coming from the other side of the Jeep.

"Oh nothing—just have to make a little pit stop," Franklin motioned his head toward Mitch and grinned. "Seems ol' Mitch had one too many."

I pulled into a driveway nearby, shut my lights off and smoked the last of my Drum pouch joints. The kitchen light came on in the house I was parked in front of and I saw a real, honest-to-god Midwestern housewife in curlers peering suspiciously out the window. Looked like she even had a rolling pin in hand.

We had to drag Mitch from the car and up the stairs to his bed. I was disappointed, because I wanted to sit up all night and talk shit with him just like the old days. But instead, I just drank beer, played card games with Joanna and the other great friends sitting in the living room and went to sleep face down on the floor some hours later.

The next morning, Joanna shook me awake with a goofy grin, "Come upstairs for a second, you have to see this."

We tip-toed up the stairs and into their bedroom. Mitch was face-down on the bed, sagging and broken on one side. It was the bed that he always talked about—some wooden monstrosity of a bed that he built himself and lugged to college and back. It was one of his most prized possessions.

"He got up in the middle of the night and started jumping around on the bed," Joanna whispered in my ear. "He broke the whole damn thing!"

We shared a nice laugh at his expense and enjoyed a lazy day. I cut my hangover with a morning beer and a couple movies on T.V., until Mitch finally stumbled down the stairs scratching his head, confused, and looking like a truck had just hit him.

"Uhhh, do you know who broke my bed?" he asked groggily.

I slapped my knee and laughed at him, "*You* did, you crazy bastard! Your sacred bed! Ha!"

He snorted his nose and put on his glasses, collapsing on the couch next to me with the remote in his hands, "Man, I feel like shit."

"Well, you gotta follow me to the airport so I can drop this rental car off," I slapped him on the chest. "C'mon, let's go get this over with."

The attendant at the rental car counter tried charging me an extra day because I returned it an hour late, but I threw such a fit that he gave in and promised to reverse the charges (which he never did, in fact).

We drove back to the house and lazed on the couch for the rest of the day, too hungover to do anything but watch movies and smoke weed. Joanna returned from working at the battered women's shelter and we ordered a pizza and passed out early.

"Sorry we didn't do anything fun today, man," he said at the end of the night. "Kinda boring just laying around the house, eh?"

I shook my head, "Nah, don't worry about it… I needed a day like this. I been moving too fast lately."

The next morning, a Monday, Mitch and Joanna both left for work early and I slept in late, then put on a scarf and jacket to wander around in the sunshine. They lived in a beautiful neighborhood of old Victorian houses and smiling mailmen.

Around noon, Mitch called and asked if I wanted to meet him for lunch.

"My dad told me to take an extra long lunch because you're in town," he explained. "So I think we should go down to this sweet little sandwich place near campus."

He pulled up to the house a few minutes later and tooted the horn. I ran out and hopped in, startled to see him wearing a suit and tie.

"Dude, what the hell are you *wearing*, man?" I cackled.

"Nyeh, I know," he grumbled. "I hate wearing this shit, but it comes with the job."

"How's that all going?"

Mitch had just recently moved from his post-college hippie lifestyle in Colorado to take a marketing job at his father's company in Columbus.

"You miss Colorado?" I asked.

"I do, I really do," he said. "But I'm making good money and Joanna and I are pretty happy with this house and all. It's just a trip, y'know, *dealing* with all this—mortgage and all that shit, and plus we're starting to plan the wedding."

"You're not getting nervous are you?"

"Nah, it's just a lot of shit to deal with," he sighed.

"Well, you've done well for yourself, Mitch," I said. "You can always go back and visit Colorado, y'know?"

"Two weeks a year," he shrugged. "That's all the vacation time I get, not including the honeymoon next winter. I think we're gonna try to put together another sailing trip this summer, though—whaddaya think about Belize?"

We ordered at the sandwich place and ate them outside on the curb. Fine little college girls cut down the street smelling of papayas and herbal skin treatments. They looked just like the girls I saw in Fort Collins.

"Belize, eh?" I asked.

"Yeah dude, we just gotta be careful about the weather, y'know? Can't go too late in the summer because of the hurricanes."

"Who's going this year?"

"Let's see," he counted his fingers. "Me and Joanna, *you*, Ani, Franklin… I've told a couple friends from here but they're flakey on stuff like this, and Derrick from Fort Collins said he wanted to go. I bet we could get a crew of ten on the boat."

"Well, the more the better," I said, munching on a pickle. "Helps make it cheaper."

"Hey, did you get a chance to see Ani in Colorado?" he asked suddenly.

I flushed, "Uh, *no* actually, I didn't."

"Hmph, that's too bad."

Although Mitch is one of my best friends in the world, I never did tell him the way I felt about his sister—it was one of those things I thought would be better left unsaid.

"You'll be able to come right?" he chomped into a thick steak sandwich.

"What?"

"On the *Belize* trip. You're gonna try to make it, right?"

"Oh, yeah… I *hope* so… I don't really know what's going on this summer, but I don't have any plans against it."

"Good, because you and I are the only ones who know how to sail the boat. And Ani."

"God, that was a helluva trip, huh?" I asked.

"Dude, you know what I think about all the time?" he asked suddenly. "That crazy fucking road trip when you drove me from L.A. to Colorado after I got back from Australia."

The memory hit me like a warm flash, "Oh man, that's *right*, god, what a great trip that was!"

"Except when I had to hang around your house in Hollywood that week with your coke-head roommates."

"Ha! Because I was shooting that McDonald's commercial in the desert... *man*, I forgot all *about* that! That must've been horrible hanging around with those bastards."

"Dude, your one roommate, the short one... *Bernie*, he was the *weirdest* motherfucker. I caught him in the bathroom one time cutting his pubic hair with a Flowbee!"

"You never told me that!" I hooted. "What a strange dude—I still owe him two grand for back rent that I'll never pay."

"He kept asking if I wanted to go 'pick up chicks' with him, you know the way he talked, all whiny and nasal, '*hey man, you wanna go try to pick up some chicks?*'"

"Man, and we took off that night when you'd been working like thirty hours straight," he continued, his eyes smiling. "You drove all the way to the fucking Grand Canyon before we passed out—remember waking up right at the *rim?* Wondering where the hell we *were?*"

"And that drive through Monument Valley at sunset?" I shouted.

"And camping out by that huge crater in Canyonlands that night?"

We were now cutting down the street shouting back and forth to each other like old times, making our way back to the car.

"And that flat tire we got right next to that weird hitchhiker who kept trying to help us change it for a ride to Denver?"

"Man," he shook his head wistfully.

"We had some good times," I said.

"It's so strange now, not having time to do that kinda stuff," he frowned. "Well, at least I don't have time to do it anymore... you still seem to make it happen."

"Well, it sucks sometimes doing it all alone, y'know?" I

said. "I don't mind it most of the time, but it sure was nice to have a road buddy."

Mitch sighed and climbed back into his Jeep, battling with the inevitable tide of growing past the road wandering years of youth and becoming an adult, getting married, raising a family, buying houses, and wearing suits to work. Just like Liz, he was looking back while constantly moving forward. Always the forward motion.

"I wonder sometimes if I made the right decision taking this job back here," he said. "I mean, I'm *happy* and everything, but I never seem to have time to do the shit I used to enjoy, like taking road trips and going to concerts and all that. You remember how many times we would just pack our shit and cruise up to Mishawaka for the bluegrass shows up there? And camping on the river?"

"Well, I guess it's all part of getting older, man," I said. Fuck, what a stupid thing to say.

"Bah!" he barked. "Sometimes I just wanna be back in college, getting drunk and playing frisbee golf again."

He dropped me off at the house and drove away, back to work, back to the wheel, back to his adult life.

I stayed one more day and told them I'd be taking a Greyhound to Cleveland that night.

"Why you gotta leave so *soon?*" Mitch growled. "If you stay this weekend, we can cruise up to the lake and then there's a good bluegrass show in Columbus on Saturday— it'll be just like old times."

"I gotta get moving on, man," I said. "I want to try to make it into New York by the weekend."

"What's the hurry? New York'll be there," he said.

"Well, I don't know really," I scratched my head. "I just feel like I gotta keep moving."

We grilled up a great dinner of hamburgers and sat around on the back porch as the sun went down, smoking bowls and looking at the ever-fleeting time.

"I wish I didn't have to work so much while you were in town," Joanna said. "I feel like I barely got to see you."

"It's all right… after that crazy night in Chicago, it was kinda nice to sit back and chill for a couple days."

"Well, don't take too long coming back, all right?" she said.

She then wrapped up some bread and cheese in tin foil for me to eat on the train and all of a sudden it was time to go. We lugged my gear out to the Jeep and took off toward the station.

"Is this it?" Joanna asked later. She pointed to a dimly-lit building with a crowd of travelers milling around stamping their feet and blowing into their hands.

The station was squat and had grime on the corners of every edge. A few buses grumbled noisily around the back and grim-face attendants took tickets for beat passengers. Where is everyone going with their long faces?

The fare to Cleveland was $21 and it left in twenty minutes, so we just sat off to the side with my big pack and said our goodbyes.

"Well shit man, it was good to see you again," Mitch said. "It's never long enough, eh?"

"I know, man," nodding my head guiltily. "But you know I'll be back. Sometime... someday."

"I hope so fucker, you're gonna be here for the wedding right? You're one of my groomsmen."

"Yeah, *course* I'll be here," I said. We hugged and Joanna came back from the restroom.

"Here," she handed me a small Buddha the size of a pinky finger. "I know you won't travel safe, because that's just not your way, but it can't hurt to have a good luck charm, right?"

What a great girl, that Joanna. I'm so happy my old buddy Mitch found her and that they're getting married and living in a great home with good jobs and probably with some kids on the way soon. They're the type of people you know belong together. I wondered what it was like being in love with someone you *knew* you were going to spend the rest of your life with... feeling that you found something incredible and permanent... but the thought vanished and I waved goodbye to them passing through the back door and onto the road again.

The bus grumbled through the outskirts of Columbus into the darkness of Ohio, two hours to Cleveland, where I'd meet up with the train and continue east through Pennsylvania up and over the rolling Alleghenies, Pittsburgh at the small hours of the morning, Philly in the early afternoon tomorrow and pulling into the big godfather of them all—New York City—right at mad mad rush hour. Catch the underground PATH to Hoboken and meet up with Seda for some sweet sweet sex at the end of the coast. Ah, how good it will be to lie next to a warm hot girl and smell her smells, feel her heartbeat, taste the salt of her skin and look at her fluttering eyelids while she sleeps. Aaah. I love women. Every one of them. They all hold some secret inside that they'll never show you, but us men go hunting after it none-theless.

I arrived in the midst of a frozen Cleveland night with a winter chill blowing in from Lake Erie. Two hour bus ride into the glum city streets—negroes blowing into their hands outside the Greyhound station in great clouds of mist into the frosty air, almost like I could pick out and read the very depths of their beings just by the talking clouds they emitted.

I hoisted the old rucksack on my back and meandered over to the information counter.

"Excuse me, how far is the train station?" I asked a lethargic station attendant. She was thumbing through a Danielle Steele novel.

"'Bout five mile," she said, not looking up.

"Five miles? The bus driver said it was only a few blocks."

"Bus driver was wrong," she yawned. I could've been stark naked with spaghetti noodles draped over my head and she'd have never noticed.

So I hailed a cab outside the Amtrak station, which was deserted at this quiet hour of the morning, except for a spry old man behind the counter with fantastic bushy white eye-brows and a beady, intelligent cast in his grey eyes.

"Can I get a ticket to New York?" I asked him.

"I don't see why not," he grinned and turned to his com-puter screen. "Which way you wanna go, young man? The Capitol Limited stops in D.C. for two hours and the Lake-shore stops in Pittsburgh for an hour and a half. They both get into New York about the same time."

"Hmm, hot 'bout D.C.?"

"A fine choice, son," he nodded. "I'd rather spend two hours in D.C. than Pittsburgh. You can stop in and have lunch with President Bush—that prick."

"Yeah, that'd be a hoot," I chuckled.

He printed out my ticket and told me the train wouldn't be in for another three hours. I hauled my gear over to a corner seat and read the last twenty pages of *The Dharma Bums* in the silent station.

These graveyard train stations—seems that every train leaves either in the middle of the night or first thing in the morning. All these lonely hours spent watching the brown, grainy carpets, the faux brick walkways, the stained columns and hard fluorescent lights. Men's room here, women's room there—vending machines full of plastic wrapped confection, national route maps posted on the walls behind scratched panes of Plexiglass, wilting fake ferns dusty with the years of travelers brushing past—and that old standard sign above the door leading out to the tracks: "To Trains." I stare at this sign, stare at the words, the big, simple white letters. I think about what it means. I stare outside at the lit-up skyscraper with a red key atop its highest floor. I think about what that means. I stare at the vertically draped American flag with wrinkles near the bottom from passersby. I stare at the lockers painted red and blue and the white world beneath them. Easy listening music on the quiet house speakers—songs from a decade passed. The shadows on the walls, the great electric hum of heaters rushing air through ceiling vents—a buzzing, subconscious din that you hear only when you want to, only when nothing else makes noise to drown it out.

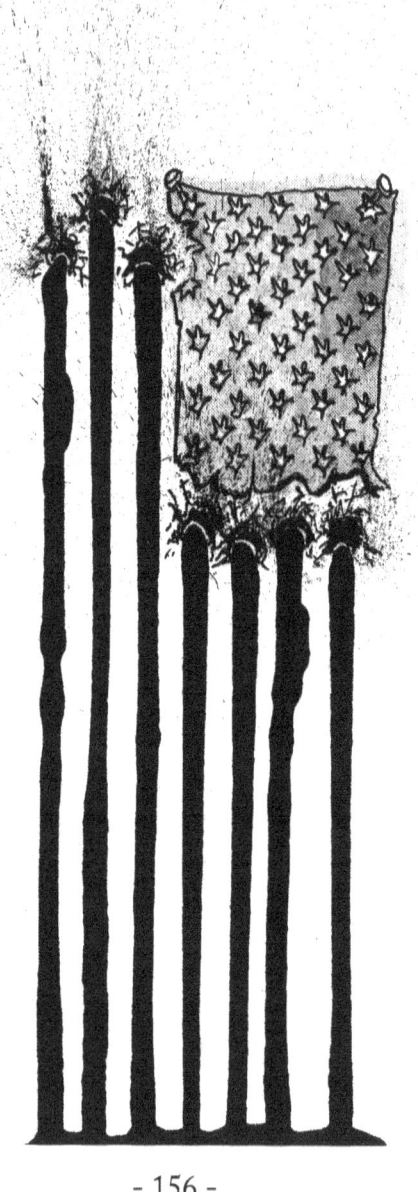

The train clanked to a halt at the platform finally and I nodded goodbye to the old hoary station attendant.

"Be sure to say 'hi' to ol' Bush for me, all right?" he called after me.

The whistle blew and I was off—into the night—back on the tracks. All I could do was curl up and sleep with the lull of motion spinning fabulous dreams of wandering bliss. I felt like I was home again, back in my train seat. The hissing air vents, the lull of buckles and turns in the track. I dreamt I was a giant, twenty-five feet tall, lumbering around Venice Beach in Los Angeles, casting a huge fifty-foot shadow, but nobody seemed to notice I was so large—they just whizzed beneath my feet on rollerblades and beach cruisers, walking tiny dogs in sweaters and eating ice cream cones, stepping around my huge feet. "Hey! Lookit me!" I yelled. "Lookit how *tall* I am!" But no one heard me. The only person who even saw me was one man in a strange orange suit who stopped talking into his cell phone long enough to gaze all the way up at me with a sneer, before continuing on his way, walking right into the ocean and disappearing forever.

I awoke as we wound alongside the Ohio River leading into Pittsburgh—city of rivers and steel. Strange looking tugboats shoved barges into indigo slips lit with yellow twinkling lights, the reflections dancing over turbulent, inky water.

It was all factories and industry with houses wedged somewhere in between.

The match struck at dawn and I peered out my window to the Allegheny Mountains rolling by. Sleepy Pennsylvania towns popped up between long stretches of rural countryside, leading onward into West Virginia at midday, all brown and barren.

I brought out my camp stove and cooked a can of beans. It was a small three-prong burner that screwed onto the top of a butane bottle the size of a softball. When the burner lit, it hissed and spat fire onto the little aluminum cooking pot. I ate the beans and chomped on the bread and cheese Joanna packed for me while an old black man watched curiously from the next seat.

"That sure is a helluva contraption you got there," he said finally, licking his lips.

"Yeah, it's better than eating that crap they have in the dining car."

"Boy, ain't that the truth," he frowned down at his dining car crap on the tray table.

Rolling along on this eastern commuter train bustling with businessmen and women reading the *Wall Street Journal* and wearing suits, typing into laptops and PDA's. Trains are much different in the east than they are in the west—more people, and everyone seems to look important and busy.

A lady behind me blathered on and on to some poor old man while I wrote a poem in my journal, until she suddenly turned to me without skipping a beat and said, "You ain't writing about *me*, are you? Cuz if you are, I want royalties."

We pulled into D.C. with cranes and construction everywhere. I lugged my pack off the train, into the station and got my ticket for the Silver Star heading into New York.

I called my elderly father from the station and told him where I was.

"What the hell are you doing in Washington, D.C.?" he grumbled.

"I'm on my way to New York, Dad. I'm touring the country right now on the train."

"Hmph… seems like a hell of a waste of money to me," he sniffed.

I hung up, sorry that I even told him in the first place. He'd never understand a trip like this. Maybe in the past, when he used to travel around all over the place and quiz me on the state capitals he would've understood. But not anymore. It has no purpose to him, no practicality. Just another one of my nonsense ideas. Like becoming a writer. Like dropping out of college and moving to Los Angeles to work in the film business. I should be joining the army or going back to school, becoming a pharmacist or a doctor or something of worth—whatever profession that he read is on the rise in *Consumer's Report*. My writing was always a bit of a let-down to him—a phase that he hoped I'd grow out of soon.

To my father I'll always be a misunderstood potential that never had the chance to prosper. To him, I am a completely different person than what my friends see, or even strangers too, for that matter. Because they can all accept my reality. If they don't, fuck 'em. But my dad… my dad deserves to feel pride in his boy, right? To feel that maybe he did something right in raising me. To see that I don't grow up as a miscreant dope fiend. He wants me to be part of society. He wants to feel that I'll eventually find my way, that I'll raise my family, that I'll continue the line. That old Nordic And I hope I will someday "find my way," but it'll never be quite what he envisioned. Such different lives we lead, my father and me. He will always just be the figure, the persona, the father who was just a father, nothing more. He was 50 years old when I was born, and divorced my mother before I'd entered high school. I know so little of who he really was… mostly because I never took the time to ask. Was he always just the frugal, Swedish, close-minded, stubborn Midwestern Great Generation molding? What was he passionate about? What did it feel like to shoot another man? What was it like when that bullet ripped apart his guts? I always wanted to know those things, always saw that irregular scar, that ancient scar that he received in Korea decades before I was born, to the left of his belly-button. I always thought it was a second belly-button, in fact. My father, the injured veteran of foreign wars. My father, the patriot. My father, the bigot. My father that never really knew his son, not for lack of trying, but for lack of understanding... no simpatico vibes... hanging out with my father was on par with hanging out with my great-grandparents when I was a little kid; it's never fun, almost like it's "doing time," everything smells funny in the house, the dog pees when it gets excited, the back yard is overgrown and sinking, FOX News is always on the television, in the background, a surrogate stream, the ice cubes taste funny, the neighbors are just as boring, you can see them watching their own T.V.'s through the picture window. I love these people because they're related to me. But I can't relate to these people that love me. Oh, I guess my family isn't that bad—I'll forever be the black sheep, though. It's just one of those things. I never gave them a chance, because secretly I always wanted to be born of a dysfunctional family so I had something to run from. I resent them for being so normal.

Soon we passed through Baltimore, the rows of faded brick tenement buildings cutting by, brown soccer fields lonely and dry, derelict factories with broken windows left to rot with hobos warming themselves by cooking fires in the gravel lots. Eastern architecture—not a whole lot of new strip mall type places... mostly skyscrapers and old buildings built hundreds of years ago before we realized we'd all be whizzing around like we do now.

Cars trundled by on the turnpike, wires and telephone poles everywhere, railroad men in modified trucks that ran on the tracks, wearing heavy jackets and doing something or other in the waning hours of their workday. Everything brown and sullen, stoic, barren... but alive somehow with a historical edge of significance you just can't see west of Denver, or west of the Mississippi for that matter.

Poor bleak trees shifting in the chill breeze, yellow caution tape leftover from a recent construction at this platform where we've stopped. Gulls circling above the river, diving down and picking at floating junk making way to the ocean.

The river getting wider, spreading out into a fan delta as we neared the city—oil refineries with flaming pyres exhausting into the atmosphere, nondescript white buildings with some sort of purpose—industry industry—here we go—steam rising into the air from the smokestacks—big oil tanks with Sunoco decals on the sides, oh and there we have it, a small shanty town with houses right on top of one another—each one connected at the sides with no space to breathe—quiet Delaware bars (The Love Palace Tavern) zip by, church steeples, giant spanning bridges leading over the delta—rolling—just an hour to go now. Almost into Philly with her hard streets and patriot history living strong, silent, and still. Cranes from a dock, longshoremen scrambling like ants loading boxcars onto giant barges heading up the river to deliver our goods inland, or perhaps out to the Atlantic for export to foreign lands.

School bus graveyard flashing by, yellow and rusty in the golden sidelight. Old school building with windows busted out and boarded up. A lonely bum strolling through a wooded area chained off by the railroad with his hands deep in tramp pockets… oh how I wish I were him for just a few moments, to see the way he saw the world, this world I'm so in love with, this world that I despise.

Storage units with white plain bread trucks, "Stargate Diner," rabbit ears poking out of drafty houses butting right up to the tracks—brick chimneys, wood siding, shingles missing on the roofs. Wandering kids in hoody sweatshirts and headphones crossing the tracks above an overpass, looking down at me as we whoosh by, 60, 70 mph and gaining speed—I swear one of them caught my eye and smiled, but maybe I just dreamed the whole thing. Row of houses built around a square high-voltage enclosure—back yard pools drained and covered with black tarps, overgrown weeds and shrubbery at the edge of the rails.

Heading into an unknown… a city I've never seen with adult eyes. A region I know next to nothing about—for miles and miles we have been passing industrial and residential areas cohabitating together—no open space anymore in the east—at least not here in this track leading into Philly.

And there she is now, downtown Philadelphia—I remember the skyscrapers, the downtown layout, the brown smell. A very modest skyline dominated with several phallic buildings and smoking chimneys. A city of masons and smoking breath, pulling into the 30th street station, cars cutting by on the turnpike—mostly cabs and mini-vans.

A woman argued with her husband on a cell phone behind me.

"Well I don't *care* how much she said it was, we have to make this work," she shouted. "*Why?* Because she needs *braces*, John, she needs *braces*… Oh, I don't want to talk to you when you're like this."

Last stop before New York at Trenton, New Jersey. I watched trench-coated easterners feeding dollars into automated ticket machines at the platform and scarved old housewives waddling along with sad eyes looking out from the glass, young hoodlums yapping into cell phones. Cell phones, we're all bound by the wireless fury. Who are all these people talking to? Old black man in white beard and black beret hobbling along, girl in khaki scarf waving and blowing a kiss to her boyfriend on the train, newsstand clerk picking his teeth lazily as the light turns low and golden.

Shadows dancing on the rock walls beside the tracks, black crows flying aimlessly through the aquamarine sky. Goddamn, what a day on the other end of the country. More busted window factories with dull red paint and air conditioning ducts and pipes and tubes sagging from third story windows, opaque panes of glass in the windows still intact.

A Giant statue of a man on a horse, white marble or granite—I wonder what *he* did for *his* immortality.

Piles of dirt by the side of the road, gullies underneath a phalanx of birds drifting through the air unhurried, graceful. Really moving now—the toothpick trees just blurring by—I can see the townhouses and shanties between them, like you can see through the slats of a fence when moving at a good speed. These are sights these green eyes of mine have yet to see, and I'm glad to get them in—the eternal checklist.

More and more construction—how do we find the space to build so much so high? Pink light now, salmon hues, mahogany trees and long shadows casting whole houses, whole neighborhoods, whole cities in darkness. New York should be all lit up and twinkling when I arrive.

I wrote in my journal:

LINES LINES, RAILROAD SIGNS
LOOK OUT THE WINDOW,
EVERYTHING'S FINE.

and we pressed forth into the greatest city in the world.

I EMERGED FROM PENN STATION at dusk with my rucksack and stared at the sea of moving people rushing by with cabs honking and hot dog venders yelling and lights blinking everywhere around Manhattan. My god, the beautiful noise of a big, bustling city; a *real* city, a city with *character*, nothing like hated L.A. Wrestling with my load through the crowded sidewalks, I made my way down to the PATH station at 6th and 33rd, feeling for the first time in my life that I belonged somewhere. No one noticed me. Even if they did, they didn't care. I was just a rucksack wanderer—nothing more, nothing less.

Before dropping under, I called Seda in Hoboken.

"You're *here!*" she yelled. "Call me when you get off the PATH and I'll come pick you up—I'm only a few minutes from the platform."

I'd first met Seda in summer, when I was in L.A. working on another bullshit commercial. Her sister lived in Venice and let me crash on her couch whenever I was in town, and Seda just happened to be visiting during a school holiday (she taught second grade).

She'd just broken off a long engagement when we met

and, being newly single in her early 30's, was looking to have a little fun. We spent long, beautiful hours sleeping on the hide-a-bed couch with her dark black, shiny hair and deep green eyes staring into mine, her thin figure and raspy, sexy voice. She always had a ragged, sensual look about her, like she'd just finished running up two flights of stairs naked.

Before she'd gone back to Jersey, we'd agreed that any time we ran across each other's paths, we'd hook up and have no-consequences sex—each a safe harbor for the other.

I bought a ticket for $2 and waited for the subway, which finally arrived with the sound of a boiling teapot rising and finally spilling over with that honk and whoosh of air, the people all piled in the cars and rushing out clutching newspapers and handbags, and even a robed Indian carrying a damn *falcon* on his gloved hand. I got on and sat with my pack between my legs, watching a bored businessman read the *Times* over a Jewish woman's shoulder. She looked over and raised her eyebrows before turning the page, and he nodded approval. Oh, those moments are the best. Strangers communicating. They make me feel whole again.

I ran up the stairs and waited next to a newspaper stand, digging the steady stream of people coming and going from the platform. Soon, she pulled up in a new Toyota Corolla and we sped away to her apartment.

"God, I'm so glad you're here," she glanced over at me and raised her eyebrow. "I took tomorrow off from work, but you're not obligated to hang out with me or anything… I know you like your 'alone time,' I just thought…"

I leaned over and kissed her as we stopped at a red light, tasting the sweet nectar of her breath, the warm sigh and wet lips. Her eyes fluttered and a car honked us away from the trance when the light turned green.

"My mountain man here in the big city," she shook her head. "Never thought I'd see this."

We found a parking spot and ran up to her apartment,

locked the door and started tearing each other's clothes off in the hallway, breathing heavy, slowly dragging our way toward the bedroom.

"Wait, wait," I broke away from her. "I've been on that train for a coupla days, I gotta take a shower."

"No you don't," she whispered into my ear and started undoing my belt.

I pushed her away again, "Yeah, I do… just gimmie a minute."

There were at least seven different kinds of shampoo and conditioners, plus body washes, apricot foot scrubs, shea butter facial masks, loufas and papaya cleansing creams in the shower. I read each bottle in frustration to figure out which was the soap, then dried off and walked into her room with a towel around my waist, smelling very feminine.

"It's so weird to see you without crutches," she said. She was lighting some candles and putting a Dave Matthews CD on the stereo. "How *is* your knee anyway?"

"I think you'll be pleased," I leered and we collapsed on the bed and made love a half dozen times throughout the night, sweating, tearing skin, biting lips, curling toes, pulling hair, finally crumpling naked into each other's arms listening to the night sounds spinning below.

I ran my fingers all over her olive skin, watching the goose bumps follow my fingertips like energy particles, like wheat fields in the wind, like spring waves crashing to the beach.

"Do you have, like, a girl in every port, Max?" she said into my ear.

"What are you talking about?"

"I mean, you're always traveling, always moving around from one place to the next… I just wonder, am I just a pit stop, or do you care about me?"

Ah, how to answer that one? Of course, she *was* just a pit stop, but I *cared* about her. How do I explain that I love her the moment we're together, but when we're apart, I could go the rest of my life without seeing her again? I only love the time we spend together because I know it won't last.

"Of *course* I care about you," I smooched her on the cheek. "You know how it is, though."

"But don't you ever get tired of just coming and going? You enter people's lives and leave these impressions, then you're off again, leaving them to wonder if we might've had the same effect on you. After that week in L.A. last summer, my whole outlook on everything changed."

I ran my fingers through her dark hair and thought carefully about forming my words; "Who I am right now is a direct mix of *all* my experiences. Everyone I meet, all the friends I have, the girls I've slept with and fallen in love with… everything. Some have a bigger impact than others, but *everything* affects me. It's all a chain reaction—if I hadn't dropped out of college, I wouldn't have moved to L.A., I wouldn't have met Chuck, I wouldn't have met your sister through Chuck, I wouldn't have had a place to stay when I came back into town when I worked, I wouldn't have met you that week, and I wouldn't be staying here in your great little apartment, and I wouldn't be lying here exhausted and sweaty after having sex all night. If only one of those factors had been different, I would be sleeping somewhere else right now, maybe not even have taken this trip in the first place. Shit, maybe I'd be *dead*. Who knows?"

She smiled and kissed me, "I don't think I've met anyone quite like you, Max. You just do whatever you want and go wherever you please—never worry about reality or consequences or any of that other stuff the rest of us are all bound by. You just do your own thing and make it work."

I'm always fascinated with the way people see me; my lifestyle. They don't see the hard nights I spend alone, sleeping in rest areas and scraping change out of my truck's ashtray for gas station burritos and fuel. They don't see the piles of rejection letters in my cabin, the stacks of notebooks and journal writings that nobody will ever read or care about. They don't have to avoid calls from collection agencies wanting to know where their money is and avoid people in the grocery store because they owe them money.

"I only wish it were that simple," I sighed.

"What do you want out of life? I mean, what do you expect you'll end up as?"

"I'll tell you what I want," with our heads side by side, looking up at the ceiling, "I just want to earn enough money to go wherever I wanna go, whenever I want, and maybe someone to come with me, too… and I guess I want to be remembered someday."

Immortality… the age old quest of man. What is it that gives him the desire to live forever? Is it the mere thought that when our bones are laid to rest in the void, all of our life's devotions are lost? All of our efforts? All of our love? All of our failures? Everything we've learned as humans, and tried to pass onto those who will carry on?

Sunlight crept through the blinds in the morning.

I watched a spider crawl along the ceiling for a few minutes. He stopped to investigate his upside-down world every few seconds, then disappeared in the corner.

I leaned over and kissed Seda on the forehead. She came awake with a pleasant sigh.

"Good morning my little Armenian friend," I slid my fingers down her stomach and felt the warm moisture between her legs, which opened invitingly. There's nothing better than sex in the morning.

We took a shower together and lazily put our clothes on for the day.

"What do you wanna do today?" she jumped on my lap.

She rattled off a list of places to go and things to do, but I just shook my head and said, "Why don't we just head into the city and see what happens?"

We ended up getting off the PATH at Penn Station with newsboys hawking the *Times* on the street corners, a sea of yellow, honking, mad-town motion; cabs cutting down 7th Avenue, people walking everywhere, listening to iPods, wearing scarves and trench coats, waving their arms in the air, talking and shouting and reading newspapers, hooking arms around bus stop railings, spitting in the street.

People walk in New York like they drive in Los Angeles, always at a blistering pace, cutting around the slowpokes and crossing busy streets against the lights, coming and going eight million different directions in shadows of magnificent buildings reaching high into the cerulean sky.

On up to Times Square; the big, flashing advertisement with gawking tourists snapping pictures and standing stupidly in the middle of traffic, unable to cope with the magnitude of it all. It was a beautiful sunny day, but cold, and street vendors were wrapped in scarves, doffing pageboy hats, selling pirated DVDs laid out on the sidewalk and "I ♥NY" tee-shirts, dirty water hotdogs and pretzels, yes.

We took a subway down to the World Trade Center memorial and sighed. Here, two buildings once stood tall and proud, now just a dirty hole of construction surrounded by grated fencing and milling, sniffling people staring at it, gazing at the end of the American Century. Streetwalkers selling pictures of the planes crashing into the towers in huge fireballs, couples holding hands and kissing each other's foreheads, firefighters with tears in their eyes, conspiracy theorists screaming unheard to the masses, tender graffiti on the walls, like one that read:

yo New York
I hope you are feeling better
I see that nasty scar is starting
to heal ... a ... little.
I will always pray for your losses
Stay strong. you are still the
greatest city in the world
I Love you

"Let's get out of here," Seda said, and I agreed. It was too sad... too real.

We caught a subway up to Central Park and meandered around in the quiet chill, people sitting on benches reading thick books with plumes of white breath dancing from their noses, dogs catching frisbees, a little black kid about six years old dancing like Michael Jackson to a boombox playing "Thriller," pigeons poking at the cement, school kids throwing footballs on field trips. Everything was moving, everything was alive. Even though we were mired in winter, the sunshine and rebirth made it feel like spring.

"This is so great!" Seda beamed. I had my arm around her on a bench. "I live right across the river, but I never come into the city anymore just to walk around—I'm always going to a show or going to the bar to get drunk."

We walked over to 1st and 58th to drop off a scarf Franklin left in Ohio. He lived in a shabby tenement building with hallways that smelled of urine and body odor.

"Hell of a view, eh?" he pointed out the window to a brick wall about two feet away. "But this is a mansion compared to the last place I lived. This is my roommate Dave."

"Yaap, nice to meet you guys, hey Franklin, you gonna move or what?" Dave whined. They were playing an apparently heated game of Risk.

"You want to roll with us to the bars later?" Franklin asked. "I don't think we're gonna do anything special, maybe just hang out around Sutton or something."

"Nah, I think we're gonna meet some of her friends in Hoboken tonight," I said. "But maybe we can get together for lunch tomorrow."

"Yeah, gimmie a call, I don't have shit to do. I had an audition, but they called me back and said not to come… I guess that means I didn't get the part."

Franklin's apartment was like any of the other shabby dwellings of fledgling actors trying to make it big in New York. They lived in the valley in Los Angeles and in dives like this in New York, but their goals were always the same, and so rarely accomplished. But something always kept them going—dreams of success and recognition, or maybe just enough dough to pay the rent on a place without cockroach armies.

He showed us out the front door.

Back on the street, Seda suggested we hit Washington Square Park to get some "burgers at the Shake Shack!" It was closed for winter when we arrived. Some film school kids were shooting something over on the sidewalk involving a body bag and a blow-up doll. "What're you shooting?"

I asked. "A movie," one of them muttered. Everyone's a smart ass. We took a subway to the Village and ate great big slices of pizza at Lombardi's. Best pizza I ever ate.

"I think my feet are gonna fall off," she groaned after dinner. The PATH brought us back to Hoboken, where we lounged around the apartment for a while—her napping and me writing into my journal on the fire escape, trying to capture the feeling, the moment, the era of my life when lonely moments on fire escapes mean everything in the world, especially when you got a pen cap in your teeth and a clean white page to dirty with your words.

That night we walked down cobblestone Hoboken streets to Irish bars, meeting up with Seda's teacher friends so she could show me off, the big "mountain man writer" they had all talked about between classes. Upon meeting them, I could tell they knew everything about me—the way I kissed, how long I lasted in bed, how big/small my penis was, how many/few orgasms I gave her.

They all had flat, boring teacher asses, and drank way too much, and whined about men and grading papers—I was right in the middle of a hen circle of women in their early 30's jaded on love—they were all jealous of Seda for her younger man; the traveler. And I acted the part that Seda oh so wanted me to play—the out-of-town writer drifting around the country and stopping in for secret affairs with her, buying shots for them, knowing that every time I went to the bar for more drinks or to the bathroom, they would bow their heads together and discuss me, what did they think, was I cute, blegh.

And I supposed I enjoyed it greedily—the man on display, living gloriously inside their perception, albeit false, but what is reality but our own attempts at running from it?

We finished up at some bar called O'Brien's or O'something-or-other, and met some other friends of Seda's at a dance club packed full of sweaty, silk-shirt-wearing Armenians and vomiting girls, sweaty thugs grinding and dry humping on the dance floor, muscle-bound bartenders in torn tee-shirts and shaved chests, cokeheads railing lines off the porcelain and dreadlocked deejays spraying sweat everywhere. It was all so sad and pathetic. I wanted to go home, but Seda only got two days a week to go out and drink, and I didn't want to spoil her night.

After that place we met up with *more* teacher friends; also raging alcoholics who couldn't hold their booze. One of the women vomited in her purse as I played pool with her goofy husband, and another went home with some sleazy guy at the bar with a toothpick in his mouth. I had no idea teachers were all so horny and sad.

"Do you wanna get out of here?" I asked Seda. "I'm kinda tired."

"Wait, lemme introduce you to my friend Tommy," she dragged me across the room. "He likes to travel too, you'll love him."

And I shook his hand and listened to him about "that one time he was in Amsterdam," finally excusing myself to sit on the curb outside to smoke. Seda came out some time later to look for me.

"There you are, c'mon, we're gonna go and catch closing time at Dooligan's."

She tried to pull me up but I resisted.

"Ah, why don't we just go home?"

"I thought you liked to *party!*" she howled.

"Well, sometimes I don't."

We got back to the apartment finally and I put leftover slices of pizza in the microwave while she yakked in the toilet. I tried to imagine my *own* second grade teacher—little old Mrs. Herzogg with her blue Chevy Nova and polyester pantsuits—boozing it up and vomiting in bathrooms when she wasn't teaching us cursive writing and arithmetic. It just didn't fit.

I put Seda to bed with a popcorn bowl on the floor and sat again on my fire escape in jacket and scarf. Drunks shouted to each other in dirty alleys. The night was winding up for the masses. I missed my train... my motion. I missed falling asleep with a book on my chest and waking up in a different state. I always missed the things I could never hold onto. I didn't want to be here anymore—it was just as depraved here as it was anywhere else. Oh, when will I find what it is I'm looking for?

WHAT DOES THIS ALL GO DOWN TO?
AM I A WHOLE TO THOUGHTS THAT
LIVE INSIDE MY OWN HEAD?
WHY AM I AT THE WHIM OF A
LIFESTYLE THAT HAS SPUN
BEYOND MY CONTROL?

AM I IN CONTROL OF MY
OWN DESTINY ANYMORE, OR DOES
THAT CONTROL LIE WITH THOSE
WHO HAVE SOMETHING TO
OFFER ME? WHY ALL THESE
QUESTIONS.

THIRTEEN

THE NEXT DAY, Saturday, I woke up early and left Seda a note:

> Seda,
>
> Went into the city to wander around.
> Be back by dinnertime —
> Hope you feel better —
>
> — Max

I slipped out the front door and caught the PATH into Manhattan, wishing I'd brought a book to read on some park bench.

Another beautiful sunny day—two in a row. I made my way to the Empire State Building, stood in line for 45 minutes behind every imaginable form of tourist—all clutching cameras and talking excitedly.

"Mommy! Mommy! When are we gonna get to the *top*?" a little girl screamed to her dumpy mom wearing, yes, an "I ♥ NY" sweatshirt.

"I heard if you drop a penny off the top it'll go clear through someone's skull on the sidewalk," a little boy boasted to his older brother.

"Nu uhh," his brother sniffed. "It only goes, like, two *inches* into the skull—not all the way through."

The little brother looked down, disappointed, "Oh."

I felt enormously foolish standing in line with all the chatty tourists who stood out wherever they went, it seemed, but I hadn't been up to the observation deck since I was a little boy with my father. On our travels back east every summer, he'd stop at every attraction and historical landmark along the way—from the world's biggest ball of twine in Darwin, Minnesota to the grave of Stonewall Jackson's arm in Fredericksburg, Virginia. The head of the world's largest dog in Huntsville, Utah to the anchor from the USS Maine in Reading, Pennsylvania. The famous drive-thru redwood tree in Bear Valley, California, the world's largest killer bee in Hidalgo, Texas, the birthplace of T.V. in Rigby, Idaho—he stopped at them all and dragged me and my two sisters out to take pictures and then ushered us back into the car to continue down the road to the next one.

And now all he does is watch FOX News all day long like the rest of the trembling masses and take handfuls of pills to help slow the congestive heart failure ruining his body. Is there anything sadder than a traveler who'd lost his desire to go?

I felt just as stupid being ushered through the line to the top of the Empire State Building as I did then, as a kid. Before they let you out to see the skyline from the now tallest building in the city, they take your picture next to a *fake* NYC skyline and tell you to pick it up on your way out. Then they feed you through a massive souvenir stand selling key chains for $9.95 and Statue of Liberty dolls for $15.99, which the people schoop up and drag home with them in neat plastic bags, throwing them in attics to gather mold with old LP's and photo albums of relatives dead and gone.

I walked clear around the observation deck and tried to look out on the city, but too many people were crammed close to the railing. Everyone elbowed one another and stuck cameras over my head, snap snap, pushed me out of the way, asked to take their picture. God dammit, I just wanted to stand at the railing and look at what we've created, and feel something good behind it. Is this all we are anymore? Slack-jawed tourists handing over gobs of money to say we saw this, visited that? *Take my picture! Validate my vacation!*

The herd lined up to exit, but we were fed through an area where they had our pictures from the fake skyline printed out. The hardworking man behind the counter found mine and handed it over—I had the biggest scowl on my face in the photo, and thought it would be funny to hang it up somewhere, but then he asked for $25 to keep it.

"Twenty-five *dollars?*" I yelled.

"Oh come on," the concessions man whined. "Show your friends you went to the Empire State Building, have this memory to keep forever! It's a small price to pay to show where you've been!"

"I'd rather show them the ticket stub."

He snapped the picture back, tore it up and harassed the next person in line. What a complete waste of money.

Almost two hours later, I was back on the street in a foul mood, sore that I stood in line like a lemming and spent $20 to go up in a building to look at a view I couldn't even see for only five minutes.

I wandered over to a lunch cart and bought a bratwurst for $3, ate it greedily, and crossed the street.

"Man… flyest hat I ever saw on a white dude," I heard a black guy mutter in passing, referring to my beat hat. A man cut by carrying an American flag wrapped around a Rasta-colored pole. A mulatto girl led a smiling, blindfolded Cuban boyfriend down the sidewalk, whispering the sights into his ear. Such fascinating people we are.

The subway at Broadway and 34th took me down to Battery Park, where I moped around the water's edge for a couple hours staring at the tiny Statue of Liberty and writing in my journal.

So many different people strolled by on that sunny Saturday. Yawning Muslim women in blue shawls, soggy-bottomed Midwesterners pointing video cameras out at the water and gasping, talking too loudly, Armenians in sharp suits, reeking of expensive cologne, joggers panting along with the words to hip hop songs, urban blacks in stiff-billed caps and baggy pants sneering at the world, gaggles of Asians yabbering in their native tongues, snapping pictures of each other flashing peace signs, always flashing peace signs.

The Staten Island ferry horn blasting from across the East River, cell phones ringing crazy tones, helicopters buzzing about the sky, gulls screeching and diving into the muddy water, couples holding hands and speaking German, smiling Mexicans with little brown kids in tow.

Hup, a white droplet of bird shit almost hit my foot—close but no cigar, bird.

All these people coming and going and laughing and honking. Where do they go? What do they do? Are they as lost as I am? Do they feel? Do they see? Do they listen?

I called Franklin and asked him if he wanted to get a bite to eat.

"Sure, where you at now?"

"Battery Park, just about to hop on the subway."

"Okay, I'm at 5th and 48th doing some shopping, meet me outside Radio City."

A few subways later, I walked up to the street and saw him leaning against a fire hydrant, thumbing through the *Village Voice*.

We cut down 5th Avenue amidst all the life blowing by, clear past Midtown, yapping about girls and travels and reminiscing about our sailing trip. I stopped to pick through a stack of old books from a hairy Polish street vendor on 28th. One Dostoyevsky and a Salinger.

"That's a *great* book," Franklin flipped through a few pages. "When I was in college, I wrote this huge paper on symbolic meanings in literature, and I used the red hunting cap as a symbol for Holden's attraction for unusual things that people usually miss, or gloss over, or whatever, y'know, which also transferred to his obsession with *people* that are weird too, and his whole thing about the phonies an' all that shit."

"Right."

"But my stupid-assed lit professor gave me a bad grade for it, sayin' it wasn't a symbol for *anything*, just a stupid hat he bought for a buck."

"What the hell, *everyone* knows about the red hunting cap," I said.

"I know! I don't even think she *read* the fucking thing," he spat. "Junior level lit professor who didn't even understand a simple symbolic meaning… shows you just how useless college can be if you get bad professors. I ended up dropping it and took a bowling class instead."

"That's showing 'em," I chuckled. We ducked into a Chinese dim sum place and ordered big plates of food.

"That's a pretty cute chick you brought over yesterday," he said, shoving a whole potsticker in his mouth. "What's her deal?"

"Ah, I don't know, she's just a chick I met in L.A. last summer, nobody special," I said. "It's' nice to have a place to stay near the city, though, and a warm body to lay with too."

"Yah, that never hurt anyone," he nodded. "When you takin' off?"

"Tomorrow morning, I think… I'm gonna bum around D.C. all day and catch the night train down to Florida to do some fishing with my buddy I met in Thailand last year."

"Are you still thinking about going sailing this summer? In Belize?"

"I hope so," I said. "Mitch and Joanna sound like they're down for it. We just have to watch out for the hurricanes, y'know… supposed to be another rough year."

"Is Ani gonna go?" he asked with cocked eyebrow.

"Ah, I dunno, maybe."

He smiled at me and took a drink from his beer, "You never told Mitch about you and Ani, huh?"

"What do you mean?"

"I saw you guys together," he leaned back and crossed his arms. "You mean to say that nothing went on between you two?"

"How *could* anything have happened? We were all on the same *boat*."

"Well… I remember talking with her like a month afterwards and she said some pretty nice things about you."

"*Did* she?" I asked eagerly. "Like *what?*"

"I dunno, just good things… she really liked you, y'know?"

"Are you fucking serious?" I dropped my fork. "I never

knew *any* of this! I've been so hung up on her ever since that trip… but I never did anything about it, partly because, y'know, she's Mitch's sister an' all."

"*And* my cousin," he added.

"Well, whatever… but also because I didn't think she felt the same way about *me*."

"She kind of felt the same way, you know, about the whole 'Mitch best friend' thing… it's probably a good thing the two of you never did anything… especially since she's getting married now."

Plunk.

"What? She's getting *married?*"

"Yeah, I thought you talked to her in Denver," he said. "She just told us a few days ago, right after you got to Columbus. He's a pretty good guy, too… I guess they're gonna wait until she's out of school, though."

"I can't believe it…" I trailed off. "I guess I always had this secret little fantasy that we'd get together someday, y'know? I know it's totally impossible, and *wrong*, y'know, to date your best friend's sister, but still… I dunno… I guess I just…"

He took a long swig of his beer, "Look, it's probably for the best, y'know? I mean shit, you only spent two weeks together, and on a *boat* for chrissakes. You barely *knew* each other. You didn't even kiss her, did you?"

"No," I said, the memory coming back to me.

It was the last day of our trip and Mitch was loading gear from the sailboat to the airport van with Joanna and Franklin. My flight left eight hours after theirs, so I was just lounging on the dock, drinking a beer. Ani'd walked up to me with a sad, graceful smile and given me a hug. I smelled the salt in her hair, the tender, soft skin of her back, god, how she felt in my arms.

We didn't say anything for a moment, both struggling with the reality of the situation, perhaps. She'd go back to school in Colorado and I'd go back to L.A. Back to both of our worlds. Nothing would ever happen between us, despite whatever desire there might have been. All my life I've met amazing people, only to watch them go.

And there was a moment after we'd hugged, with our faces inches from one another, when we almost kissed—a forbidden, taboo kiss that would've changed everything. But Mitch yelled from the street and the cabbie honked the horn, and she gave me a last look and fluttered away.

I looked down at my mess of Chinese food on the plate. What is that feeling when you meet someone and fall in love with their momentary flash through your life? Is there a name for it? Someone you sat with on the bow with feet dangling and warm salt water lapping and laughing and long nights of talking when the rest of the crew had passed out by the bonfire on our own sandy island, and the reality that it will never be as sweet as it was then, you're not in love with an actual person, but an *idea* of a person that somehow fits so magically with one that just happens to be someone you'll never be with.

"I guess I've always regretted not giving her one smooch, at least," I told Franklin shamefully.

He nodded his head and motioned for the check, "Well, I'm sorry to bring it up, Max... I didn't realize—"

"No," I looked up. "It's not a big deal... it's probably best this way, like you said... it was just a stupid fantasy anyway."

We paid the check and hit the street again, the sun growing faint, throwing hard shadows down 5th Avenue.

"There's a PATH down there at 14th, that'll take you back to Hoboken," Franklin said.

"Thanks man, you headin' home?"

"Yeah, I got an audition on Tuesday for some gay ass play, gotta study my lines," he said, as so many struggling actors have before him. "It was good seeing you again. Ohio, now New York... where the hell you gonna turn up next?"

"You never know," I smiled.

We shook hands and separated; him heading back up-town to his shabby apartment, and me back to my hungover schoolteacher with vomit breath.

Seda and I ate a late, tedious dinner at the Italian place down the street and had late, tedious sex once before I passed out—all the life taken from me—waiting for tomorrow when I could get back out there again and move, move, move on down the line.

The train left at dawn the next morning, Sunday, and we were running late due to morning lovemaking.

"I don't think I have time, Seda," I pushed her off.

"Oh c'mon, I need it one more time," she pleaded. I submitted, but missed the PATH by five minutes, so she had to drive me into the city and drop me off at Penn Station.

"Ooh, I don't think we're gonna make it, Max, I'm sorry," she said, racing through Hoboken toward the Lincoln Tunnel. I stared across the Hudson at the New York skyline silhouetted in a fiery pink sky.

"We'll make it," I assured her. "God, lookit that sunrise! I've never seen anything more beautiful." I felt it again, the movement, that feeling of being alive yet again. The mere notion of hopping on that train again stood my hair up and lit a little fire under my seat.

She didn't notice, just continued through the tunnel to Manhattan with the red sun rising fat and lazy up 33rd Avenue—the Empire State Building looming overhead with its windows sparkling. Glory be the first light of day spilling into this mad, wonderful city.

"This way, *this* way," I pointed, but she missed the turn.

"That says Madison Square Garden," she said.

"Well, the Garden is right next to Penn Station," I said. "C'mon Jersey girl, don't you know your way around the City?"

"Is it? Shit, okay, hold on," and she veered right, squealing the tires and going down some alley with bums sleeping next to trash cans and vendors shaking floor mats out of back doors.

I hung on as she hopped over a curb and tore down 31st back toward the Garden. City birds flew lazy loops in the blossoming sky.

We pulled into Penn Station with ten minutes to spare and I thanked her while hurriedly lugging my gear out from the backseat.

"No, thank *you*," she grinned devilishly.

"I don't know when I'll be back in town, but maybe we'll meet up sometime in L.A., or… wherever, y'know," I said.

"Yeah, that'd be nice," she nodded her head wistfully. "Take care of yourself, all right?"

I smooched her on the lips and hoisted my pack aback once more, happy to have the weight again. I looked back before dropping underground and saw her watching me with a forlorn look. I waved and she re- turned it and drove off slowly, merging with the quiet Sunday city traffic and disappearing around the corner.

FOURTEEN

THE TRAIN PULLED OUT of the station under rose herringbone clouds. Heading back along this same section of track through Trenton, Baltimore, Philadelphia, and, eventually, arriving in D.C. around noon. I planned to spend the day walking around digging the sights and hopping on the Carolinian at nightfall going all the way through to Florida—maybe stopping in South Carolina for a day, maybe not—I could do whatever the hell I wanted.

I resolved to stop torturing myself over Ani's impending marriage... but I wondered why Mitch and Joanna never said anything about it when I was in Ohio. Did they keep it from me, and if so, why? Ah, hell with it. Let it all go.

Inside the station, the Amtrak attendant shook her head sadly and told me the Carolinian was "full to the gills."

"What do you mean it's full?" I asked. "*Every* seat is sold out? That's impossible."

"Yeh, sorry sir," she sympathized. "We have a full train of high school students traveling on a field trip to Florida. The next available train is this same one leaving tomorrow."

"Well, what about other routes? Can I connect with anything?"

"Let's see," she clacked her inch-long fingernails on the keyboard for a moment and sadly shook her head, "No, there's nothing else. Sorry."

"But where am I supposed to stay?" I asked her pointlessly. She just shrugged and called for the next person in line.

I left disgusted and decided to forget about it until later. I transferred some essentials into my daypack and checked the heavy rucksack and my computer case at the baggage locker.

Weird cops whizzed around the station in "Segway Human Transporters"—those two-wheeled stand-up electric scooters. They looked incredibly foolish… like some sort of space pod soldier. I watched one try to go through a door that was cordoned off with velvet rope. He backed into the door, ducked under the rope, rammed the door over and over again, catching on the rope and almost fell off, finally got it open and buzzed away. It must've taken him five minutes to go through the door when he could've just gotten off, opened it, and gone through. What a waste of time. What a fucking idiot.

It was grey and pissing rain outside, but I didn't care. I pulled a poncho over my head and my backpack, then trudged across the street toward the Capitol—a hunchbacked drifter. It was closed for repairs, just like it was when I saw it fifteen years ago with my father.

"Can I help you?" a stone-faced cop said, standing guard outside the chain link fence.

"No, I'm just looking around," I said vaguely.

"The Capitol's closed, y'know," he said. I could tell he wanted me out of there. so I just scowled at him and wandered all the way down the Mall to the Washington Monument where a teacher led a gaggle of Japanese schoolchildren tethered together in one long chain, all wearing bizarre yellow day-glo hats.

Everything looked so sad and solemn that day in our nation's hollow heart. Here the leaders of our country walked the alphabet streets and made decisions on my behalf that I rarely ever agreed with, or even *knew* about for that matter. They don't represent me. This democracy is not transparent. We are not the people, we are the plebs. The day they elect a poor, sad, lonely drifter into the halls of Congress is the day they represent me.

I sat with my back against the Washington Monument and stared down past the reflecting pool—a muddy scar drained for the winter—toward the Lincoln Memorial. Millions have trampled this grass for causes great and small—wars come and gone, civil rights and equality solved and forgotten. A fanny-packed father dragged his two whining children behind him, all wearing $2 ponchos.

"Tyler, Andrew, I'm *not* going to tell you again," he yelled. "If you don't stop this bickering, we're going back to the hotel."

"Fine!" the older boy said. "This is *boring*. I'd rather be at the hotel *anyway*."

"This is our nation's *history*, Andrew," the father stretched out his arms. "Don't you care about where you came from?"

"I came from Ohio," Andrew waved his arms in the air.

"And where do you think *Ohio* came from?" the father countered.

"I don't care! I don't care about any of this!"

"Well, someday you'll feel differently," the father sighed. They stormed down the muddy lawn still arguing all the way to the Smithsonian. All I could do was smile and think of my own father saying exactly the same things to me and my two sisters. My god, who the hell wants to have children? Little ungrateful bastards.

I broke out a pack of peanuts and ate them one at a time, savoring each bite. I'd lost about ten pounds from not eating much the past two weeks.

A uniformed ranger appeared out of nowhere and stood over me, "Excuse me, sir?"

"Yes?"

"We ask that you don't eat inside the national monuments," he said kindly, head tilted to the side, hands clasped together. I looked down at my bag of peanuts and back up at him with my best *are you fucking kidding me?* look.

"I'm not *in* the monument, I'm outside in the fresh air and I don't plan on littering, so why don't you go bother someone else?" All these rules and guidelines that meant nothing. Who the fuck cares if I ate some peanuts and leaned against a national monument? Was the world going to end if I continued?

He sighed patiently and smiled, "Yes, I'm sorry about bothering you, but we have *rules*, and—"

I threw up my hands and got up, "Okay, okay, I'll put them away. God forbid anyone break the *rules*. God forbid I sit out in the open free air eating some fucking *peanuts*."

He nodded and walked away satisfied and I finished the bag anyway, putting the trash in my pocket and continuing down the Mall toward Lincoln's shrine. It seems you can't walk five yards in this country anymore without some asshole hounding you about something.

I stopped at the World War II memorial in a sour mood and sat at the edge of the fountain to roll a Top—I switched from Drum to Top tobacco because it was cheaper. I resolved to spend less money, to suffer a bit more, to eat less, to roll my own cigarettes and not buy stupid things like Coke in the bottle at tourist stands. I felt the need to wean myself away from these extravagant habits of my era, if only to distance myself further from the fact that I was one of them too.

But then I saw another tourist stand to the right of the

memorial and ended up buying a bagel and some popcorn for $5 after waiting in line for ten minutes behind two couples buying prepackaged sandwiches, little bags of Doritos, hot dogs, Lipton iced teas, Budweiser beers, and cellophane-wrapped chocolate chip cookies that all had the same amount of chocolate chips and looked exactly the same.

There were tourists everywhere, despite the rain. They were all pointing little digital cameras at everything—snapping then looking, snapping then looking. Instant results. I tried to stare up at Lincoln's gaunt face behind those stone columns and feel something move me, but I couldn't stand it because everyone kept running in, snapping pictures of each other with peace signs and then moving on to capture the next sight. Nobody seemed to look at his big frozen hands, or the delicate cracks that ran like epigraphs down his pant legs, or the dignified look on his face.

Seems we only look at the important stuff through the lens of a cheap camera nowadays. These 21st century locusts, who consume and consume, and that's patriotism, I guess.

A fat-bottomed mom with big droopy underarms flapping around ushered two fighting kids in front of Lincoln and screeched for them to, "Shaddup you two, lemme just take this pitchur, then we'll go get some hot dawgs, okay?" and they stopped fighting for a second and smiled with their arms around each other while the false memory was preserved, then pulled hair and slapped each other again down the steps.

Over to the Korean War Memorial, where I dropped a small flower at the feet of a stone soldier with cape and B.A.R. slung over his shoulder, held in immortal silence. My father was wounded several times in Korea. He had already fought for his country and almost died numerous times before he was 21. Here I was at 25 feeling useless and stupid, as if the world owed me an explanation. A purpose. What did I know about sacrifice? About honor? What did I know

about anything? The world owed me nothing, yet I took from it everything I could and expected more. More, more, always more. I expected everything she could give and nothing less.

The Vietnam Memorial, all solemn and black, a queer silence echoing across the open space while veterans sat weeping against the Wall. All those names etched in the granite, all those lives lost. My god, what was it all for? So I could stand here with my pack aback, munching on peanuts? So we could place pictures under magnets on refrigerator doors? So we can watch Monday Night Football and pass out with hand in pants on the living room couch?

Washington, D.C.—the city of memorials, the city of graves and hallowed remembrance. Somber tears mixed with falling rain.

Oh, what will become of us all? Will there be another memorial for this pointless war we wage in Iraq? This shameful quagmire we refuse to acknowledge as a defeat—America doesn't lose wars! We win! We are powerful! We are the ones in charge! We tell *you* when we've had enough! Oh it all makes me so ashamed to be American… and I want to believe in this country… and I want to feel as if I belong here, that I'm a native son… but won't we eventually run out of space and stop remembering our fallen soldiers who died for reasons we never knew or understood in the first place?

Everything so grey and melancholy that day in the yawning heart of our nation. I couldn't take it anymore. I sat at the steps of the Lincoln Memorial in the rain and tried to write into my journal, but no words came. The ink just blurred and the paper curled. The thoughts of an outlaw American matter not to those on their pedestals. They wanted so much for us—and we've let them all down.

Just then, the presidential helicopter swooped low overhead, engines whining, rotors throbbing, slicing through the rain-bloated clouds, winging toward the White House. Everyone pointed their cameras to the sky and snapped and looked. Gulls cried and scattered in the heavy air.

"There he goes!" screamed some happy little girl, waving up at the helicopter.

Yes, there he goes; our child bully president looking down on his people like ants. Our smiling, swaggering, democratic dictator reading somber missives from cue cards and running this country right into the ground, destroying what it is we fought for and remembered with these many memorials.

I moped away from all those tombs and walked through town to find a store to buy some more rolling tobacco. Homeless people mixed with power tie-wearing politicians on the sidewalks. All I could do was shake my head. Nothing makes sense.

But later, after the sun broke through the clouds in early afternoon, I began to feel saintly for some reason—a shrouded wanderer moving through the earth and her people, seeking only the Truth and nothing else. At one point I stopped and saw a parking meter that had expired and plunked a quarter in there—to assuage my lifelong guilt, perhaps, from being born white and mediocre with a roof over my head and a family that cared about me. Then I saw *another* expired meter and started digging in my pocket for another quarter. Then it dawned on me that it was *Sunday*. I just stood there laughing at myself. What a fool I am sometimes. All the time. Here I was thinking I was solving the world's problems one quarter at a time, when I was just padding the government's profits.

I meandered past the White House and peered through the iron gate of the back lawn surrounded with Secret Service agents and cops and picture-snapping tourists. I wanted to get a glimpse of Bush so I could throw rocks at him and yell "Fascist!" but he wasn't there, of course. He's never there. It wouldn't have mattered anyway.

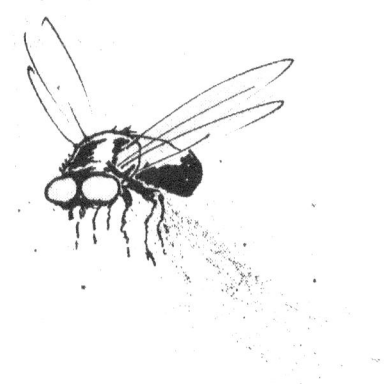

I WONDER IF THERE _IS_ ANY TRUTH IN THIS WANDERING... THIS AIMLESS JOURNEY THAT KEEPS TAKING ME FURTHER & FURTHER FROM HOME BUT CLOSER TO THE SOUGHT-AFTER WORD I CAN'T HELP BUT CHASE, LIKE A DOG AFTER MY OWN TAIL. WHEN I FINISH THIS SILLY TRIP & SIT BACK IN MY DIRTY LITTLE CABIN IN IDAHO WITH ALL THOSE BUGS SMASHED ON THE WINDOWPANES & TRASH CANS OVERFLOWING WITH PIZZA BOXES & POP BOTTLES, I'LL TRY TO PUT IT ALL TOGETHER. I'LL FIGURE OUT HOW MANY MILES I COVERED, HOW MANY STATES I PASSED THROUGH, HOW MANY HOURS I SPENT ON THE TRAIN... AND I'LL TRY TO VALIDATE IT WITH MY WRITING, MY PICTURES, MY BARROOM STORIES. BUT LIFE WILL MARCH ON AS IF I HADN'T LEFT AT ALL. I'LL MEET ALL MY PSEUDO-INTELLECTUAL FRIENDS AT THE 419 & WE'LL DRINK OURSELVES SILLY, READ MEDIOCRE POETRY AT OPEN MIC NITE, SEARCH THE ROOM FOR WOMEN I HAVEN'T SLEPT WITH YET — BUSINESS AS USUAL — BUT MAYBE THIS WHOLE THING WILL CHANGE ME & OPEN A DOOR INTO MY DISMAL PURPOSE. MAYBE I'LL STOP TALKING SO MUCH & BEGIN TO LISTEN AGAIN. TO OBSERVE. TO WATCH WHAT'S HAPPENING WITHOUT ME IN IT. MAYBE I JUST WANT TO RECORD EVERYTHING I CAN WHILE I'M STILL YOUNG & STUPID ENOUGH TO FIND BEAUTY IN THE MUNDANE THINGS WE ALL FORGET ABOUT WHEN THE YEARS TURN US OLD & BORING.

I made my way back through town slowly. The lights at the Capitol suddenly blinked on right as I looked up.

A middle-aged man with a knapsack walked up to me outside the Navy Memorial. He asked if I'd snap a picture of him next to a marble statue of a sailor with a sea bag.

"I'm an old Navy man, y'see," he explained. I took his old battered Wal-Mart camera and snapped several pictures of him and the statue, arm-in-arm.

"Thanks a million," he said and rushed away to catch the next attraction before the light dimmed into darkness. I pulled out my camp stove and cooked another packet of ramen noodles, then noticed I was seated on a giant, circular world map laid out in granite. I walked over to north Idaho, where my journey began, and took five great steps across the country to where I was then. I was a giant, trudging across the earth. A strange hobo midget sat and watched me with a wry grin, eyeing my noodles.

D.C. seems to be overrun with midgets... or "little people" as we're supposed to call them. I saw *five* of the little fuckers in less than an hour—all randomly, not like they were there for a convention, if such a convention existed. One a smiling little woman who waddled heavily with each step, crossing Pennsylvania as I scowled away from the White House, another at the Department of Archives trying to read the Constitution on tip-toes, another walking down the grass at the Mall wearing a beret of all things, one more near the Lincoln Memorial and the final one my hobo at the Navy Memorial. Never saw so many midgets in all my life. Poor little bastards.

The light was fading quickly on the way back to Union Station. I checked for open seats on the Carolinian one more time before giving up and sleeping in the station that night.

"No, sorry sir, there's a school field trip—" the Amtrak attendant started to tell me—a different one than before.

"Yeah, I know," I said impatiently. "I was just checking to see if anything had opened up."

"Well, you could take the Crescent down to New Orleans and take the Sunset Limited into Jacksonville," she offered. "Then you could catch up with the Carolinian. There's plenty of open seats on that one."

I raised my eyebrows, "Really? The lady before said there were no other options."

She shrugged her shoulders, "Well, this one leaves in about twenty minutes. You wanna take it?"

"Hell yeah, just lemme get my bag out of the lockers."

I gave my claim ticket to the fat black woman behind the counter, who grunted and moaned herself up from her perch next to a tiny television set to get my pack. "Everybody Loves Raymond" was playing.

"Lawd *me!*" she cried from inside the baggage room. She re-appeared a second later.

"That yo bag there, that big ol' green one?" she thumbed back to the room with a harried look.

"Yeah, do you want me to grab it?"

"I think you're gonna have ta, I can't *lift* it."

I came behind the counter and hoisted the pack on my shoulders.

"You in the military or sumpthin'?" she asked.

"Oh no," I chuckled. "No, I'm just a bum."

I ran away giggling, leaving her with forehead all wrinkled in confusion. Hopped on the train just in time, my feet aching from all the miles I'd covered, and fell happily asleep as we chugged south toward New Orleans. I wouldn't have to sleep in the station. I wouldn't have to lose a whole day. Everything would work itself out. It always does. Right?

FIFTEEN

WE CHUGGED THROUGH the Smoky Mountains and into Atlanta at dawn, aglow with sunshine and gridlocked traffic spilling into downtown. The air was warm and crisp when I got out to smoke a cigarette—I was finally out of winter.

I had long since run out of weed, so I was always on the lookout for young kids ducking off to smoke out of the conductor's field of view. No luck this stop, however… just a sweet old black woman who walked up and asked if I had a lighter.

I lit her long, thin cigarette and she nodded thanks. Her face was ancient; deep, leathery wrinkles like that of an apple left in the sun. She held kind eyes inside inside that old face.

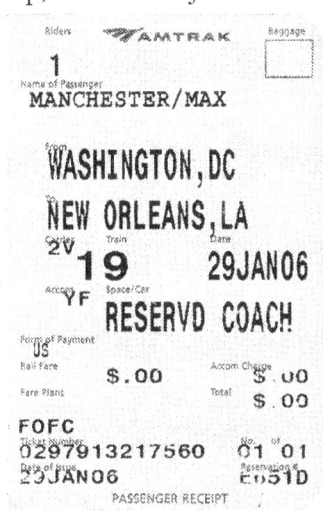

"Whatchoo smokin' there, chile?" she asked with comic expression.

"Tops," I said, showing her the pack from my pocket.

"Ahh, roll y'owns," she smiled. "I used t'smoke those when I's a little girl.

the pack from my pocket.

"Ahh, roll y'owns," she smiled. "I used t'smoke those when I's a little girl. Haven't had one since I's 'bout nineteen years ol'."

"I can roll one up for you if you like, ma'am."

She laid her hand on my arm and twinkled her eyes, "Oh, thanks the same chile, but I'm fine with these ol' totem poles here."

"How far you going?" I asked.

"All th'way down Tuscaloosa. I's up in New Yawk visitin' my daughter fo' the week—jes' had surgery on her feet and needed some ol' Southern cookin'."

"That sounds like a fun trip," I said. "Nice of you to help her out."

"Well, tha's what mama's *do*, chile," she glowed. "I'm eighty-fo years ol' and I never stopped takin' care o' that chile… she's a sweet angel too."

"I'm sure she is," I smiled.

The conductor called us back aboard and I wished the old woman a good trip.

At the next smoke stop, some weird meth-head dude came up to me out of the blue, twitching and jerking and scratching his face, saying something like, "You know when I got on the train in D.C. it was so durn far from the station and I was so durn late, they had to take us out in a *scooter*," and then he laughed maniacally, like some drunk hyena, and slapped his knees while I lit my cigarette. "A *scooter!* Can ya believe it?"

I just smiled and nodded, as I do when all morons speak to me. He kept talking, spouting all manner of bullshit—none of it understandable.

"Then the conductor, the conductor sez, 'ho there boy, you gotta check that,' and I sez, 'what' for? It's only my KIT-bag,' ah ha haaaa! My KIT-bag!"

I kept smiling and nodding, avoiding eye contact and

finally dashing out my cigarette before I was finish just so I could get away from him. Fucking nutbags.

An hour past Atlanta the train stopped and sat idle for a while. Unrest spread about the train car.

"What the hail *now?*" a hee-haw southern man drawled. "We been stoppin' an' goin' this whole trip, got *dammit!*"

The conductor appeared at the head of the car and asked for everyone's attention.

"I'm sorry about the delay folks," he said. "There's a lot of freight congestion ahead, but we should be on our way in about twenty minutes. I've been hoping it would be different for the past month, but it hasn't happened that way. We left Atlanta an hour late and we'll most likely lose another hour or two up ahead before N'Orleans."

Everyone groaned and asked their pointless questions, but I just read Dostoyevsky silently. I got nowhere to go but everywhere, and nothing to be late for anyway, so who cares?

And hoo boy, we're really getting into the South all right. Great piles of rural junk sat everywhere along the tracks, run-down shacks next to muddy brown forests and car graveyards and trailer parks on the horizon with tattered trampolines in their back yards. It smelled of southern woe.

The train emptied most of the passengers in Atlanta—just a handful of us left for this last push through to New Orleans. Hup, there's a brown golf course with two old fat women in the whipping wind getting ready to tee off—one of them swats at the ball and it dribbles ten feet and stops.

And there's another Junkyard Sam—this one king of *southern* junk. Stacks of rusting crap everywhere. Railroad men in hardhats erecting a new track next to this one, factories out in the middle of nowhere, water tower that says

"Tallapoosa—the Dogwood City" on the side. Every house has rain streaks and rotten siding, linens hanging motionless on the line, life inside the cavity.

Every neighborhood looks like it had suffered some past calamity, like civilizations built atop swamps and slowly sinking into the earth—strange clingy weeds growing like canopies over the ground. Lots of old buckets lying around beside the tracks—wonder what for? Ah, a nice green meadow I'd like to stretch out in and take a nap—wee little birds hopping around the heather pecking for worms and bugs.

A man in a red pickup truck full of logs waiting for the train to cut through—another peaceful meadow with little trickling creek cutting through the middle. I wanted to go romping around the woods looking for frogs and crawdads and come home with muddy shoes and a sniffling nose, just like so many days of my youth.

These southern names of towns and cities; Charlottesville, Lynchburg, Danville, Greensboro, Salisbury, Kannapolis, Gastonia, Spartanburg, Greenville, Clemson, Toccoa, Gainesville, Birmingham… once just names on an atlas, and now we pass them all and leave them behind.

What a nice old man that conductor was back in Gainesville—I forgot all about it until now. I went into the café car to sit and write, not being able to sleep, and he told me I'd better put on my shoes for FDA regulations, but he said it in a kindly way, so I obliged—he was an older guy, early 60's, probably a career railroader—combed his hair in a strange duck-ass in back, both sides meeting and creating a stiff grey ridge. He then came by some time later and asked if I smoked—I said yes and he told me we'd have a smoke stop in about 30 minutes, then reminded me twice more. I rolled up a Top and put on my jacket, went outside when the train stopped and saw him there with his conductor cap on and heavy coat, holding a cup of coffee. He carried a look of a man pleased with his lot in life, content, comfortable in the routine. A new conductor strolled up with some sort of safety glasses on and this old duck-ass man handed him the cup of coffee and smiled, said hello and welcome to work and all that jazz. Just a nice old guy who probably watched trains chug by when he was a kid and fell in love with the lifestyle, the sounds, the motion, and has been working on them for his entire life. Probably has an old picture of a locomotive or steam engine in his living room back home, on the mantle, and a chubby old Mickey Rooney wife washing dishes quietly, waiting for his return.

Gad these run-down towns—streaks of rain on my windowpane, a sleepy day here in wherever we are— somewhere in Alabama. Dead automobiles everywhere. Gas is $2.29 at the Chevron there—Old Edwardsville Road with white cars swooshing by, Orkin pest control man racing the train to the crossing. Ha—beat you to the track, sucka.

Hoo! A small wooden footbridge over a tiny lake, decaying forests with fallen logs outlined in blankets of leaves—I bet this is a hell of a trek in the fall when all the leaves explode with color. But I kinda like this melancholy winter trip—puts my mind right where it needs to be.

"Smile On" it says written in graffiti there, and I did. Rain's really coming down now—overflowing a back yard pool of this house built down in a gully with a saggy volleyball net and beer cans sparkling everywhere.

What weather today—from rain to snow to sun to overcast to sun to rain.

Hayfields throbbing by, we're really moving now—the engine driver stepped it up a notch. Everything is whizzing by faster and faster. Trying to make up time because we're oh so late now. Oh, and there's a sad little graveyard next to a grey church. Southern houses with columns out front and a wraparound porch, people sitting around listening to the raindrops on the roof and probably drinking rotgut bourbon of some kind, talking about god knows what these people talk about—NASCAR I suppose.

I really am out here on my own, aren't I? So far from home. Never been here before—no stories to remember, no trick of comfort this time... just the drizzling rain outside in the overcast, depressing, run-down, po-dunk towns clicking by—and I'm hungry but I don't want to spend any more money in that fucking snack car.

I rummaged through my pack and found a granola bar to fill my grumbling stomach.

A leather-faced road man got on at Birmingham carrying a guitar case and sat down in the row next to mine. He struck up a conversation with the black couple behind me.

"Music is a good thing," he said. "Some of my darkest hours came light at just the sound of my old guitar plucked by m'own hand."

Then he cracked open the case and strummed a little song. It was a simple melody, using just three chords:

"*Oh my baby, I'm a-comin' ho-ome,*" he sang sweetly. "*Oh sweet angel, why do I ro-am? Been so lo-ong since I seen your face. Been so long away from that place... called... home.*"

A few people clapped when he finished and he nodded to them modestly, putting the guitar away.

"Music's good for my soul," he said to the black couple. "It's good for *everyone's* soul. I just hope I can play down in N'Orleans. They need it down there, those poor people."

"Bo' ain't that the truth," the husband agreed.

And my god we've broken through to the sunshine again; warm weather, big puffy clouds down there around the Gulf a few hundred miles south. Picked up a few more passengers at Birmingham, and now we're rolling through the rail yards—a conductor sits idly in an engine reading a book, waiting for his boxcars to come clanging up behind him—elbow out the window just like he's waiting at a stoplight, but he's in a big mother engine instead. The backstreets of Birmingham; old brick buildings splattered with graffiti, hard black brakeman checking his cell phone and peering over at us, grumbling out of the platform.

Closer and closer we get to New Orleans—where I've been only once, before it was destroyed. I'll either sleep in the station tonight and explore tomorrow or splurge and get a cheap motel room... sure would feel nice to stretch out on the bed, watch a movie, find some weed somewhere perhaps, and take a hot bath—not a shower, but a *bath*—can't remember the last time I took a damn bath.

Before we pulled into the Birmingham station I got some hot water from the café car and poured it into my trusty green mug, put some ramen noodles in there and the sauce packet and ate about half of it before realizing that ramen is bad enough when it's fully cooked and ten times worse lukewarm with hard noodles. So I threw it out with a grimace and ate a cold can of beanie weenies to satisfy my hunger without spending a cent. I didn't feel like hauling out my camp stove and dealing with all the strange looks people gave when I cooked with a bottle of pressurized gas on the train; explaining what it was, that I wasn't a terrorist, I wasn't going to blow them up.

Gad, what a beat town, this Birmingham—roads dead-end into the tracks, tents set up outside of ramshackle houses for some reason, spare bedrooms perhaps, rusty schoolyards and project housing stretching blocks and blocks and blocks right by a sweet old cemetery full of dead bones and lost souls—one old man out there standing before a modest gravestone with his hands in pockets and head bowed—a split-second portrait of sorrow. Man, and this cemetery goes on for miles and miles, thousands of bones, *millions* of them. To think, a final resting place beside this ratty old rail yard and tracks cutting across the earth.

Skidmarks down the embankment of the highway where some drunk slid off the road and probably flipped his car end over end one rainy night.

Memories memories, playing out in my mind from the times I've lived, the places I've been—I'm 25 years old and I've already done so much, yet it's never enough. It doesn't take. Scary to think—how much *is* enough? But I have no memories of this place in western Alabama, beside this wide open field of muddy grass, the sun poking through the cloud layer. It's all a clean slate from here.

Hoo, just whizzed by a strange swamp with stick trees poking out, seemed to stretch for miles deep away from the tracks, up and over a draw and suddenly there is this big heavenly meadow all green with a useless cow loping away from the tracks as the train whistled and a single shaft of sunlight broke through a momentary hole in the cloud layer. Getting down into the thick Mississippi country now. I'll eat you someday cow, and for that I'm sorry.

The sky slowly reddened and caught fire as we pushed through the Mississippi towns of Meridian, Laurel, and Hattiesburg. The dining car called for dinner, but I won't be eating there—gotta hold out until tonight when I can have a hot gumbo dinner in N'Orleans.

We pressed on, with steely-eyes and blazing fury, further and further south toward the refugee city. I spent hours watching and listening to two kids ahead of me flirt with each other—one a young black FUBU kid with stiff-bill Yankees cap and baggy urban pants worn low, the other a bubble-butt chick with strange looking stiletto boots, crazy long fingernails painted bright pink and a cell phone that played Nelly whenever it rang, which was every few moments.

She answered it the same exact way each time: "Hullo? Hey, whassup Shantay." The guy drank Heineken beer and watched "I'm Gonna Git You Sucka!" on his little DVD player. He stopped the fat girl on her way back to the bathroom and said something smooth, which convinced her to sit down next to him.

Over the next three hours, I watched them get closer and closer, and eventually the guy put his arm around her shoulders and she put hers between his legs. They started smooching and whispering and then disappeared for a half-hour, coming back with clothes post-coital disheveled.

When the guy smiled, I saw his full row of golden teeth. When the girl ran her fingers through her hair, I saw the weave come detached. Little did they know I was sitting there, the eternal peeping tom, watching everything they did and writing it into immortality.

Long hours on that train. I wrote Flannigan a text message asking how he was doing; life, women, whiskey, etc.... he wrote back:

```
"Life - an unanswerable, ever-changing
frame of mind. . . women - a magnetic pull
I try to ignore. . . whiskey - a band of
brothers that beat the drum of my soul. . .
you - an unorthodox soldier. . . I - a won-
dering carpenter."
```

Only Flannigan could write something like that—probably while sitting in the bathroom at work, killing time. Flannigan, who bent his head to every task with such determination and fever, but always ended up throwing it aside to go chase after another—the quintessential A.D.D. child of the 21st century who refused to take his meds. Flannigan, who read the first 30 pages of every book and tossed it aside for the next, who thought idealism was still a good thing, who wanted to believe in something, anything, who wanted to feel, who wanted to bleed. Flannigan, who was so naïve, yet so wizened by this naïveté. Flannigan, who understood what it was to want, what it was to dream, what it was to believe in believing in something, which was really just nothing in the end. It made me smile and miss him and miss the whole lot of them back in Northsaint—my Others—collecting at the bar for nonsense conversations, playing chess at the Green House, thumbing through 75-cent shirts at the thrift store, buying packs of cigarettes and bottles of cheap booze on their way to somewhere interesting, composing poems on bar napkins, making change for customers behind the bar, searching for the lost pair of panties in the bedroom in morning-afters, sitting upside-down on couches with books in their hands, papers in their trembling, restless fingers, disease in their hearts, fire in the eyes.

I wondered if this period of time in our lives, this strange, holistic, horrific, beatific era of our defiance and expansion and searching for meaning was just a normal phase of "growing up." Does everyone goes through this? I hoped not. That would somehow cheapen what we're striving for. No, we're unique. We're different. We're just as unique and different as everyone else. We're all swimming in the same shades of grey.

I wrote him back:

Us all - happy without ever knowing the definition of the term except by its opposite.

And, as a matter of fact, I did feel strangely happy. No

reason to be. My teeth hurt, my feet stank, my back ached from sitting in that god-awful train seat for weeks, my stomach grumbled with hunger, my money running out… but I felt a purity only attainable on the *go*, in transition from one place to the next without knowing what looms ahead. Heading into the darkness with a light radiating from the eyes, into a city recently destroyed by a hurricane without knowing anyone to shelter me—completely on my own. In charge of my own destiny. What a feeling. What a world.

Then I realized I still had *two more weeks* on this ol' train and rubbed my hands together. I always had a quiet, nagging doubt festering in the back of my brain, since I'd begun. I was worried that I couldn't make it around the country in the month I had to travel. But it wasn't even February yet, and I was already making my way into New Orleans.

I smiled and realized I had nothing but *time* to do *whatever* I wanted—and I didn't ever have to spend any money on a motel room or fancy dinners if I didn't want to. I was in charge. I was in control. By god, I was happy. But something still felt amiss. The happiness didn't take.

Ah hell, there goes bubble-butt's phone again: "Hullo ? Hey whassup Tommy." So much for *that* train of thought.

These solitary street lamps illuminating the trees, casting eerie shadows, bayou shadows… we're in the swamps, all right. The lowland delta where this big muddy river empties her burden into the sea. Except the sea spat it back up and flooded everything, and I had no idea what to expect. For the first time, it dawned on me there might not even be motel rooms *available*. There are thousands of displaced people without homes, and *I'm* seeking a motel room.

Oh, but to take a long hot bath—to lay on a comfortable bed and watch the evening news, to sleep in late and walk around without this heavy load on my back.

A few seats ahead I heard a man say, "My time is entirely my own." I smiled in silent agreement.

God damn right it is.

Agh, this fucking train—we stopped again to let that damn freight congestion clear up. An hour outside of New Orleans now. Goddamn this freight congestion. If Amtrak ran on time, we'd have been there two hours ago.

I open my Dostoyevsky again and the book tears completely apart at the bindings and pages go flying everywhere. I take it as a sign and bundle the rest with a rubber band, saving the end of *The Idiot* for another day.

Hup hup, I thought we were moving there for a second, but it was only the dark train beside us—and here we go, here we go, clank clank, nudge nudge, I think we're moving now—the guitar man back there started clapping and yelling, "Let's go you bastids!" and everyone gave a little sigh of relief and harried cheer to finally be underway again. Poor bastard automobiles piled up at the crossing, about twelve deep, I wonder if they had to wait this whole time.

We reached Slidell, a small town just north of New Orleans and a man behind was talking with someone on his cell phone. I wasn't really listening until the subject turned to motels.

"Yeah, muh brother sez they's nothing open except for the big places downtown, at four hundred bucks a pop, no thanks," he said. "I dunno, I haven't been there in a few weeks, but it can't be that much better… oh yeah, the whole fucking *town* is destroyed. It's a dead city… ain't never gonna be the same."

I waited for him to finish and leaned over the back of my seat to ask about the motel situation.

"Yeah bo', there ain't shit available down there," he said matter-of-factly. "I gotta stay with muh brother and his family in their FEMA trailer."

"That can't be right," I argued. "In the whole city there's not *one* room available?"

He chuckled, "Well, they's rooms downtown at the expensive places, but who wants to pay that much?" He looked at me sideways: "You mean you headin' down there and don't have a place to *stay?* What the hail you thinkin', bo'? Hurricane ripped that sumbitch apart!"

I dismissed him as a pessimist, but prepared to sleep in the station that night if I had to. The whole trip down I hadn't really thought of the seriousness of the situation… like every naïve American, I just figured things would be cleaned up and back in business.

The closer we got to the city, however, the more damage I saw. Even in the darkness, after we crossed Lake Pontchartrain, I saw small fishing boats overturned and splintered on front lawns, billboards ragged and trailing electrical wires, cars piled on top of one another. There was debris everywhere. This was no city—this was a war zone.

For the first time of the trip, I worried.

Right then, a baby started wailing a few seats up—a piercing, shrill cry. I frowned at the two black kids necking, thinking maybe I should've found a girl on the train. Then I would have a place to stay… now I'm fucked…*figuratively*, not literally, like them.

The baby kept shrieking, destroying my nerve. How can sex be so beautiful when little shit-screamers like that come out? Thirty-six hours on that train and I'd had enough. I was fed up, ready to run off screaming. I needed fresh air, I needed a cigarette, I needed a hot meal and a bath and a moment alone. Well, I guess *need* is a relative term. I guess I didn't *need* any of those things, compared to what the refugees needed. But I sure as hell wanted them.

In the midnight darkness and dank mist of New Orleans, the train finally *screeeeed* to a halt and I ran out the door with my pack aback, lit upon the platform and ran toward the station, ready to be anywhere but that smelly train seat.

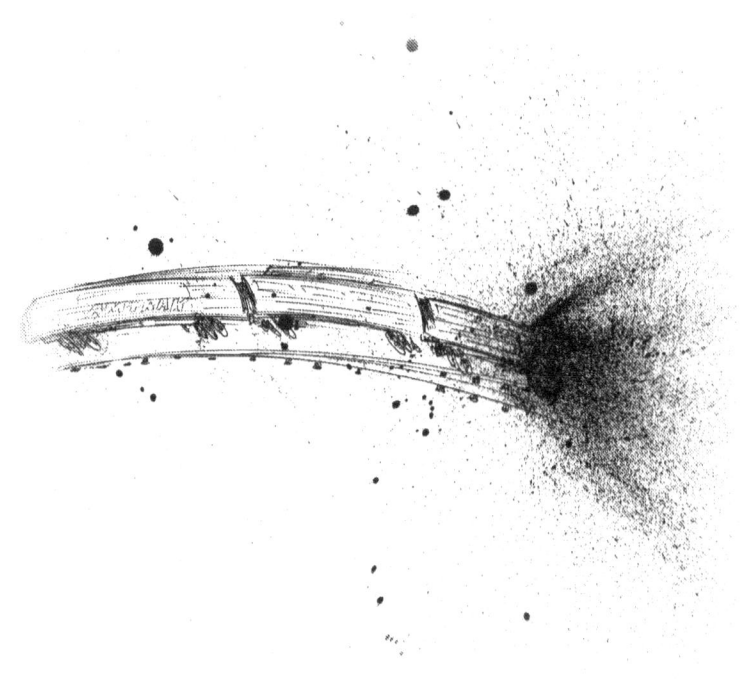

SIXTEEN

Everything fell apart when I reached the station.

It was musty and smelled of bleach. There were crying babies and poor families sitting with garbage bags full of clothes waiting for the Greyhound at the other end. Armed guards with bulletproof vests patrolled the tiled floors with heavy boots.

There was a buzz in the air—something was wrong—the vibrations told of the recent disaster. The looks on passengers' faces weren't the standard bored traveler looks... instead there was a vacancy in their sunken eyes, an emotion somehow missing from all the exhaustion. No one was smiling. No one was laughing. They had pale cheeks and nervous tics. They wanted out. And there I was, coming in for a visit.

I dropped my pack at the counter and waited five minutes for the attendant to acknowledge me.

"What can I do for you?" he snorted finally.

"I just got in from D.C. and I'm a little out of sorts," I tried to be affable. "I have a rail pass and I'd like to book a ticket to Jacksonville if I could... do you know when it—"

"Tracks are down from here to Jacksonville because of the hurricane."

"What?"

"The *hurr-i-cane*," he enunciated, like I was a simpleton. "It washed out the tracks in Mississippi— they've been down for *months*."

"But the lady in D.C. told me I could connect here into Jacksonville," I whimpered.

"Well, she was wrong."

"So what do I do now?"

"I'm sorry, I'm closing down. You'll have to wait until morning," he said. "The only way you can get to Florida is to take the Crescent back up to D.C. and then take it south through the Carolinas... it's a four-day trip."

"I just *came* that way! I spent 36 hours on that train!"

He grew impatient with me. The way people get when they're off the clock and stuck dealing with work matters, like waiters when you walk into the restaurant five minutes before closing, or DMV tellers at the stroke of their lunch break. They don't care, they've been pushing their rock all day, all week, all their miserable lives. "Fuck you!" they say with their eyes, and feel no shame or remorse for it.

"There's nothing I can do, sir," and he shut the window.

I stood motionless at the counter for a moment, my mind running through the options. Keep it together, keep it together. I lugged my gear over to the Greyhound counter. The attendant was even worse than the last.

"What do *you* want?" he growled.

"Uh, when does the Greyhound to Jacksonville leave?"

"Do you have a ticket?"

"No, I—"

"Bus is full."

I took a breath, "Okay, well, when's the next one?"

The people behind me shuffling their luggage along the floor, grumbling impatiently and clearing their throats.

"Next one leaves tomorrow at nine, but it's full too... *next!*"

"Wait! I'm not done yet!"

Someone nudged me from behind. The lobby was boiling, spilling over.

"Look, I don't have *time* for this," the attendant barked. "In case you haven't noticed, we've had a bit of a disaster here. There are passengers waiting, we got a bus leaving… now *please*, step out of line sir!"

I hauled my gear through the station again and found a bank of payphones with a board listing motels in the area. I tried every one of them and only got through to a couple. They were booked solid. New Orleans was a third world country and nobody understood my dialect.

"Ain't any motels available," a man said in passing. I whirled after him.

"You know anywhere to stay?"

"Nope," he shrugged and marched out into the night.

The only light moment came when I saw the two black kids that necked the whole way down on the train sitting with their spouses that had picked them up. Sinners. They sat right across from each other while waiting for the baggage—obviously ignoring the existence of the other.

Wellll, I thought, *guess I'm staying in the station tonight.* I'd figure out what to do tomorrow morning when the counter opened again. Sleeping in the train station wasn't so bad—a little boring and uncomfortable, but not too bad at all. Just crack open a book and listen to some music—it would be morning before I knew it.

But, suddenly, around 2 a.m., the station guards marched in and announced that everyone had to clear the building.

"Only ticketed passengers can stay!" one of the helmeted guards yelled. "C'mon, everybody out! Move!"

I sat silent on my pack, thinking I was safe with my rail pass, but one of the guards suddenly demanded to see my ticket. I showed him my pass.

"What's *this?*" he grunted.

"It's an Amtrak rail pass," I said. "I've been traveling around the—"

"It's not a *ticket.*"

"No, it's a *pass*, you use it to book the tickets—"

"Awright, you're gonna have to leave the station," he handed me back the pass.

"What? What do you mean?" I yelled. "I *have* a ticket! Here, right here!"

"That isn't a ticket. Only ticketed passengers can stay. Let's go."

I looked around and noticed everyone was watching with dull interest—I was just a minor car wreck. I was just a bum to them, just a nomad, just a hobo with a beat pack and nowhere to go. They didn't give a fuck about me.

"This is *bullshit*, you can't kick me out on the streets, the guy at the counter said I'd have to wait until the morning to book my ticket!"

"Then you'll have to come back in the morning," the guard grew impatient, grabbing my arm. "C'mon, get up, you can't stay here."

"But where am I supposed to *go?* I don't have anywhere to stay!"

"Not my problem," he said coldly. "I'm not going to ask you again."

His partner came over and stood at my flank, ready to whip out a club and beat me if necessary.

"Can you at least let me stow my pack in the lockers?" I pleaded.

"Lockers don't work, c'mon, get moving, NOW!"

"Goddamn you Fascist bastards! 'Protect and Serve' my ass!" I shook my fist at him. "You're going to make me stay on the street? There're no motel rooms available! Fucking pigs, no wonder no one trusts you!"

The second guard grabbed my other arm and they both

ushered me out the front door, pack and all. They gave me a final shove and locked the door, then continued frisking the passengers for tickets. I was on my own… stranded in the dead city.

That was the beatest night of my life.

I had no choice but to lug my 70 pounds of rucksack and gear with me, through the rubble and debris lining every street. All that talk before about me being "on my own" and "in control of my own destiny" flew right out the window. I was scared shitless and had nowhere to go.

I wandered around the salty air for a while smoking cigarettes and trying to figure out what to do. I had only been to New Orleans once before, and I was college drunk the whole time. I had no idea where anything was. The long train ride down filled me with exhaustion, but I kept moving. I wandered aimlessly down the tracks next to a chain link fence, passing the Superdome to my left and entering a deserted neighborhood with destroyed houses on every block. Sirens wailed all across town. Helicopters buzzed in the night sky, throwing spotlights down a few blocks away. Pools of fetid water shone stars for moments in passing.

At one point I sat down on my pack and cried into my hands. I stared up at the stars and prayed to a god I didn't believe in. My feet hurt, my shoulders ached and my soul came apart. I'd never felt so alone and lost in all my life. I felt it was only a matter of time before a marauding gang of looters hunted me down and stripped me of all my possessions before knifing me, ending my life before I had the chance to do anything great. All of our trappings and technologies, all of our conveniences, all of our worthless possessions—none of it mattered that night in New Orleans.

About a mile down the tracks, I came across a derelict

brick factory with high water marks along its façade and a littered gully around back. Graffiti speckled the walls, and broken bottles and used condoms were scattered about in the dirt. An upside-down boat sat on top of a house across the street.

I pulled out my camp stove and cooked a can of beans in the sad little pot, the hiss of the little gas jets sounding so lonely, so sad, so loud in the queer, quiet ghost city. I ate them slowly, starting to hate the taste of beans. But it satisfied my hunger and put a little drop of warmth in my belly. There was only a little water left in my Nalgene, so I wiped the pot and camp spoon clean with a dirty tee-shirt and packed them away meticulously.

In back of the factory I cleared a space in the piss and broken glass and laid my sad Mexican blanket in the dirt, then climbed into my sleeping bag and sighed. The old crescent moon shone down and the stars twinkled into my tired eyes. I thought of all the miles I'd covered, all the places I'd been, all the life I'd lived, and how this was the first real hang-up I'd had in two weeks. Most of all, though, I wondered how the hell I was going to get *out* of this mess.

"You're really in the shit now," I whispered to myself. "Is this what you wanted? What are you proving to yourself? Why can't you just be satisfied like everyone else? Why are you such a fucking idiot?"

Too afraid to close my eyes, I just lay there staring at the bugs and the stars circling around each other, looping crazy in the charcoal night, exhaling peaceful clouds of smoke above my head. I thought of all my friends back home, my poor mother having no idea where I was or what I was doing, my little cabin all dark and lonely in the woods. I cried for the things I took for granted every day. I cried for the darkness, the night, the earth swollen with sadness and the yearning of voices unheard. I cried because I can't seem to ever find my home. I cried because I wasn't strong enough to handle this like a man. I cried.

Throughout the night, police cruisers patrolled by with spotlights, but I was hidden well and they didn't bother me. I must've drifted off to sleep for about an hour before the sky grew light to the east—fantastic shades of crimson and orange in this pastel dawn. It brought everything through the circle, a hard, carefree peace. A solace. I felt the warmth wash over me, take away the night, take away the danger. A few lonely gulls screeched overhead in the mist and an alley cat padded by my head without taking notice. When I awoke, everything was fresh and new inside.

It all came to me in a fine flash. With dawn breaking on this world and life emerging from the decay, I sat up in my sleeping bag: I would hitchhike to Florida… it was the only way.

SEVENTEEN

I CRAWLED OUT OF THE BAG and packed my rucksack quickly; a new surge of life burning through my bones, twigs in my hair, grime on my jeans. I even started whistling. I made it through the night and had a hell of an adventure ahead of me. I'd been hitchhiking a few times in my life, but never in a foreign place such as this. This… this was all going to be something new and dangerous, like stepping out into the bloodstream of what you once believed America to be, in all those books and in all that rhetoric, and seeing if it was at all *possible*. To stick your thumb out and hitch a ride in 2006. To have faith in a humanity that has given up on itself. To believe in the inherent goodness of human nature. It was worth it to try.

The sun shot up hard and pierced the haze like a bullet. I looked around and saw, for the first time, the devastation of Katrina in daylight. Like everyone else, I'd watched the news footage and shaken my head, feeling sorrow for the people whose lives were destroyed by a gust of wind, and then turned my attention to more important things. Not until I saw it all with my own eyes did it finally register.

Palm trees sat horizontal in the streets, houses sunk at

queer angles in various states of demolition, whole car engines sat on sidewalks, stripped and junked, lying next to boats and stacks of broken wood and vinyl siding. Pools of stagnant, fetid water, women weeping, shaggy men with their heads in their hands on curbs. They all picked around the rubble like junkyard dogs… dumpster-divers searching for what used to be their lives. My god, it *was* a war zone. Seen from ground level on the way out, this city was dead.

I put my great pack aback and shouldered my daybag and laptop case, then lumbered out of the gully like a hobo down to where I-10 cut through the city. A FEMA trailer on the corner handed out bottles of water to refugees. A sad black man picked through his own personal junk pile by the street corner, searching. All of them searching.

I dug through my laptop case and found a manila envelope and Sharpie marker, wrote, "MOBILE" on the front and held it up by the on-ramp. I figured that was a good place to start. Thousands of cars rushed by in the next hour, all glancing over at me with curious, suspicious eyes. One threw a bottle, but missed.

Whenever I spotted a police cruiser, I brought down the sign and pretended to talk into my cell phone, but they just whizzed by. They didn't give a shit about hitchhikers.

At one point, a young black hoodlum cut by and said, "Shee-it, ain't nobody gonna see that little ass sign."

I looked down at it, "You don't think so?"

"Whatchoo got in dat case there? Guns?" he motioned to my computer case.

"Nah, sorry… no guns."

He walked away playing with a yo-yo.

All the faces passing by, their gaping eyes, their split-second reactions, their sarcastic sneers and timid waves, their thumbs-up and thumbs-down, their shrugs, their purposeful look away.

Then, WHAM, a black pickup truck with flames painted on the hood slammed to a dusty halt at my feet. The window rolled down.

"I'm goin' as far's Biloxi," the man yelled and I said hot damn and threw my pack in the bed. He was a middle-aged machine worker named Orlando with a dirty baseball cap and jeans caked in oil and grease. Hoo boy, as soon as I shut the door, he hit that ol' gas and we flew off in a blaze of dust and squealing tires and he balled that sumbitch all the way to Biloxi at 100 mph, banging on the dashboard and pointing out parts of New Orleans that had been washed away.

"This whole area was under ten feet'a water," he yelled, waving his arm over the wide destroyed bayou of East New Orleans with a beer in his hand. "Mostly poor people lived there—it's a goddamn ghost town now, bo'."

"Man, I never thought I'd see anything like this," I shook my head.

He looked over at me queerly, "What the hail you doin' hitchin', bo'? Dangerous out here, y'know."

I told him of my predicament at the station and he nodded his sympathy and said, "Wail shee-it, guess you gotta do what you gotta do. Why din't you jes' get a plane ticket?"

"Ah, I hate airplanes."

Twenty minutes later, he pulled off the freeway.

"I gotta stop fer 'nother drink," he explained. But when he pulled into the gas station, he banged the dashboard suddenly, "Sheee-it! I left muh wallet in muh locker, dammit!"

"That's all right, I'll buy you a drink," I said. "Least I can do for the ride."

I bought him a beer—it wasn't even noon yet. I bought myself one too and we sipped our way down the road.

He told stories the whole 100 miles, mostly about getting drunk and the best strip clubs around. I told him about my trip and he seemed mildly interested, but I could tell he wanted to talk about himself, which was fine with me.

"Lissen to this," he motioned to his phone. "Muh ex-wife jes' sent me a text message an' asked if I'd come over an' fix her damn sink, so I sends her back: 'fuck you whore, fix it yerself'." He belly-laughed and spilled his beer.

I asked him why he picked me up and he said, "Wallll, you looked pretty normal an' all," as he took another swig of beer and passed a handful of trucks at 110 mph. "Besides, I gotta .45 under the seat."

Before I knew it he was coming up on Biloxi like a charging bull and slowing to let me out on the freeway.

"There's a truck stop somewhere up ahead here," he pointed. "You shouldn't have any trouble getting' a ride, jes' stick on 10 and keep a sharp eye fer queers."

"Thanks a lot for the ride, man," I gathered my stuff and shook his rough, callused hand.

"Shore, shore, jes' be careful out there," he nodded slowly. "Lotta weirdoes 'round here. Have a good rest of your trip, god bless, and don't do anything I wouldn't do, which isn't a hell of a lot, haw haw haw!"

He said so long and peeled out in the same cloud of dust he met me with—god's own soldier of speed.

I hoisted up my bag with a grunt and trudged down the ditch by the freeway, and climbed up a small embankment to an adjoining road. The nearest access back to I-10 was up a frontage road about a half mile, so I spat on the old pavement and made my way for it, bound to get there one way or another. Grasshoppers clapped wings in the dusty weeds by the freeway, fat, lumpy clouds sailed lethargically across the sky… oh road, I'm in love with you and the rocks I kick on your shoulders. I love your smell, your grains, your purpose.

Onto the littered on-ramp, dumped my pack down for just a moment, and didn't barely have time to put my sign out before a silver PT Cruiser suddenly stopped 50 feet ahead.

I grabbed the bags and whoopeed up to the car. A Bulgarian man leaned his head out and yelled, "I can take you to Pensacola, hop in."

John was his name and he was hitting all the boatyards looking for work, "I have to get off this next exit after the bridge up here to see about a job, so I drop you off and if you're still there, I come back and getcha."

I didn't mind—a ride is a ride—so we cruised down the road talking about sailboats. He just bought a 26-footer in Biloxi for 711 bucks and he was planning to live on it with his 7-year-old son. His idea was to build boats for a spell while his kid finished the year in school, then head down to Florida to live on the boat and build a bigger one.

"I just bought plans to build a 62-foot custom design for 200 bucks and they regularly sell for 600—but I want to have some practical experience before I build it, so that's why I'm checking on these jobs," he explained. "After that damn hurricane, there's lotsa work on this Gulf Coast."

And just as quick as that, he pulled off and left me at the exit. He tore away before I realized I'd left my sign in his car. Damn. I rummaged through the pack for another piece of paper and just finished writing "FLA" on there when he came buzzing back.

"They were building Navy boats there—I don't wanna get mixed up with any *war* business," he grumbled. I hopped back inside and we resumed the conversation about sailboats.

"I tell ya, there's something about the idea of owning your own boat," he said with eyes looking out on the horizon. "Just take off whenever you get bored of this stuff, just sail off into the ocean and don't ever gotta come back if you don't want to. *That's* what freedom is, that's what this America is supposed to be, don't you think? That's why *I* moved here."

"Sure," I nodded. "That's the ultimate freedom; living on a sailboat. Y'know, I went sailing one time in the British

Virgin Islands. I fell in love with a girl…she's getting married now."

The words came out before I'd realized it. But, who the hell cares? I'd never see this man again. I could say whatever the hell I wanted.

"Well, you probably fell in love with the sailing life, and she just happened to be the one you associate it with," he said. What a wise thing to say.

We drove awhile longer, ten miles up to a road leading to Bayou LaBatrie, where he let me off again and said he had to check on another job. Same deal as last time.

I grabbed the sign this time and propped it against my pack while rolling a cigarette. I felt enormously good, enjoying the simple pleasure of rolling my own cigarette by the side of the road in the midday sun, some other state, some other world, no direction but forward. I was hitchhiking my way through southern Alabama, of all places, just cruising and seeing and sighing and smiling. This is what They were all talking about.

After twenty minutes, a battered Jeep Cherokee rattled to a stop on the shoulder and the goateed driver leaned out the window over his chubby pig-tailed wife.

"You got any drugs or guns?" he yelled.

I said I didn't and he harrumphed, "*All* right, *hold* on a second," and huffed out of the car, dove into the trunk to clear off the backseat. It was full of bags and spare tires and garbage and even an old blind mutt named Buddy. This whole process took about five minutes.

He finally pulled the backseat forward and thumbed for me to hop in.

"How long you been standing there?" he asked, looking at me in the rear-view. I could barely hear him over the wild air rushing in from his broken driver's side window.

"Not long," I yelled back. "About half an hour," and I told them about my trek from New Orleans and why I was hitchhiking.

They were A.J. and Stella—hurricane refugees relocated to Pensacola. They told me all about evacuating and losing their home, moving what possessions they had to a small house that smelled like cat piss and salt. Luckily, they were out of town when the hurricane hit. They've spent the better part of three months salvaging their flooded house and finding a new place in Pensacola, trying to start over their lives.

"But there's nothing to *do* in Pensacola," A.J. grumbled.

The conversation died and Buddy nuzzled his snout under my hand, sighing deliciously when I scratched behind his ears.

"You can swat 'im if you get tired of him sitting on your knee," Stella shouted.

"No, I don't mind at all," I yelled. "I love dogs. Sometimes they're a lot more intelligent than half the people you meet."

"Hey, sorry about that drugs n' guns stuff," A.J. said finally. "You can never be too careful, y'know?"

"No problem."

Stella asked if I had any rolling papers, which I did, and she rolled up a couple joints with them.

"I've got this bag of dirt-weed I been meaning to roll up," she said. "It's not very good, but it'll get you high. Might as well give it to you."

We passed around the J and the sun grew golden in the Gulf sky. When I told Stella I was a writer, she turned around suddenly and told me she used to write for *High Times* magazine, and asked where I had been published. I suddenly felt ridiculous with my piles of gibberish writing lying unread and unpublished back home in the cabin, so I lied and told her I'd written for some weeklies in Seattle and Portland. She nodded her approval.

I don't know why I lied. Sometimes they just pop out, and before you can stop yourself, the deed is done and you must follow through with it. I was only a writer because I *called* myself a writer—I hadn't earned any right to use that title yet... so I lied to cover up my own shame and failure.

They were both sweet people who said they picked up every hitchhiker on the road.

"We both used to hitch a lot when we were younger," Stella told me. "But man, we get some characters sometimes."

She turned to A.J. and elbowed him in the ribs, "Remember that one guy in Mobile who kept saying he wanted to live in a tent on the water? That crazy old guy?" She leaned back to me, passing the joint. "He kept saying he wanted to build a raft of logs and put a tent on top, and live on a river somewhere, or something like that."

"No, he said he wanted to float down the Mississippi in his tent, like Huck Finn," A.J. corrected her.

"Oh yeah, that's it," she laughed. "Gad, what a crazy old coot! He was hilarious. We even gave him ten bucks because he was so damn entertaining."

"And what about that blond kid with the squirrel?" A.J. drummed his fingers on the wheel. "This blond kid said he was heading to Miami to find his pet squirrel that ran away... what a fuckin' kid!"

We all laughed and I scratched ol' Buddy's ears again, glad to be moving down the road with these strangers, making it closer and closer to Jacksonville, gettin' there man.

"What you heading to Florida for?" Stella asked.

"I'm gonna stop and hang out with an old friend that lives near Tampa. He's taking me fishing if the weather holds up, and I kinda just want to lay on the beach and do nothing for a few days."

"I guess I'll make my way west from there," I continued, "Probably stop in on another friend in Texas and eventually make it to L.A., then up the coast back home... I kinda wanted to hit the four corners of the country on this trip, y'know? Seattle, New York, Florida, L.A."

"Hell, you don't gotta explain it to us," A.J. said. "We know exactly why you're out here—same reason we liked to do it too—those that pick you up usually always hitched themselves. There's something you feel hitchin' that you just can't get anywhere else. Just keep an eye out for weirdoes."

They let me off at a gas station outside of Pensacola and we said our so long's and see ya's. I trudged back over to the road and started to cross, feeling something was missing, then noticed it was my *hat*, my lucky beat sweat-stained pork-pie hat that has followed me around this earth for so many years, and I clutched in the air where the bill would normally have been, yargh, where's me hat?

I dropped my pack in the ditch and sprinted back to the station just as they were pulling into traffic.

"Stop! Stop! Hey, *stop!*" I waved my arms in the air. They finally saw me and pulled over. I ran up to the car and doubled over panting.

"What is it?" Stella poked her head out the window.

"My hat!" I gasped. "I forgot me hat... *my* hat."

They fished it out and handed it to me, and I breathed a sigh of relief—don't know what I'd do if I lost that old hat. I trudged back over to my pack.

Across the street and over toward the on-ramp heading east. It was growing dark, and I knew the likelihood of a ride grew slim with the fading light. The tight pinch that reaches you when you realize you must get that last good ride, and get it *soon*.

Along the way I passed a strange bum on the side of the road. We met in the ditch and he ambled over and hooked a thumb in his belt to talk. He had nothing with him except a handkerchief tied in a bundle in his hand. The cars buzzed all around us.

"Where ya headed?" he called over.

"Jacksonville." He scratched his ratty beard and measured my response.

"Wellll, I 'spect you should head on down to Donnersberg," or some such place, "they got some kinda rainbow festival or sumpthin'... what you *do* is, see, you take 98 to 85 and head north 'bout ten miles or so," and so on, telling me directions that I couldn't possibly remember. He was all hung-up on that town because they were having a big chili feed and were handing out free bowls to vagrants.

It was that moment I realized, quite suddenly, that he wasn't panhandling or asking for food or trying to get something out of me. He was sharing road wisdom with a fellow hobo. He thought I was a drifter, like him, and I guess I *was*.

My whole life I'd lived under the guise of American respectability; wearing clean clothes and eating in nice restaurants, discussing gas prices, sleeping warm and contented in soft sheets and comfortable beds, punching clocks, not questioning the things that need to be questioned, passing myself off as just another productive member of society. But always, deep inside, I never fit. I was always a jagged edge. I felt like a hobo that somebody had given a few bucks to shower up and look respectable. Behind my mask, all I wanted to do was squat in dirty alleys and cook beans over a fire, to sit on street corners and watch people walk by, to put up a sign and throw out a thumb, take me to the next town, always the next town. I wasn't built to deal with bank accounts and insurance bills and "free movie Friday" at the video store. Something was missing in the chemical make-up.

All during the voyage, I had subconsciously tried to pass myself off as a drifter, a hobo, a bum with my ragged beard and sorry pack. I felt it important to get back to roots that never formed. But not until that moment, on the triangle of grass between the boulevard and the on-ramp to I-10 outside of Pensacola did I finally achieve my true position in life. I *was* just a bum, like this man here. I may have been born in a better hospital and raised by better parents, but sometimes you can't take the nature out of the man. He didn't question it. He smelt his own. I felt more accepted than I ever had. This strange man saw something in me I'd wanted the entire world to see.

The moment passed like a sigh in an elevator.

"Well, think I'll try to scare up sum grub here t'night and put muh sign out tomorra… man, shore wish I could git *drunk* t'night," he scratched his withered beer belly.

I contemplated giving him my bottle of Wild Turkey for a moment, but decided against it and bid him fare thee well. Something told me I was going to need whiskey later.

"Y'ain't gonna git a ride t'night," he called after me. "Might's well find a good place to sleep, bo'."

"Ah, we'll see, eh?" I called back. "Take care of yourself, all right?"

He just scratched his beard and continued on to wherever he was headed, muttering and shaking that old head.

After ten minutes of thumbing, a pickup stopped about a hundred feet up and started reversing. I ran up to meet him and he opened the door, a golly-gee happy old bald guy with enormous bull head and sad grey eyes set far apart on his face, lending him a look of simplicity.

"Pile on in here, pardner, I'm going up the road a ways."

"How far you going?" I asked eagerly.

"Oh, a ways," he said.

His name was Chester and he was a cheerful old guy that kept saying, "I always pick a guy up, y'know? Gotta hep each other out, y'know? I used ta be homeless, y'know, fer 'bout two years, and you know *what?* I really *loved* it, just travelin' 'round at yer own speed, not carin' 'bout a thing."

I asked him what he was doing now. He said he was

a janitor at a hotel. He was very interested in my rucksack and my travels, and, when I told him about my trip around America, he looked over at me with a glad look in his eyes. A look that people get when they're running through the golden memories—when they think of something they wish they could've held onto, but lost somewhere along the way.

"I'd prolly be out there travelin' 'round like you if I didn't have a wife an' kid now," he sighed. "Do it while you can."

I couldn't argue with that, but shit, we only got about five miles down the freeway before he turned and said, "Welp, this's my exit here," and pulled over to let me out. We hadn't even made it out of Pensacola yet. I hopped out and thanked him for the ride, now stranded on the whizzing, bustling, dark road with the nearest on-ramp a mile away through a series of ditches and culverts. Why the hell did he pick me up if he knew he was only going a couple miles?

It was getting dark. I harrumphed and trudged down to the on-ramp. Along the way, I stepped on a god-awful railroad tack of some kind that went clear through my shoe and into the bottom of my foot. I yowled and pulled the bugger out, then limped over to the on-ramp.

Nobody stopped for me, of course. It was pitch black and people couldn't even read my sign, let alone get a read on who they were picking up. Hitchhiking is a game of first impressions; you only get about a second to give someone the impulse to stop. At night, nobody wants to stop for anyone—darkness is evil and only evil comes out in darkness.

Stuck… standing there by the freeway smoking butts for hours, the air growing cold, my foot hurting from the tack and my back sore from all the bent head trudging. There was only one clear choice remaining.

I trudged two miles back to the outskirts of Pensacola and checked in at a roadside dive. It was cheap and dirty, just how I liked it. Right away, I walked across the street to buy a few beers at the 76 station and was accosted by two thugs.

"You got two dollas?" the taller one demanded. I said I didn't and his shorter friend snorted.

"The hell you mean you ain't got two dollas?" he stared. "You the Man, right? You the Man, ain't ya? You the Man. Shee-it, ain't even got two dollas. You the Man, right?"

I ducked into the station and hid in the bathroom for a minute, then bought the beer and crept out of the store.

They'd moved along. I lugged my six-pack back into the room and sat on the balcony all night staring up at the stars with a fine breeze in my face, the bottles emptying slowly.

"This is what it's all about," I whispered to the night. "I never knew... I *never* knew."

EIGHTEEN

I WOKE UP LATE and hiked back to the on-ramp outside of Pensacola after a small breakfast of chicken noodle soup and saltine crackers bought from the 76 station. My sad pile of cigarette butts were still lying in the dirt where I'd struck out the night before. Two drifters had a sign out on the ramp leading west, but no one stopped for them either.

It was around eleven when a white Ford pickup with construction lights finally stopped. I threw my gear in the back and climbed in the cab.

The man offered his paw, "How you, pardner?"

"I'm good, thanks for the ride," I shook it. "I'm Max."

"Howdy Max, I'm Dan."

Dan was a 300-pound Georgia good ol' boy who worked as a road construction supervisor. He drove back and forth through Florida, checking on his road crews placed all over I-10. He had a sickly bald head and bushy blond mustache like Wyatt Earp, and he clicked his teeth and chewed hard candy the whole time he wasn't smoking cigarettes. His fleshy cheeks were covered in burst blood vessels. He said he picked me up because he was tired of driving by himself and wanted someone to talk to.

"That's just it, Max," he clicked his teeth. "I get god-awful lonely out here, y'know? Nice to have someone to chew the cud with on these long drives."

We discussed the work he'd done after the hurricane, the impact it had on the area, how many days a week he spent on the road, and how many times he'd passed certain landmarks in the past month. Dan was pretty vague about how far he was going, but he said he'd get me "close to Jacksonville."

"Boy, you ain't like any hitchhiker I ever picked up b'fore," he chuckled when I pulled out my bag of Tops to roll a cigarette.

"How do you mean?"

"Wail, fer one, ya got y'own cigarettes. Most times I gotta give 'em my *own*. And another is you seem to be an in-*tel*-ligent person. Like you said, y'ain't hitchin' because you got no other choice, but more fer the *experience*."

"That's what I'm all about," I beamed with pride.

We chatted on amiably about places we'd been, things we'd done. Dan informed me it was tough being a Southerner and open to new ideas and experiences.

"They's so many people all hung-up in they close-minded worlds down here, Max," he said. "Specially in the South."

"Oh, I agree completely. If people would just open themselves up to new experiences every once in a while, I think we'd all be the wiser for it."

"Boy you hit the nail on'na head there," he said quickly. He popped in a hard candy and sucked on it aggressively.

"I had a friend named Robby from high school that I lost contact with for a number of years," he said. "An' one day outta the blue he calls up and sez he wants me to come visit him in South Dakota. He's just split up with his wife an' needed an old friend to talk to, see, so I booked a ticket and went on up there in the dead'a winter few years back."

"When I get there, they's nothin' to *do*," he spread his

fingers out on the wheel. "Big snowstorm blowin' through, cain't see a thing, *T.V.* didn't even work. Mostly we just sat around his old trailer talkin' 'bout the good old days and shit like that. Then, one night after we'd put away a case of beer 'tween us, he looks me inna eye and sez to me, 'Dan, I gots somethin' to tell ya,' and that sumbitch tells me he's gay. You believe that? Right outta nowhere, I tell ya."

The hairs on the back of my neck. They tell me instantly what's going on... he was *getting* to something. He was buttering me up—all that "close-minded" talk and "experience" bullshit... he was playing redneck chess with me, but I saw all of his next moves.

"So he tells me, 'Dan, I'd really like to do somethin' I always wanted to do since we were kids,' and I sez, 'What's that Robby?' and he sez, 'I'd like to give you a blowjob.'"

Ah shit, I thought. I sat quietly, listening to his story and trying to not seem too interested.

"I never did nothing like that b'fore," he continued. "But I decided, hail, if this is somethin' that's gonna help ol' Robby out, I'll go ahead and let 'im do it. And y'know what? It was the best durn blowjob I ever had."

He looked over to judge my reaction, but I just stared out the window, my mind going over the exits from this situation. How the fuck did *this* just happen? One minute I'm out there on the side of the road feeling good about it all, and now this guy... shit.

Then he hit me with it. His tone suggested he was merely asking a waiter what his daily specials were: "Saaaay, you ever let another man suck yer dick?"

"Aaah, no-o," I said nervously. "Never was interested in that, y'know."

"Wail, why not?"

"Um, well, because I'm not gay," I said. "I'm not attracted to men."

He banged his fist on the steering wheel, "It's not about

bein' *queer*, dammit, it's about tryin' new *things*. Ya said yer-self it's important to try new things every once in a while, right?"

"Well, *yeah*," I stammered. "But I was talking about hitchhiking and traveling and stuff—"

"Is it any *different?*" he asked.

And I knew he was right. I walked right into his trap. The bastard tricked me. Fuck.

"Look," I told him finally. "I *love* women." I was completely lost for words.

"Boy, I tell you what, you ever letta 'nother man suck yer peener, you'll never go back to women. They shore know what to do. It's just lips, when you think about it. Lips is lips, tha's all."

I tried to change the subject back to traveling, but he kept bringing it up, getting more aggressive each time. We were moving down a fairly desolate section of freeway west of Tallahassee, so I didn't necessarily want to get out and start hiking, but at the same time, if Dan didn't stop with his propositions, I didn't see any other choice. I had to stall him.

"Boy, they's this one hitchhiker I picked up a while back," he lit up a long cigarette. "Said he wanted to be some kinda porn star or somethin' like that, and I sez, 'Wail, how big's yer peener?' and he whips that ol' sumbitch out and got *damn*, I'd be a liar if I didn't tell ya it wadn't the size of a Pringles can." He chuckled and rolled his fingers and thumb around to indicate the girth.

We passed a sign for a rest area and he said, "I wanna show you this rest area up ahead here." I started to protest, but he looked over and grinned, "Relax, I jes' wanna show you the view from the parking lot. It looks down on the Choctawhatchee River. Great fishin' in there."

He drove through slowly, scanning around the parking area (maybe for cops), then got back on the freeway. Tension hung tight in the air as we moved down the road, each calculating the other. He got to sucking on a hard candy and formulating his words. Sure enough, he started in again.

"Y'know, even though I let a lot of guys go down on me, I never have done it muhself. And I tell you what, I 'spect if I did it'd prolly be with someone like *you*."

"What?" I sighed.

"Wail, you seem ta be a pretty clean person, prolly wash an' take care of yerself down there, an' I wouldn't have to worry about doin' a good job or ever seein' you again. In fact, you get the hankerin' suddenly, you just let me know an' we can pull off on the shoulder an' I'll go to town. These construction lights are good for that kinda shit, nobody ever bothers a construction truck with yella lights flashin'. I pull off all the time to whack muh pud right there on'na shoulder, or have hitchhikers do it for me."

"So?" he leered. "Whaddaya think?" His knee bobbed up and down, his fingers drummed the steering wheel, and the hard candy was thrown around inside his puffy cheeks while I put together what it was I said to him.

Finally, I turned and stared right at him. "Dan, you seem like a real nice guy and everything, and I appreciate the lift, but there's no way in *hell* I'm gonna let you anywhere near me. I'm *not* gay, I'm *not* attracted to men, and even if I *was*, it wouldn't be with some stranger on the road who gets blowjobs from random hitchhikers. I mean, what the fuck, man? You ask me again, I'm gonna get out and walk the rest of the way. God dammit!"

That shut him up for about an hour. We passed through Tallahassee in awkward silence and pressed further east as the sun dipped into mid-afternoon.

But about fifty miles west of Jacksonville, he suddenly pulled into a rest area and looked around again.

"What are you doing?" I asked him suspiciously.

"Oh, jes' thought I'd take a stretch, y'know," he said kindly. I got out and stood nervously near my pack, debating whether I should just try my luck with another ride or see if I can make it the rest of the way into Jacksonville with Dan. He didn't seem particularly dangerous, but still, there was definitely something weird about him.

He got back in the truck and leaned out the window, "You comin'?"

"Yeah," I wavered, then got back in the truck.

It was fine for another couple miles, through the Florida pines before he grew fidgety and clicked his teeth again.

"Got dammit, Max, I can't hep it… you know when you wanna say somethin', but you don't know if it's right to say?"

"Then don't say it," I said through clenched teeth.

"I can't hep it," he whined. "I really got muh goat up now. What if I tol' you I'd take you all the way into Jacksonville an' dropped you off right at the train station an' everything? Would you wanna—?"

"NO, goddammit!" I yelled. "*Fuck!* Pull over here, I'll *walk* the rest of the way. I can't *take* any more of this shit."

"No, c'mon, you don't—"

"Pull this goddamn truck over now," I pounded the dashboard. "I want *out* of here."

He sighed and pulled over on the side of the freeway. There was no sign of a town or anything for miles—just a clean horizon and a hot sun—but I didn't care.

"Shore you won't change yer mind?" he asked.

I slammed the door in his face and grabbed my rucksack out of the back. He pulled away finally with a toot on the horn and I was left with myself on that lonesome highway. I felt sorry for him immediately. Poor man was just lonely, like all of us.

I stuck my thumb out and started walking, the sun hot on my back, five miles down to the next intersection where Highway 301 intersected with I-10. So much for all that nonsense about hitchhiking being quixotic and pure.

NINETEEN

IT WAS A TOUGH STRETCH in the hot sun. No one picked me up, of course. The freeway was void of any exits or on-ramps for a long time… only a dusty ditch filled with mounds of litter and broken glass. Some bird of the swamp sung out *cheema-la-seema-la?* in that woeful way they do. Weird droning insects buzzed by drunkenly.

By the time I reached the first intersection, I was a sweaty mess. But my mood improved quickly; there were several truck stops at this exit. It wouldn't be long before *someone* gave me a lift the thirty miles or so into Jacksonville.

The Flying-J Travel Plaza was loud and busy, full of grumbling semi trucks and air brakes and intercoms announcing shower stalls that were ready inside. I set my pack down outside and leaned against the wall. Sure enough, there was an open wireless signal to pirate. Funny how you can go from hitchhiking through a swamp to checking your email. I must've looked strange to the customers coming inside to pay for fuel, purchase Mountain Dew and Twinkies and beef jerky—a scrubby hitchhiker with a $2,000 Apple laptop.

Jack had sent an email asking how the trip was going, If I'd been killed yet, etc. I told him about Dan the road queer and all the rest. He probably didn't believe anything:

> "Hoo boy! Did I ever have some shit happen
> to me in New Orleans. I got stranded and
> had to hitchhike into Florida and just had
> to escape from a 300-pound Georgia queer
> who kept asking if he could suck my dick."

I imagined ol' Jack sitting in the Corner Booth holding court with the Others, the booze-shitters, regaling them with the stories while they banged the table in disbelief and hooted with laughter. The quick vision of home, of Northsaint by the frozen lake… quick pangs of emotion… and I wished I could share these sensations with them completely, with Jack and Flannigan and the Others, but I'm just alone out here, telling stories.

A moment later, his reply came:

> "Jesus, man! What in the holy hell are you
> doing messing around with southern homos?
> I'm in the office now, in my ratty corner
> drinking a stale bottle of wine and trying
> to find something to put in the paper – and
> you send me this shit. Christ. Now I won't
> get anything done. Keep yr chastity."

I sat for a while in the shade smoking and watching clouds—it was a long stretch. I still had lots of daylight. Besides, truck stops have always fascinated me for some reason. All the people, all the transitory moments. They're designed as resting places, where you can hang out as long as you want and no one thinks twice. But they're also designed as quick stops where you can buy everything you need and go.

The truckers ambled up to the fuel desk with Leathermans attached to their belts, carrying huge jugs of Pepsi and grunting hellos at their brethren. Mexican families piled out of rusty cars at the pumps. College kids bought cigarettes, told loud stories and zoomed away in sleek sedans bumping rap music and packing them on the heels of their palms. A soldier in uniform carried his giggling girlfriend into the store with a cast on her foot. Drifters pecked about the parking lot, searching for spare change and hitting passersby for wine money. I watched them all, every one. I study their faces, their habits. I am the quintessential shit fly on this highway wall, recording these men and women into notebooks, burning images into my brain, trying to make sense out of them. They're all different, but somehow all the *same*.

Weekend tourists in pastel polo shirts get out of shiny cars and slam the doors—*flump flump*—swipe credit cards and put gas nozzles into the tank—*ruttley-kink*—fill 'er up, top 'er off, tighten the cap, back into the car—*flump flump*—start up the engine and speed off with blinkers blinking, radios blaring, seatbelts clicking, hands at 10 and 2… off to consume, off to consume. I never saw their faces.

I brought out my camp stove, fished around in the bottom of the pack and found one last can of beans, cooked them up and ate luxuriously. Then I rolled up another halfdozen cigarettes and placed them in the pouch, folded my handkerchief into my back pocket, hoisted my pack aback and hoofed over to the on-ramp whistling.

Hours rolled by. The sun dipped toward the west. No one stopped for my sign—now with "JAX" written on the front. A whole heaping shit ton of big rigs cut by, the drivers all banging the shifters into gear at precisely the same moment and drinking coffees and fountain drinks and lighting cigarettes in passing. Some actually met eyes with me—say one out of five—but the rest just passed by invisible and unhurried, not allowing me into their bubble.

They carried everything imaginable; lumber, cattle, farm equipment, polka-dot Wonder Bread, flammable gases, bulldozers, shiny new cars stacked atop of one another—a never-ending stream of goods and industry. Two college hippies passed by in an old Volvo and hesitated for a moment, but kept driving once they saw me up close. I must've been an ugly sight in my sweaty hat, snap-button thrift store shirt with tears at the pockets and cigarette burns, grimy jeans and flapping shoes.

The light was fading. I dragged my albatross of gear back over to the truck stop and stuck my sign out there. The big rigs continued to pass by, releasing air brakes and spitting throaty exhaust in their wakes.

"You need a shower?" a leathery old woman yelled from a van parked by the grumbling trucks. She was sitting on an old burned-out lawn chair, drinking canned beer and scratching her ass. Her husband was in the driver's seat snoring at the sun. They looked *settled in*, like they'd lived at that truck stop for years.

"Uhh, no, actually I need a ride into Jacksonville," I yelled over to her.

"Oh, well, I got a free shower coupon if you need one. Worth six dollars."

"No thanks," I waved her off.

On the way back to the on-ramp for another try, I saw a charter bus marked "Amtrak." I jumped and waved at the driver with my rail pass in my hand, "Stop! Stop! I have a ticket! *Stop*, you asshole!" But he just kept barreling along.

Before long it was dark and I still didn't have my ride. I walked back to the truck stop and bought a Coke, drinking it slowly and savoring the bite of caffeine in my throat. The gas station clerk eyed me curiously, and the janitor asked me to lift up my feet so she could mop the floor with bleach. I briefly considered mixing some ammonia in with the bleach and trying to get a lift by ambulance.

"You waiting for somebody?" the clerk asked.

"Ah, kind of," I said. "I'm trying to get into Jacksonville

to catch up with my train."

I told her about New Orleans and my hitchhiking journey, leaving the part about Dan *out*, of course.

"Well, why don'tcha ask some of these truckers for a lift, hon?" she said. "I'm sure they wouldn't mind taking you into town—it's only thirty miles."

So I bummed around the noisy din of the diesel pumps and approached every trucker with the following greeting: "Excuse me, sir? You wouldn't happen to be heading into Jacksonville, would you?" and they all barked, "Nope, sorry," and went about washing their windshields and checking air in their tires.

Time dragged by. The sun went down, the air grew cold and lights flickered and caught and shined their lonesome arcs across the parking lot. Flying pests crackled in the bug zapper hung near the front door. At midnight, as I sat on my pack in the cold, head in my hands, I thought of how ridiculous this was. I was so damn *close* to Jacksonville, but I was all hung-up at this damn truck stop. But there was no way I would be able to hike thirty miles with all this gear—especially in the middle of the night on the freeway.

Inside the store, through the cracked windowpane, I stared at a bauble on the shelf for hours—it was a tiny angel with motorized wings that flapped back and forth. It was in a back corner on a dusty shelf. Just a trinket nobody ever bought or looked at. It just sat there flapping those wings for eternity on the highway.

I thought of how much worse this situation would be if I didn't have any money. As a side thought, I called the bank to check my account balance, thinking that maybe I could spare a little cash to call a cab if nothing materialized soon.

"You have… forty-*one* dollars," the mechanical voice droned dispassionately.

"What!" I screamed. "What! What! *NOOOO*, that can't be *right!*"

I tried again, the terror creeping up my spine, but I got the same answer. Forty-one dollars. Forty-one fucking dollars. I thought I had at *least* a couple hundred left.

SHIT!

I pulled out my smelly ol' wallet and found $60 in cash.

FUCK!

In a heartbeat, the gravity of my situation became painfully apparent. I was stranded at a truck stop at midnight in a town 3,000 miles away from home with only $101 left to get me home and to live on thereafter. All my plans fell apart—I wouldn't travel west through Texas to see my buddy Nate. I wouldn't stop in Arizona to see my mother at her desert home. I wouldn't stop in L.A., wouldn't take the coast up, wouldn't' eat any more hot meals or drink anything but water from here on out. Everything just vanished—replaced by the urgent need to get home. To get *anywhere* except for this nomad's road.

Reality had caught up to me.

All that hoping to be a bum, that romantic nonsense about being free and loose in the world... now I was *really* out of money, out of options... now I had to face the demons.

Where could I have possibly spent it all? In the bars of Chicago? New York? All those bags of rolling tobacco and burritos and six-packs and bottles of Coke in vending machines caught up to me. Unfortunately, this isn't the first time I've run out of money on the road. It seems to happen just about every time I go anywhere. But goddammit, I was hoping this trip would be different—that I could just not worry about the almighty dollar for once, that I wouldn't be controlled by it. I went on this trip to escape these bad habits, these trappings of money… I wanted to live pure—but here I was again, right back where I'd been too many times before; stuck, broke, forced to figure a way out.

The truckers kept shooing me away and my mind kept dwelling on money… evil fucking money. Somehow I'd have to pay my rent in two weeks, my phone bill, my car insurance. Even if I did get back to Northsaint before going completely broke, what then? What was waiting for me? I'd just have to borrow some cash and go right back down to L.A. to work another goddamn T.V. commercial. The cycle repeats itself.

Ah me, why is it like this? When will the break come? This life is wearing me down, dragging everything out of me—always being on the edge like this, teetering back and forth between poverty and motion, always three steps ahead of the ghost and not caring about the long fall down until I slip and hang from broken fingertips. Dealing with consequences after the fact, instead of planning ahead. I'm just not built that way—to save money and plan for the future. Is it the curse of my generation—the Curse of the Non-Generation? Will we ever figure it out? Or is it just me and my inability to do anything right?

The only thing left to do was to get to Jacksonville and figure out what came next. I could continue down to visit Ed near Tampa and go fishing and sailing for a few days, then make the long trip back, or cut my losses and head directly home. But the key was to make it to the train station—worry about the rest later. Just get my ass out of this lonesome truck stop.

Long agonizing hours there at the Flying-J, the angel's wings from Taiwan now mocking me, flapping and laughing and taunting. I pulled out one of the books in my pack and wrote a little poem inside the front cover:

MIDNIGHT LONELY TRUCK STOP POSEDIAN NITE.
INVISIBLE. $41 IN MY POCKET AND 3,000 MILES
TIL HOME. THROATY DIESEL SPIT & ANGEL'S
WINGS INSIDE THE BROKEN WINDOW. RUCKSACK
SEAT. SHIVERING FLORIDA WINTER COLD. 32
MILES TIL THE NEXT STATION — 60 POUNDS TO TOW.
7 PIECES OF KNEE CAP MELDED INTO ONE.
ONE.
DRIPPING RAIN GUTTER SPOUT. CIGARETTE BUTTS
FLOATING IN INDIGO SPIT OF INTERSTATE MOTION.
WHERE YOU GOIN'? ROOM FOR ONE MORE?
HUNG UP.
NEON S MISSING FROM YELLOW WAFFLE HOUSE SIGN.
WAITING FOR A RIDE — SORE ARM, SORE THUMB.
WHERE IS MY HOME?
RUCKSACK REVOLUTION 50 YEARS TOO LATE.
MELANCHOLY OF SO FAR GONE WITH MILES & MILES TO GO.
GONE LIKE A SIGH IN THE WIND
A LIGHT UPON THE ISOLATE EARTH AND
FALL FREE INTO THE ETHER...

With all that darkness, all that hunger, all that unknown staring down at me, I wrote a *poem*, and a *bad* poem at that. I slammed the book shut and hid my face in my hands.

All my words dripping into the apathetic void. All my attempts. All my yearning. Nobody cares. All my life I've been searching, running, festering... restless and weary and all torn-up inside because I couldn't get there fast enough. And so has everyone else, and maybe all of our efforts are just canceling the others out. Maybe we're stymied. Maybe this is as good as it gets. Maybe a truck stop morning is the death knell of this lifestyle I thought I'd mastered. Maybe the pursuit of this truth has created only lies inside of me.

All I ever wanted was to feel this freedom we're supposed to have here in America. I wanted to believe in what those people clap for when the president speaks borrowed words and tired slogans. All I ever felt was the great American Knot bunching tighter and tighter around my neck, squeezing the life right out of me, day by day. Conform, accept, turn-over. I'm an ex-patriot living inside these American walls, too dumb to escape completely.

Finally, around 1:30 a.m., I saw a barrel-shaped, jeans-wearing trucker ambling up to the fuel desk. He caught my eye and nodded.

"Hey man," I said doggedly. "You wouldn't happen to be heading into Jacksonville, would you?"

"Yeah, why?" he asked.

"I'm trying to get a ride into the train station—I've been here for eight hours… if you could just get me anywhere close, I can walk the rest of the way."

He thought for a moment and looked me up and down, "Well, hang on a second, lemme pay for my fuel, we'll see."

It was the best answer I'd received in eight hours. "Sure thing," I said and gathered up my things.

A few minutes later, he came out and walked halfway to his truck, ignoring me. I thought he'd changed his mind until he suddenly turned around and waved me over.

"You comin' or ain't ya?"

I was up like a shot and lumbering over to his old beat-up brown rig hauling farm machinery.

"S'long as I don't gotta go outta my way, or nuthin'," he grinned.

"I don't care, you just get me anywhere close to Jacksonville and I'm happy."

I threw my gear in the cab and hopped up into the passenger seat. He looked over at me, "You ready?"

I hooted, happy for the first time in hours. Fuck the money, fuck the truck stop, fuck the glory tide of old age reaching the young, fuck the stars, fuck everything. I'm gone now, brother... got me a ride! Got me an answer. Fester in your heartbroken echo. Dream in your forgotten tomorrow. Die in your leather cocoons.

"I know she ain't that big in here, but we'll git where we gotta go," he slammed that mother in gear and took off in a hail of curse words, grabbing the CB mike and yelling, "Awright there boys, this is ol' gold-niner-six-seven, but y'all can call me T-bird on the radio—lookout fer me now; I see ya in muh way I'll ram yer ass right off the damn road!"

Finally. Just a normal spitting, swearing, ignorant harmless Georgian trucker willing to help a brother out. Finally. Finally, I was going to make it.

But a mile down the road, he suddenly leered over at me and said, "You ever let another man suck your dick?"

Ohhhh Christ, not again.

But it was dark and cold out there, and I was getting closer and closer to my destination. I thought maybe I could stall him until we got close enough for me to walk. I was so goddamn desperate to get out of that truck stop.

"Ehhh, no," I said.

"You married?"

"Well, no, but I'm *engaged*," I lied. "My high school sweetheart back home. We're getting married next month."

"Yeah, well, I'm bi-sexual," he stated proudly, pronouncing it "seckshall."

"Hmm."

He even used the same exact terms that Dan used earlier—some sort of demented Code of the Road. It turns out they were even from the same small town in southern Georgia. What in the hell is going on in the South?

"Bo' I tell you what," he grinned. "Y'ever lett'a 'nother man suck yer peener, it'll be the best durn blowjob y'ever had. Ain't nuthin' like it."

I said I wasn't gay.

"Hail," he barked. "It ain't about bein' *queer!* I ain't no

- 248 -

queer! Do I look like a queer? I don't like them *feminine* type a men… I just like to get me a nut, y'know? Lips is lips, tha's all. Lips is lips."

Jesus Christ, it was maddening. How is this happening again? What the fuck was I doing to bring this on? Why me? It was early in the morning on the freeway and I was a hitchhiker in the cab of his truck. He was a pretty stout guy, too… probably could've done something to me if he had it in him. I fidgeted my fingers and watched the miles click by, halfway there now. Quietly, I reached into my pack for something to use as a weapon. The vibrations were all wrong. Something bad was going to happen. All I could find was a tin box of Altoid breath mints. I hid it in my palm.

"There was this kid I picked up one time outside a Houston," he recalled. "Boy couldn'ta been more'n sixteen, maybe less. Blond hair, clean baby face, and sweet blue eyes. I told 'im, 'Boy, you just as purty as can be,' and he said he wadn't innerested in gettin' no BJ either, but I tell you what; half-hour down the road I finally had 'im convinced and he let me go down on 'im and shore as shit, kid had the best nut of his life. Rode with me all the way to N'Oleans, stoppin' every hour or so at the rest areas."

"Well, let me tell *you* something," I gnashed suddenly. "I just rode 250 miles with a 300-pound road worker who kept trying exactly the same shit you're trying, and I finally told him to fuck off and hopped out of the truck, so you ain't gonna get anywhere with me, buddy. I'm just tryin' to catch up with my train, that's all. I don't want to suck anyone's dick and I don't want anyone to suck my dick. Is that too much to ask? Hmm?"

He mulled this over for a second and took his foot off the gas, started pulling the truck over to the side of the road.

"What are you doing? Why are you stopping?" I darted my head around, seeing nothing outside but what was lit in his headlamps.

"Y'know what I like about pickin' up hitchhikers?" he asked with an eerie grin. "I can do whatever I want with 'em and nobody'll ever have to know."

He hit the airbrake and the rig stopped on the shoulder in total darkness. He reached over and grabbed my leg with his hand, but I shoved him back against his side of the cab and opened my door.

"C'mere got dammit!" he lunged again.

Everything happened so quickly. I flailed at him with the Altoids tin, accidentally bloodying his nose.

"You sonofabitch! I'm *bleedin'* dammit!" he whined with hands over his face, but I wasn't there to listen anymore. I grabbed my pack and the rest of my gear and bailed out sideways, rolling down into the ditch. I hit my feet and ran as fast as I could, ears ringing, eyes darting, knees trembling, not sure if he was following me.

"Come back here, you sonofabitch!" he yelled.

I just kept running away from the freeway, into a patch of trees and doubled back the other way. A patch of squat shrubs grew in the ditch, which I ducked behind for cover. My heart pounding, my fist hurting from the damn Altoids tin, my knees shaking… I sure as hell wasn't gonna let this happen. No sir.

Evidently he wasn't up for a chase.

The airbrake released, finally, and the big rig pulled off into the night leaving me crouched in silence by the side of the road. I couldn't move. I brought my shaking hands to my face and took deep breaths. I was convinced he was still out there, waiting for me to come out of the brush. God damn these nights, these setbacks, these evil omens. And damn these people who don't Understand, who refuse to let me Understand. Who destroy my efforts to love and trust and believe. Who provide so many justifications to all those living in the grip of Fear. They will not destroy me.

The lights of the city were still very far off—there was

only one choice left.

"Well, this is your grand adventure, you fucking idiot," I said to the crickets and crescent moon. "This is what you wanted, right? You fucking happy now?"

I peered out of the bushes and saw nothing but the quiet freeway and darkness. A few headlights whooshed by, bound for their unknown destinations. The truck was gone.

Grunting under the strain of my pack yet again, I bent my head to the hard grains and walked east, toward the sea.

TWENTY

THERE WAS DEW ON THE DESOLATE DITCH beside the freeway and a cold, wet gust blowing in from the Atlantic. I could feel it out there—the other coast. Ghastly clouds raced across the moon. Crickets serenaded my forlorn foot-falls. Plumes of crystals billowed from my nostrils, mixing with the air, mixing with the world, living free of my body. Oh, what was I doing out there all alone?

Traffic on Interstate-10 had died down at this quiet hour of the morning when only drug fiends and yawning whores are still awake. And hitchhikers. Every so often a semi truck would trundle by and nearly blow me aside, but I was mostly left alone for my mind to brood.

About a mile down, the ditch narrowed and eventually turned into a long bridge, leaving only a tiny shoulder to navigate. All it would take would be one trucker nodding off and veering slightly over to end this poor struggle I've led these many years.

Gradually, the lights of Jacksonville grew closer and ex-its began to appear. I knew I had to catch the 295 connector north to get to the Amtrak station, but I had no idea how far it would be. I ended up counting six mile markers before I made the turn. Six hard, cold miles; constantly readjusting the straps, shifting the weight and stopping to rest whenever I tired.

It was another mile north until I finally saw what I was looking for, what I'd been dreaming about every moment since I stuck my thumb out that sweaty morning in New Orleans—just yesterday, though it seemed like so long ago; an exit sign that read "Amtrak" with a picture of a passenger standing at a station platform next to a train. Sparkly green highway sign paint flashing on and off with the sporadic headlights hitting it.

Hot damn, I climbed down that off-ramp clumsily and expected to see my station all warm and lit with streetlights and smoking passengers milling outside. But it wasn't over yet. Oh no. The exit connected with a wide, four-lane road that ran east. A sign up ahead told me: "Amtrak 3 miles."

I just laughed like a loon. After all, what's another three miles after this crazy fucking trek from New Orleans to here? From New York to here? From all the way in snowy, sleepy north Idaho to here? From the womb to the wormy grave? What's another three miles?

There was a nice dark bus stop bench at the corner that looked inviting. I set the pack down with a grunt, fished to the bottom, pulled out my bottle of Wild Turkey and took a long swig. It washed down into my stomach, throwing warmth into my body, prying open my eyes, setting fire to my legs. Wild Turkey—it hits you like gasoline running from a spark, sending shivers through your limbs, the leg kicks out spastically, the mouth puckers and salivates and you can't help but let a bellowing howl into the night, "HOOOOaah!" I walked on with the bottle in my back pocket, feeling good. Whiskey is a beautiful thing, as long as you're an ugly person.

The air grew colder and colder as I slogged onward, past the run-down motel courts on the outskirts, taken over by knee-high weeds and graffiti from another blighted generation. Mean trailer park dogs barked and thrashed against their chains when I passed. There was a long swamp ditch by the road that I kept shying away from, thinking stray alligators might be lurking in wait for tired hitchhikers with whiskey bottles in their pockets.

I kept moving, taking pulls off the bottle every five minutes or so, bound to get there, bound for glory, bound for ruin… with every drink, my fear gave way to a strange feeling of confidence.

Though I was still scared shitless, it was a reckless fear—like a man with terminal cancer picking fights with gang-bangers, just *willing* them to do something. I was curious what else could go awry, what other misfortune could hit. They always ran in packs, these wolves of adversity. Consequences are for the living. Long shadows and foreign vistas at that ungodly hour of the morning. Fuck it, whatever comes.

Suddenly, in the bowels of the pack, my phone rang. God knows what time it was—maybe 3 a.m. I dropped to my knees and tried to fish it out. No one calls at three a.m. except for the ones you love to talk to at three a.m. I knew it was probably one of my booze-hound friends back home, probably calling from the bar (it being midnight back home) filled with crashing bar noise in the background.

But, to my great surprise, it was a message from Arianna, my red-haired pig heart dissecting friend, telling me she loved me and just wanted me to know she was thinking of me. That voice—the spark of familiarity—oh, it was like a warm blanket over my shoulders, a set of open arms to wrap myself in… it brought me out of my void, out of this crazed voyage, back into the warmth and compassion and acceptance as basic as one human being loving another.

WE TRAVEL THROUGH THESE DARK TUNNELS & PASSAGEWAYS, WAITING, WAITING, FOREVER WAITING FOR A SIGN THAT THINGS WILL GET BETTER, THAT EVERYTHING WILL BE "OK," THAT A SPARK WILL CARRY US FURTHER, THAT THE BAD WILL WASH AWAY THE GOOD & VICE VERSA. WE HOPE THAT THE SCALES WILL BALANCE & WE CAN ALL BE LEFT WITH A PETRI DISH IN WHICH TO CAST THE NEXT FOREIGN OBJECT, SO WE CAN STAND BACK & WATCH THE GROWTH WITH WRINKLED BROW & CURIOUS EYES; BUT A FIRE NEVER UNDERSTANDS THE SPARK THAT CREATED IT — IT JUST BURNS MAD INTO THIS THATCHED WORLD OF HALF-TRUTHS & BROKEN DREAMS, FUELED BY SOME INNER FORCE THAT WILL NEVER BE RECOGNIZED BY THE HEART OF MAN.

I dialed her number and stumbled onward.

"Hey *you!*" she answered, her voice husky (probably from lying in bed). "Wait, lemme guess, you're in New York riding a pack of wild elephants down Broadway…"

What a great thing to say. That Arianna.

"Nooo, not even *close*," I panted. "I'm in Florida on my way to the train station right now."

"*Flor*-ida! I just can't keep *up* with you Maxy!"

"Oh, that's not even the *half* of it! I got stranded in New Orleans and had to hitchhike over to Jacksonville, and just had two rides in a *row* where they asked to suck my dick!"

All I could do was laugh.

"What are you *talking* about?" she cried. "Are you *serious?* You're *hitch*-hiking right now? You crazy man!"

"Ah Christ, it was a fuckin' nightmare... I had to escape the last one and I've been walking with all my gear for about eight miles now, and I'm freezing, and I'm sweating, and my knee is killing me, and dogs keep barking at me, and, and, and... and I feel fucking *great!* Oop, shit, there goes a cop right now."

And it *was* a cop, cruising by slowly and hitting the brakes like they always do—cop scare tactics. Apparently I didn't warrant a stop, because he kept on going.

Arianna was overwhelmed with all this maniacal gibberish. Poor girl probably just got home from the bars and had a little too much to drink, maybe she's lying in bed with the covers pulled over her head, snuggling her beautiful little body into comfort, maybe listening to Bob Dylan or Iron & Wine on a low stereo, maybe reading a little bit of *Siddhartha* or writing a poem on the back of her medical textbooks.

I could taste the warmth right over the phone; the familiar, comforting, loving aura that Arianna radiates without doing anything but breathing. I wished I were with her then, sitting on a couch with our arms interlocked, talking about adventures and good books and her tousling my hair and smooching me on the cheek when I said something that pleased her.

But I *was* there with her, through the power of her voice. It put me right back on top again—someone to listen to the story I was telling; not after the fact, but right smack dab in the middle of it. Someone knew me and someone cared about me, and someone listened to what I was saying... and I felt glad, for the first time in a long while. Glad I'm the way I am... because if I were any different, I wouldn't be *me*. I could've married her the very moment she left the message.

"Are you gonna be all right, Max?" she asked. "I can stay on the phone with you if you want."

"No, I'll be just fine, A. You go to sleep and dream about something wonderful."

"I'll try to dream about *you*," she said. We said goodbyes and I hung up a new man.

A train whistle blew across the eerie night! I was getting close—maybe another mile to go. "I'm a-comin' you bitch!" I bellowed, my legs aching and my shoulders cut and bleeding from the straps of my pack, but it didn't matter. That train whistle was salvation… church bells calling the poor to mass, mothers singing wayward sons in from the cold, that highball blowing from some outbound freight, the call of the buffalo, last hurrah of dying soldiers.

I just wanted to be off this road, safe behind four walls and a book. I'd never been this far out on the edge before, this close to the yawning abyss.

Not until I saw the cool glow of the Amtrak sign and the lights of the station did I think everything was all right. The end was in sight—this strange journey was almost over. I had *made* it! Hot damn.

I burst out from under my pack and straggled up to the front door with a dumb, goofy smile on my face; my knees shaking and tee-shirt drenched in sweat, the seeker climbed up the mountain top for an audience with the grand yogi. But when I got to the door, I stopped suddenly and dropped my jaw. There was a sign taped to the glass:

Closed until 8 a.m.

Son of a *bitch*.

That was it—the last straw. I broke down and crouched on the pavement, laughing hysterically. It lasted ten minutes… I couldn't stop. I thought maybe something inside my brain finally snapped… that I'd lost my mind. Everything oozed out onto the cold sidewalk.

All that I'd gone through to get there; all the setbacks

and half-starts—how fitting that the end of the line be closed. Like reaching heaven and seeing a "closed for eternity" sign.

Ah, but what choices do we have when Amtrak rejects us and heaven spits us out? I sat on the cold wire bench outside the front door and drank my whiskey, rummaging through the pack for warm clothes. I pulled every sweater out of there and put them on, then my jacket, then a heavy rain poncho, scarf, long underwear, two pairs of socks and an extra pair of jeans. I shimmied into my sleeping bag sitting up and read Thomas Mann, shivering for four hours, breathing thick plumes of fog into the frigid air. It couldn't have been more than 40 degrees.

We seek and seek until there is nothing left in us, and we fall and die.

How ironic that I almost froze in Florida... that I finally had a chance to utilize all this gear I'd been lugging with me in one of the warmest parts of the country. Not in snowy Denver or the great blizzard of Chicago, but in sunny Florida.

It was a miserable four hours there under the buzzing halogen lamp of strong silence—stamping my feet, rolling cigarettes with numb fingers, trying not to look at the time. I must've dozed off a bit at the end, because I woke up sharp at the sound of a car door slam and alarm *chirp chirp*. An Amtrak station attendant shuffled up to the front door jangling keys in her hand, looking bored. I threw my hands in the air and yelled, "Hoo-AH! Thank *god* you're here, I'm *freezing!*"

Apparently she didn't notice me there because she screamed. She actually *screamed*, Hitchcock-style.

I thought for a moment she was going to pull out some mace and hose me down. I must've been an upsetting sight there; huddled on the bench in my sleeping bag, with a woeful rucksack beside me, bottle of whiskey clutched in my hand, and Thomas Mann in still life on my lap.

But she opened the door and told me to come on in.

"How long have you been sitting there?" she asked.

"God, I have no idea," I rubbed my eyes. "Too long."

"You have a ticket, right?"

"I have a rail pass."

"Where you headed?"

Well, where *was* I going? To Ed's or home? To Ed's or home? North or south? Which way? Which way?

"I need to get to Bradenton," I said at last. "I think it's south of Tampa."

"Can I see the pass? And your passport?"

She scrutinized my papers, turned them over, examined

the pass, and looked up questioningly.

"You're from *America?*" she asked.

"Uhh, yeah," I responded. *What the hell now?*

"This is a *foreign resident* rail pass," she handed it back. I stood there blinking.

"What do you mean?"

"This is a pass Amtrak issues to foreign residents traveling the country. You're an American, so you should have the North American Pass. This is an invalid pass."

We met eyes like tigers in the jungle. I breathed slowly, sizing her up.

"So what does that *mean?*" I repeated, feeling the alarm rising in waves up the back of my neck.

"Well, I'm sorry, but you're going to have to upgrade to the North American Pass, which will cost you... $300. I can't issue you a ticket with this."

She slid the pass back across the counter; my old faded, creased, barely legible pass that's been folded in the back pocket of my jeans for three weeks and taken me clear across the country without any problems.

I slapped both of my hands on the counter and leaned in with a mean glare.

"Let me tell you something, lady, I'm at the end of a very short rope right now and I claim *no* responsibility for my actions if you don't issue me this goddamn ticket. I've lost hours and hours from delays on the track, goddamn *freight* congestion, what the fuck *is* 'freight congestion'? I was stranded in New Orleans and had to sleep in the *street* because one of your half-wit attendants didn't know the tracks were down in Mississippi. I hitchhiked seven *hundred* miles through the heart of redneck southern America and almost got raped by truckers—*twice*—and I hiked ten fucking miles with 70 pounds on my fucking back just to get back to this fucking station to catch the train without a fucking cent in my *pocket*. And now you're telling me that one of your other idiot employees issued me a foreign resident pass by mistake, that, by the way, *nobody* else in the *entire* country has had any problems with, and that I have to buy *another* one or else I'm stuck here in your shitty ass city? Is that what you're saying? *Is* it?"

Fear glazed over her brown eyes and hung thick in the air. She recoiled, sensing violence and death and carnage and doom from this flipped-out nomad hobo suddenly punching her face flat and ripping into her guts with his sharpened fingernails.

"I'm sorry, sir… I—" she yammered.

"*Don't* tell me that you're 'sorry'! Don't you fucking say that! Just *book* the fucking ticket! *Do it!*"

She pursed her lips, looked around (I was the only other person in the station), looked back into my blazing eyes and started clacking on the keyboard.

"This… this will get you to Winter Haven, and then you'll catch a bus to Bradenton, and it should arrive at six this evening," she said officially. She dropped the ticket on the counter and quickly disappeared to the back room, probably to weep into her hands.

I scooped it up and walked to the furthest corner, slumped my head to my chest and fell asleep with a smug smile. My train was due in an hour.

TWENTY-ONE

BUT THE TRAIN DIDN'T COME IN AN HOUR, of course. Passengers filed into the station and sat worthless on the benches. They fidgeting with their knuckles, they read romance novels by hack authors, they ate pre-packaged Lunchables from nearby vending machines. They listening to headphones, held lame conversations about the weather and sports teams and the Supreme Court swinging to the right. They did what people do when they wait together.

"What the hell's going on with this train?" an old man grumbled. He had a crossword book clutched in his liver-spotted hand and erasable pen in the other, walker waiting nearby. "We were s'pose to leave two hours ago."

"Train's stopped somewhere in South Carolina—freight congestion," another man said. He wore typical Florida snowbird attire; knock-off Birkenstock's with black socks, madras shorts, and god-awful Hawaiian shirt, smelling of aftershave and Jolly Ranchers.

"Sow Caro*lina?*" the old man scowled. "Where'd you hear that?"

"Attendant told me."

Just then, the attendant—the one I'd reduced to tears—

came out from behind the desk and addressed the murmuring passengers. She avoided eye contact with me.

"I'm sorry to announce that the 8:45 train is having problems somewhere north of Georgia. The conductors say it'll be another hour or two before they get an engine switched over, so the new departure time will be around 1 p.m. unless there are more delays."

Groans and bellyaches from all the passengers.

Goddamn this Amtrak. This stupid fucking worthless train. All I could do was sigh. I gathered up my gear and trudged out to the patio by the platform. There was a wire bench out there, and I stretched out in the sun, resting my head on my jacket and fell asleep with my hat over my eyes— Indiana Jones style. I was so weary, so tired, so beat down and worn out with life and my attempts to live it. It was a beautiful nap of misery, and I had plenty of company.

After a few hours of sleep in that sun, I felt better again. It's all smooth sailing from here, m'boy. I called Ed and told him I'd be in that night and he said he'd be ready with a nice big dinner, then we'd go out on the boat the next day—good ol' Ed… he's gonna hear some crazy stories when I get there.

I boarded the train, which was running *five* hours late, and collapsed in the seat, feeling like I'd just climbed a mountain and fallen off the other side. We rolled south through the bearded wetlands and misty midday sun, heading for Winter Haven. There, I'd disembark and catch my bus into Tampa, then Bradenton for the end of the line. A couple of days at Ed's place to rest and regain my strength and momentum again, then blast off in one final direction; northwest… all the way home.

A long way to go with no money, but what the hell? I didn't come this far to falter and die on the other end of the country with my dick in my hands.

All that comes in the future—just then it was sunshine and cold beers… enjoying this nice purgatory at the very peak of my travels—far, far away from home, and spreading my arms wide before sliding down, down, back down the crumbling decline from which I climbed so far. Back to the low-lying flatlands and bitter realities I tried so hard to escape. But not quite yet. I was still free.

Just got a call from ol' Flannigan and we shot the shit for a while, talking about our writing, plans for the future, crazy trips we want to take, and how we've got to get together and do some serious *talking* when I get back to Northsaint, always *talking*, scheming, figuring it out. He was packing a bag to, "A—have sex, B—get out of Northsaint for a bit, which I'm sure you know all about, this town is *stifling* me, man, C—hang out with some young college motherfuckers instead of all us jaded intellectual post-modern dipshits without a thought in our brains, and D—" talking the way that only Flannigan talks, switching from subject to subject, lightning quick, telling me about new poem he wrote that's "not great or anything, but it's *ree-ally* fucking *goo-ood*," about how I was an "unorthodox soldier" and he's a "wondering carpenter honing my skills and sharpening my tools" and saying thing like "I don't know man, I'm still learnin' my stride, but I'm droppin' bombs an' when I'm on fire I write like mad an' when I'm not I just say fuck it an' sit in my bathtub an' jerk off an' write in my notebook about Sufjan Stevens an' folk music an' quiet moments in the Palouse with my thumb out to the winds of fortune an' all that shit… we'll get there someday."

Yeah, I don't know anyone quite like Flannigan—he's got this crazy bug stuck up his ass just like me, at this torpid point in our mid-twenties when we're not ready to accept the shroud of normalcy that falls on us all, forcing us to give up to embrace a mediocre world, when we're still idealistic enough to think we can rise above this shit and somehow make art eternal. To make it worthy of its creation. To seek it above the rest of this methodical madness pulling at our earlobes. We're both chasing after our own ghosts and saying "Fuck *yoooo*" to those who naysay and hmm and haw their ways through life, hung-up on obstacles that they create for themselves. We're just enjoying being young.

Yeah, it feels good to know he's out there. Somewhere. Bending his head to whatever new task, whether it be reading Buki or cajouling some nice young woman home to his bedroom or picking his butt behind the counter at the bookstore, sniffing his fingers out of total boredom, spreading napkins out at the bar and writing poems about the daytime customers he serves, staring out the bunker slit window at the grey world beyond, wondering… always wondering.

We continued south through immense pine forests and low-lying glades, houses with strange little greeneries sometimes dotted between. Sleepy towns with schoolchildren playing in back yards of modest shanties—a factory of some kind up ahead with a red and white striped Dr. Seuss smokestack poking out, spilling waste to the heavens. We're moving again. We're safe inside the motion.

I closed my eyes and realized that I covered more ground in three minutes on this train than I did all last night on foot. But the walk needed to be done.

Freight congestion lost us another hour. When we finally pulled into Winter Haven, I was an astounding *eight* hours late. No matter—haul my weary bones off one vessel and onto another. This time it was a Greyhound charter bus cramped with people in various foul moods. A deaf woman kept talking to me, asking where she had to get off, where we were, but I couldn't understand a word of what she was saying. She ended up writing on a tablet and handing it to me:

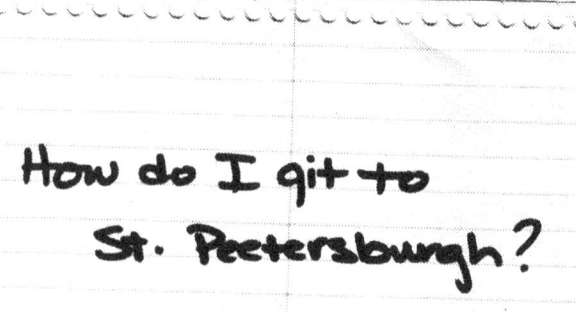

How do I git to
St. Peetersburgh?

I wrote back:

Just Follow Me — My stop is
the one after that — ill tell
you when to get off —

She nodded her thanks and went back to staring out the window at nothing. Night had fallen across the sands of Florida. The earth spun out, dry and abandoned.

I called Ed and let him know about the delay.

"Jesus, *eight hours?*" he said.

"I know, it's ridiculous. It's been like this the whole trip. They think we'll get into Bradenton around midnight."

"All right, well, call me when you're crossing the Skyline Bridge and I'll head over to pick ya up," he said. "I've got a couple cold beers in the fridge for you."

"Thank god."

Down the dark interstate in that rumbling bus, growing ever closer to my final jumping off point—this end marker of my eastern and southern journey before heading back over the long hump of America… back home.

I struck up a conversation with a 73-year-old Canadian named Dave who had come all the way from Edmonton, Alberta—a breathless four days on the train. He looked like an old mafia don, with his dark glasses, sharp-edged goatee, tucked-in wife-beater, and leather fanny pack tied around his pudgy waist. He played the guitar and was traveling down to visit a son he hadn't seen in seven years.

"What do you do?" he asked.

"Ohh, I just travel around and write about it," I replied. "You?"

"Ohh, I play guitar in a band and ride the train to visit my kids," he shot back.

We were on the same page.

The bus dropped me off in Bradenton around midnight, along with Dave.

"Max, this is my son Wayne," Dave said. Wayne shook my hand politely, a mid-thirties clean cut kid all grown up into a self-supportive, affable worker bee of the world.

"Nice to meet you Wayne," I said.

"You need a ride anywhere?" he asked.

"Ho ho, where were you yesterday?" I snickered. They didn't understand. "Nevermind, I'm all right."

They trundled off to Wayne's waiting SUV, glad-handling each other. I looked around for my ride, but it wasn't there. Ed must be close.

It was warm and the town was quiet. The bus left me outside the stucco courthouse, amidst the silence. For two minutes I sat looking up at the misty heavens and smoking a cigarette, feeling the weight of all the miles in my wake. Such a long way I'd come, and still so far to go. Breathe it in, the humid air. Will I ever cease this futile motion; batting around, looking for a reason to keep going?

An old couple walked a toy poodle on a retractable leash. It stopped and pissed a silent stream on a mail drop box. A young couple sat in a beat-up Ford pickup idling in the lot across the street, her head dipping down and he trying to convince of or something sexual perhaps. Lonely cocktail party man with blazer over tieless shirt, hands deep in pockets, coughs twice politely into his fist and spits on the sidewalk before cutting right and disappearing forever. Oh these people… I wonder what they think about on nights like these. Do they feel love? Is anyone really happy? How come comfort is so confining?

There was a garbage can with a white cover housing that had all sorts of writing on it—mostly local political slogans; "No on Prop 775," and "Egertson is a fraud," and a few lewd comments; "Fags go home." I pulled out my old trusty hitch-hiking Sharpie and wrote:

THE END OF THE LINE
2.2.06 M.M.

and smiled, wondering if I would ever be back this way again to see those words.

A great thunderstorm was moving across the Gulf with brilliant flashes of warm lightning defining the horizon. I discovered the next day there was a tornado watch across Florida, and am honestly surprised—with my luck—that one didn't touch down and suck me up into the clouds.

Ed's pickup lugged around a corner finally and stopped at the curb. We shook hands with smiles and hugged, ("C'mere you big bear!") loaded my gear in the back and made our way out of town to Anna Maria Island.

I had met Ed the year before in Thailand, when I volunteered for disaster relief after the tsunami hit. He's a 70-

year-old retired air force test pilot with a big Buddha belly, who walks hunched over from ditching a fighter jet in the Gulf a long time ago. He spends his days fishing and grumbling about "right wing nuts" taking over the country, travels around the world every year and smokes joints occasionally on his patio overlooking Tampa Bay. We clicked immediately because he'd spent the past twenty years working in the same business I loathed—the T.V. commercial production industry. He was a producer and just recently retired. We talked shop and swapped horror stories from shoots that went awry.

"This is real easy living here, Max," Ed told me, and I believed it.

The canal out back, behind his patio with a pool and hot tub, houses his fishing boats—a 17-footer he used for fishing backwater and tidal flats in the shallows and a 26-foot Mako open cuddy cabin with two 140 hp engines hanging over the centerboard. If the weather cooperated the next day, we'd go offshore. If not, we'd think of something else to do.

So that's that… after all that shit and all that struggle to get here, I think, right now, it's all worth it… I feel at ease finally. I've been out there for so long now, I don't remember the last time I felt as safe and serene as I do now, sitting here with my shirt off on this comfortable bed, propped against a bunch of pillows and smelling the salty breath coming in the open window, rustling through the palm trees and afterglow, smiling because I know it doesn't get any better than this. Sure, we'll have good dinners and fish on the Gulf and I'll have some great times here, but this moment is what it's all about—this little space of time all to myself when I know that I can finally put down the road guard and sink into a state of rest. I made it. It's going to be a long trip back, and not an easy one either… I've got about $90 left but I'll be damned if I'm going to let that stop me.

TWENTY-TWO.

THE NEXT MORNING I rose around noon, sleeping through several of Ed's attempts to awaken me. It was the first restful sleep I'd had in over a week, and it felt glorious.

"*Well*," he looked up from his newspaper when I emerged like a zombie. "Thought you were gonna sleep all day."

"That's a damn comfortable bed," I yawned.

He crushed up a couple of hand-picked oranges from the front yard and poured the juice into a glass for me. We reclined out on his shaded patio chatting while birds sang somewhere unseen. His wife Ru sat in front of the computer, writing a letter in Russian to her mother still back in Siberia. She was in her mid-fifties, and had met earlier that year when Ed was traveling through Siberia.

"She's always on that damn thing," he grumbled. "Ru, why don't you come out and sit with us on the patio?"

"So?" he turned to me, "How's the knee? You look like you're walking pretty well on it."

"Yeah, it's getting better every day. Still hurts like a bastard, but all this hitchhiking has been good for it I think. A lot of walking with my heavy pack on this trip. It's been almost a year, y'know?"

"I was just thinking about that," he nodded. "Can I see the scar?"

I pulled up my pant leg and showed him the six-inch long surgical scar plastered vertically across my bulbous kneecap, little dots on either side where the staples held the stitching together. He winced.

"God *damn!*" he muttered. "That's one ugly son of a bitch."

"I know, but hey, at least it works, eh?"

"They put steel pins in there, eh?"

"Yeah, there's two big vertical ones and a horizontal one—kinda like a big H—the bone fragments are all wired together through the pins."

"I bet you set off the metal detectors at airports with all that junk in there."

"I'm not really sure… haven't gone through one since the accident."

"Boy, that's gonna be a painful bitch when you get older."

"Shit," I snorted. "Who says I'm gonna get older?"

He chortled, "Ho ho, lemme tell you something, you young shit; just wait. You're gonna get old and shitty, just like me. You won't be able to go anywhere without taking a piss every five minutes, you'll forget people's names, you'll have to pop Viagra just to jack off… it's *terrible*, I tell ya."

"Ahh, so much to look forward to."

He leaned in, suddenly sober, "But really though, are you doing all right with everything? With the accident? I can't imagine all the shit you've been through—you got banged up pretty good."

I looked down at my fidgeting hands, the memory of the accident still raw inside, flashing through my head, the long months of physical therapy and bed rest, walking on crutches for another three months after that and the constant pain that never recedes. It stays with me, this pain, and reminds me of that fateful night in Thailand.

It happened on our last night of the volunteer period of

disaster relief, in a small fishing village by the Andaman Sea. Ed was in my crew, along with Bama from Northsaint and my friend Chuck from L.A. We were all eating dinner at a small Muslim family's restaurant after working that day.

There was a beautiful 20-year-old daughter of the owner who brought us lunch while we built grass huts and hacked evacuation trails up mountains. She was a little Thai princess and I lusted after her.

One of our translators, a Thai man named Zie, was miffed because we kept teaching him American slang that wasn't correct. Earlier in the week, we taught him: "Hey douche-bag, how the herpes?" which we said meant, "Hey, how are you?" and he tried it on some random English woman in the market one day to disastrous results.

He decided to strike back.

I rushed back to camp before dinner and splashed water in my face, combed my hair, sniffed my armpits and put on the cleanest shirt I could find. I even picked wildflowers and painstakingly tied them together with a strip of palm frond.

I was going to woo this girl.

It was a wonderful night. The whole crew was there, along with a Scotsman named Eric who built boats in a nearby camp, and we all laughed over the communal curry dinner and beers.

I asked Zie the correct pronunciation of *"Khun sooy maa,"* which meant "You are beautiful."

"Don't say *that*," he shook his head. "Tell her '*pom pen kay*.' It means, 'I think you pretty.' Other one too formal."

I practiced the lines and announced to the table that I was "going in." They all ceased talking and watched me make the move.

The girl was sitting atop a beer cooler like a delicate flower, surrounded by her large family. They were all chatting loudly and swatting flies on the little concrete porch.

I walked right up to her, handed her the flowers with a

wai—the traditional Thai greeting; hands together in front of face and slight bow of the head—and said, "*Pom pen kay.*"

She slowly accepted the flowers and stared for a moment with puzzled eyes. Then she slowly craned her slender neck over at her family. They had abruptly cut their conversations short and were all gaping at me with disbelief.

An awkward moment passed.

I thought maybe I'd offended them somehow, so I retreated back to our table red-faced and cowering. As I sat down, the entire family erupted in laughter. They slapped their knees and wiped tears from their eyes, pointing to me and shouting, "*Pom pen kay! Pom pen kay!*" The little boys rolled around in the dirt clutching their shaking guts.

I whirled around and glared at Zie.

"Why are they *laughing* at me?"

Wiping tears from his merry eyes, he told me that I had just walked up to the most beautiful girl in the village, handed her flowers in front of her *entire* family and announced, "I am gay."

The bastard tricked me.

Now our table joined in the roaring laughter. I chased Zie around the dirt for a few moments in comical horror, finally caught him and put him in a headlock, "You bastard! Tell her I'm not gay! Tell her!"

The evening was winding down, and everyone was getting ready to turn in for the night. But, around midnight, Bama got drunk and started being an asshole, as he always does. He started whimpering and bitching about the fact that Chuck and I were ignoring him and not listening to any of his stories. He'd just finished telling a story about catching a fish in Alabama for the tenth time that week—no one really listened or cared, because they'd all heard it before.

"The hail, y'all ain't even *lissenin'* to me," he shouted with bleary eyes. Everyone at the table felt awkward at his outburst.

"That's because you tell the same fucking stories, man," I

yelled back. The sight of his bloodshot eyes and constant cigarette smoke blowing in everyone's faces annoyed me. "Maybe if you learn how to shut the fuck up and stop talking about yourself all the time, people wouldn't *have* to ignore you."

It had been a long three weeks with Bama in our crew—getting wasted every day, offending the locals, alienating the other crew members who just wanted to do something good for humanity. We just wanted to build houses, to clear brush, to get dirty and sweat and contribute what we could. Nobody in our crew came to Thailand to drink beer all night and play power all night, telling stories about fishing and getting busted for selling ecstasy. He gave us all a bad image. He represented the typical American that the rest of te world believes us to be: drunk, fat, ignorant and arrogant. I was sick of trying to overcompensate for him.

"Ah, fuck *yooo!*" he swept some bottles off the table. They shattered on the ground where the children played in bare feet. "Think y'all so fuckin' *great* or somethin'… I own a got damn *publishin'* house! My daddy's got the biggest lumber yard in *Alabama*. Y'all are nuthin'! *Nuthin'!*"

I was ready to kill him, but Chuck—the eternal peacekeeper—stepped in and drug Bama away from the table, followed by Eric the Scotsman.

"Now, c'mon Bama," Eric said, laying a kind hand on his shoulder. "You guys are mates, calm down a bit and deal with this at another time, right? This isn't the—"

"Fuck yooo!" Bama yelled and punched Eric right in the jaw. Everyone at the table sprang up and dishes clattered all over the ground. The poor little matriarch Thai lady who ran the place stared with sad eyes at us; these drunken coddled Americans who were supposedly in her village to help rebuild, but were really just spreading our viral hatred. Chuck held Bama back while Eric picked himself off the ground, rubbing his jaw. Eric had at least fifty pounds on Bama and could've pummeled him into the earth in a second, but he was a good guy and just shook his head. He walked out to the road to cool down his anger.

"What the fuck is *wrong* with you, Bama?" I yelled. "Why do you have to *ruin* everything like this? This is our last fucking night here, and you have to pull *this* shit? These people don't give a damn about you, about how much *money* you have. They don't *give* a shit, because you're a bastard and you... *you* represent all that's rotten and filthy about America! It's because of *you* that the entire world hates us!"

"Git off'a me," he squirmed under Chuck's hold. "Git yer fuckin' hands off'a me, Chuck."

He shook free and swung at Chuck, but missed and fell on his face.

"I don't need any yoo fuckin' guys!" Bama blathered. "Jes' keep on whisperin' an' tryin' to talk shit 'bout me."

"Nobody's whispering," Chuck said.

Such a sad end to such a beautiful night, a beautiful three weeks of doing something good. No matter how far away from America I went, it always caught up to me—the evil, privileged American ego. Gimmie this, gimmie that, cater to me and let me do whatever I want. Soulless wealthy families breeding stupid ignorant children like Bama in droves and letting them loose in the world to piss all over everything, then sending them to white-collar rehabs to clean up and be released again to repeat the cycle. There was never any accountability, never any respect. All their life a waking moment between rehabs, between moments of clarity, between the sheets. All their life stillborn.

"Fuck this," I said. "If I stay here any longer, I'm gonna kill that fucking guy."

Eric came over and talked real close to me, his hand behind my neck, "Look, why don't you give me a ride back to my camp? Cool off for a bit, right?"

His crew of French volunteers was at the other end of the mangrove swamp, about 10 kilometers down a lonely stretch of jungle road with a few shrimp farms and a Muslim fishing village along the way. I drove the motorbike and Eric rode behind with his guitar strapped to his back.

"Don't worry about all that stuff, mate," he yelled into my ear as we whipped past the dark mangrove swamps away from the sea. "He's just drunk."

"He's *always* drunk!" I yelled back. "I'm so sick of everyone's nights getting *ruined* because of him. He's done this so many times before, and never remembers anything the next day. He's a selfish bastard."

"Well, what are you gonna do? Let him *win?* Let him succeed and ruin this trip of yours? You guys have done some great things the past three weeks—building that grass hut, making that evacuation trail up the mountain... I mean shite, look at us right now, look at that view... we're flying along on a motorbike in Thailand while our friends back home are working at their desks and sittin' in pubs smoking butts and talking about T.V. shows and the like. You just got to put things in perspective sometimes, mate."

And I knew he was right. There was no way I would let Bama win. This was *my* voyage, *my* trek... and there was still a whole week of sailing and traveling before we returned to America. I'd be damned if I was going to let Bama cheapen it with his bullshit.

"You're right," I said. "You're absolutely right, Eric, thanks. God, lookit that moon! Hoo!"

The wind danced through my hair. The smooth bike cut corners down the lonely road. I smiled a secret smile—one understood only by those who've run a fast motorcycle down an open, moon-drenched highway.

I was *alive!*

I was on top of the world and on the eve of a great sailing trip in a matter of hours. Nothing could hold me down anymore. Fuck Bama. We'd spent three long weeks doing our good for humanity. Now it was time to explore.

Eric jumped off the bike at his camp and I tried to flirt with one of the French girls in his crew, but she just yawned and slogged off to her bunk. Eric and I shook hands and he wished me luck on the high seas.

"Remember to check out Kho Phi Phi," he said.

"Right—thanks for everything. I'll come see you in Scotland sometime, I hope."

I took off down the road, heading back toward the ocean breaking softly, somewhere out there in silvery gloom.

Cruising back along those lonely curves and bridges, remembering them all after hitchhiking this road into town for email and food or building supplies and tools. The electric hiss of cicadas in the trees under the windscreen, bullfrogs hooting in the void, aah.

I leaned left around a turn before the second bridge, about halfway back to camp. I didn't see the water buffalo until it was too late. He charged out of the mangroves, the wide arc horns lowering and snout sputtering, his dumb staring eyes glowing in the headlights. I swerved instinctually and missed him by inches, but when I leaned hard the other way to correct, the tires hit a patch of soft earth and I went into a slide.

"Shit shit shiiiiiit!"

I felt it coming... WHAM!

Going about 40 mph, my right knee slammed into a concrete post on the side of the road. I was thrown from the bike. The next moments are hazy memories of tumbling end-over-end in the air—tree branches and bushes thwack thwack—then *sploosh*, I sank into the murky swamp water.

It all happened in a matter of seconds.

I sprang out of the filthy swamp, teeming with bacteria and disease, and dragged myself out and up the ditch like a wild animal. The wreck had sent me flying about twenty feet.

"I'm okay, I'm okay," I chanted, dragging myself clear of the ditch and onto the road again, fingernails chipping and breaking on rocks, clutching my way up the bank, "I'm okay, I'm okay... I'm *okay!*"

The bike was crumpled in the ditch near the post I'd demolished. Somehow I managed to haul it out and get it upright. It wasn't until I tried to kick start the engine that I noticed my right knee was completely shattered.

Pain like I've never felt before—a sickly *snap crunch* as the bones ground together. I fell to the ground screaming, clutching my knee. The bike crashed back down the ditch. My left foot had been slashed open and was swelling and turning blue. My left elbow felt strange—I tried to extend the arm and felt it snap too.

Then I tasted blood and realized my entire face was covered in it. I felt weak. Horrified, I passed trembling fingers into a deep wound in my forehead and traced the gash another four inches or so up the scalp.

I was definitely *not* okay.

A lot went through my mind out there on the side of the road; my body busted and bleeding and nothing but the dark sounds of the jungle all around. I screamed for help in every language I knew, but no one heard me. I thumped my good arm on the ground and cried and kept wiping warm blood from my forehead so I could see. My eyes stung with it. It just kept pouring out. My god, it was everywhere.

It dawned on me that the chances of someone coming by after midnight on this road were slim. It led only to the sea and the Muslim fishing village we were staying—still about five kilometers away—neither very populated destinations.

I knew if I didn't get help soon, I'd die. Well, there was a chance I'd die. No, I couldn't die… *could* I? Too much blood lost. Too much blood lost.

I began to panic. I became delirious. I rolled in the weeds and punched at the air; I threw rocks into the swamp and screamed unheard. Then I quietly laid down in the grass and heard nothing but my own irregular breath and pounding heart in this hollow abyss.

I just laid there… wallowing in pain. Suddenly I heard my own voice shrieking, "*You little pansy, GET UP, get the hell up, GET UP!*"

I gritted my teeth and struggled to a standing position, then started my trek, whimpering and screaming for help. I hopped along on my wounded left foot and dragged the right leg behind for a while, counting my steps. Five meters, 10, 20… I made my way to the next concrete post and rested there for a moment, then continued on.

My left foot eventually gave out after about 100 meters. It felt broken and wouldn't support any weight. I collapsed on the highway and tried to stand again but couldn't. I had already tied my shirt around my head to stave off the bleeding, but it didn't help much—I could feel the mosquitoes and gnats rummaging around inside the wound, gorging themselves on all the warm blood, burrowing deeper into my skull.

With only one working limb, I dragged myself down the road on my ass.

At this point I completely lost track of time—I imagine about an hour passed since the accident. It must've been another hour of painful, methodical crawling before I finally saw what I'd been waiting for: *headlights!* They were coming from the east! I pulled myself erect and leaned against a concrete post waving my good arm frantically, shrieking for them to stop. I saw the end in sight—I was *saved!*

The truck never even slowed down as it passed me. I couldn't understand why they would *leave me there* like that—I know they saw me.

After losing so much hope, my momentum was shot. Movement became sluggish, lethargic. I was faint from the blood loss and something was infected in my mangled foot— it kept swelling and leaking yellowish fluid. My knee felt like jagged marble pudding. My left elbow swelled and blood oozed from dozens of cuts and gashes all over my body.

Then another set of headlights appeared—also from the east. I staggered to a crouch and waved desperately. I screamed, sighed and collapsed again as it, too, passed by without so much as a sideways glance.

"What the hell is *wrong* with you people!?" I yelled to the uncaring night. "I came here to *help* you! Fuck!"

I dragged myself down the road for another hour.

In the pale moonlight, I saw a small shrimp farm to the right and called out for help, in English, in Thai, even in French. I had passed this farm often and had always seen a group of Thai children out front riding bicycles and waving to the Americans, saying, "Hel-LO! Hel-LO!" And there was a *truck* in the driveway. I yelled, "Help me, I'm an American, I'm injured, please *help* me! *Aidez-moi! Chûay! Pom Chûay!*"

After a few minutes, a figure emerged and ran to the truck. A warm feeling spread over me as I saw the brake lights glow and heard the engine fire up.

"*Finally!*" I cried and drug myself to the middle of the road. If he wanted to pass me he'd have to run me over. The truck backed into the road and hesitated for a moment, then swerved around my outstretched body and quickly drove off.

That was it... I gave up completely. I must have made it a kilometer or two down the road in the two or three hours I'd been out there, but I didn't have anything left in me.

I collapsed on the asphalt and stared up at the stars with tears in my eyes. I listened to the electric hiss in the jungle, the cicadas simmering and screeching, thousands of bugs flying loops around the heavens. Everything so peaceful, so quiet. The pain was fading away, the sounds seemed to drift in and out, rising, falling. Sometimes I heard nothing but the air struggling through my lungs and my heart beating, thumping, pounding in my chest.

So this is it, I thought, sniffling. *This is dying. This is how I die—I'm going to bleed to death here in this jungle in Thailand.*

And I was certain of it, in fact. There was no "life flashing before my eyes" or any of that nonsense—just fading consciousness and darkness, darkness, darkness.

I closed my eyes and felt the night take me.

Somewhere in a dream I *heard* something. Far off, very faint, but getting closer. I opened my eyes and saw a peculiar glow in the distant mangrove trees—*headlights!*

This time the truck stopped.

Three young Thai men jumped out and helped me into the pickup bed. They all asked me questions, but I didn't understand anything. I just sat there weeping and shaking my head, unable to believe that I was still alive.

They sped me back to camp, but for some reason, didn't go inside the gate.

"I need to you wake up my friends!" I told them. They stood there blinking, wanting to help, but refusing. *"Hòk,* cabin number *hòk,* PLEASE!"

They refused to enter the camp.

"CHUCK!! CHUUUUCK!! HELP!" I screamed. They were probably all passed out drunk in their beds. "SOMEBODY, ANYBODY, HELP!!"

I screamed for at least ten minutes before Chuck appeared cautiously at the front gate in his shorts. He recognized my voice and came running over, but stopped short when he saw me lying there in the back of the pickup. The look in his eyes will haunt me forever—it was the look the living give to the dying. Primal fear, shock, disorientation, glazed disbelief. He dropped his jaw and tried to speak several times, but nothing came out.

"I thought someone was being murdered out there when you were screaming," he told me later. "When I ran up to that pickup and saw you lying there... well... *god,* you looked so *horrible.* You were *covered* in blood. Your entire face was red, the shirt around your head was soaked—I really thought you were going to die. It was one of the most disturbing images I've ever seen, man. I thought we were gonna lose you."

Chuck woke the others and they all rushed me to the hospital in another bouncing, tumbling pickup truck bed. Over four hours had passed since the accident. All I remember is him holding my hand the whole way there, squeezing me, and the sunken, horrified look in his eyes looking down into mine.

For the next two days I was laid up in two different hospitals. I learned that my kneecap was shattered in seven pieces, my elbow fractured, my foot severely infected with bacteria from the swamp and the gash on my head had required about 25 stitches.

I was also told the reason no one stopped to pick me up; there is no "Good Samaritan" law in Thailand. If a local picked me up and tried to get me to a hospital and I died in their care, *they* would be blamed for my death. A wounded Westerner is the last thing anyone wants to deal with in Thailand. The three men that finally got me were the Chief of the village and his two sons. Apparently the shrimp farmer heard me screaming and drove fifteen miles to the Chief's house to tell him.

Naturally, our plans to sail around Phuket were cancelled. Chuck spent a day on the phone arranging new flights from Ranong to Bangkok. From Bangkok we would head east toward Los Angeles, stopping briefly in Taiwan. Bama, as usual, didn't remember anything from the night before and tried to console me in the hospital bed, but I pushed him away. I never wanted to speak to him again. It wasn't his fault I got in the accident, but I'll always wonder what would've happened if he hadn't caused a scene that night. I never fully forgave him.

The next few months were filled with painful reconstructive surgeries, physical therapy three times a week with me screaming as the therapists manually bent my frozen knee, the bones cracking and snapping, the tendons ripping, long, lonely hours in my cabin, popping pain pills and believing I'd been crippled for life. In fact, the doctor was sure I wouldn't recover completely—the trauma from pulverizing my kneecap was too much. He said I might have a lifelong limp.

But I was *alive*. I was still breathing. Throughout my life, I'd been in countless scrapes and close calls, but never have I smelled it like that. It changed me like nothing before ever had. I was no longer invincible. I was no longer young and immortal. I was just as fragile as mashed squirrels on the highway. I came face to face with my own mortality, and by some chance of luck or divine intervention, I didn't die on that road in Thailand. I lived. I lived.

And now, sitting here on a quiet retirement island in Florida drinking freshly-squeezed orange juice with Ed, the memory is not one that gets filed and put away into the corners of my mind. It stays with me. It will always be fresh, raw, full of haunting images. Every step with my right leg brings a little jolt of pain; a pain that has been tolerated and accepted as the default. A pain that must be managed. A pain that I Live With. The scars on my body, the scars on my mind… oh, I'll never forget.

"I think about it every day," I told Ed quietly. "It changed my life, y'know? I really believed I was going to die after that third truck passed me by. It's an extremely strange feeling knowing that you're going to die… *accepting* it. I thought of all the rotten things I'd done in my life, everything I wished I could take back, opportunities I'd blown, girls I wished I'd kissed. But mostly, I thought about the things I'd never get to do. How I was essentially going to die a failure. It was so awful."

"Yeah, but you're *alive*," Ed said. He searched into my eyes and we stared at each other for a second.

"You're goddamn *right* I am."

"What ever happened with the insurance situation?"

I scowled and slammed the glass down, "Ah Christ, don't even get me started on *that*. The travel insurance company claimed since I left Thailand to have my surgery done in America, I voided my policy. Even though they couldn't even *do* the surgery in Thailand. They sent all my bills from the hospital back and now, since I don't have insurance of my own, I owe like $20,000 to the doctors. Our relief organization stopped taking my phone calls, saying they couldn't do anything either. They all just dropped me. It doesn't matter though—just more bills I'll never be able to pay."

"Jesus," he shook his head and clicked his teeth. "Funny what happens to a guy who just wants to help humanity, huh?"

TWENTY-THREE

THE WIND WASN'T BLOWING the right direction for fishing, so Ed suggested we hop on a couple of old beach cruisers and take a tour of the island. It was full of neat cottages with "For Sale" signs everywhere—everyone getting out before the next hurricane season.

We stopped at a beach club and had beers on the deck overlooking Tampa Bay.

"I forgot my wallet at home," he said. "You mind picking these up?"

"Yeah... no problem," I said, looking at my poor wallet. Shit. Now I was down to $70.

"That's the Skyline Bridge you called me from last night," Ed said. He pointed out to a crazily designed bridge with two tall masts and hundreds of suspension guy wires running in between them.

"It's the longest cable-stayed bridge in the world—1,200 feet across, I think."

"I like the design," I squinted across the water to the humongous bridge. Sand sprayed in fine mists from the beach and settled underneath our beers in wet rings.

"It's actually the second one," he said. They rebuilt it after some asshole freighter slammed into it in the '80s. Killed a bunch of people and everything. But there was this one guy whose pickup truck hit the deck of the freighter instead of going into the water, and he actually *survived*. The rest of the cars that fell all sank and everyone drowned. Someone smiled on him, eh?"

"Jesus, how far of a fall is that?"

"Oh, I think it's about 200 feet."

I whistled. Inside the bar were typical Florida beach retirees arguing about politics.

"Well, I don't care what the goddamn liberal media keeps saying," a pig-faced old man said to his Italian buddy with pale legs and sandals. "We can't pull out of Iraq *now*. I don't like our boys dyin' over there any more than the next guy, but can you imagine what kinda stuff would go down if we just up and left? We have to *win*."

"An' them towel-heads'll think they won and start bombing us again, too," the Italian man said.

"You bet they will," Pig-Face said. "I think Bush is doing a *fine* job—he just shouldn't listen to all the naysayers. Man knows what he's doing."

Ed snorted loudly and took a drink from his beer.

"You hear that shit?" he pointed his bottle to them. "What a buncha assholes. They have no idea what's going on out there."

"Yeah, and it's only gonna get worse, too," I added. "We'll probably elect some other dipshit in 2008 and America will dissolve into a theo-nationalist oil regime."

"Nah, there's no way in hell that'll happen," he shook his head. "You really think the American people are that stupid? I think they're waking up a bit."

"Of course they're that stupid! Look who they elect into office! We elevate these fools, year after year."

"Yeah, but things are going to change, I bet," Ed said. "There comes a point where people have had enough. I think things'll turn around."

"Well, I wish I had your optimism. All I see happening in this country is more division, more blind patriotism, and more of the same ignorant mentality. Everyone is wrapping themselves in the flag and pissing all over the constitution. Lookit the Patriot Act! We're giving up so much of our freedom just to protect our freedom… it's ridiculous. Where do you draw the line?"

Ed sat back in his seat and crossed his fingers over the Buddha belly, "I tell you what, Max, I'm damn glad I'm not growing up in the world you live in. In all my life I've never seen things this bad. And I lived through Nixon. It makes you wonder how it's affecting people your age, growing up with all this shit."

"Well, we're growing up without any kind of center, or purpose. We don't believe in anything anymore, we only know what we *don't* believe in. All these generations of the past have all defined themselves from major wars and conflicts that had clear sides of good and evil… but then, starting with Vietnam, everything just stopped making sense… nobody understood *why* we were at war anymore, why we meddled in the affairs of sovereign nations. It's not our place to be in the middle of a civil war, and that's exactly what Iraq is right now. It's their war, not ours. They didn't bomb the Trade Centers! They didn't have anything to do with it. Plus, we seem to be just as corrupt as who we're fighting against. How do you pick which side to believe in?"

"Hell, *I* don't understand, that's for sure," he nodded.

"This whole Non-Generation of youth is so numb to all this shit, nothing seems to register anymore," I continued. "Our enemies are all sound-bytes on the T.V. news and third-page blurbs buried under headlines about celebrities' divorces an' all that shit… we care more about who Jessica and Nick are than who we're at war with. Did you know that more people voted for 'American Idol' this year than for the president? And shit, everything gets spun over and over again until no one has any fucking clue *what's* going on anymore... I mean, we've been *raised* with such widespread disaster and messy politics for so long, the only thing we can do is flip the channel and find something to entertain us."

"It's like you've all been desensitized."

"Right. Oversaturated. And we *have*. We're so consumed by Fear that we'll sacrifice anything just to feel complacent again... everyone's waiting for the other shoe to drop, but it never will... it'll just keep hovering over us."

"I just think we need to learn from history and not ignore it," he said. "That article you wrote a couple months ago was right on. Ever since September 11, we've been so gripped in fear that anyone in a power tie that says they're fighting for freedom can bulldoze the shit out of our constitution in order to protect us. I can't believe we've let it get this bad."

"There's no more checks and balances... it's been replaced with fire and brimstone."

"I read this poll the other day that said more than half of Americans believe *most* of our Congress is corrupt in some way," he said. "Isn't that incredible?"

"That doesn't surprise me."

"Did you also see that *Times* article last week?" Ed asked. "That one that said Bush gave the NSA authority to eavesdrop on U.S. citizens' phone calls without a warrant?"

"You bet I did," I said. "Pretty ironic that Nixon was impeached for the very same thing. But Bush can get away with it because of the fucking War on Terror. What a mess. It's amazing! Bush has accomplished the impossible—he's actually *vindicated* the ghost of Nixon... in Bush's America, Nixon is beyond a doubt, *not a crook!*"

We shared a good laugh and finished our beers. The old men must've overhead us, because they both gave us evil glares when we walked past their table to leave.

"C'mon, let's head back to the house," Ed said. "I'm gonna cook up some snapper I caught the other day for dinner."

The next day was Superbowl Sunday. All across America we sit glued to the tubes for the biggest spectacle of the year. I told Ed I didn't really want to watch it, but he sneered and said, "Why the hell not? I'm making my famous bi-annual chili!"

He had a gigantic cauldron on the stove full of sliced veggies, fresh flank steak cut into strips, beans, and spices. It smelled fantastic.

"Well, I don't really give a shit about football, and I hate the fact that the whole country is expected to watch it, you know?" I told him. "It gets worse and worse every year—all this hype. It's no longer just a football game—it's a corporate drum of bullshit. Like watching one long commercial with a little bit of football in between."

"Oh, get over yourself," he sneered. "You *work* in the commercial business for chrissakes, *remember?* So did I."

"Yeah, but just because I worked on a few commercials doesn't mean I have to *watch* them."

"You're damn *right* you have to watch 'em," he wagged a wooden spoon in my face. "You're part of the hype, too, whether you like it or not. This is our America right here, as hideous as it is," he pointed over to the pre-pre-game show on the set with two old hack players in ties and coats talking about drive techniques and passing percentages with a giant Bud Light banner waving behind them.

"Besides," he grinned. "I rolled up a joint for us to smoke."

"Ho ho! Why didn't you *saaay* so? When's that chili gonna be ready?"

"It's just about perfect," he tasted the wooden spoon.

"What do you have in there?"

He smiled secretly, taking off his apron, "I'll never tell. I don't ever follow a recipe. It comes out different every time. This year it's a little spicy."

We watched the game with tremendous bowls of chili

on our laps and hunks of bread torn off the loaf. Later we smoked the joint and scowled as the Rolling Stones played for mainstream teeny-bopper crowds who paid hundreds of dollars per ticket to scream when the TV producers said to scream. Funny what happened to rock n' roll.

The weather finally calmed down Monday. Ed kept getting up to squint at the flagpole across the canal like Ahab. Finally, he muttered, "It's blowing out of the southwest now a bit, that means we should hit this hole over on Eggmont Key. C'mon, lessgo fishin'!"

We piled the gear in the boat and yelled at his neighbor Harry across the canal to hop in, then rummaged around in the live bait net for several large shrimp. Every house along the canal had the bait nets stocked with shrimp, tied next to their docks. With the sky exploding in sunshine and a warm breeze blowing in, we puttered out of the canal and cruised out into the bay, throwing a white wake across the green, green water.

I took off my shirt and drank off a couple of beers while Ed and Harry argued over the results of the fish finder. Along the way we saw diving pelicans and dolphins surfacing just feet away, blowing their spouts into the air and diving back under. Magnificent creatures.

"Where there's dolphins, there's fish," Ed said, so we threw our bits in, but didn't catch anything. In fact, we didn't catch anything all day.

"It's a dead sea today," Harry muttered. He was a 78-year-old from New Jersey who seemed to be some sort of fish fanatic. He stood ready on the balls of his feet at Ed's left, pole in hand, saying, "Wellll, this is *great*, hot *damn*, haven't been out in a few days, golly, let's get some fish, eh?" He seemed to be the type of guy who could go all day without a bite and still come home happy afterwards.

We patrolled up and down the leeward side of an is-land that housed several pillboxes from the Spanish-Ameri-can War and tried to get the little fuckers off the sandbar, but that didn't work either. I wanted to catch something, of course, but just getting out on the water was enough for me. I was free.

There were moments out there in the clear green water when I almost forgot about the long, looming voyage still ahead of me—back through the whole heap of America with barely enough money to eat. And my eventual fate when I returned to Northsaint, broke and busted.

But these times come and they go. Sometimes there's nothing to do but just enjoy the moments as they come and worry about the rest later. We have a whole lifetime of jaded mediocrity ahead of us, hair growing in our ears, teeth rot-ting out of our heads, joints breaking down, nights ending at 9 p.m., mornings with no hangovers, whole weeks and months without excitement… these are the days that matter. These are the days we'll remember. These are the days that will never die. This is *my* time.

"So you're planning on leaving tomorrow, eh?" Ed asked on my last night. We were sitting on the back patio having a beer. "Can I give you a ride into St. Petersburg to catch the train?"

"Well, sure, that'd be great if you don't mind," I said. "I don't mind catching the bus here in Bradenton, though."

"Nah, no problem. We can even go visit the Dali mu-seum in the morning if you want… Ru's been wanting to check it out for a while now."

"No shit, I *love* Dali! That'd be *great!*" I exclaimed, then frowned, remembering my money situation. "Oh, well, *shit*…

I don't know if I can go, Ed."

"Why *not?*"

"Uh, well, I'm kinda out of money," I confessed. "I've only got like 70 bucks left to get home with, and to live on when I get back."

He leaned back and laid his arms across his chuckling belly.

"Boy, you *are* a crazy dude, aren't you? You mean to tell me that you're gonna try to take a four-day trip back to Idaho with only 70 bucks in your pocket? Plus live off that when you get back? How are you gonna *eat?*"

"I'll probably just buy some cheap cans of soup or something. I can go a few days without eating."

"And then what're you going to do when you get back home? You got anything coming in there? Any savings?"

"No, not really," I said. He laughed again.

"Jesus, I've never known someone with so much talent that was so damn *broke* all the time! Shit, all you gotta do is just head down to L.A. and do a few commercials, right?"

"I know, that's probably my only option left. I'm just so sick of it, though… selling out like that."

"You need some cash? I can loan you a little bit if—"

"No, no," I waved him away. "Thanks, but I'd like to see if I can make it back. I get myself into these situations, I like to be able to get myself out, y'know?"

"I can respect that," he nodded. "But you *will* let me buy your ticket to Dali tomorrow. You don't wanna pass that one up."

"If that's cool, Ed… I don't wanna be a—"

"It'd be my pleasure, Max. It's been nice having you here, catching up and everything. You give us old farts hope that maybe your generation isn't all doomed after all."

"Oh, we're plenty doomed, don't worry."

He and Ru went to bed and I slipped outside into the warm night, rolled a cigarette on his dock with feet dangling in borrowed slippers. The half-moon shone like a lamp and the brilliant swath of stars; Cassiopeia, the Big Dipper, Orion the magic hunter... ahh, and the breakers on the windward side of Anna Maria, and the night breeze on my neck, and, and, and... well, it was a nice moment.

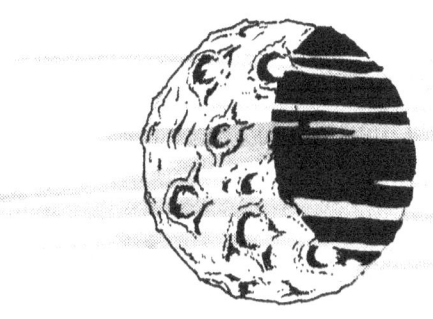

Here, on this last night of my eastern journey, standing at the furthest edge of it all, I will gaze once more into the unknown, the abyss, then turn around and make the long fall back from whence I came. Sitting there listening to that breath somewhere out there, that incessant breath that never stops, unlike my own, but every once in a while, it seems we link up... we synchronize... almost as if we breathe as one—Man and Sea.

Back up through the Carolinas and Virginias to D.C. and over to Chi-town with her stormy Mondays, hop on the Empire Builder ("*The Empire Builder, takes me ho-ome*") past Milwaukee and Minnesota chill, Wisconsin sorrow, North Dakota winter flurries and long, flat Montana monotony until I'm home, clanging into the Northsaint station at midnight—home again—home again—to my lonely little cabin sitting there in the dark snow, to my warm circle of friends all rushing about their lazy lives, to my life left in limbo when I escaped it some three weeks ago.

I'll pull into Northsaint with just a few dollars in my pocket and who knows what I'll do then. No real money coming my way. No job. No future. I don't even have enough to make the drive down to L.A. to work for more. I'll have to borrow from someone. I don't know… somehow I'll find a way. Always do. Always the eternal loophole and my fruit-less efforts at finding it. It always comes down to these situations of me being tapped dry because I've lived too hard and not thought about tomorrow. I don't know when, or if, I'll ever get out of this cycle—this live-hard-devil-may-care lifestyle of freelance bliss—but I know that it's the only way that seems to work for me right now.

I know it's all going to come out in the end. When I'm 30, or 45, or maybe 70 like Ed, I'll have plenty of money and I'll have a house and all that bullshit weighing me down… it's not even a question… I just have to get myself through this strange period of time between; because *this* is the meat that counts. The pit and pinnacle of something that I'll re-member the rest of my days, when I was young enough to do crazy shit and bat around the country like a jellyfish on acid… to *not* think of the future, to *not* save money, to take exotic drugs, and spend all my paychecks on booze and kicks and crazy road trips that are useless to anyone but me. When else will I be able to do this without being too wise or rich to care? These are the days that fade too quickly, when all that's left are golden sidelights of a life lived too quickly.

I'm 25 years dumb and growing older, every day. There's smoke in the air, chill in the tips of my slippered toes, anger in my brain and sorrow in my heart for something that has never been… for an era that I'll never see, I'll never breathe in… I'll never experience. For a loss that was never mine. For a feeling that will only come as I go… magnetic op-posites in this misguided world, always chasing each other around like Orion and Artemis in the night sky.

Tears… tears for neurons. Tears for synapses. Tears for these crashing moments of time—the past a death shroud on my future. Always running from something, never settling for anything, always extracting the juice like milk from a cow taking a dreamy crap in a lonely fallow field—analogies, banalities—curses and cream. We all live lives we wish were something else, and we all wish something else was in our lives. Eternal conundrums that have existed before the word "conundrum" was printed and bound with a thousand million other words in a thousand million blue hardcover books to be sold to a thousand million people all over the world, all over the ocean and land—the expanse of the human stain upon the earth. Homogenize the masses, ally the people, defy the enemy—don't you know? In the world of the sheep, the *blind* are king.

Oh this American life. This American Dream. Who *are* we? What goes through our drawstring minds? Is it really as bad as you read in the newspapers? Are we really that evil? Are we actually that stupid? If dreams were diamonds I'd be wearing white linen suits. If struggle was chili I'd feed the world a thousand times over and leave them trotting to their outhouses and back yard shit trenches for days. "I wish I could open my eyes and see in all directions at the same time," to see what happens when I turn my head, when I run away, when I leave those behind on the constant surge onward. I wonder what that would be like, to swing around the undergrowth at an unknown and irrelevant velocity, bound for glory, bound for pain, seeking both as my Truth, my faux surrealistic Truth, and to *know* what it looks like from the other side.

And what *is* Truth? What *is* death? What is all of this? Where am I going with these ideas? How come they come so quickly? So fragmented? So clearly? So fucking muddled? Goddamn, how come everything? Why can't I anything? Where shall I nothing? Words, words, thoughts, emotions, pain, fear, heartache, sorrow, indifference, wander-lost… let it go, let it go, get thee to a taverny and drown this boiling bile piss of a reality 'til it ceases to be, no more unrest, burn it *down*, burn out the Truth, hide in the leeward shadow of motion, toddle after this ghost of my mind on the side roads and back alleys stinking of winter chills and freedom.

Oh, I can smell it out there; that smell of road oil, the pine smirk of the woods, the salt mist of coastal starlight—a smell of *life* out there where I don't belong, and neither do They—neither do any of us, for we are all just wreckage, debris, baggage—fleas on the back of a winged monster, swooping low over these scorched plains of the American Dream, the brown rolling hills of giants sleeping, the draw of the glowing horizon, magnificent hints of sunfire in the grass, unfocused, uncentered, unsure—junkie's fix, nomad's cure—blow the smoke out the window and feel the warm wind in my eyes, my watering eyes, my yearning, burning, *boiling* eyes, god *damn*, gotta keep moving down this dark highway, always looking for a point, that fine point where I'm here, I'm there, I'm nowhere and everywhere, when all those false epiphanies cease to be, just bug smears on the windshield in yellow and brown and red and maybe some Bob Ross color I can't remember—happy clouds... *fuck* that, clouds are angry, trees are angry, rivers and streams and creeks are angry... we're *all* angry, Bob (or is it just me?)

Why must this linger? This useless melancholy that tears through my veins, and a train blows a whistle somewhere in the black shroud of a dark and lonely night out there in the wheel, turning somewhere in the sky, beyond our eyes. Something is lost in the transfer, something is left behind, can't drive fast enough, can't go far enough, can't lose it, can't shake it, can't move on cuz all I'm moving *to* is *from* that thing that chases me. That thing that's me.

"I give the world a thousand sighs and don't get any back." I bleed for dreams, I suffer for ghosts... I run and sweat and jump and curl and shake for a myth—the eternal vision, the final answer to all this madness—all this turning, suffering, loathing, writhing inactivity when the earth stands silent and all-knowing like Lincoln's hands, grabbing you in, grabbing you first at the back of the eyeballs and spreading like cancer through the bloodstream to your fingers, down the pant legs to your shaking knees, the calves, the ankles, the bottom of the cracked soul skin of your feet and you're walking, brother… you're moving, you're *running*, god dammit, you're *drifting* out there free and full of confidence—a silent scream—filled with the desire to see over that mocking horizon, that hazy point you'll never reach unless you keep chasing it—the dog at his tail, the butcher at his meat—chasing it around this world and secretly knowing you'll never get to the end of it, but fooling even yourself most of the time—cuz when you're treading the earth on a mission to get somewhere or to escape from somewhere else, running from people, from the past, from the future or lack thereof, from anything or to anything, it don't matter—on the road there *is* no story, there is no memory, there is no breath in tandem with things you'll never understand—a forlorn man sighing with the crashing Atlantic waves at sunset as birds circle about the bay and dive for sand crabs, the sand cold and all-powerful in between your toes, the wind a living whisper in the center of your ears, the stinging surf like tears on your cheeks—crying for a moment that you don't want to die, crying for that moment you'll never find—crying for that unanswered ache you've felt inside all your life—the void—the emptiness that serves no purpose and remains devoid of anything but the ill will of men and Hope. Hope buried somewhere beneath his cold, black heart.

We're all growing up so fast, but I just want to keep in this holding pattern for a while longer—why not? Sure, money would be nice. So would a little bit of a safety net. But it will only come if it comes. I cannot determine if I'll ever be a successful writer in my life, or a photographer, or a film producer, or a hamburger flipper… I just know that when the chips come down, and the end credits roll, I'll be on the winning side, unless I die early as a failure and never get my shot at greatness. You see, I'm just like the rest of America: I want to do something spectacular.

That's the only thing that really scares me—dying before I'm able to prove myself and prove to everybody else that I knew what I was doing the whole time. It's not so much an "I told you so" moment. It's more like, "*There—that's* what I was talkin' about all those years." A final understanding, where instead of just being a dreamer with empty water in the vase, I blossomed and squeezed the nectar out of what I had held deep inside for so long.

I don't know any final wisdom I may have learned from this trip—any "life lessons" or morals. I just know that I came, I saw... I wrote. That's all I intended to do in the first place.

TWENTY-FOUR

WE CRUISED INTO ST. PETERSBURG in the morning and poked around the Dali museum for a few hours. I was mesmerized by his circular mind in this angular world; his bleak, surreal landscapes and hypnotizing symbolism that jumps from the canvas. Clocks dripping and bone-weary women staring out of windows up close, but step back and you see Abe Lincoln's face if you de-focus your eyes a bit—every canvas like a Technicolor dream distorted by peyote visions. Finite strokes of paint from the darkest corners of his mind.

Born into a family that never understood his genius, raised in a world he knew he didn't belong in; so he created his own. He lived his whole life in the shadow of an older brother who died before he was born. In fact, his father named him Salvador after the dead brother, and refused to believe the second son was anything more than just a reincarnation.

And now you can buy postcard-sized prints for $5.99 and fine art puzzles and Dali teddy bears in the gift shop.

We drove into the old Cuban part of town filled with sweet-smelling cigar shops and stucco buildings. We had some lunch at a noisy grill with gawking tourists arguing over prices and poring over maps, clogging the sidewalks like useless, hairy clumps in the drain.

"I'll give you one piece of advice, Max," Ed said, forking a piece of grilled ahi into his mouth. "God forbid, if you ever decide to get serious about a girl, look for one thing and that'll tell you if she's worth the trouble."

"Oh yeah? What's that?"

"The length of her fingernails," he smiled. "That's one piece of wisdom you'll thank me for someday. If you're dating a girl with long talons, run the hell away and don't look back. The longer the nails, the more of a bitch she is. Trust me, I've done my research on this."

Ru grinned and looked at her own fingernails, clipped short and neat.

"I guess I passed the test, huh?" she chided him.

"You wouldn't have gotten *anywhere* if you had fingernails like that waitress of ours," he said. And sure enough, the waitress came back and we all studied her nails. So obviously, in fact, that she looked at them herself and smiled.

"I just had them done yesterday," she beamed. They were at least an inch long and painted bright purple with little flowers painted on the tips. She walked away and, a moment later, dropped a plate behind the bar with a loud crash.

"*See, see?*" Ed elbowed me with merry eyes. "What a fuckin' idiot."

"You're horrible!" Ru swatted him.

Ed paid the tab and drove to the station a few blocks away.

"What are you gonna do about *food?*" he asked suddenly.

"Oh shit, I was gonna try to pick some stuff up from a grocery store."

"You still got an hour until the train leaves, c'mon, there's got to be something around here."

We made a few circles and eventually found a seedy Cuban market with hoodlums leaning against the sun-faded brick walls smoking butts and jingling change in their pockets. This was, what Ed called, the "bad part of town."

"Just run in and we'll wait here for you," he parked on the street and left the motor running. I bought a loaf of bread, a jar of peanut butter, a can of soup, some oatmeal cream pies, two small bags of peanuts and two pouches of Top tobacco—all for $11. That would be the extent of my food for the next four days.

Back at the station, Ed and Ru got out of the car and hugged me goodbye.

"I really had a good time," I told them. "Thank you so much for the meals and the room and everything else. It was nice to be comfortable for a few days."

"Well, we had fun too, Max," Ed nodded his head and patted me on the shoulder. "You let me know if you ever need help with anything. I'm always willing to give someone a hand that deserves it."

"I will," I promised.

"I think you're gonna go places, Max. Just keep working and keep taking crazy trips like this—you're onto something, even if it's disaster. After all, it was a disaster that brought the two of us together, right?"

I smiled at this. Sometimes people say some really great things.

"You be careful on your way home," Ru called after me.

"*Course* he won't be careful," I heard Ed grumble to her as they got back in the car. "He's probably gonna derail the train on accident and end up hitchhiking home with a god-damn serial killer. Nothing we tell him will make any difference."

They waved and tooted the horn, then drove away on cobblestone streets, off to continue their own lives and me heading back to mine. Good ol' Ed, my Jewish Buddha in the Florida sun. I stood there in the parking lot with my pack aback, closed my eyes into the sun and felt the warmth on my face one last time. The salt air teeming with city noises, passengers filing in through the beat doors of the station with expectant, eager looks that only people getting ready to board a train can truly achieve. I was one of them, and they were me.

TWENTY-FIVE

OH AND YES YES *YES*, back on the train, back on the rails, back on this slipstream track across the country—a four-day journey at my feet and nothing to do now but wait and watch and read and write and listen to Mason Jennings and Ray LaMontagne in my headphones while the New Yorker guy behind me talks to his apparently hard-of-hearing mother back in the city—describing his journey in every detail: "I saw an *owl*, ma… an *owl!* I saw an owl, ma! You know, the *boid*."

We're moving now, pulling out of the old sun-faded walls of these nondescript buildings in Tampa, past the "bad part of town," where all the hoodlums are wandering around looking for rape victims. A good song playing in my ears, bright sunshine out that old windowpane, and 3,500 miles to go… heading home. Heading back to my old Northsaint sitting there waiting for me… man, what a feeling. There's just something about those first few moments on a train, in the late afternoon, when you first get underway—everything giving birth to everything else.

I think I'll make it fine. Of course, when I arrive I'll be in another heap of trouble with no money to my name and an overdrawn account and rent due and phone bill due, but no matter… that's in the future. Now I just gotta let this ride for four more days—this Gulf Stream train, the Silver Streak they call it, and all I can do is gaze out the window with my fist in my chin and sigh.

We're leaving it all behind. The lonely chain link fence sagging in a field of hurricane-swept foliage, the pebbly litter-strewn ditches on the side of the freeway, cars smashed into neat cubes stacked in junkyards with trucks in waiting to haul them away.

These scenes that pass by unnoticed by most, but not me. I watch them all and take something away—every second. Every blink a refreshed image, every breath a new thought. Soak it up, ol' boy… soon you'll be stagnant and crazy back in the night streets of Northsaint, drinking and whooping into the wee hours of the morning. Or driving through mad traffic in L.A. Or sleeping in rest areas in Oregon. Or standing atop cliffs in Colorado. Or tapping my foot underground in New York. Or whatever else comes next. It's all out there, waiting.

Melancholy… woebegone miles ticking down the track… is this really the end? Can't I go a little further? A little longer? Can't I live a little more? Ah, but everything ends and then begins again, fresh and new… nothing to do but accept it and move on, move on, move on into the next.

Agh, but I don't *want* it to end… I don't want *anything* to end… I want to keep living in this suspended animation where I'm not quite here, I'm not quite there, but *somewhere*, gloriously *somewhere* in between it all where the real juice and pit and marrow lives… the space between it all, the gap, the void, the unconscious fury and joy and kicks of moving through the miles and feeling the weight of motion again… truly nomadic with the roots trailing behind reckless and distended. *That's* where it is… wanderlost. I've never known a drug or a high or a woman or anything else that can make me feel as I do now, this day, 25 years, one month, and eleven days old… dumb as shit and right smack dab in my prime with nothing to show for it but my long face gaping into the Dali horizon, waiting, yearning, hoping for something to come along and show me where to go next. How can I be so lost and so found? Does a tear shed at sixty miles per hour make any difference to this crazy mixed up world?

Let it all go, let it all go, the cement factories and the causeway bridges over canals leading out to the Gulf with crystal blue water rolling underneath. The sleepy Florida towns slipping past with front porches of sagging in winter sunshine. Let it all go. The porch-sitters with cheeks that sag in the autumn years of their lives, the sad-faced housewives in their Oldsmobiles waiting at the train crossing, sighing, always sighing. Let it all go, the field of rich green clover beside the ditches with broken glass, the discarded bicycles left to rot and rust and fade away, the lids from soda fountain cups blowing in the wind, the errant little butterflies scampering about the ground in search of whatever they seek on a bright day in February. Let it all go.

The old pale Florida woman eating an apple delicately in the seat beside me, taking a bite every minute or so and chewing lazily, holding it perched in her chicken-skinned hand and staring off into space, a napkin on her lap and her old sinewy fingers grasping at the edges, pinky sticking up like she's been trained, then she lunges for another bite, leaning forward, turning the apple to search for a good spot to chomp, lashes into it, then leans back again to chew lazily, still staring cow-eyed ahead, just waiting for death to come and chomp into *her*. Wearing nylons under her polyester old woman pants and open-toed white sandals, a thick well-worn trash romance novel on her lap with that burlesque raised font title saying something like *Eye of the Beholder*. Now she gets up and tosses the apple core into the trash bin slowly, as if she's proving to everyone that *she* deposits her litter in the proper place, then harrumphs back down to read the book about romances that never were.

Riding this white noise back across the whole teeming country—up through the seaboard Carolinas and brown Virginia again, back into winter, back into the cold, with a quick stop in Washington, D.C. where I had to kill two hours in the station and ended up staring at a buffet with savory food under freshly-wiped sneeze guards; pasta salads, steamy lasagna, spaghetti with meatballs, green Jell-O with pineapple chunks, garlic bread, stuffed chicken breast, steak cutlets, chicken strips, Caesar salads, tater tots, ah me, I was *so* hungry, a hunger that festers and boils, a hunger that makes you squeeze your guts, a hunger reaching so deep, you can feel the walls of the stomach lining grinding and churning, a hunger for something to fill you up, a hunger for life, a hunger for death, and the sign said it was only $6.49, so I said "fuck it" and loaded a plate as full as possible, piling it thick and high, and walked up to pay with a five and two ones, but the clerk lady cleared her throat and pointed to the total on the cash register read-out—$22.49—and I realized it was $6.49 *per pound* and just groaned, but had to eat it all because there were no returns, three whole pounds of food, and in fact didn't eat anything for another two days I was so damn full. And back we go through steely Pittsburgh through the small hours to Chicago socked in with another massive snowstorm, the Amish people with their neck beards and wonder-eyed kids in plainclothes lugging beat square suitcases, getting off to visit their progressive relatives in the big city, changing trains again, one last time, the Empire Builder takin' me home, rumbling like a big steel caterpillar past frozen lakes of Wisconsin with psilocybin in my brain and visions of fish trapped under the ice, and those fish are me sometimes, and dark tundra of North Dakota with teardrops in the void and shivering cows and Bob Dylan in my ears, and the sun rising behind us now, due east, one last day of travel, one last day out here in America, one last day of wayworn bliss, cutting into Montana with just a little bit of whiskey left kicking around in the bottle and a drunk man in NASCAR jacket burping up and down the aisles, shoving raw hotdogs in his mouth and sayin' "Ah'm a race care driver," and stripes of sienna sunfire undulating under the big oscillating firmament and big grey wheat silos creaking in dusty solstice winds with lonely names of towns in cracked paint and farmers stopping the winter plow to watch me roll by, catching eyes, matching sighs, heading west, and what a fabulous direction is West, my favorite of all, like you're rolling downhill with the sun a ghost behind low lying clouds and burnt grass waving and power poles cracking and silhouetted in the pink sky, I'm heading home, heading home, Glacier Park sundowner and by god, we're almost there, nothing but a few hours of fidgeting and beard tugging and feverish gasps to go, peanut butter sandwiches and oatmeal cream pies for breakfast, whore's bath in the toilet, change of clothes, climbing the hump, never making it over, the struggle is what I seek, crossing the border of Idaho in gloomy darkness with my forehead pressed hard against the windowpane to catch the first familiar sight, but all I can see is my own reflection, my own moon face staring right back with a dumb, glad smile a whole looping horizon wide, gaining momentum by the mile, each second passing bringing me closer to something, away from nothing, pinpoint stars cutting across the heavens, looking down on us all, everyone's asleep and sprawled in shades of supine indifference, but not me, not me, I'm wide awake watching the migratory night birds invisible and reeling with unknown velocity, moving, drawing, spinning fabulous loops, circling this old lump of land called America in one month's time to see her people, to see her soul, *to believe in something instead of the absence of nothing,* to bleed her slogans and accept her faults, to love, to die, to *go*... and the rock is still rolling and I am stronger than it, I am better than it... I *am* the rock and I ain't gonna budge, and I'm home, I'm home, only home I'll ever know or care to find... pulling up to Northsaint, stop with a hiss and squeal of brakes and clash of metal on metal as the cold blows through the door while the passengers snore and I'm drinking whiskey, hoo! The train has ceased, the movement gone, and holy god, here I am, blasting off in a new direction onward, lessGO!

TWELVE THOUSAND FIVE HUNDRED MILES IN 27 DAYS. Thirty-six different states—by train, bus, rental car, subway, fishing boat, thumb, and foot.

The Sierra Nevadas at dusk, the blizzard blues streets of Chicago. Warm Gulf waters lapping with dolphins cresting beneath my feet. Sad starry nights in New Orleans back alleys. Lonely cigarettes smoked up to the crescent moon on-ramp Alabama air.

Abe Lincoln's feet, the Empire State in winter hush. Fishing boats chugging out of the harbor in Portland; heading out to sea with nothing but the sun and the whole hump of America to their backs.

These flashing scenes outside my windowpane. The people that make up our nation; our brothers and sisters and enemies and lovers. We're all one. We're all related. We're all the same. The opulence, the struggle, the comic tragedy that is American Life in this strange new century.

But the best sight of all came right at journey's end, when the lights of Northsaint twinkled and spilled in through the windowpane, refracting and breathing over the still water, the smoke coming from chimneys, the snow crunching under car tires and smells of home, smells of home. One last sigh. One last moment on the rails.

"There he is!" I heard someone yell from the platform.

"Hup hup!" I yelled back, pulling a cigarette from my ear and lighting it with a smile. Jack, Wrenn, Flannigan and Arianna were huddled in a group by the tracks, my old faithful friends waiting in the cold for me to return. Is there anything sweeter in the world?

I hoisted my pack, stepped off that grumbling steel ghost and resumed my life once again—right where I left it in suspended animation those many days ago. Except now I was broke. And I didn't care. My voyage was finished, my traveling done... but it'll march on, and I'll come shambling along after it with hands digging deep in pockets for a pen to record the moment before it's lost for an eternity, because there *is* a brighter view over that mountain, beyond that cliff and across the heather, down the coast to that spot on the horizon that never becomes anything more than a thin line, moving beneath your feet in dashed patterns, yellows and whites, while the crickets and thistle-brush scream warm breath through the open window as I pass by—*whoosh*—look up and see that ol' sun, always that golden sun shining down life to lost souls like mine, filling me up, taking me further, for we live and breathe its glow, we mourn its passing... at night, we chase it around this world as it chases us, never to let the darkness settle in.

SPECIAL THANKS to Zach Hagadone for all the time he has spent helping with this book; illustrating, scheming, late-night talk sessions in the Corner Booth, editing in Mexico with Havana Club Rum in a $33 motel room—I couldn't have done it without you. This book is just as much yours as it is mine. To Brannigan, the wondering carpenter, the man who wants to believe, the hitchhiking partner. Believe. Write. BE GOOD! To my family for having the patience and unconditional love to raise a wayward child who'll never amount to anything worth a shit. To *The Reader* for publishing my gibberish and all my friends in Northsaint that make life interesting, the Others: Adriane, Jenna, Josh Hedlund the folk singer that you'll all know about in a few years, Jenn my sighing ballerina, Brian and Loni and Jill at the Crossing, Nance, Nat, all those degenerates at the "419," the Shookies and the people I see on the street from time to time and chat with. To Mike and Marie for being my L.A. support group, Marisa for letting me crash on her couch like a bum while I'm selling my soul, Chris and Jocey in Ohio, Al on his fishing boat, to the bloodthirsty water buffalo in Thailand, to my campfire buddies; Schuck, the Bopp family, Tate, and

J.P. the (reformed) Pirate. To Mark and Pam Story for all the assistance and opportunities. To everyone at Crossroads Films and all my production buddies in smelly old L.A.; Greg, Dave, Dan K. (sorry for rolling your truck on Sunset Blvd.), Dan S., Stevo, KO, Murwarid, Lesley. Thanks for giving me work and keeping me fed. Also, special thanks to my new publicist Renee, who is working for nothing but booze and a chance.

AND EXTRA SPECIAL THANKS to George W. Bush and his surrounding miasma, for giving me a reason to hate, and a reason to seek America again, because you're destroying it. We're trying to find it again; the Others... and you'll be nothing but a stinky chapter in history when we prevail. May you hang by your thumbs for eternity and get flogged by the ghosts of all those you've killed.

About the Illustrator

ZACH HAGADONE IS A MAN with a lot of free time. He is a dabbler in the illustrative arts, jazz saxophone and piano, trap shooting, writing, editing and the collection of rare rumba records. He is also an appreciator of classical requiems, an armchair historian (specializing in the occult roots of National Socialism), an aficionado of fine whiskeys (and whiskys) and something of a specialist in military memorabilia.

His association with illustration, however, is his longest-running hobby, predated only by his fascination with the history of the Third Reich and Soviet Russia. His early works focused on out-of-date editorial cartoons lampooning such long-dead figures as Adolf Hitler, Josef Stalin, V.I. Lenin and Benito Mussolini.

Considering this, his associates are not surprised at his longtime collaboration with Ben Olson. Olson is a tyrannical asshole. The two have been friends since their days as political operators at Sandpoint Middle School, located in their hometown of Sandpoint, Idaho.

Both returned to Sandpoint around 2003, and begun work on several freelance articles. None of which received any more attention than not-so-polite rejection letters from various national publications. Frustrated, Hagadone, together with two fellow classmates from Albertson College of Idaho, founded a weekly arts and entertainment newspaper, *The Sandpoint Reader*, in which Olson served as main news and feature writer for about a month.

Olson's articles, "Notes From the Rails," were originally published in *The Reader* as a four-part series, edited and partially illustrated by Hagadone. The nonfiction dispatches served as the foundation for the fictional *Wanderlost*.

Today, Hagadone lives in the Portland, Ore. area with his wife, Danielle, and works with *The Reader* and Olson via electronic mail. He is currently accepting damn near any job offered – illustration, writing, editing or vintage German helmet consultation (he is also open to any spots on trap-shooting teams on whiskey (or whisky) drinking associations).

About the Author

Ben Olson was born and raised in north Idaho, in a small mountain town of hillbillies, realtors and hippies. He wrote "Wanderlost" in 37 days, when he was 25 years old.

After dropping out of Colorado State University in his third semester, escaping the "institutional hand" he fled to Los Angeles, home of the Weird. There, Olson lived for three years in disrepute, working as a production assistant on TV commercials and eventually documentary films. He recently worked on the Academy Award winning, "An Inconvenient Truth," and was *Time* Magazine's "Person of the Year" in 2006. In 2004, he was hired to produce a fine art photography book by renowned director/photographer Mark Story called "Living in Three Centuries," a book of portraits of the oldest people in the world. For a year, he wandered around America searching for "supercentenarians" (people over 110 years old) from California to to Georgia. During the scouting, Olson took constant notes on the American People, and began formulating the idea to write a novel.

He is also an inveterate traveler; a sailor of Caribbean Seas, a tsunami relief volunteer in Thailand (where he was nearly killed by a charging water buffalo), a hitchhiker down lonely highways to see the Dying of the West, a backpacker through canyons of Utah, and a roman candle shooter at drunks in the streets of downtown Seattle.

Olson writes occasionally for *The Sandpoint Reader,* which his friend and illustrator Zach Hagadone owns and publishes. He has been rejected by some of the best publications in the world. He used to live in a small cabin by the lake, but was recently evicted for non-payment of rent and is roaming around America without a cent in his pocket, trying to figure out what the hell to do next. Pick him up on the highway if you see him with thumb out and cigarette aglow.

Etc.

What follows are several poems and miscellaneous gibberish from my friends and fellow Others. I include this section in the ass-end of the book for several reasons.

First and foremost, I believe in what they have to say. I know these people. They Understand. They Get It. I write about them not because I'm bored and unimaginative, but because they are all my muses. They inspire me. I owe all of them money, dinners, drinks drinks drinks. They've supported me during the down cycles, and endured me in the high times. If this is the least I can do to show my belief and appreciation, so be it.

Secondly, no one else will publish them, just like no one else would publish me. Except for a dunce. Unless you have the secret formula for Shit, nobody seems to take a chance on anyone with actual talent anymore. All that matters is the market. These people are the bartenders who serve your drinks. The waitresses who clean your crumbs. The worker bees of daytime hours turning the other half, the Night, into their outlet. And they shine gloriously in their defeats.

Finally, because I want to share Our Art with you. We're proud of it. It's a pain in the ass, this life; but, when you have people like the following artists that show you their innermost petals, it almost seems we're all dipped in amber.

-Ben Olson

AMERICA

By Erin Brannigan

●●

America I broke up with you in a bathroom in Prague
at the age of 27 after walking on my own feet for only
a year or two... America, like my father, you told me
everything but I had to go and learn it for myself
Ameria I scare all the pretty girls away with my words
about you but then they come and knock at my window
late at night when they see that my light is still on...
America you fooled me for so very long... America you
are an inanimate object in the eyes of Others... America
your winters are harsh and cold and dark... America your
seasons are round America you are so pretty you make me
feel worse and worse America your breast is well ex-
cercised but what has become of your heart today, your
legs are long and thin America you are cursed with
consciousness America, in the bookstore I work in your
self-help section is overflowing America your people are
only monkeys and sheep and lemmings, worrying about
what all the other monkeys and sheep and lemmings think
America you care too little about the rest of the world
America I bought you over and over again America when
I am drunk and hi on some front porch of yours smoking a cold-handed cigarette I have no remorse when I
throw it down on you and put it out and smother it and
burn your face America what happened after the creator
gave itself to you America what will happen after the
baseball game and the football game and the basketball
game is over, what will we be then America America
Whitman, Emerson, Thoreau, WCW, Pound, Elliot, Plath,
Ginsberg,Wakefield America why does no one know of our
third civil war America I've no direction home America
the invisible history books of explosion will not paint us
like the reflection we see America we are Sparta America
we are Narcissus America why are the book shelves empty
and storage units the next big thing America is L.A. all
Ben says it is, the noxious streets, the plastic lips,
the bums pissing themselves in Venice America where is
my hope, I already live in the rural Northwest country
I've no where else to go America the Northeast is my

only ally here America the couch is not a bad place to sleep America you gave me cocaine, terrorism and insomnia America who's gonna back me America what you are saying is not true America walk down your perfect streets there is a syringe lying in the gutter America it is raining and the gutters are full of Israelis, Palestinians, Sunnis and Shiites America when I'm in the mountains I forget that you exist and start to miss you, I followed your white stripe to the coast this summer and I found your real beauty America what are you clapping for when he says those things in the round rooms of Congress America why so many billboards America you are right out of high school, a badass dude with a girl in a poodle skirt and clean-shaven, but why wont you admit that your insides are hurt America your bars are full of rising smoke and cheap regurgitated thoughts America you talk about television programs too often America you've scared the dreamers America the best way is honesty America please don't throw away your leftovers America Cat Stevens isn't such a bad guy America listen to Ray LaMontagne, listen to Collin Oberst, listen to Sage Francis America the communists have turned brown America slap me in the face so I know that you are real America one of my brothers is stumbling drunk with a back pocketful of sorrow, another is painted white hiding in his room and locking his doors his stomach is burning and his mouth is full of crooked teeth he is beautiful nonetheless, and yet another is trying so hard to be what you want, with his wife and his job and his bills and all, he won't cry America, he resents me America my sisters are sad with idealism America I brought the paper home from work today, I'm not sure why America I am you America I live between your borders, between your overly nationalistic ideals, between your cloning rules, between your expensive medicine, between your insurance, insurance, insurance America your hippies no longer vote they only talk and dance and spin America exactly how are we going to win? America my 5-year-old niece is a hobo, her life is in a backpack, she is nothing like the ideas and pictures you paint America I am already two wars old America I am afraid of the outcast kid who gets made fun of incessantly in the corner of the classroom, his name is North Korea America I don't think detention scares him America I made my room for you so many times America hide your habits you hypocritical Limbaugh addictions America your words are thin, the

lines you draw don't matter America is rambling illegal
it seems that it is America we are in debt, constantly
trading loans America small businesses are disappearing
America homes are hard to buy America that same 5-year-
old niece wants McDonald's and doesn't know why America
no one will pick me up when I stand along the road with
my thumb out, we're afraid of each other, afraid of our
own America our rules don't work America why did you
tell me that the world owes me something, why are our
streets in chronological, hierarchical, and alphabeti-
cal order America why are we laughing lonely by the
1000's simultaneously watching TV in the dark America
why not more like Canada America I'll deal with you as
you are not as you ought to be America Castro is dying
yet your tables are not clean America what about Spanish
and Ebonics and Art America how do you really feel about
Sameer Hadid, Shai Manzuri, Ben Olson America the west is
dying America you have the power to abolish all forms of
human poverty, the power to abolish all forms of human
life we have forgotten America that we are the heirs
of that first revolution America Rolling Stone Magazine
is gone America California is no longer an angel in my
heart, a flower in my hair America Idaho is not the Midwest Put out your papers America the bums need blankets
America I love you but you are a whore America I have
a rolled up dollar bill resting behind my ear that I
forgot about America look what you've done to Jeffery
Miller America your good looks will only take you so far
America an eighth of herb a week America you're a strip
mall America we are free falling America an atomic bomb
will drop on you some day America Einstein was a paci-
fist America kiss my cheek, my thighs and blow me, then
hold me to Radiohead, I'll never see you again the next
day America the rooms are empty every time I move somewhere new America if you were naked you'd be beautiful
America turn out your light and go to sleep.

CHRIS
by Erin Brannigan

He takes
Jim Beam
doubles
and I pour
them strong.

He's got
a moustache
like Custer
and a nose
like a
Cherokee
Indian.

He plays
harmonica.

He plays
guitar.

He listens
to Little Feet.

He sings
like Bob Dylan
with a cold.

He lives
way up
on marijuana
mountain

and he thinks
they should all,
"Go to hell!"

In fact
he quit his job
at the hospital.
"I finally told them
to fuck off,"
he said,
"No more blue
scrubs for me."

He smiled big
with all three
teeth.

His good old
dog lying
right beside him.

He has
4 or 5 or 6
and then he
drives home,
sideways,
in his old
blue Suburban.

He always says,
"Thank you my
good man"
and tips his hat
when he leaves.

He's the
nicest
drunk
I ever met.

A SMALL AUDIENCE
by Erin Brannigan

One day
a young man with a
five o'clock shadow
and sideburns
will pick my shit up
while thumbing through
used books
at the thrift store
on his day off.
His girlfriend still in the
back looking at clothes,
he'll find one of my
chap-books out of boredom.
or maybe he'll find something
that's published after I'm
dead.
No matter,
he'll thumb through the pages
then,
he'll read a little
not knowing why.
Then he'll read a little more.
Maybe two or three of them.
He doesn't even read poetry.
Just like I didn't ever read
poetry.
And he'll think
Damn
this guy is like me
just the way I did when I
found
Jeffery Miller that day.

If this never happens,
no matter,
it's the way I'm going to
go down thinking
nonetheless.

PUNCHED OUT
by Erin Brannigan

They sat
and smoked
and talked
about their trailers
they talked
about
how no one will
let them "hook em up"
anymore.
Because
they aren't
"up to code,"
"Fuck that,"
and
all this kind of shit
then
they drank up
and went
over
to Roxy's
so they could
smoke
and talk
some more.

Afterwards,
all that was
left was an
ashtray full of
cigarettes
and one
beautiful
burning
amber
cherry
that didn't
get
punched out.

by Erin Brannigan

I know he's my boy
we never have to tell each
other
"I love you"
or anything like that

when we travel
we argue
(he hates my poetry)
we agree
and it's good

we don't care where we go
we just sit on the side of the
road
& "chew on it"
like cows
but ideas
instead of grass

When he's gone
I don't miss him one bit
I think "good riddance...
it's for the best,"
& I get my life back
I sleep well in my bed
no one bothers me

But then I get bored
and start wrestling with
hefty tattooed whores at the
bar
late at night
by the corner booth

Then I call him up in L.A.
and say, "hey, lets plan our
next trip,
I'm ready."

He takes the train up
we drop a few darts on a map
and we're off again.

At first I worry about
getting fired

He just sits there and smokes
he says, "you'll be all
right,"
"I know," I say,
"I know."

Then the sky starts moving.
The words start coming
and their faces turn into
inanimate
objects like Tupperwear
and used-up sandpaper

Then the angels start rising
they start picking us up in
their trucks
and telling us about their
world
how, "they're bleeding over
the
hills,"
and so on.

It's living.

Then we return home
and he returns to L.A.
& I read his shit online
late at night
In the quiet
when the jokers are asleep
and the next door neighbor
dog
stares at me through
the window.

I read his shit and think
"you fucking asshole, you
got it all wrong,"
knowing well that we'll
have
something to "chew on" for
next time.
As I lie there in the dark
with the heater on.

- VII -

TWO OLD FRIENDS
by Erin Brannigan

They sit and they drink
like they never left
because they never did
one of them tells me
about how he switches between Kokanee
Rainier
and Pabst
every couple of months

the other just sits
there and drinks and stares
with his elbows on the bar
like he always did
like he always does
he's got two pairs of glasses on his head
one on his hunting hat
one on his eyes

then
he gets this unordinary look that I've never quite
seen
before in the bar
and says,

"Got any of them Hawaiian chips?"

"Yes."

I picked the Hawaiian chips off the rack
and handed them to him

he ate them
and took a drink from his
mug

and his friend watched in awe
smiling,
as if it were the most exotic thing
he ever did,
because it probably was

OFF THE TRACK
by Adriane Albertowicz

A hundred thousand tons of steel
Narrow metal spinning wheels
Stopped here and its only rider
Staggered off, not drunk, just stiff
From the bumpy railroad lines

I don't know what his state of mind was
The thumping of the train car
Must've kept him from sleeping
Most nights

He showed the itching need
To get from here to the next new place
Only to seek
           Again and again
           The future
                On the tracks
                On the seashore
                Across another horizon
He was uneasy in a crowd
Uncomfortable when he wasn't moving
He was always chasing sunrise
     always folding dusk

In the darkened lid of night
In the tawny cups of beer
The town people encountered the vagabond

Like quarters in a jukebox
     He started to play
     A spinning record of questions aloud
From every consort arose
     A barbarous retort and
My friend the freight train
     Started an argument
     Personally offending
     Each and everybody

Spittle coating faces
                Cold drink
        Hot red cigarette between two lips
Smoke and confrontations
                Billowed out
Before too long
Everybody was pissing, pointed, shouting
Thinking
On their broken TV sets
Their sister with cancer
The war overseas
The highway above city beach
The concept of quality
Love beyond lust
The meaning of compassion
And the big idea behind
bathrooms with decorative themes

Then the lights
Came up
Although the sun had not yet risen
And when we heard the train roar away
We - the town's people
Looked bashfully at each others' eyes
        Haggard
                Changed
                        Fiery
A little readier to do something about all the
Indignation we'd been trying not to feel

Later
        Under the foggy dawn of day
I thought about that ragged traveler
        How he must have been at peace
                Knowing the momentum
                Started in the small town bar
With a group of good hearted people

I realized
Even when the train's not moving
He's out turning other wheels.

STOPPED

by Adriane Albertowicz

Requiem highway
Delirium dream
lulled to comfort
In my music
In my car
I came upon
Contorted metal forms
Bleeding human bodies
In the road
In my way

The collision stopped
A body's breath
travelers
On the same path
Turned off their engines
Behind a barrage
of orange and red
light flashing
Caution
Someone here is dying.

Dying like Kamber Johnson did
When we were eight-year-old
Kids in the same grade school
class.
He didn't beat the car
Across the highway that day
And afterwards his mother
Broke all those glass bottles
against
The outside wall of their
house.

Dying like my father did when
I was eleven years old
Carrying that ragged bear
Next door to wait for
My sister
My mother
Came in with the news and

Sis was worried he would never
Be at her wedding
And I was worried
I'd miss the next day's school
picture

and the
Bigger picture shows me
That we all die
Unexpectedly
Or after a long life
It doesn't matter
Cause we all blink out someday

Last Monday about six p.m.
The same fire trucks
The same emergency workers
The same scene unfolded

A life
Hanging in the balance
Between
the asphalt and heaven.
The lifebird
touching down for transport
The ambulance
driving to the hospital
Slowly
The nervous onlookers
Knowing
It might have been them.

Why not me?
Why not today?

I get to appreciate
Color
another day
the sky is lavender
the fields grow chartreuse
while the firefighters
Make everything ordinary again

The onlookers
Straight faced
Begin to pull away in their cars
Some girl leans close to her boyfriend
Helmeted motorcycle-riders invoke their gods
An old iris of a woman squints behind spectacles
With tears in her eyes
I let the rainy day come in my window
And I selfishly think
It is not convenient for
Me to wait
It wasn't convenient for that
lady to die
On my way to the airport

I am afraid and
I bless the woman
Her life now spilled
Along the highway
soul passing through
Vehicular exhaust
Clouding
the Cocolalla air
the long line of stopped cars
starts to move again
All of us a handshake
Away from our own funeral song
And blink
We will be gone

Dying is not the soul's redemption
That is life's work.

UNTITITLED
                    by Jenn Witte

••
Part I

figurehead, how do you feel
perpetual flashlight
life goes on behind you
it is easy for the crew to navigate
within the ship's walls
you go face first,
and all the waves hit you hard

how can you know anything for certain but yourself
and how can you know what that means
what do you feel
and how do you know what that means

it is your lonely job to part the fog

••
Part II

Why does the girl
who, as a young child
was hospitalized for dehydration
still never drink enough water?
Why don't I write?
Staring at the bottom of the sink,
toothbrush in hand, frozen still,
wondering why I never do anything
I've lost it, and I know it's not at the bottom of the
sink.

••
Part III

I will go on walk after walk after walk
at night, tricking death, until
the poem jumps out at me from
around the corner.
You will be the first to hear me scream!

••

ah my friend, the canon, the pisser, the drunken fool
wanderer, the believer, the non believer...driving
across this big wide country plunged me into myself.
so much thinking my mind ate itself in circles. so i
did drugs. and wrote text message poetry. and had a
dream about moving through time and space,
encountering my soulmate in different realms. he was
also an interdimensional traveler, though neither of
us could stay put long enough to be together. i awoke
with a sore neck, which got worse by the day, until i
woke up two days ago unable to move. i attribute it to
cocaine (damn that bama!) emotional recklessness and
angst, crazy astral dreams, and too much time in the
car staring out the window at the lines and the
changing leaves. new york was serendipitous, i was
swept along on one zephyr (poignant word, dont you
agree?) to another, spent the night with our beautiful
corin, wandered from the east village to the west, and
then found myself in a car, speeding through eastern
states faster than i could turn the pages of the road
atlas. when i saw the sign for the wild turkey
distillery i made kate veer rapidly off the road to
search for it. i wanted so desperately to find it, i
have never been to a distillery, but even more, i
thought it would make me feel closer to you somehow,
on the other side of the map, not to mention the
fantastic opportunity for a pic message. sadly, we
drove around in circles for a half hour before giving
up (not my choice, but i was really just along for the
ride on this one) kentucky was not a complete failure
however, as i fulfilled my life long dream of having
my very own cauldron. i found a perfectly funky and
magical little specimen at an out of the way antique
shop, and i couldn't be happier about it. finally a
place to brew my potions. from there we detoured south

to nashville, where we indulged in debauchery
for a few hazy days, we spent the next 2 days driving
driving driving from nashville to burlington colorado,
from burlington to jackson, wy. we stopped in jackson
for more merry making (see photos) hiking, hot
springs, hangover recovery, before heading upward
through the grand tetons and yellowstone, where we
wept at the beauty abounding. into montana, and you
know the rest. upon arriving home i had a complete
emotional break down. more confusion more angst more
love. you plunge yourself into poverty to feel alive,
and i use love for the same purpose. is it masochistic
to willingly indulge in something that brings as much
pain as it does joy? can i live with both peace and
passion, or must i choose between the two? when i am
full of one i want the other, but have yet to discover
a way to feel both, i fear they are too conflicting,
on opposite ends of the spectrum, and i must decide
which is more important to me. i am going to hawaii,
dec 7, for a couple of months, maybe longer. i am
hoping for perspective, for some sort of clarity,
which will surely come in a most brutal blow. i can't
predict what lies in store for me there, but i have no
doubt that truth will take a powerful position, being
intensely undeniable and painfully intense. i am
literally throwing myself into the volcano. a new me
will emerge, one way or another. i am terrified. and
completly driven to face what i must to enter the new
phase of my life. and i think thats enough rambling
for now (induced by hydrocodone, bong hits, and wine)
more to come, whether you like it or not...

I STEPPED INTO CHURCH TODAY
by Jenna Bowers

I stepped into church today and didn't burst into flames
I held my breath as I crossed inside
Waited to be struck down by this god's fury
But it was remarkably uneventful
High ceilings
Rows of pews and piety
People of faith
Believing blindly in an answer
I turned backwards in my seat
Facing the other direction from the rest
And wondered what it felt like to accept
Tried singing their hymns
Amen's in unison
Broke bread and drank blood
Wearing red lace panties under my church dress
Silently rebelling
My quiet pagan allegiance
Last night I held my own worship
Among pine trees and starlight
Moon rising over our lake
Took sacrament in shared laughter and campfire smoke
Spirits whispering soft enchantments
spinning spoken spells
Today we prayed together and I realized it's the same thing
We use different names
To make god feel like ours
To bring salvation closer
Putting our faith into something
Anything
To help us feel significant
To justify our existence
We can't accept that there's nothing
Such an empty actuality
So we'll believe what they tell us
Or even in magic
Nod our heads through the sermon
And stand up and sing
Alleluia

LOVE IS LIKE HITCHHIKING
by Jenna Bowers

Love is like hitchhiking, sometimes you get a great ride, but most of the time you're on the side of the road with crutches, just getting passed by

Almost lost faith in humanity, again, if I saw another "lucky" red pickup truck pass us by I swear I would have given up completely - every time it got dry we got that way, hardened our hopes, with a growing disbelief in a world where people are good, and real, like us, we are the others, odd men and women out, and everyone else just drives by in their big empty suv's, burning gas, windows up, a/c blasting. Most of em don't even look our way, a few did and then scowled, even an occasional wave, mocking, saying 'I see you, but am in someway unwilling or unable to give you a ride' we throw our thumbs out at everyone, even the semis, the shinys, the rvs, the vanity plates, we want to give them a chance, people can surprise you, after all, like ron, who picked us up on one side of town and drove out of his way to drop us off on the other side, knowing in his wise old way that the other side is the best place to get a ride, and of course I can't walk it, seeing as how I'm all laid up with crutches and wounded ankle. Ben carrying my sleeping bag and water bottle, me clumsily wielding my too-long crutches, hobbling up to the few cars that do stop, throwing em in the back and making conversation until we get dumped off again. We are praying for another ride like the one on bull river highway, hop in the back of a pickup and share headphones, take in the scenery, drink a beer, sit back and believe in the good of the world. We can't afford to stop at any roadside bars this time though, we are out of money and time is more of the essence, Ben must get back to his grind, and my ankle hurts too much to allow for any excess traveling to and from the saloon parking lots. It all started when we decided to sleep in that little ghetto park in Kalispell, too tired and drunk to try for the last 15 miles at midnight. I split my toe open, the sprinklers doused us and moved us to a far less comfortable uneven rock pile, where we slept fitfully until the cops rousted us a few hours later to get on our way. The wounded toe led to a huckleberry catastrophe, which led to my wrapped and damaged ankle. It was somehow all worth it though. I couldn't walk through glacier park like I wanted to, so we had to slow down a bit, and appreciate what was offered from the other perspectives. I am humbled, asking Ben and Adriane to bring me that and carry this, they are gracious, helpful, and ever loving. After a few days of our trio Adriane brought us back to her lucky place and we begin again. The sun is hot, Ben is writing on the back of our sign and I am singing to the clouds and passing traffic. It's getting dry again and we are wondering if people like us are getting fewer in the world, or if they are all just at work right now, some pointless day job, slinging booze and daydreaming about being on a road side, thumbs out, catching the winds of fate. We agreed that we always have and always will pull over for hitchers, (unless it's some crazy looking guy wielding a knife) and where the hell is our karma for all those times of faith, where we restored someone else's by finding our own, faith in goodness and truth, in a silver line of connection that runs through us all. It's easy to lose, takes a little more work to get it back, but luckily for us today its all pretty simple, and we are brought back by every person who pulls over, by every shared smile and story, by the bend in the road and the blue summer sky. Our last ride was by far the best, a like spirit, artist, a little different, had to detour to the ross creek cedars, we happily tagged along, ate wild berries and spoke about living our dreams. Shared laughter took us all the way to my doorstep, where we couldn't stop smiling and hugging - not only did we make it, we made it well, beautifully, with courage, humor and grace. A dozen good luck charms in our pockets and the dirt of the road on our grinning faces, we part with a deeper connection, to each other, to the world around us, to ourselves.

"SAVING GRACE"
a song by Josh Hedlund

Hey hey pretty grey, why don't you take me somewhere,
somewhere that I deserve to be.
Cause the Raine would like to meet the sun,
kiss rosy cheeks and then come undone,
on a beach despite the roots from which we came.
Hey my majesty why don't you wrap me up,
in a flag with a map and a sparkler in my hand.
Though the moon looks true from where I'm at,
give me a wheel and awhile and a welcome mat,
and I'll prove to everyone this is my home.
Be my saving grace.
Old Ben awoke the other day bought a ticket for the train,
he said all my love is deserving more.
Can I take your picture, steal a moment,
and press it hard against the wall,
he says all my love now let's have a drink.
And now I'm skipping down the sidewalk
eyes wide open, sleeping words
cover every house on this old block,
and I'm only feeling worse,
this place is tired, but still it grows,
I never said it, but still she knows,
when to wrap it up, and when to call it as it lays.
And to be my saving grace.
And though the moon looks true from where I'm at,
give me a pier, and a lake, and a looking glass,
and I'll try to say what's on the other side.
Just be my saving grace.
Hey hey pretty grey, why don't you show me something.
Sing a song of the comfortable between.
Cause the night's too dark, and the day's too bright,
and your love is strong, words still push,
for time and space inside my spinning head.
Hey my majesty, why don't you wrap me up
with a picturesque refrain and changing shape.
Cause the moon looks grey from where I'm at
give me a smile, and awhile, and a perfect past,
and I'll prove to everyone that this is my home.
Be my saving grace.

"YES SIR"
a song by Josh Hedlund

Yes sir that is me in a painting
I'm a sad face with a burning bush behind me
it's far fetch story and with all its glory
it's not real, but it's still nice to feel
Yes sir that is me I'm an apple with me
poison seeds I'm still green but I'm happy
have I ruined your garden I'm no serpent
but I know I've made mistakes
and I've done just what I done

But my book is written, oh so many versions
way too many eyes and ears to know quite what has happened
stones are cast and hearts are broken
apologies are a timeless token
suns they set and it's so easy
to forget & we're fast asleep
in the soil turn to oil and then we'll sell
In the soil we will sleep

Yes sir that is me I'm a native
and this place is changing soon I won't afford to be here
ahh, it's so lovely, California bought me
this is true, but I still like you
Yes sir that is me I'm a dollar
wait, no I'm a twenty, no wait, maybe a fifty fuck it,
I'm a diamond, can't you see the sparkle in my eyes?
so are you surprised?

But my book is written, oh so many versions
way too many eyes and ear to know quite what has happened
stones are cast and hearts are broken
apologies are the timeless tokens
suns they set and it's so easy
to forget that we're fast asleep
in the soil turn to oil and then we'll sell
in the soil we will sleep

Yes sir that is me in wolves clothing
did I show my teeth while chewing meat
oh was I smiling did I get my kill
did I get my fill, well I don't know
but I had a dream in all it's glory,
on a bed of leaves on passing morning
a brief reminder than a waking moment
and I woke up as a child

"SMALL TOWN HUNGER"
a song by Josh Hedlund

I think it's my pride that holds me under
and this television screen isn't helping me see a thing
I can't see a goddamn thing
This is a pack of wolves I run with
Hungry for love, and for truth, and for love, and for truth
and for all of the above; but I've been sharpening my teeth
and I'm hungry for the sun and some perfume in my nose
and we're all built from what we used to be
and so I won't let it bother me when your eyes are on my love
but I've been sharpening my teeth

I think it's my mind that gets me going
and the way that she moves isn't helping me see straight
just like smoke stuck in the light
and when it's so cold in this little old town
and the blue-skies-sunshine-bright-days see so distant
and so very far away; you need a little love
But I've been stuck beneath the moon; and sufficiently consumed
and so I'll warm my boned by the fireside
and I'll grow my hair down past my smile
and I'll tie my thoughts to you

This is a pack of wolves I run with
Hungry for love, and for truth, and for love, and for truth
and for all of the above; and I think I see the sun.

"THE 419 SONG"
a song by Josh Hedlund

In came a storm of stinging bees
faces made like hurt me someone, please!
lips curled it's time to show some teeth
well you better just smile my brother
cause hey I don't know you
and no you don't know me
so unless we're shaking let's keep our hands to ourselves.

In ran a frightened little boy
Finger on the trigger screaming please!
Eyes closed it's time to make a change
voice rose it's time to take a stand
well you better just think my brother
yeah, you better just keep it safe
cause hey I'd like to know you
and the truth is you could know me too
so unless we're OK let's walk out separate ways
so unless it's our time let's try and walk it off

and this place is alive and it's buzzing tonight
can't you hear the working bees?
Jaws just jacking teeth are clapping
at their own hot air and hard release
and this place is alive and it's spinning tonight
can't you smell its cheap perfume?
Fingernails and lips and eyelids all dressed up
with nothing else to do.

In came the truth with lights so bright
and then locked the doors up for the night
last chance to try and make a kill
well you better just sleep my brother
I know you don't want to
and no I don't know what's best for you
but you're a worker bee and it's ten to three
and you're just like me and you're just like me and
you're just like me
you're just like me you're just me

and this place is alive and it's buzzing tonight
can't you hear the working bees?
Jaws just jacking teeth are clapping
at their own hot air and hard release
and this place is alive and it's spinning tonight
can't you smell its cheap perfume?
Fingernails and lips and eyelids all dressed up
with nothing else to do.

If you pick up a hitchhiker and give them a copy of this book, write to the following address and tell the story... I'll send you a replacement copy for free:

Ben Olson
P.O. Box 2494
Sandpoint, ID 83864

Otherwise, if you have too much money and nothing to do with it, by all means, send it to me. Check, cash, money order, gold ingets... I don't care. I'll find something interesting to spend it on.

www.ingramcontent.com/pod-product-compliance
Lightning Source LLC
Chambersburg PA
CBHW022004050726
47499CB00002BA/303